ORDER OF THE GRYPHON

UNDER THE ROSE

BY

L. N. FREEBORN

AND

D. W. WILLIAMS

"Dedicated to Patty. I'm sorry it took me so long."
D. W. Williams

"Dedicated to Kalina and Declan. Even if it takes you twenty years, never let anyone tell you it's impossible."
L. N. Freeborn

PROLOGUE

The carriage shook from side to side as it made its way down the dirt path into the wilds of Forever Forest. It was drawn by four black horses and two guards sat up top in the blistering cold. One, a fat oaf with a thin mustache, the other a thin and young man fresh out of childhood. The Queen sat comfortably inside the carriage, wrapped in heavy and luxurious furs, staring at the young girl across from her. The queen's face was narrow, stony, and wore a look of disgust and contempt for the girl who in comparison was fair, rosy cheeked, and filled with youth to be spent on the promising tomorrows after. The girl did her best to avoid looking at the Queen's awful glare but the gaze was too much and she burst into small sobs.

"Why are you doing this, your highness?" it came out as a sob.

"The King is dead and had no heirs to the throne" the Queen eyed the bundle of cloth wrapped tightly in the girl's arms "Except him."

The girl held the baby closer to her and buried its face into her bosom; large and filled with mother's milk. She didn't have on much more than some peasants gown, which was torn and tattered, and a thick cloak of heavy wool to keep herself warm. She averted her gaze from the Queen now. Her fears had come true. The Queen knew of her and the King's affair and also about the boy she had given birth to in secret. The baby in her arms was the only blood heir to the throne. Tears began to roll down her cheeks and upon seeing that, the Queen gave a thin lipped smile.

"Crying will get you nothing now, dear. It's nothing personal. I just can't allow the bastard to take my crown."

The carriage came to a stop and the Queen sat up straight now doing as she always did to look as prim and formal as possible. She made sure to fix her hair and then offered a smile so terribly fake that the girl's stomach lurched. The carriage door was opened letting a cold brush of winter air in. The girl shivered and looked at the Queen with wide and tear filled eyes.

"Please, your highness, he is just a baby. I won't cause any trouble, I swear." her lips trembled on every word

"Out." the Queen replied while wearing that terrible smile.

The girl was grabbed by the fat guard, who had opened the carriage, and dragged out into the winter air. She let out a cry as she fell to the ground with her baby still wrapped tight and protected for now. The guard then gave the girl a kick causing her to cry out once more. The Queen let off a small laugh and leaned out the carriage. Her words were colder than the frigid wind that blew around them.

"Now run, girl. I never want to see you or that baby again. If I do, I'll kill you myself." The smile was gone as those final words left her lips.

The girl stared at her for only a moment before she scrambled to her feet and started off into the deep wilds of Forever Forest without looking back behind her; even if for a moment.. The baby was pulled close to her chest as she ran as fast as her bare feet would allow. The sharp pain of little twigs and other things that laid on the dead forest floor bit into her flesh but at this moment of urgency, that was not a concern. She was only worried about getting as far away as she could so she could raise her son. The Queen watched as the girl faded into the woods until she could see the young mother no longer. She leaned back in the carriage and spoke very cooly as she adjusted her furs.

"Kill them."

The guard nodded before shutting the carriage door. He walked to the front of the carriage and grabbed a bow and quiver. The driver looked down at his companion and frowned.

"Don't look at me like that, Glen. She gave me an order."

"A defenseless woman and a babe?"

"Easy to say that when you aren't the one being ordered to do it." he slipped the quiver around himself "I'll be quick enough."

He set out from the carriage with the bow in hand. He started off at a fast walk but as he got into the woods he began to run. Glen watched with a pain in his heart. He knew the poor girl and kid were going to be slaughtered out there. He even knew that if it weren't for the cold, the guard would have taken her by force and raped her until he was satisfied. Having her in every hole available and if she bit, he'd beat her until she was unconscious and then continue. Things had gotten strange since the King's death a few weeks prior. He drew in a deep breath and let out a long exhale.

Twigs and dead leaves crunched loudly under his heavy boots as he chased down the girl. A hawk had swooped down directly over his head and soared off ahead of him. It flew towards the running girl and then back into the air. It continued to circle the three of them as he tracked the woman. "Getting ready for a meal" he laughed to himself knowing there would be some fresh dead bodies for it to pick at. The terrified mother finally looked over her shoulder and saw the guard, as big as he was, gaining on her. She tried to run faster all the while letting out a woeful sob as she desperately tried to get away. He stopped, pulled an arrow from the quiver slung around himself, notched it, drew it back, and let it loose. Her pain, something like a snake bite in her back, caused her to cry out. She fell to the frozen forest floor sending a spray of fresh snow forward.

The child spilled from her hands with his pink face barely visible beneath the wraps. Her eyes met the baby's and she let out a sob only a mother can while the snow around her began to turn scarlet.

"I'm so sorry" she whispered to him.

The guard stood and watched her lie still for a moment. The blood around her was enough for him to be satisfied that she would not survive. He contemplated on putting an arrow through the baby as well and as he decided it was best to do as told; the hawk swooped at him again. He swung his hands around "Get away from me ya bastard bird!" He loaded the arrow and shot it at the hawk. The bird dodged it easily and flew low behind a tree. The guard loaded another arrow and aimed at the tree waiting for the hawk to reappear. Instead of a hawk, a bear appeared with its jaws open and large claws ready to swipe at anyone within range. The beast stepped from behind the tree, seemingly out of nowhere. The bear was massive and had thick brown fur. It let out a hard roar and to this sound the baby began to cry. The guard startled at the roar and took a few steps back before turning and running the way he came. The baby would die out here in the wilds and that was okay. His job was done and he could report that to his Queen.

Once the man had disappeared the bear lowered itself to all four feet. The massive thing stomped over to the red snow and sniffed at the woman laying there who looked at the creature with wide watery eyes. Her breathing quickened as she reached around in her cloak and pulled from it a scroll sealed shut with the crest of Normoon. She stuffed it into the baby's wraps hoping, praying, that the bear would leave her son alone and by some grace of the gods someone would find him.. She kissed her fingers and placed it on the baby's head and then died without getting to say one last I love you to her son.

CHAPTER 1

The sun crept over hand carved stone buildings and cobblestone streets in the great city of North Normoon, capital of the kingdom of Normoon. The very recent death of the ruler of Normoon, King Dorian Sorrin XII, left the city in mourning. What was supposed to be a great festival celebrating the peace and prosperity of the kingdom now turned into a funeral. The now ruling Queen Alasandra Sorrin, once Princess Alasandra Temple of Morrenval, dedicated this year's festival to her husband and declared that it would go on without delay and so preparations were made and fulfilled.

Couriers were always the first to be out in the morning light, most even before then, getting letters and parcels to where they belonged in a timely manner. These of course included letters to friends, lovers, businesses, as well as nicely wrapped packages pertaining gifts or products.

Following the couriers who had already had a busy and productive morning, were the volunteers who decorated the city from the front gates all the way to the palace and even the bridge to Whiterock, a Dwarven stronghold. Blue banners trimmed in gold and bearing the crest of Normoon, which was a tower standing tall before the sun, hung from balconies of the larger buildings and homes. Flowers were placed on every corner. The streets had never looked cleaner thanks to the volunteers who made sure to sweep their areas regularly. Torches were placed and prepared with powders that would produce colored flames when lit later in the night. The city would be well luminated and ready for its citizens to be out and about partying until the sun rose the next day.

Following the volunteers were those who owned and worked the shops of the city. It was big business on days of celebrations. Food vendors made sure to get extra stock to accommodate as many patrons as they possibly could and even hired on family members and friends to do a bit of extra work to earn themselves a bit of spending coin for the night. The smell of bakeries and grilled meats filled the air along with the sounds of industry. Crates were hoisted and stacked with back breaking groans from the laborers. These sounds were soon joined by jovial chatter as people began to start their day along with the songs of birds who lived there in the mountain city.

On one of the smaller streets a little more than an alley sat a house of humble designs and lacking in both class and craftsmanship. A lovely painted wooden sign hung near the front door depicting a potion bottle and simply read *Apothecary*. The building belonged to a young Elven woman who had been awake for a while but still laid in bed. Plum colored eyes rimmed in gold glimmered in the sunlight as a ray of glorious and bright light shined crossed her face. She sat up, rust colored hair a terrible mess, and got herself dressed so that she would be ready for the day.

Rennyn, one of the few Elves who lived here in North Normoon, braided her hair and dressed herself in modest trousers and a shirt. Over her shirt, stained with the ingredients of potions past, she wore a brown leather apron. She carried with her a broom and with her other hand she opened the front door. She stepped outside and drew in a breath of the cold mountain air. She looked up and down the street with a frown on her red lips. It would not be much business coming her way and she knew it already. All the bigger shops would get it while the smaller ones suffered as they always did. Still, she began to sweep the little area in front of her door. A clean shop is a welcoming shop she would say to herself. Once she was done, she stepped back inside and opened the windows to allow fresh air to come in. She dealt with ingredients that could cause a foul smell and she would rather not keep it boxed inside. The pale, but beautiful, Elf headed to her table near the front door and opened a large wooden chest that sat on it. Once opened, trays extended outwards carrying bottles of different colored liquids. She organized them all and had no need for labels but for the customers she labeled them anyway. Her shop was ready for business, that is, if there were any to be had.

As she stood there taking inventory of her goods and what she needed to collect for stock, she could hear the gossip that passed by her home. It was hard not to hear it with a street that small. These were the same discussions that they always were. Things such as *Her husband did this* and *I can't believe she wore that* and *Did you hear about what happened in Karren's Call*? The last she had heard several times already this morning but nothing more on it and like the other gossip, she paid no mind to it for there was work to be done.

Once she was finished making her list for restocking, she placed the parchment down and sighed. She stepped outside once more and noticed a familiar face coming up the street. An old woman wearing a basket on her back gave a wave partnered with a smile that lacked a few teeth. Rennyn, Ren to her friends of which she had none, waved back.

"Good morning, old mother," Ren called out. Her voice floated like a song bird's call "I see you're moving slow this morning. Here for the usual?"

"No dear, not today. Too busy." she jabbed a short thumb at the basket on her back. Ren could see now they were filled with ribbons of blue and gold. "Very tempting though."

"Why would you volunteer for that?" Ren asked, hoping to not sound disgruntled at the lack of the woman's patronage. "I'd have thought you'd be out hunting for a man for the night."

The old woman let out a laugh that sounded like a dying horse. "I wouldn't have but, with the King's death I felt it was my duty. Much business today?"

Ren shook her head. "Not yet. I'm hoping that I'll see a bit later today though." in truth, her business was barely keeping her afloat, but she managed to keep the roof over her head and that was enough at the moment.

"Well," nodded the old woman, licking her lips to moisten them "I wish you the best of luck today, dear." She started off but only two steps in she turned around with the face of a young girl who had a great secret to be told. "Did you hear about that business in Karren's Call?"

Ren shook her head; the move of her head forced her braid to sway behind her. "No. I mean I've heard mumblings from those passing by, but I do not know much about it. Why is that sleepy little town making such gossip?"

Old mother stepped close as Ren leaned against the door frame and folded her arms. "Murder!" the old woman spat out in a harsh whisper that was joined with a smile that revealed how much she fancied the gossip. "Some poor whore found herself mutilated in an alley behind the local brothel. They say she was ripped open and torn apart. Innards all over the place. Body parts removed."

Ren's mouth hung agape, "That's terrible!"

"Oh it gets worse, dear. They say-" the old woman took a brief moment to look up and down the street. They were not alone and so she dropped her voice as low as she could. Ren's Elven ears would hear every word. "They say not only did the brute murder and mutilate her, but they say he left his seed in her too."

Ren grimaced and the old mother nodded in approval of the response.

"She was a whore" the old woman said glumly, "but still. Nasty way to go."

Ren agreed. "Well I hope he rots."

"That's the thing, love. They ain't caught him, have they?" old mother shook her head. "Nope. Some say it was a man. Others say it was a beast. Then there's some who say it was a monster of great size." Old mother nodded again at Ren's look of shock. "People go missing out in the wilds, sure, but a murder right out there in the town? That quiet little town? Tsk tsk. Nasty business."

Ren felt sick and attempted to change the subject, "Are you sure you don't need that drink with the little extra something?" Ren offered a wink and the Old woman cackled.

"Temptress!" the old woman adjusted her basket and blew a kiss to Ren. She made to turn again but spoke once more "You do dangerous work, girl. Keep your eyes open, hm?" she groaned and stuck her pelvis out giving her back a nice pop. "I'm off to handle this business of mine. Be well, Rennyn."

"Don't overwork yourself!" Ren called out as the old woman slowly moved down the street. Once old mother was lost in the crowd, Ren took a deep breath and stepped back inside to begin mixing commonly bought potions.

It was soon lunch, or perhaps a little after, when her stomach growled it's displeasure. She locked her front door and took a little stroll down her street and around a few corners to the bakery in her area. She passed by many who were also looking for a bite to eat when they had the moment to do so. There were actually a few bakeries in the area, but this was her favorite. Not only was it delicious, but it was cheap. When she reached the place, she opened the front door causing a little bell to ring as she did so.

"Just a moment!" a big voice called out from the back "I'm just getting something out of the oven!"

Ren stepped toward the counter and leaned against it. The nearly seven foot tall baker, with the most massive mustache Ren had ever seen, stepped out wearing his own apron and a large smile.

"Ren! My favorite customer!" he threw his arms out and up to showcase his joy. "The usual?" he asked though, he had already started to prepare the order.

Ren nodded with a friendly smile while eyeing some of the pastries in the glass case which, sadly for her, were a luxury she rarely could afford. "Yes, please and thank you. Busy today, Harold?"

"Well" he wrapped her order and placed it on the counter. Ren placed two silver coins next to it, but Harold didn't reach for it just yet. "I'd like to say we are but probably less than usual. You know how the festivals are. The city square businesses get all the coin today. The rest of us won't get much of anything. I don't even know why I opened up this morning."

"Where else am I going to get lunch?" Ren teased playfully.

"Ha!" Harold clasped his hands together. "Well I'm glad I opened just for you then!" he then placed a beefy hand on the counter and shifted his weight to it while the other rested on his hip. "You happen to hear about that business in Karren's Ca-" he was interrupted by the door's bell chiming as it was opened. "Hello friend!"

A figure cloaked in brown cloth stepped in. The light from the window behind them made it difficult to see their face.

"Bread" the voice of the cloaked figure called out in a husky rough voice "Your cheapest please. I do not have much coin, but I have been traveling for quite awhile and I need food."

Harold nodded and spoke while slapping his hand on the counter, "Sure thing. Just a moment." Harold headed to the back, but before exiting the room he called out "One silver crown."

The cloaked figure shuffled around for a moment before reaching out with a gray hand fitted with fingernails that could easily be mistaken for claws and dropped a single silver coin on the counter. The stranger did not look at Ren but kept staring ahead. The very fine hairs on the back of her neck stood up. She tried not to give herself away as she did her best to try and see the stranger's face. She was unsuccessful in this endeavor. Harold the baker, wielder of the thickest mustache, returned and slid a loaf of unshapely bread across the counter.

"Here you go, friend. Thanks for stopping in." Harold offered a smile.

The cloaked figure grunted his thanks and took the bread. As he turned, the light shining through the windows illuminated the face within the hood revealing an ugly beast of, of what? A man? No, it was far too monstrous looking. A wide crooked nose rested on a face that looked as though it had once been chewed on by some wild animal. Jagged teeth hid behind fat lips. Thick brows hung over yellow eyes. Had the baker seen the face, he would not have served him for anyone, especially Ren in her line of work, would recognize an Orc when they saw one. Not just an Orc though, he was not big enough. No, this Orc, by the way of tales Ren would have heard over many years, was one of those Orc and Human hybrids. What a great mystery it was for her that the creature got so far into the city, but it was here now and Orc kind were brutal monsters. One would not be sure about the Orc Human mutts, but it would always be safe to assume it was a monster waiting to rip someone open. Orcs were savage warriors. They ate any and everything including, but not limited to, deer, wolves, people; it simply did not matter.

Once Ren had pieced this together, an audible gasp escaped her lips and she looked away while stepping back slightly. When the figure was gone, she took a deep breath, gathered her lunch to her chest, and nodded a quick goodbye to Harold who returned it with a wave. Her feet rushed her along outside and back towards her small home, casting a small glance over her shoulder now and again to ensure she wasn't followed.

When she reached her safe haven she sat down with a huff and felt silly for being afraid of the cloaked figure. There was no way an Orc could make it into the city in daylight and not be captured and killed on the spot. He was just a very, most extraordinary, ugly man. She unwrapped her lunch and took a bite. She decided to leave her door open for anyone to come by and make a purchase. The day stretched on and more customers did indeed stop by Ren's home. There were actually more than usual that stopped by, mostly asking for a love potion or sorts for silly girls and boys wanting to entice their secret love. Others picked up materials for dirty business that Ren found it best to not ask questions about.

The sun had finally begun to set behind the mountains in which North Normoon was settled. The palace spires stretched high and cast a shadow over parts of the city. The sky had turned to those beautiful orange and lavender colors right before dark. The torches that were placed out were now being lit by merry makers. Blue and yellow flames danced from the braziers. There was music, from all parts of the city, that could be heard up and down the streets. Voices singing into the darkening sky clashed with the sounds of bottles breaking, signaling that the people had begun to celebrate early.

Rennyn had cleaned herself up as best as she possibly could to make sure that she was presentable. She knew that most of the bigger spenders wouldn't come to their area of town with all the shops that were available in the main square but she didn't want to risk it in case someone important decided to stop by. The hours passed by and what was once dimming light had faded to darkness completely.

The cathedral bell rang its song signaling that midnight had come and yet the festival was still in full swing. Nearly all the city guards were surrounding the city square. The rest patrolled the streets. A knock rapped at the door, light and gentle, and then a voice called out.

"Oh apothecary! It's Martin Sarn! Are you home? I need to resupply!"

Rennyn had dozed off in her chair by the dying embers of the fireplace, but was awakened by the sound of Martin calling her. She got up, rubbed her eyes gently and walked to the door. She opened it slowly, put a smile back on her tired face, and spoke warmly.

"Good evening, Martin. It's quite late, what can I help you with tonight?"

Martin, a handsome noble from a very wealthy family, pushed his way in without an invite and began talking. "I actually need another order for that poison that puts people to sleep for a few days. Business is booming lately and I have run out. " Martin did not shut the door behind himself as he hadn't planned on staying long. He was already digging the gold out of his purse.

Ren tried to keep a patient look on her face as his gold would line her pocket nicely. "I am more than happy to take care of getting that together for you but I will need a few days to gather ingredients and get everything mixed together. That is a mixture that should not be rushed." She turned around and walked to her supply cabinet to make a mental list of what she had and what she would need in order to give him a cost. "If it doesn't sit long enough, it can be too potent and can be more dangerous than what you want to use it for." She was silent for a moment. "If I am making the same amount for you as the last time, it would be fifty-six gold crowns." She pulled out her tattered ledger bound in soft leather and began to write down some notes while she waited for his reply.

"Better make it double." Martin said in a rather relaxed tone while dumping his purse out onto a nearby table. The sound of coins hitting the wood were followed by the sound of the front door slamming shut. The gust of air caused any candle light to be blown out leaving them nearly in complete darkness except for the faint red glow from the dead fire. "What in the world- " was all Martin was able to get out before the sound of, what could only be described as a wet or juicy ripping, filled the room followed only by a strange but alarming cracking noise. Then there was a gurgle and on the floor, lit by the red glow, fell the body of Martin whose head had been ripped in half. That is to say his skull had been split and torn right down the center. Martin's blood poured out onto the floor and would continue to do so until he was bled dry.

Ren stumbled back. She tripped over herself and fell to the floor. Her mouth opened as if to scream, but no sound escaped her. She sat there, completely frozen, unable to move a single muscle. Her purple eyes widened as she realized what she was seeing. Stepping out of the shadows was the cloaked figure she had seen earlier that day at the bakery. This time however, his hood was down and in the dim light Ren could see that his hands were covered in crimson.

"You're the apothecary?" he asked, watching her with eyes that in this light seemed orange and bright, staring deep into her own plum colored ones.

Rennyn nodded quickly, pushing herself back and away from him as much as she possibly could before backing herself against something. She wasn't sure what she was leaning against. She had forgotten her own home now and she only knew she felt trapped. It was dark, and though her Elven eyes would allow her to see much out in the natural dark, the faint light of the dead fire seemed to bother her. She felt blindly for something, anything at all, on the floor near her. Her fingertips would graze a long thin bottle that, she assumed, must have fallen from the table and onto the floor in the commotion. Her fingertips found it's broken edge and she slit a finger upon it, but did not wince. She knew she mustn't give herself away like that. She gripped the makeshift shiv and waited.

"Then you are the one supplying this poison," he motioned to the chest of bottles on the table "that this dead man used to kidnap women and children. That he used to sell them off as slaves. " his last words were more of a snarl turning to a bark. "Do you have any final words?" he gave her no time to respond "There is no honorable death for you tonight, I just want to hear your pathetic excuses for your hand in this."

Her grip tightened on the broken vial. She was ready to strike him if he came closer, but then she saw another bottle. This one was intact and was filled with a flammable potion. It was in fact the same tincture she had prepared for the old mother. Without so much as a second thought she threw the broken bottle at the beast and immediately grabbed for the bottle on the floor. When her hand wrapped around it she wasted no more time in throwing it into the fire. The once dead fire immediately sprang to life as a gulf of flame shot from the fireplace causing the cloaked man-beast to shield himself for a moment. This was the moment that Rennyn needed. She scrambled to her feet and darted to the table where she grabbed the first thing she could see that might provide protection.

"I don't ask questions," she tried her best to sound intimidating, but it was not working "I just sell what is asked of me" Her eyes went from an undefeatable calm to frantic when she realized that the knife she held was used for nothing more than scraping seeds from plants. She held it up in front of herself anyway. "You need to leave. I won't tell anyone you were here," her next words sounding more like a plea than she intended "please."

He stepped forward to grab at her. Just as his gray hand, one that Rennyn thought looked like the grasp of death at the moment, reached out to grab her throat; they both heard voices coming from down the street.

"I saw it run this way, lads! It was a bloody Orc!" one of those voices cried out.

The Orc snarled once more. If he stayed, he'd be captured, but to let this slave driver live seemed dishonorable. The Orc found himself in a strange position. Sadly, there was no more time to contemplate his predicament. Armored guards were already banging on the doors of homes that lined the street asking if anyone had seen the beast. Finally, the knock came at Ren's door.

"Open up! We're looking for an Orc! It's on the loose in the city!"

"Please," she whispered quietly, her eyes fixated on his "I will get rid of them. Just please, don't hurt me" and with that she took a few cautious steps towards the door. As she reached to open the door the hand holding the knife went behind her back.

The Orc said nothing, but stepped into the shadows of the room. His glowing orange eyes could still be seen quite easily and even now, as Ren looked over towards him, she could see he was not the size of an Orc and nowhere near it. If he was indeed a full blooded Orc, he was the runt of the entire Orc race. Ren took a deep breath to calm herself and opened the door slightly.

"Good evening, gentlemen" her eyes flashed their best smile "Is there a problem?"

"Sorry to be a bother ma'am, but we have an Orc loose in the city. We chased him this way, but the bastard is fast. All of House Sarn has been ripped to shreds by the beast. We need to put him down before anyone else gets hurt. Have you heard anything?"

Ren put on a sweet smile for them "Oh my goodness! That's terrible! I haven't heard anything this evening. Do you suppose it's the same person who is responsible for the murder in Karren's Call?" She could feel the Orc's eyes upon her as she stood there lying to the guards. Every instinct in her body told her to run, but she knew in her heart that wouldn't end well for her.

"Might be. Kinda looks the same the way I hear it-" the guard paused for a moment. The glint of scarlet gold, illuminated by the fire, had caught his eye as it rested on the ground behind Ren. He followed the little trail of red until he saw what he assumed was a pool of blood. "Sure is hard work chasing down a monster" he said with a deep hard voice "Mind if we come in for a little bit of a sit down?"

A brief flicker of fear crossed her face without her even realizing it happened. She did her best to continue the charade "It's quite late, boys. I have already turned in for the evening so I must politely decline." She tightened the grip on the knife behind her back. "I will keep an eye out for anything that might be suspicious," she nodded. "And will report it immediately of course."

The guard eyed her with a cold stare that screamed he didn't believe her and then he gave her a solid nod. "Yeah, it's late. Keep an ear out." he took a step back but continued to stare at her until another guard pushed him along so they could move to the next house.

She smiled and shut the door quietly, releasing a deep sigh of relief. She waited at the door until she heard banging on other doors again. When she turned around she saw the Orc standing at her chest of potions. He grabbed one and held it up to the light. The bottle looked to be filled with a black sludge.

"This-" he held the bottle out to her "How do you have this?"

"I made it. It's what I do." she replied, sounding more annoyed than intended.

"This is made by Orc kind. It sends Orc kind into a blood rage when taken. None outside of Orc kind would know it." he was glaring at her again and clearly not believing her words. "You speak pretty words too easily. Even when faced with death you lied to the guards. How am I to believe that you, a pretty little Elf, know how to make something only Orc kind knows of?"

Her back was pressed flat against the door, nervous at first, but angry all of sudden at the doubt of her skills. "You ask for proof?" Waving her hand towards the table where he stood, she stepped towards him "I have been doing this my whole life! If you want a quick pick me up you can go to these other shops. If you want a bottle with power, you come to me." she was indeed proud of her work. She glanced over at the body on the floor. After fighting the urge to lurch she spoke softly, more to herself than him. "I am going to be out of work for days trying to get this cleaned up."

"You should be out of work entirely for the things you have had a hand in!" he roared at her. Ren shrank back and the runt did his best to calm himself and spoke once more "Still, you have shown me kindness by getting rid of the guards. Even if it was to save your own neck." the Orc placed the potion of sludge back on the table "You will not die on this night. Maybe another." The Orc faced her "The guards *will* return."

"So?" she flared up, her eyes looked bright as a flush crossed her cheeks. "The guards mean me no harm. They're looking for you!"

He nodded "Yes, they are looking for me. I have killed every single one of those slavers in that house and then this one" he pointed to Martin's corpse "But slavers keep ledgers. Too much gold to keep track of. I might not be able to read but I'd bet my life your name comes up in one."

She crossed her arms "I can take care of myself", but even as she said the words, the doubt showed on her face. She depended entirely on her skills to keep her safe , but of course it wouldn't be enough in this situation. She was nowhere near as strong as she was skilled with mixing. Not even close.

"I will leave when things calm down in a few hours. When it is safe to escape the city." the Orc said, pulling off the cloak and revealing a bare and scarred chest. Below that he wore leather leggings with a belt that had two hand axes hanging at the side. Even now, Ren could see they were sharp. "What is your name?" he grumbled at her "What do your people call you?"

Ren wore a frown on her face as she examined him. She felt sick. This was a creature who had seen many fights and survived every one of them. She had no hope. She replied in a sulking tone "Rennyn." She took a moment before shaking her head, trying to clear some of the anxiety she was feeling. "If you are staying, make yourself useful and figure out what I am supposed to do with this body."

Ren turned from him and headed into the kitchen. It was small but she didn't need anything large for she was a tiny Elf. She grabbed a handful of rags and a dish of water. Returning to the room where the body lay. She sat the dish and rags down near the corpse and began to work on stoking the fire. She knew the evidence would have to be burned. Her stomach turned once more at the idea.

The Orc grunted and grabbed one of Martin's arms, "I do not know what to do with him. I did not plan on sparing your life." He dropped the arm and looked at her, "People have complicated names. My mother called me Alastor. That was her father's name. My Orcen brethren call me Orc'oth. It means impure Orc. It seems more fitting to me. I do not care for names."

It was a strange conversation Ren thought, but she tested his name on her tongue, "Alastor". It was nothing more than a mumble as she tried to keep her gaze away from the corpse of the well known nobleman while scrubbing the floor.

Alastor let out another grunt as if disapproving of his name leaving her mouth, "We can chop him up and burn the flesh."

"Not in this house!" she fussed. She had only planned on burning belongings, but burning a body would cause such a foul stench. Ringing a cloth out in the bowl of now brightly colored red water, she went back to her work, "I suppose if we wait a few hours, everyone will either be sleeping or too intoxicated from the festival to notice us moving a body."

The Orc sat down on the floor and ran a finger over the crudely sharpened axes. His glowing gaze was fixed on the Elf, "Why do you li-" his head tilted to the side, "Did you hear that?"

Rennyn perked up and listened closely. Her hearing was always pretty good, but she was unable to quite make out what he was hearing. She placed her crimson soaked cloth down and stood up. The Elf blinked a few times and she said quietly, "I think I hear-" it was just as those words were spoken that the door to her home was kicked in, sending the wood flying in halves and splinters.

"She's hiding something, boys! Burn her out!" is all she heard now, but even before those words were spat out by the guard outside, bottles of booze with flaming rags stuffed inside the necks came flying in. They broke upon contact with whatever they hit and sent a spray of fire in all directions. One bottle, two bottles, then more. "They'll come running out like rats in no time. Kill them on sight."

Ren let out a yelp as wet burning liquid hit her bare arms. She frantically swiped at it trying to get it off her skin. She spun around and looked at Alastor, "You need to go! Now!" and without a moment's hesitation, dove under her work table. She scooped up a locked wooden chest in her arms and held it tightly.

The air was now thick with smoke and she covered her mouth with the neck of her shirt. There wouldn't be enough time to grab everything, but she needed to find her book, a special book, one she would not leave without. Alastor was fairing no better. He let out a roar of both pain and anger as the liquid fire splashed against him as well. This may have been the one time that not being as big as his full blooded Orc kin paid off. He stood up remarkably fast. In fact, he was faster than one would assume of him.

"We go now!" he grabbed the Elf by the collar and pulled her along with him "They'll kill you too!"

Rennyn let out a choked sob "Please! Alastor, I need my book!" She coughed, her face now covered in dirt and small scratches, "It's the only thing I have left of her!" The fear and sadness in her eyes were very clear.

"Argh!" Alastor drew his axes and ran the blades through some of the burning booze on the floor. Both sharpened edges of the weapons ignited and he was pleased to see such a thing. "Find it! Then out the window!" and without another word, he gave a terrifying war cry and charged out the front door.

Rennyn sobbed, eyes barely able to see, as she ran towards her room. Her feet burned as she trampled over the burning floor. She looked around in a panic for nearly a minute before she spotted it. Resting peacefully on a table near her bed was another small leather bound book. She sat the locked chest down and ran a finger over the lock. The chest popped open with a small green flash and she stashed her book inside. She shut the chest and locked it by running her finger over the lock once more. She grabbed a cloak hanging on the wall and her boots that rested near the wall. She hurriedly slipped them both on and grabbed the chest once more. She looked around and was dismayed to find the flames licking at the bedroom door. She wanted to cry. She was trapped until she remembered Alastor had told her to go through the window. The door fell off the hinges as she thought about the window and she swallowed hard. All her courage had gone and the only thing left was instinct. She started at a short run and leaped through her bedroom window. The glass shattered around her as she went through and as far as she could tell she was not currently injured.

She laid there for a moment, though brief, it felt long to her. She stood up, her wooden chest still clasped tightly to her, and stared back at the house. The heat from the flames felt as though it was baking her skin, but the cool spring air was helping. Her eyes checked her surroundings and saw only more wooden and stone homes. The fire, if not contained, would spread and put others out. She felt terrible. In a moment of clarity, Ren saw that a crowd of guards were gathered at the front of her burning home. Every one of them yelled and fought as they too became engulfed by smoke. The yelling carried on, only for a moment, before the voices dwindled down. She stopped for a moment and looked out to the south west.

"The forest. I have to get to the forest." she said to herself out loud.

Out of the smoke appeared the charging Orc and her eyes widened. For a moment she thought he was going to kill her now. The Orc, painted in blue and yellow fire light as well as blood, lowered his head under her arm and shouldered her stomach. She clutched onto the box tightly as she was lifted by him and carried away from the burning house whose timbers had begun to fall. Her hands touched the blood that covered him. It was warm to the touch but she saw no wounds. She grimaced when she realized it was likely not his own.

"I have to go to the forest!" she cried out in a sob.

"Not to the wood, girl! To the Dark!" he snarled back.

Ren clasped her belongings even tighter as she blinked away tears that threatened to fall. That of course released a torrent of tears as she watched her home of many years fall to ash. Neighbors scrambled to get away from both the fire and the dead bodies of guards they'd stumble across. She knew now she could never return home and it pained her greatly.

Alastor, or maybe he was Orc'oth at this moment, was fast. He was a lean muscular creature and more than likely running off on pure adrenaline most times. He ran through the alleys and the back streets that were the darkest, doing his best to avoid well lit areas. It would seem that they were heading toward the bridge leading into the Dwarven kingdom of Whiterock, but the Orc turned away from that path and again ran in the dark alleys which eventually led them to the sounds of rushing water. The deafening sound of running water became louder and louder. Ren only took a single glance behind her to see what was happening when she, to her alarm, saw that they were racing towards a wall. It was a wall which she knew to be the barrier between them and the waterfall that fell down the mountain side.

"Hold tight and hold your breath!" Alastor shouted as he leapt on to a crate and then over the stone wall.

Below them was a tremendous drop that Ren could not even fathom. Her gunt wrenched at the sensation of falling and she closed her eyes tightly, squeezed her wooden chest against herself, and took a deep breath; anticipating nothing more than death.

CHAPTER 2

Ren allowed herself one quick scream before she held her breath again. Her eyes watched the wall disappear as they went over and fell. The drop itself might have been several seconds, but to Rennyn it felt like an eternity of falling. Their bodies hit a pool of water that was thankfully deep enough that they were not injured. The waterfall would continue to spill over the edge of rock and pour down another tier. Ren was set free by Alastor before they made contact with the pool. She felt the air leave her lungs from the force of the contact, but not once did she loosen the grip on her wooden chest.. Still holding tightly to the box that contained her most special and cherished possessions, she kicked her feet to propel herself to the surface. Her eyes scanned her underwater surroundings to find some sign of the Orc. Just as she thought he might have gone over the next tier, she was grabbed from behind and propelled upwards even further.

Once both of their heads were above water, Ren saw that Alastor was shouting something to her, but she couldn't hear a word he was saying. The water was freezing and she had not realized it until now. Alastor had grabbed hold of her cloak and started swimming back towards the waterfall. It was a struggle, but Alastor managed to do it fine by keeping close to the edge where there wasn't much of a current. He found a ledge and lifted Ren to it before climbing on it himself. They both took a moment to catch their breath and thanked all the gods that they were still alive. Ren examined her wooden chest. The seal had not broken and she had hoped it was tight enough to not have let water ruin her things. She would have cried about the idea if she wasn't already so shaken over the night's events.

It was a long while before Alastor stood up. Ren watched him try to speak to her again but heard nothing. Instead of trying to yell, he waved her on and pointed to the waterfall beside them. He stepped near it, then behind it, and vanished. Ren stood, clutching her wooden chest again, and did as he had. Taking great care to not slip and fall beneath the crushing might of the water flowing down the mountain side. The sound was so loud in her head that she felt it in her bones as though she were going to vibrate right out of her body. Then, the sound began to ease and as she looked around she saw that they stood in a large cavern. Alastor moved slowly, the adrenaline had gone and he was tired.

"Thank you" she spoke quietly, her voice unsure. Moving slowly to him, feeling her own fatigue within her sore body, she asked "Are you okay?"

"Yes," he grunted, turning to her and letting out a long exhale. "I've had worse. Do you know where we are?"

Ren shook her head. She wanted to check her wooden chest again. She wanted to take stock and examine everything inside. She fought to find an excuse, "Any wounds that require attention?"

"No. If it is time to die then I shall die with honor. Save your medicine for someone who fears death," Alastor mumbled as he stepped further into the cave. His hands kept patting his thighs where the axes would hang. Ren assumed he had lost them. "We are beneath North Normoon, very near the kingdom of Whiterock," he grunted "One of the nineteen Dwarven holds. This cavern is connected to a series of tunnels and passages that once belonged to them but have been taken over by Orc kind."

Ren didn't think her night could get any worse. Her wet hair clung to her face and she stammered, "What?"

"There is no need for your worry, Elf. Our path, though through what is called the Dark, will lead us high above the Orc camps. Even if they knew we were up here, they'd not know how to get to us. We are not intelligent creatures."

She shivered as she tried to keep up with him, "You would be safe regardless, wouldn't you? Me however-" her tone was muted when she was cut off.

"You do not know much of Orc kind, do you?" he asked without looking back.

"I know that I would not be welcomed. I would be robbed of my possessions and then killed." she said finding relief that he hadn't looked at her. She didn't want to showcase the worry in her face. Alastor let out a laugh that upset her for some reason she wasn't sure of. "I stayed very safely in my home doing my work to help people," she snapped back, "forgive me for wanting to live some type of normal life."

He ignored the snarky comment and started heading further into the Dark. His Orc eyes would guide him just fine. He assumed her Elven eyes might even have some of the same qualities. It was a long silence before he spoke again "Orc kind do not look on Orc'oth favorably. If caught, they would beat me. Force me to do slave labor. Starve me. Orc'oth are nothing but abominations to Orc kind." Ren shivered hoping they would find some sort of warmth soon. Alastor continued, "And you, they'd take what meant something to them. Then they'd rape and enslave you. And it would continue until they grew tired of your tears. Then they would kill and most likely eat you." his tone was rather matter of fact like. "None of us are safe with Orc kind."

"And I am supposed to trust that where you are leading me is safe?" she asked angrily "I can't go home now! My livelihood is destroyed because of you. How am I supposed to survive?" Even though she questioned him, she found herself still following behind him. Her eyes, just as his, could see in the dark just fine when there was no other light.

He spat out, "You think I am leading you to your death when I could have easily killed you a handful of times already?"

"You think I'm so weak that I can't defend myself?" Her reply was sharp and cold.

He stopped and immediately turned to her. His hand moved down to his thigh but found no ax. He growled out, his voice echoing in the cavern numerous times until it became a low rumble "Then have at me! Let's see if your mettle is as sharp as your tongue!"

Her eyes seemed to flash brightly as she clenched her fists tightly at her sides. Alastor never noticed the pebbles on the cavern floor around him vibrating. "Fuck you!" she spat out angrily.

He bared his ugly misshapen teeth at her. The Orcen lust for bloodshed quickly became strong inside him. "You would not be the first pretty little Elf that I have carved up. I-" there was a loud roar that echoed in the tunnels beyond that cut off his threat. He turned his head only momentarily, the wheels turned slowly in his mind but turned nonetheless. "I hope they did not find our path" he glared at her one last time before turning away to head deeper into the cavern. "Let us move. You'll be rid of me soon enough."

The rocks that once danced on the floor of the cavern fell back to their still selves as she followed behind him. "Do you have a plan as we walk through this potential death trap?"

"My plan is to die with honor; fighting till death won't allow me to continue. Only then will my ancestors be pleased. What is your plan?" his words were but gnarls.

Ren's bravado was wearing off as she followed behind him "I don't know. I wasn't expecting my evening to take such a turn." She was cold, tired, and now fearful at the possibility of being left alone.

They walked for hours. The growls of Orc kind grew distant and closer all at the same time. They crossed over ledges where with a single glance over one could see Orc camps littered below. It seemed the silence would go on until the faint sound of whispers caught their ears. Alastor looked back at her.

"Keep your guard up. I hear something ahead and I know not what it could be." his own voice but a whisper.

The color had drained from her face, yet her cheeks were flushed bright pink. She only nodded as she glanced around. She wasn't sure how much further she could keep going. The early morning and excitement of the evening had taken most of her energy. Ren stumbled and fell to her knees after another long while of walking, how long she did not know. She took a moment before she muttered.

"Can we take a short break? I'm so tired" it was almost a whine.

Alastor, with a face displaying his disbelief in her weakness, meant to turn and face her. He had all intention to give her a tongue lashing but found himself being interrupted by torch light blinding him from around the corner. He lifted his arms to shield his eyes.

"Oh aye" said a rough voice in a thick accent " Ye all hide from the light but the darkness saves none. State yer' business, Orc'oth, and ye may yet live. What'cha doin' in my halls?"

Rennyn got up again and stood near Alastor. She could feel her body vibrating, whether it was the cold or nerves, she was unsure.

"Seeking passage through Whiterock." he called out.

"Oh aye, I bet ye are" the reply had a hint of jolly retort in it. "Half Orc and" the voice paused, "What's that behind ye?"

"Elf, sir" Ren had peered out slightly to look at the torch bearer "Rennyn. If it pleases you."

"Elf with a half Orc?" the voice asked questioningly. Voices behind him mumbled. "Are ye' a prisoner, lass? We've got arrows on em' if ye' are. "

Ren shook her head. "No! He saved me. We are making our way through the caves to-" she stammered "to get to-" another pause "Well I don't really know where we're going."

The torch was handed off and held up by another. The light revealed a short and stout Dwarf with nearly gray-blonde hair. His beard was braided and hung down his armor. His armor was dented and worn, but clearly taken care of. It was made for him and it fit him perfectly. Other features of the Dwarf were hidden at the moment.

"We 'ave no quarrel with the half Orcs nor the Elves. Though, I must say we nay see yer' kind down here often. Or ever really." he half turned to face the other Dwarves behind him. "Hassir."

"Aye?" came another thick accented reply.

"Go fetch the wagon. The lass looks like she's gonna faint." the head Dwarf said, giving a finger jolt towards Ren.

"Aye. Going get the wagon." was the reply and the Dwarf shuffled off.

Turning back to face Alastor and Ren, the head Dwarf spoke again. "What trouble are ye' in to wander in the Dark?"

Ren looked at Alastor and gave a slight yet tired looking smirk. "Yes, Alastor, what sort of trouble?" her comment trailed off as she swayed. Her knees buckled from beneath her, and she collapsed against the Orc.

"Go get 'er, lads! Be gentle now!" the head Dwarf barked out. The rest faded out fast for Ren as she gave way to unconsciousness "And make sure he nay has any weapons."

Hassir returned with the wagon and they loaded Ren in it, making sure to keep her wooden chest safe. Alastor was also invited to join them. He declined. The head Dwarf and Alastor talked a bit longer while the wagon carted Ren off into Whiterock. Alastor shared the story of how they came to be in the Dark and when the story was done he declared that he would continue to venture through the tunnels as he knew of an exit that would lead him out the base of the mountain that was far too dangerous to have taken the Elf with him.

"Will you take care of her?" asked Alastor.

The Dwarf nodded. "Aye, best as we can. I doubt anyone from the Human city will recognize her when she returns in a few days. At least nay enough for her to leave."

Alastor nodded. "May I have a weapon? Mine are gone and the area I'll be going through will be dangerous."

The Dwarf eyed him for a moment and then nodded. He took one of the remaining Dwarf's swords and handed it over. "Good luck to ye'."

Alastor nodded and turned heading back into the darkness. The Dwarf watched him go and nodded back to the others. They followed the same path that Ren was taken down. It was a long walk for a Dwarf but they finally returned to the great Dwarven hold of Whiterock, so named after the white stone of the mountain that it was carved from. Homes and businesses were carved high and deep into the mountain. Large ornate faces of Dwarven Kings from the past loomed over the city in grandeur. As they marched in they were greeted by some guard and jovial banter was exchanged. A young Dwarven lass had come running up to the group.

"Lord Frothfire!" she was out of breath "They've been requesting yer' presence in the Hall of Kings."

The Dwarf nodded. "I'll head that way now. Make sure this lass is seen to my quarters. I want her treated with the honor a guest of the holy order deserves. I'll come back when I'm done with that business."

The Dwarven woman bowed her head and did just as the man had asked. He placed his large hands on his iron helmet to take it off, decided against it, adjusted his braided beard,and set off for the Hall of Kings.

A decorated hammer struck the anvil in the center of the room signaling silence from the Dwarven nobles sitting in the seats that formed a circle around the anvil and the striker. The voices, once loud as well as filled with laughter one moment and anger another finally calmed. All eyes were set upon King Romic Silverwheel, who held the hammer at his side. Silverwheel was a mighty tall Dwarf standing a little under five feet tall. He had well groomed gray hair brushed back from his receding hairline and though his beard was not long, it was full and thick. Silver rings laid as ornaments in his hair and beard, as most nobles did in Whiterock. He wore an elaborate decorated robe and large gaudy rings on his fingers. Brown eyes surveyed the mass of Dwarven nobles and he inhaled through his wide nostrils.

"Ye all know why ye here." he started in a low husky voice "The High King of the Nineteen has passed at the honorable age of one hundred and eighty-four. "

"Good man! Great King!" someone shouted. The crowd agreed.

"Aye" Silverwheel nodded "Aye he was, lad. Still, as our tradition, it is time we select a new High King. That means every hold selects one worthy of the title and sending them off to King's Hold where they shall be judged and possibly crowned as the High King of the Nintenteen."

"And who is worthy?" one called out "B'cause it's not ye', Silverwheel."

The crowd erupted into laughter. The King hammered on the anvil to call for silence once more.

"And why not me? Whiterock under my rule has been prosperous!" Silverwheel exclaimed.

"And prospered under the Kings before ye' as well! What have ye' done, really?" another called out.

The King grumbled to himself, muttering something about the ungrateful and then shouted out "And who would ye' select? Who among ye' would be an honorable High King?"

A fat, brown haired, pocked skin Dwarf stood up. "Ow's about me son, Mervis? As tough as the mountain he is!"

"Tough as a mountain with the brains of a rock!" someone shouted. It was followed by laughter.

"Then how about me?" boomed a voice from a man who had a long luxurious braided red beard that was held by one large golden cuff "A *real* man with a *real* beard!"

"Your daughter has a nicer beard! Sit down ye' fool!" more calls and laughter

Even Silverwheel had a laugh at that. There were more calls and shouts but none of which were taken seriously. The King was becoming annoyed as the selection needed to be made. He had almost given up on the idea of it happening when a Dwarf with wispy white hair stood up. He leaned on a wooden cane and shook as those of old age do. The hall went quiet, a sign of respect for the old timer, and the King nodded. He addressed him formally as he knew the old timer honored the old ways and would not speak until he was acknowledged properly.

"Hannok of the White, I recognize ye'. Speak yer' wise words for us." Silverwheel called out.

Hannok bowed his head. His beard, in patches now, wavered as he did. "I think I know just the Dwarf for the job."

The crowd laughed. "Surely not this old man? He's older than the High King was!"

Silverwheel also laughed but hammered the anvil again. "Enough. Let the old man speak."

Hannok waited for a moment, unturned by their mockery. "May I suggest a Dwarf of noble blood but humble in heart?"

"And what Dwarf in Whiterock would ye' name High King, Hannok of the White?" the King asked.

"Dwim Frothfire also known as Dwim of the White." Hannok spoke with confidence, pride, and was most earnest in his suggestion.

"And where is Dwim now? Why nay he speak up himself?" Silverwheel asked, a small bit of contempt in his voice.

"Dwim is at the moment reclaiming our halls lost to the Dark." Hannok replied.

There were no jeers. There were no jokes. Only quiet mumbling. This was then replaced by agreement and cheers. To the King, it would seem the decision might be made. This was okay. He didn't really want to be High King anyway. There was too much burden that came with that crown.

"Aye. Dwim is noble in both name and heart." the King spoke out. "Let it be an official request! We, the nobles of Whiterock nominate Dwim Frothfire as our choice for High King. All in favor, say Aye!"

The reply was thunderous. The King nodded. "And those against?"

There was no sound uttered. The choice was made. King Silverwheel hammered the anvil and the room applauded.

"Go and fetch Dwim Frothfire!" the King shouted out to a young Dwarven attendant. She bowed and left immediately to summon him as requested.

Some time had passed before Dwim was able to make it to the Hall of Kings where he was summoned. The chamber was cleared when he entered and King Silverhweel was sitting on the stone throne near the anvil. Dwim nodded to the guard and stepped in further. His boots made his footsteps heavy on the cold stone floor causing them to echo. King Silverwheel eyed him from the throne. Dwim went as far as the first row of noble seating and dropped to a knee. He removed his helmet and placed it on the floor at his side. He had a full head of thick hair where braids lay on the sides and held together with silver cuffs. He had big blue eyes filled with care and devotion, which is how Dwim attended to everything he did. His nose was large, hooked, and colored red like his cheeks.

"Yer' majesty." he dipped his head and looked back up. "I was told ye' requested my presence? How can I serve ye' and Whiterock?"

"Stand up, Dwim of the White." the King raised a hand to signal the request. "Ye know of the High King's passing into the next life, aye?"

Dwim, getting to both feet, nodded. "Aye. Very sad, yer majesty. He was a great Dwarf and warrior."

"Aye" the King nodded "Aye, he was. A good friend too. It is by official decree of the King and the council of nobles that you, Dwim off the White, Dwim of the noble name Frothfire, be chosen as our delegate for High King."

Perhaps the King expected some sort of thank you or praise for such an honor, as he waited there on the throne with a smile on his lips and looking favorably on Dwim. Dwim, however, did not feel the same.

"Yer majesty, I mean no offense, but I nay want that title." Dwim said softly, almost pleading.

"Are ye' insane?" Silverwheel exclaimed. "Ye' didn't have a single vote against ye'! Why in the world would ye' pass on this?"

"I'm a Paladin of the White, yer highness." Dwim replied apologetically "My life is devoted to protecting others and serving Olm's holy purpose as well as-"

The king cut him off. "Too bad, lad. Yer' goin'. That's the way this all works. Maybe ye' will get lucky and the other holds chose someone better. You have time to get yer' affairs in order before ye be levin'"

Dwim let out a sigh. He was disgruntled that he didn't have much of a choice and being a man who loved his people and their ways he would do it if they so wished. As he turned all this over in his head though another maiden was let into the Hall of Kings and she called out in a terrified voice.

"Yer highness! The Oracle!" she was breathless, "The Oracle has gone into a fit! He has collapsed and is muttering incoherently. None of us know what he is sayin'!"

The King groaned and gave Dwim a nod. "We best go have a look, aye? This seems like it might be yer' line of work anyway."

Dwim gathered his helm and followed the King out of the Hall of Kings and to the chambers of the Oracle. Dwarves did not put much faith into the mysticism of the universe and all the powers within or beyond, but they have always had an Oracle, who on occasion was able to intercept divine visions. One had not been divined in many generations and while the current Oracle was spry for a man of his age, Dwim had hoped it wasn't just the old man finally giving in to death. He thought about that and then about the strange Elf girl resting in his quarters. He had a strange feeling that this was all meant to happen, or perhaps always meant to happen. Perhaps fate had weaved these events together. Dwim did not like the idea but by Olm's guiding light, he would do what he felt was best.

Rennyn had strange dreams while she slept away the exhaustion of her little adventure. In each dream, none of which she could recall once awake, she felt as though something were guiding her path. She felt as though an invisible hand had placed her on a road that was long and full of sadness. She whimpered and tossed under the fine Dwarven crafted sheets. A faint cold sweat broke over her brow and she cried out.

"Ye still alive, miss?" Asked a rosy cheeked Dwarf woman, lacking a beard, who was looming over her.

Ren slowly opened her eyes and blinked a few times. When everything was in focus, she examined the smiling face first, then her surroundings. She found herself lying in a rather lavish and comfortable bed in an even more lavish room adorned in Dwarven art and furniture. She sat up slowly as the maid had backed away from her. Her body ached, but she felt much more rested.

"I-" she paused and rubbed her head "um, yes."

"You've been asleep for many hours now. Nearly twelve by my count." said the maiden as she began to tidy up.

"Where am I? Where's-" Rennyn remembered the Orc "Alastor! Where is he?" She kicked off the blankets and stood quickly. The room started to spin and she nearly sat back down but fought it. "Is he-"

"That half Orc ye' were travelin' with? The way I understand it, he left as soon as ye' were taken care of. We've got yer' chest nice and safe. We were unable to unlock it to make sure yer' things were okay though. " the maid looked at her while cleaning "Strange to see an Elf and Orc as traveling mates. 'Ow'd that 'appen?"

"It's a rather long story" Ren looked at the woman "Did he say where he was going? Did he say if he was going to come back?" Ren realized she was in a sleeping gown. "My clothes, please. I would like to get changed. I really need to find him." She spotted her chest sitting on a table. Her clothes were folded neatly on top. "I didn't thank him for saving me earlier."

"Nay an idea where he was headed." the maid replied not looking away from her work now, clearly uninterested by the conversation at this point. "They said he handed ye' over along with yer' belongings and went on his way." She stopped cleaning and looked at Ren with a concerned frown. "Are ye' sure yer' feeling well? How's about a frothy beer? Puts a pep back in yer' step!"

The Elf's stomach growled loudly at the sound of a drink and she blushed in embarrassment. She also realized her mouth was terribly dry and decided she could use the refreshment afterall, at least something to take the edge off of what had happened. "I suppose that wouldn't hurt. I'm Rennyn A'sun'al, ma'am. Ren, if you prefer that." she paused, only for a moment, and pushed on "Is there somewhere that I might freshen up?" She blushed again and lowered her head. "I'm sure I don't smell as fresh as I could."

The Dwarf maid escorted her to a door in the large room and opened it revealing a steamy bathing room. In the center of the room, carved into the rock floor, a large tub filled with water. A pipe coming from the tub kept the water hot with steam rising from its surface.

"Take yer' time, miss. The master made sure to have yer' needs met. " she lowered her head. "Lucky ye' ran into them down in the Dark instead of the Orcs. Just give a yell if ye' need anything. I'll lay out some drying cloth for ye as well as some clothes. Won't be but gowns but I think there might be some we can find to fit ye." She left the room. Rennyn stepped closer to the tub, squatted, and dipped her fingers in. The heat ran through her and she let out a shiver. She was going to enjoy this much needed bath. The maid had returned just as she said she would with drying cloths and a lovely gown.

Ren stood and a blissful sigh bubbled up. "I don't think I have ever seen a room so heavenly!" The maid smiled and Ren let out a giggle "I may soak in here until I melt away!"

"Yell if ye' need anything, miss. I'll leave ye' be." the maid said as she bowed and exited the bathing room, closing the door behind her.

Ren waited a moment after the maid had left before she shed the sleeping gown and let it pool at her dainty feet. There must have been something in the water, she thought, for when she inhaled she could smell the sweet aroma of flowers. She stepped down into the basin, through the sweet smelling steam, and lowered her body into the water. "Oh my!" she exclaimed as she let her body sink in happily. The heat caressed her tiny form as she lay there, running her hands over every inch of her petite body, letting that wonderful hot water soothe her achy body. She allowed herself to sink even lower, letting her head go under as she ran her hands through her rust colored hair to get out some of the tangles. She took her sweet time, enjoying every bit of the needed relaxation. She even allowed her hands to explore the sacred space between her thighs until the heat from the water and her own body became too much. After what felt like days, she decided it was time to finally get out. Almost unwillingly, she pulled herself out and wrapped her naked form in the drying cloth that was laid out for her. Her body steamed in the cool air as she made final adjustments to the towel so that it kept up on its own. She then examined the gown and decided it was simply not her and that she would just put on her old clothes. She grabbed the gown though and headed back into the bedroom she had awoken in. Seeing her clothes on the chest, she noticed there was another set of clothes underneath. Pulling them out she found a pair of soft tan colored pants and a green shirt as soft as the finest silk. Ren got dressed and pulled her hair into a loose braid and wrapped it around her head in a messy bun, pinning it with some jewel adorned pins that sat on the table.

Behind another door in the chamber, one that led out she assumed, she heard two voices conversing. One belonging to the maid and the other belonging to the Dwarf she had met in the Dark. A knock on the chamber door echoed in the room. "Are ye' decent, miss? I'd like to share some words with ye', if I may?"

"Yes" she called out. "Please, come in." Glancing at herself in a mirror that rested in a corner, she smiled seeing that she looked more like herself.

The Dwarf entered and bowed his head. He had taken off the armor of worn and dented metal and wore a more humbling attire now. A simple set of trousers and shirt while he stood in leather boots. "I nay got a chance to introduce m'self down in the Dark. My name is Dwim of the White. The White is an order of paladins serving the God of life, Olm, but that nay matters, I think."

Rennyn nodded knowing very well what the White was but she allowed him to go on uninterrupted.

"Yer' friend left ye' in our care and while ye' are indeed a welcomed guest in our halls here in the mountain, I'm sure yer' wanting to get back out in the fresh air. I don't mean to disparage yer' people by that remark. It's the same with us Dwarves. We just prefer the mountain while yer' kind prefer the wilds. I myself nay travel much outside of the mountain but turns out I will be setting out on a quest of sorts with a strange traveler. We can escort ye' as far as we go."

Ren smiled sweetly "It's a pleasure, Dwim. I can't thank you enough for your hospitality." She gestured down at the clothing she was wearing "I am afraid I have no coin to pay you for the clothes and the stay while I am here, however, maybe my services could be used instead? Healing perhaps? Potions maybe? I am more than happy to be put to work as well if you require."

Dwim raised a thick brow "What line of work ye' in?"

Ren smiled "I ran a shop in North Normoon. I was, I mean am, an apothecary."

Dwim thought it over for a moment. "Lass, there nay be a reason to repay us for anything. We are happy to help." he rocked back and forth on his heels and continued "That being said, we could use yer assistance if at all possible."

"Of course!" she replied, just happy she was able to feel as though she repaid their kindness.

"Are ye' skilled enough to produce Kalina's Mist?" he asked with a tinge of hope in his voice.

Ren nodded. "Yes. Are you having trouble sleeping?"

Dwim shook his head "Nay, can't say that exactly. We need it to relive a dream."

That was Ren's next guess. "Yes, if I can get my hands on some nightshade petals, spriggan mushrooms, and spider ichor; I can mix that up nicely. It'll take me some time though to prepare them properly." she furrowed her brow and spoke in earnest as it was something she wanted to make sure he understood. "Dwim, forgive my bluntness, but dreams aren't something to be tampered with for long. If I may be so bold to say; reliving the same thing time and time again is a quick way to insanity."

"Aye, lass" he nodded in agreement with her. "This one dream is a wee bit important though. We nay dabble in such things often, I can assure ye'. We have an Oracle, ye' see? He had some sort of dream and came out of it maddened! Driven insane by it. He speaks of black stars and the convergence of souls. " Dwim sighed. "Besides the ramblings of things that didn't seem to make sense; he said I was there in the dream. We just want to know what has driven him so mad."

Ren listened to him carefully and with great interest about the Oracle. "If someone can escort me out at nightfall to the woods, I should be able to locate everything I need. I'll need a workspace and some tools as well."

"Aye " Dwim said, happy for her assistance "We should be able to do that for ye'. The Orc told us about the trouble ye' got into while ye' were in the Human city. We nay have plans to hand ye' over or anything, just in case ye' were concerned about that. Our peace with the Humans is based on minding our own business. It's worked out so far.." Dwim combed through his bead. "What happened is their business and theirs alone. If ye' can keep yer' head low, we can get ye' out to the woods outside the city walls."

Ren nodded and gave a lovely smile, one that even a Dwarf could say was mighty beautiful for a woman without a beard. "Then consider my services yours." She knew the potion would be tricky and required much care and skill to create but she had both. Afterall, she was able to create the Orcen sludge without a problem. She was eager to get back to work, even if it were just this. It made her feel useful. "So I may stay until you leave with this traveler?"

"Aye. Ye' can stay here in the Halls of the White as ye' have been. We appreciate yer' help, lass. I'll go get yer' escort. Be ready to do yer' work. This business is urgent to us." he gave a bow before turning and heading out. The maid chased after him.

Ren spent that time checking her wooden chest that sat on the table. She was a bit nervous to open it as she had been worried everything was ruined. She ran a ringer over the lock slowly. There was a green flash and the click of something unlatching. She opened the box carefully and peeked inside. Purple eyes darted over everything at a glance. They seemed fine. She reached out and grabbed the book that she couldn't leave behind and opened it. Nothing damaged. She held it to her chest and was thankful for such a blessing. Placing the book down on the table, she went through the rest of the chest. Everything was fine. Trinkets and small things precious to her. Her heart sang out as tears of joy streamed down her cheeks. If nothing else, these things were safe. There was a knock at the door and she wiped her eyes and tried to calm herself.

"We are here for ye', Lady Elf. The Human city will nay bother a Dwarven carriage in the dark. Are ye' prepared?" called a voice with a lighter accent than Dwim's.

In the chest was a small satchel. She unpacked it and slung it over her shoulder. "Coming!" she called. She grabbed her cloak folded on top of the pile of clothes and threw it over herself. She sat the hood over her head and gave herself one last look over before swinging the door open and stepping out to greet her escort.

The two guards, each dressed in a black cloak over heavy iron armor with the hood pulled over their heads, stood near a meager looking carriage and gave Ren a deep bow as she came out. They clearly belonged to The White for each wore a medallion depicting a shining light. She stood for a moment waiting for them to guide her but they only stood watching her. She smiled and moved to the carriage, stepping up with one foot and then climbing in. One guard followed her while another climbed up on the carriage top and took the reins of the horses. Ren was excited to get outside into the cool fresh spring air, still carrying the bite from the winter. The carriage was unremarkable and that was probably due to the fact the Dwarves did not travel above ground. Had they been going to another Dwarven hold she would have marveled at the steam powered machinery that was used for swift travel before the Dark took the tunnels. The carriage was reaching the large stone door entrance of Whiterock.

"Make quick work of it tonight, lass." said the Dwarf sitting across from her. "The Oracle grows weaker and Lord Dwim feels it important we learn what he saw in the dream."

Ren nodded. "I'll do my best to make it fast. I promise."

The carriage ride was bumpy. The wheels were uneven and jostled them about quite madly. Ren looked out the carriage and saw that the city guards were out in full force, checking down alleys and into dark spaces. She grimaced and leaned back thinking they were looking for her and Alastor. She dreaded the idea of what would happen if she were caught. The Dwarf across from her didn't seem to be concerned though and she tried to let that ease her anxiety. She was confident in what she needed to do on this night. Once they had reached the city's main gate she let out a sigh of relief. The woods were just around the bend and she'd be able to get on with her work and have a moment to herself. The jolt of the carriage stopping shifted her in her seat. The Dwarf climbed out first and then waited for Ren to do the same. She tightened her cloak around her and followed. She breathed in deeply, taking in the smell of the great outdoors. She smiled and nodded to the Dwarf.

"I'll be a bit." she said, knowing the spider ichor would be the hardest to collect.

The Dwarf nodded a response. "As quick as ye' can."

Ren headed into the woods and disappeared behind the trees. The Dwarf stood outside the carriage and waited for her. Ren walked around the woods, admiring it's serenity and how they always felt more like home than the city. She always attributed this to being an Elf. They were a people that communed with nature after all. In spots, where the moon broke through the dense collection of trees, her skin glowed in the light. She was beautiful and looked like a dream that Kalina, goddess of dreams, had devised herself. She spent a couple of hours deep in the woods, collecting the ingredients she needed. The mushrooms were easy enough to find; the nightshade a bit harder to track down. The biggest problem was finding a spider's nest. When she did though, she killed a few as fast as she could. She did so with as much mercy as possible. Once she collected them, she slipped them into her satchel and moved away from the nest. She was now ready to go. Returning back in the direction she had come, she crossed over a small stream and decided to stop for a moment. She knelt down and dipped her hands into the cold water. Her hands ached as they were submerged and she rubbed them together to clean what she could from her skin. When she lifted them, she decided they were clean enough upon inspection and dipped one hand again to cup some water and lift it to her lips. She sipped the cold water and felt refreshed once more.

The Dwarves, though not a talkative pair nor did they seem like they were doing much, were formidable Paladins of the White and were quite skilled at combat. The woods just outside the city were home to no beast or creature that could maul the girl and they were confident in that. They calmly awaited her return and upon seeing her emerge from the wood they began to prepare for the departure back into the city.

Ren smiled "I have everything I need. I am ready to return at your convenience."

The Dwarves had switched jobs now. The one who drove earlier waited for her to climb into the carriage and when she did he climbed in after her. Much like the other, he sat across from her not saying much of anything. The other climbed on top. Once ready, he took the reins and led the horses down the path until there was enough room to turn around. When turned around, the bumpy ride back to Whiterock started. They had made it through the city gates and not too far along when a guard stopped them. Ren's heart dropped and the guard across from her lifted a finger to his thick lips.

"Who's in the carriage, Dwarf?" the guard asked roughly.

"That's Dwarven business, Human. Mind yer's and we'll mind ours." the Dwarf on top replied.

The silence seemed to last forever before the carriage began to move again and Ren could see the Human guard staring at it angrily, but standing out of the way. No words were spoken after that and even upon arrival inside the great stone doors of Whiterock, when all exited the carriage, nothing was said but a humble and modest goodbye. As the Dwarves left her, Dwim approached the carriage.

"How much more time do ye' need, lass?" he asked anxiously.

"A bit more. I need to extract the ichor, dry my ingredients, and then mix properly." she responded.

Dwim nodded "Aye. We have a workstation set up for ye'." he led her to the kitchen of the Halls of the White. A small table had been set up for her near an oven. "I know it isn't much, lass, but that's what we got."

She smiled and dipped her head. "It'll do, thank you."

She placed her bag down on the table and removed the mushrooms and nightshade. She chopped them as small as she could before sliding them into the oven on a small tray that was laid out for her. She began to dissect and squeeze the spiders for their ichor when she looked up and noticed Dwim was still standing there and watching her.

"I do apologize for the time. I want to be sure the mixture is perfect for you." she said while her eyes lingered on him. "But I must warn you yet again, what you learn in others' dreams may not be beneficial to you. This can alter many things."

"Just be careful with yer' mixtures, lass. Yer' in this more than ye' know." he said, still watching her.

Ren hesitated at his words. She glanced at him again and then back down at her work. She felt nervous suddenly but did her best to try and sound cool as she spoke "I am always careful, sir."

In the next two hours, she removed the ichor and placed it into a vial. Once the mushrooms and nightshade were done baking, she mashed them the best she could into a fine powder. She measured them out and poured them into the same vial. Several long minutes passed after that and the ichor seemed to dissolve with the other ingredients into a violet colored liquid that shimmered silver in the light. It was still thick but it was supposed to be.

"Perfect" she whispered.

"Is that it then? If so, it is time to follow me." Dwim said and turned to head out of the kitchen.

Once outside, Dwim called for some of the other Paladins. He gave them orders in a low grumble and they shuffled off. He looked back towards Ren and motioned her to follow him. "They've got the chamber ready. Time to see if yer' potion works."

"It will work." she said softly. There was no doubt in her mind. She followed him holding the bottle tightly in her hand.

The halls of whiterock were long and deep and even heading to this chamber Dwim spoke of seemed to be a journey. Ren took the moment to admire her surroundings. The ceiling above her was high and carved perfectly. Some portions even painted with the scenes of great battles or Dwarven heroes. Dwim stopped at a door and knocked. It was a long moment before it was opened and the two of them entered. The chamber itself was circular and dark. Statues lined the wall, each well crafted and detailed.

Ren spotted a dais in the center where an old Dwarf was laid upon it. Even with the Dwarf on it she could see intricate carvings on the stone and before she could even ask, Dwim answered her question for her.

"Runes," he said quietly.

Ren did not respond. She had noticed the old Dwarf's hands were laid in deep carvings made for hands. The Dwarf was mumbling incoherent nonsense from quivering lips.

"That is the Oracle." Dwim whispered "I am ashamed to say his name has been forgotten to us. Even before the dream broke him, he didn't remember his own name. He's just always been called the Oracle."

Ren nodded, feeling a deep sadness for the old man. She thought it was a strange thing to forget one's own name.. Braizers sat on both sides of the dais and were putting off a lot of smoke. Ren fanned near her face hoping to not breathe much of it in.

"May I have the Kalina's Mist, Rennyn?" Dwim asked while holding out his hand.

Ren blinked, the smoke stinging her eyes "Yes of course." she held out the vial to him. Dwim plucked it from her hands and she continued to speak "He'll need to drink that completely. I suggest someone hold him down as it is not a pleasant taste." She suddenly had a feeling of deep dread. It rested in her stomach and she found that she wanted to be out of the room quite badly. She was confident in her mixture but even the slightest bit of extra nightshade could cause him to never wake. She looked towards the door to plan her escape, but was dismayed when she saw that the door had been locked by an iron bar. She thought she might be sick.

Dwim stepped over to the brazier on the left side of the dais. "Kalina's Mist is nay for him, lass. It's for us." he tipped the vial, draining the violet liquid into the brazier. The flames shot up and turned black for a moment and then silver before returning to normal. The Oracle's eyes opened wide and his body began to shake uncontrollably. His mad ranting became louder and he soon shouted his words so loudly that all in the chamber would be made uneasy.

Ren found that she wanted to cry. The room was becoming hazy and the smoke that poured from the brazier seemed to carry figures in it. She tried to step backwards but was unsure if she truly had. Her vision was becoming blurred. "Dwim-" she called out, scared. She felt that her brain was weightless and her head lifting upwards to some other existence.

"Sit down, lass. We're going on a dream walk." Dwim said as he lowered himself to the ground and breathed in deeply.

Ren covered her mouth with her cloak as she coughed, trying to fight the effects but losing. She slid to the floor, looking at the Oracle in fear before her eyes closed. She spoke only one word before drifting off "No."

Ren opened her eyes. All around her was darkness so pitch that she assumed it could be nothing more than nothingness itself. She was not light headed however and found that she could stand. She tested out her mobility by sliding a foot forward in the darkness and found that even though there was nothing beneath her she was able to walk just fine. Just as she was testing the boundaries of wherever it is she was, there was a terrible sinking feeling in her stomach as she thought to herself. *Welcome to the void for it is vast and all yours* and as she thought those words the Oracles voice boomed so loudly through the vast darkness that it brought her to her knees in fright.

"THE DOOR HAS BEEN OPENED AND A GIFT RECEIVED AFTER PRAYER! A SON OF STONE WILL NEVER RELENT UNTIL THE SOUL IS FREE!" there was no sign of the Oracle however, visions appeared in front of Ren now. It seemed to her to look like a Dwarf but there were no details that she could make out. It was still only a shadow but she noticed that one arm was bigger than the other. She got to her feet and tried to move to the shadowy figure but it vanished.

"Dwim?" She called out "Anyone? Hello?" she screamed those last words. She spun in circles, walking in any direction to find only darkness. "Can anyone hear me?" she felt like everything bad that had ever happened to her was rushing to her head. She shook her head hard, doing her best to keep it at bay. "Who are you? Are you the Oracle?"

The voice with no corporeal form boomed again "THE TWINKLE OF BLACK STARLIGHT GIVES REBIRTH TO OLD AND TERRIBLE EVIL! THE DEAD CAN NOT REST WHEN THE MONSTER LURKS!" Another visage appears. First it looked to be a tombstone of sorts. Ren tried to move closer but as she did the vision moved away at the same pace. From the grave another shadowy figure arose but then to her alarm, shifted into several other shadowy figures, each of different sizes and heights. She did her best to make sense of it but just as the last, it soon vanished and she was left in the void alone.

"A DRUNKEN CROW WILL BE CAPTURED BY THOSE WHO JEER MAGIC!" was the next cryptic declaration made by the bodiless voice. A giant crow appeared out of nowhere. Like the others, it was only a shadow. Upon its head sat a poorly made pointed hat, It's beak was entangled with a whip. Like all apparitions before it, it followed the trend of vanishing before her eyes.

Ren had resigned herself to not knowing what was going on or getting any sort of reply. Instead she stood there and waited as she had a gut feeling there was more to be seen. She was correct. The voice boomed out once more. "UPON THE DEATH OF THE YEAR A NEWBORN KING LIES IN THE BLOOD OF TERRIBLE LOSS WITH ONLY THE COMPANY OF A BEAST THAT SPEAKS LIKE MAN!" A shadowy baby lay naked before Ren. She moved to the baby to grab at it, out of instinct she believed, but as she reached out a snake appeared coiled around the child. It hissed and lashed out at her. Just as she was sure the phantom fangs were going to bite into her skin, both the snake and baby vanished.

Ren frowned but did not have time to think more on it. Beneath her the invisible floor began to rumble. A black tower started to rise under her feet and she tumbled off of it, landing on nothing for there really was nothing and yet it was all here. She looked up at the tower, her mouth hung open at its size. Above the tower were two red eyes staring down at her. The Oracle voiced out another statement. "ANCIENT CRUELTY FROM AGES PAST STILL LIVE IN THE TOWER ON THE SEA!"

Ren hated those eyes and was relieved to see them vanish as the tower itself crumbled into the void. It was replaced by blinding brilliant light as stars took the shape of two constellations. "THE AEGIS AND THE LADY MEET AGAIN!"

Ren had enough and she screamed back out to the voice "I don't understand what you are showing me!" She knew the story of the constellations. Nearly everyone knew of The Aegis and his lover. The Lady. Her head spun as she tried to gather her wits. She looked around. "Help me to understand you!" Two new figures appeared. They were nondescript but identical. One began to twist and became disfigured. " TWO HEARTS BEAT IN ONE CHEST BUT DO NOT BEAT TOGETHER! WOE IS ALL THAT IS KNOWN UNTIL THEY ARE ONE! EVEN THEN, REDEMPTION IS FOUND AT THE EMBRACE OF DEATH!"

Ren had no idea what any of it meant but had succumbed to the idea this is why the Oracle went mad. She watched the figures disappear once more while a beautiful rose bloomed in front of her. "OATHS WILL BE MADE UNDER THE ROSE AND THEIR FATES SEALED UPON AGREEMENT! UNTIL THEN WHAT MUST BE; CAN NEVER BE." The rose wilted now and vanished like everything before it, replaced by a visage of Dwim, other shadowy figures, and to her surprise, a vision of herself. "THE AEGIS AND THE LADY COME TOGETHER! THE OATH MUST BE SWORN! WITHOUT LOVE, ALL IS DOOMED! ALL IS WASTE!" There is one last loud boom and everything, even the void, seemed to be sucked back into nothingness. Ren felt as though she were falling so fast and yet being projected forward somehow. The waking world appeared to her, slowly and foggy. Ren, a dreamer without a choice, awakened.

CHAPTER 3

Ren's eyes shot open. She laid there on the stone floor, the dread lifting but not the words lingering in her head. She couldn't help but wonder how or why she was involved. She tried to recall everything, especially about the oath. She struggled to sit up but after a moment was able to lift herself up. When she did, she looked around the room and saw that everyone else was returning to the waking world as well. One of the Dwarves got to their feet and checked on the Oracle. They looked at Dwim with a frown.

"He has served till the last, m'lord." the Dwarf said in a mournful tone.

The Oracle laid there upon the dais in eternal slumber and finally, after many years of devoted service to Whiterock, was at peace. Dwim got himself to his feet and took a deep breath. "Aye. He'll get a royal burial and he will be carved into quartz. He will stand in the Halls of Majesty along with our other long passed heroes." Dwim moved to Ren and placed a fat hand on her shoulder, "Are ye' alright, lass?"

Ren nodded as she climbed to her knee and then her feet. "I think so." Looking at Dwim, with no lack of caution, she questioned him, "Why was I in this dream? What part do I play?"

"I nay know the answers or understand the riddles. I nay know the things I've seen there. They've already faded from my head leaving only fragments. We nay deal in mysticism too much down in the mountains but, our Oracle had never been wrong before. Nay any predictions like that before though." Dwim said calmly but gravely. Ren could see that he wasn't lying from the look in his glossy blue eyes.

She gathered her cloak tightly around herself again and looked to the doors of the room, "Master Dwim, I would like to go back to my room now, if I may?" Ren was eager to be alone with her thoughts and to write down what she could remember before it vanished from her mind.

"Aye, lass." Dwim said quietly. He understood the feeling and he nodded to the guard who then unlocked the door and pulled it open. "Ye' should nay go vanishing off on us now. We will prepare another escort for ye' if ye' would like to leave."

Ren had no plans to go anywhere, at least not at the moment, and so she replied, "I will stay until you escort your other traveler that you spoke of." She gave Dwim a hard look, "Can I consider my debt paid with this service?"

Dwim saw that her eyes almost dared him to disagree. He had no intention to do so however and was very agreeable in the matter, "Aye. Paid in full and ye' have our gratitude. Our traveler will likely be ready to leave soon. Get some rest while ye' can."

Rennyn managed to find her way back to the Halls of the White just fine. She was greeted by the maid who escorted her to the room while asking a hundred times if she needed anything. Ren declared each time that she needed nothing and was absolutely fine but just as she entered the room, she turned to ask for another drying cloth. The maid was happy to oblige and charged off. When alone, the Elf moved to her little locked chest of precious possessions and opened it. She removed the leather bound journal, turned to an empty page, and dug around for a quill. After a moment of moving things around in the chest she suddenly realized she couldn't remember most of the dream. When she found a quill and ink, she jotted down as many notes as she could. She made sure to mention the oath, the baby, and a few other things that had nothing to do with the dream at all. When she was done, she placed her things back in the chest.

The Dwarven maid returned with the drying cloth. Ren had decided to have herself another soak in the tub after thanking the maid and sending her away.. When her bath was done, she dried off and crawled into the bed. It was warm and smelled faintly of the oil of fresh flowers. Closing her eyes, she fell into a sleep filled with her own dreams and thankfully none that belonged to anyone else.

A good few hours had passed when the echoes of Dwim's laughter filled the Halls of the White. His laughter was soon joined by another and a voice that did not belong to anyone she had met yet. "The look on your face was priceless!" the voice exclaimed.

"Lass?" Dwim called out, "Are ye' ready to travel? Our guest has finished his business here in Whiterock."

She sat up, dressed as quickly as possible, and threw her cloak around her. She grabbed her chest, which was small enough to fit into her satchel, and placed it nice and snug inside. She threw the satchel over her shoulder and gave the room a once over to make sure she had not left anything behind. Deciding that she was fine, for her clothes were already packed along with her chest, she opened the door, pulled her hood up, and stepped out. "Hello, Master Dwim. I am ready."

"Just Dwim if ye' nay mind." he said, giving her a small bow. He then turned to look up at his new friend. "This is Leon Farharbor. Renowned adventurer and other titles he has given himself."

Beside Dwim was a tall and ruggedly handsome Human. His mustache was well maintained and large. His hair, a light brown, was parted on the right side and brushed back. His face is rough and covered with stubble. He wore regular cloth clothing, not the type to fray easily, but leathers weighed him down far too much for his profession. He offered Ren a terribly handsome smile, "It's a pleasure! I hope this religious zealot has been showing you good Dwarven hospitality." He extended a hand out to the Elf whom his chestnut colored eyes found breathtaking.

Ren smiled sweetly, brushing a stray strand of her hair behind her ear. "The pleasure is mine, sir." She placed her hand in Leon's. He grasped it, lifted it to his lips and kissed the back side of her hand. Ren blushed and tried to push on, "I'm Rennyn," she paused admiring the man and then continued once more, "Dwim has been more than accommodating during my stay here. I have felt most welcomed." She looked around, doing her best to avert her eyes from his, "I will be glad to get above ground and into the fresh air, but I will admit I will miss the bath most of all."

Leon offered a soft laugh and released her hand. "I agree. The Dwarven holds are very breathtaking, but I need the sky above me. Being able to see up a Dwarven statue's nostrils is not all that appealing."

"Oh aye, and lookin' at yer' mugs is a real pleasure for us." Dwim chuckled, "C'mon. Carriage is waitin' on us. We're headed to Karren's Call. Normally I would nay travel outside of the mountains, but I've got to meet with another Paladin of the White."

Dwim turned and started towards the carriage that was waiting for them just outside the hall like before. Ren frowned and stayed behind both Dwim and Leon. In a concerned voice she spoke up, "Karren's Call? I am unsure how safe it is there after what happened." It was also the unknown that scared her. She couldn't simply be dropped off in North Normoon as she no longer had a home to return to. Where would she go? Where would she stay? She figured she might be tagging along for quite some time or at least as long as they allowed her to do so.

"I nay know what happened at Karren's Call." Dwim said, not seeming to be all that interested.

"Some girl was murdered by some sort of monster." Ren exclaimed. She never said it aloud but she somewhat thought it could have been Alastor who had done it, especially after seeing how easily he pulled poor Martin's head apart.

"That's half the fun, isn't it?" Leon asked. "Besides, I'd think you'd be interested in such things with your profession. Dwim here speaks very highly of your skill with alchemical work." he turned and offered her a smile. She returned it. "Me? I'm more of a trophy hunter. When I heard that a monster did that nasty business in Karren's Call, I just knew I had to go investigate. I'm hoping to track the beast down, kill it, and earn myself some gold. They'll be singing songs of my bravery for years to come."

Dwim rolled his eyes, "They'll sing alright. About how ye' made wee in your trousers at the sight of it. *If* it's real."

Leon let out a laugh and Ren could see clearly that they both enjoyed the banter. She let out a soft giggle herself. "I'm not sure just how useful my skills would be in a moment that required a split second decision "she paused for a moment and then added, "but I suppose I could be of service if you needed. I honestly don't have anywhere else to go at this point." her next words felt weak in her mouth, "It's probably best if I do not travel on my own for long. Would my presence during your travels be unwelcomed, sir?"

Leon turned his head back to face her, making sure it was him she was talking to. "Not at all!" he offered her another small smile, "I'd never turn down a traveling companion as gorgeous as you are." and he gave her a small wink to accompany his smile. He faced ahead once more, "If only this guy next to me looked even a sliver as good as you, I'd swear I'd think myself dead and in the afterlife."

Dwim groaned, "Keep it in yer' pants, lad."

Ren blushed, she kept her head down hoping neither would look back to see. She played with her hair that hung over her shoulder. "That's sweet. I will try to be as useful as I can of course."

The three had come to the carriage. This one was a bit nicer than the one she previously rode in, or at least the wheels were evenly rounded. Dwim and Leon threw their bags on the back and Dwim offered to take Ren's as well. She handed it over without fuss and he strapped them down. Leon stood at the carriage door and offered to help her in. Ren smiled, took his hand, and stepped into the carriage. She sat down, adjusted her cloak, and did her best to get comfortable. Leon climbed in after her and sat across and gave her a smile as their eyes met once again. Dwim's weight caused the carriage to dip to one side a bit as he climbed it. He sat next to Leon and clapped his hands together.

"I've got some coin, lass, to get ye' some new clothes if ye' like when we get there." Dwim announced as he had started to stroke his beard. "I know we nay have much for the Elven form here in Whiterock."

Ren offered him a friendly smile, "Goodness, I couldn't take that from you." but even as she said it, her eyes sparkled at the thought of new clothes.

The carriage started off. The three of them were quiet while they rode through the stone crafted halls of Whiterock to the large stone doors that led out of the mountain. Leon, ever a curious person, was looking out the window of the carriage at the city of Dwarves, admiring all that he could. Once outside, the sunlight pierced the thin pane of glass of the carriage and blinded them. Once their eyes adjusted there wasn't much for them to do but stare out and so they did. Ren cast her eyes at Leon on occasion, but found that Dwim was far more interesting to watch as he kept fidgeting in his seat. His face was beginning to turn scarlet when he finally blurted out.

"What do ye' think it is? Really? The thing that killed the woman in Karren's call?" he asked. It looked as though a weight had been lifted off of him as soon as the words were out of his mouth.

Ren gave a shrug that was combined with a shudder that always happened when she thought about it. "I had heard it was a few things, but I can only assume it was a monster. After all, she was torn to pieces."

Leon did not look at them when he spoke, "In all honesty, probably just a bold wolf out from the woods. Seems strange though that no one saw it." He turned his gaze away from the sights of North Normoon. "Karren's Call is a harbor town. Busy nightlife there. Seems mighty weird no one would have spotted a wild animal running loose." He pulled a pipe from a leather bag that rested on his hip, "Either of you mind?" he asked, lifting the pipe up. Dwim, who enjoyed a pipe now and again himself shook his head. Ren shook hers as well before looking out the window and getting lost in her thoughts. Leon lit the tobacco in the pipe and took a long pull from it. He held it in until he was able to open the carriage window and blow it out. "Either way" he carried on "I'll take the beast down and get myself a pretty reward out of it. Some fame too, I bet."

"Saving the town is also pretty important." Ren mumbled to herself.

Leon looked at her thoughtfully, "Where are you from, Ren? Can I call you that?"

She nodded "You may, sir. I grew up here, in North Normoon. I had a small shop that I built in my home. You know-" she rambled off a few things, "Potions, powders, elixirs, that sort of stuff." Her face grew somber, "Unfortunately, my home was burnt down. I took what I could in the few minutes I had but most of it is destroyed or pillaged by now." she let out a sigh. "It will mean I will have to start over. A whole new client base. Which really just means a couple of rough years until I can gain their trust."

"Burnt down?" Leon asked, "How? Mixture gone wrong?"

"The guards were looking for someone. "She thought about Alastor for a moment. "I refused them entry and they decided to make their own way in."

"Wrong side of the law, huh? We've all been there." He took another puff from the pipe.

"I nay have been on the wrong side of the law and I nay intend to be" Dwim said giving Leon a ferocious look and jammed a fat finger at Leon but never poking him "So nay ye' go and make any trouble in my company." The face of anger vanished quickly and was replaced with raised cheeks and a smile.

Leon chuckled, amused by the Dwarf. His attention turned back to Ren. "Not to be crude, but don't you have an Elven home to return to?"

Rennyn looked out the window and wrapped herself up tightly. She didn't respond. Leon cleared his throat and muttered a sorry. The three of them went back to watching the scenery outside the carriage.

"I'm from a small town called Black Moss, in Marrenval." Leon said after he snuffed his pipe and put it away, "You've heard of it?"

Ren looked at him and did her best to keep the conversation going, "The kingdom south of Normoon?" she asked.

"Yeah.That's the one." he offered another smile, "Royal decree has made magic forbidden. They have these people called Witch Hunters who hunt down sources of magic and either imprison them or destroy them. "

Ren furrowed a brow, "What kind of magic?"

Leon casually shrugged, "Any I suppose. Anyway, there's a beach covered in rocks a good ways south of a town called Lilly Tree. I met a hermit who lived in a small hut on one of my hunting trips. He didn't do any magic in front of me but I suspect he could. I only bring this up because when we met, I told him my profession, he exchanged that he was a librarian of sorts. I laughed of course because here he is on this forsaken beach living in a hut. So I asked where his library was. Well, he invites me into this tiny hut, lifts a rug and reveals a cellar door. We go down there and would you believe me if I told you? Bookcases galore! I mean he had an odd collection of other things too but I simply could not believe my eyes. Some of them looked quite ancient too."

Ren seemed to perk up as she found it quite interesting, "What were the book subjects?"

"I'd be lying if I said I could remember or let alone pronounce any of them." Leon laughed.

"Dark magics?" she asked. Her purple eyes glistened with intrigue.

Leon let out another laugh and the three continued to make small talk. Over the next several days on their journey south east of North Normoon to Karren's Call, they made camp at night to allow their driver to rest and would start again the next morning. Leon, who was a master huntsman, was always able to get them fresh meat for meals and shared with them tales of his travels as well as his dream to create the first map that detailed the entire world. That was something that the others figured had not been fully explored and congratulated him on his ambition. By the time they did reach Karren's Call they were decent friends and had exchanged many stories amongst each other.

It was dusk when they had pulled into Karren's Call and just as Leon had said, the town was coming to life now that the night had arrived. The streets were clean and well lit by oil lamps. Trees accented the cozy looking buildings that Rennyn found very appealing. The sky was painted purple and lavender; decorated with streaks of clouds. Ren found herself enjoying Leon's company. It felt nice to laugh and eat good food. She helped as much as she could with prepping different fruits and vegetation she located out in the wilds when they made camp. She even boiled tea to help everyone get a good night's sleep. She enjoyed one particular evening where they had made camp near a crystal clear lake and she was able to sneak away in the night, disrobe, and get clean once more. She was also happy to be back to some sort of civilization.

Leon took a deep breath in. "Mm! Smell that?"

Dwim took a sniff and frowned "Old fish?"

Leon laughed, "No, my fine bearded friend. Smells like a town that's alive!"

Dwim climbed out of the carriage once it stopped and spoke some Dwarvish to the driver. The driver, who was short bearded and young looking, then climbed down and started gathering their gear from the carriage. Once Ren and Leon climbed out, Dwim faced both of them. "I'm having the driver take our things and get us some rooms at the inn here in town. It's called The Sleepy Sheep Inn. I'm gonna head to the cathedral to meet my Paladin contact. I'll see ye' two later." He gave a bow of his head and started towards the cathedral which could easily be seen looming over the other buildings. He didn't get too far when he turned back around and pointed his fat finger at them, "Stay out of trouble!"

Ren grinned playfully, "I never get into trouble!" she called back and then winked at Leon. "Shall we pick up what's left and take a walk through town? Maybe there are some shops that are open that would have something new for me to wear. I have a little bit of gold in my satchel." The Dwarf driver had nudged her just as she said that and handed over a small coin purse.

"Should be 'nuff to buy a few things. I'll be bringing yer' luggage to the inn." the Dwarf driver said with a low grumble.

Leon gave a shrug, "Sure. Why not? Been cooped up too long in that carriage. Walk would be good. Lead the way."

Ren walked beside Leon, looking up at him every so often as he talked. She was attentive and laughed at just the right times, even if what he said wasn't particularly funny. She found that she couldn't stop smiling at him either, but she was okay with it. She had a rough series of events happen and a little flirt wouldn't hurt. They passed a bakery that had her mouth watering as she remembered the fruit tarts she was never able to afford back in North Normoon. There was more walking and then she spotted a tailor's shop.

"Oh!" Ren pointed a dainty finger, "Would you mind terribly if I went in there just for a moment?" she offered Leon her prettiest smile, "I promise I won't be long."

"Go on," he said with a wave of his hand, "I'll be out here waiting. I'll even start poking around for information about our monster. I'm sure they're all eager to gossip about it."

Ren made her way into the shop trying to keep her head about her as she looked at all the dresses. She knew she needed to be practical, especially with Dwim's money. She found a couple of items that would keep her warm but that would also hold up to traveling. She also found a new pair of soft leather boots that she would be able to use to replace her worn ones. Thankfully, she was able to get what she needed without any alterations being required. She went to the shopkeeper and her total was tallied. Ren dug into the coin purse, feeling guilty for having used some of Dwim's coin but knew that she needed clothing badly, and exchanged the coin for the clothes. Both ladies wished each other a good evening and Ren headed outside to find Leon.

Cathedral bells rang, signaling the hour. The night was getting darker and much noisier. More guards were appearing out in the street. They had no intention of course to grab anyone and were more than likely out keeping an eye on the town's folk since the murder happened. Ren spotted Leon moving from group to group as well as stopping individuals in the cobblestone street. Their talks looked brief and Ren assumed he wasn't getting much information from them. When one fellow shook his head and walked away, Leon sighed and looked in Ren's direction. When he saw her, he gave a wave and headed towards her. Ren met him halfway.

"Any luck?" she asked, her brows raised.

Leon shook his head, "No. I can't get anyone to really open up."

"May I try?" she offered him a smile, "Maybe they'll be more comfortable talking to a lady?"

"Might as well give it a shot." he agreed and stood aside.

Ren picked a gathering of ladies and headed their direction. She could hear them talking over one another and couldn't really decide what they were talking about. She cleared her throat and spoke up. "Excuse me."

The group of women quit their chattering and looked at Ren, abashed by Ren's approach. "Yes?" one asked, acknowledging Ren's presence.

"How's your day?" Ren decided to open with an easy question. People were more willing to talk if you opened with small talk.

"It's a day. Like any other. " There was a long silence between the two of them. When the woman realized Ren wasn't going to leave, she found she had no choice but to ask the same. "And yours?"

"Well enough, thank you. " she cleared her throat, "Though I have been all a flutter over these rumors about the murder here.`` She got closer and lowered her voice. "I'm new in town and I keep hearing something about a monster, but I doubt this very much. It seems like something an animal would do."

The woman stared at Ren for a bit, but there was no answer. Luckily, another of the women spoke up, "What kind of animal has sex with the prey?" That woman was elbowed quickly.

"Wash your mouth" scolded another, "If it was an animal, it was one of considerable size."

Ren nodded, "Suppose it was a monster. What reason would he have to hurt this poor girl?"

"How would I know?" the first woman asked incredulously. "What causes a dog to bite? I don't know why a monster would attack the girl." She shrugged her shoulders hard and shook her head. "What I think is strange is that no one near the brothel saw anything at all!"

"I would agree" Ren declared, "I'm sure someone must have seen something. Maybe they just are too scared to talk?" She did her best to read the group. She felt like she was getting nowhere and fast with this lot.

"Probably a wolf mistaken for a dog" the woman said definitively, "No clue what else it would be."

Ren glanced back at Leon and gave him a small shake of the head when they made eye contact. She was disappointed. She looked back at the group of girls and gave a slight bow of thanks. "Thank you, ladies." She backed away and headed over to Leon. "Nothing useful, I'm sorry."

"We'll get something figured out." Leon said with a shrug. He rubbed his stomach, "I'm starving. I'm going to head back to the inn and grab a meal. We can investigate the brothel tomorrow when the light is out."

She remembered how her mouth had watered at the sight of the pastries and nodded, "Yes, I am ready for a hot meal, myself. A meal and a real bed."

They walked along the streets, passing shops and fancy homes, before they finally found The Sleepy Sheep Inn. It was nestled between two shops; one belonging to a potter and the other a leather worker. It looked cozy but run down. The sign hanging from the roof had a picture of a sheep sleeping with little crescent moons above its head. As they got closer to the inn they could hear ruckus laughter.

"Seems lively" said Leon as he reached for the door.

"Hopefully not too loud to sleep." She gave him a gentle elbow as she neared him, "You will stay out of trouble?"

Leon opened the door and held it open for her, "No trouble from me unless some sort of rare beast hides inside. " he laughed, unknowing that was more true than he could ever believe.

Ren thanked him and stepped inside the inn. Leon followed right behind her. Immediately they spotted their Dwarven driver sitting at the bar with a massive stein of beer in front of him. The inn was well lit and all the tables were filled with heavy drinkers and smokers. A thin, flat chested woman was making the rounds delivering drinks and bowls of the night's soup. The barkeep was just finishing filling up a mug for another patron when he looked up and spotted them.

"Welcome! Welcome! Come in." he slammed the mug down in front of the patron and dusted his hands off. "I'm afraid I don't have any rooms." he thumbed to the Dwarf. "He came in and rented up all the rooms. Lots of spirits and hot soup though. Make yourself comfortable."

Ren headed to the bar, "Some ale and soup, please." The barkeep nodded and started off. "Oh! And bread?" The barkeep gave her a wink and went off to get that order fulfilled for her. Ren sat down and looked around taking in the scenery. Leon took the seat next to her and waited for the barkeep to return. When the man did, he placed a mug of ale, a creamy bowl of soup that looked quite hardy, and a few slices from a loaf of bread. Ren thanked him and Leon asked for the same order that Ren did. The barkeep nodded. As he started to head off, the patron that was served before they sat down spoke up.

"Lionel. Another beer." he said, nearly belching into the mug.

Lionel, The Sleepy Sheep Inn's owner and barkeep, sighed and took his mug. He gave Leon a look, "Sorry mister, I'll get you taken care of in a moment."

Leon nodded "Quite alright."

Lionel filled the tankard and slammed it down in front of the man. "Phin, you've been tanked off your ass for nearly two weeks now. What's wrong with you, huh?"

The man, whose hair was golden and greasy, took the mug and drank from it; never giving Lionel a response. Lionel shook his head and went to fetch Leon's order. He returned with another order of ale, soup, and bread. He placed it in front of Leon and nodded "Five silver crowns for each of you, please."

Leon dug around in his satchel and counted out ten silver coins and placed them on the bar counter. Lionel scooped them up and headed to the back. Leon sipped his ale and placed the mug down. When Lionel returned, Leon spoke to him between mouthfuls of hot, delicious, soup.

"We're the company of Master Dwim of the White." Leon said and then thumbed towards the Dwarf driver who paid no attention to them.

Lionel nodded his understanding and reached under the counter. He pulled up a set of keys and handed one to each of them. "Here you go. Room number is etched on the key." Both Ren and Leon examined their keys. Lionel watched them and when he saw they were done examining them he spoke, "Strange days. A murder in this quiet town. A Dwarf coming out of the mountains. Makes you wonder what's next."

Ren continued to sip at her soup while Leon made small talk with Lionel about how strange things were the last few days, hoping to get some sort of information out of him. Sadly, nothing useful was said. Ren sat there with an overwhelming feeling that something was off in the room but she couldn't quite put her finger on it.

The drunk, golden haired man, called out for another one. Lionel looked at him and replied, nearly pleading with the man, "Phineas, I really don't-"

"Lionel, don't you get it? I've got to stay drunk to keep the monster at bay." he drooled on himself and let out another belch. "More beer. In fact-" he turned around in the chair and roared out, "A ROUND FOR THE HOUSE!" he waved drunkenly as he faced Lionel again. Those behind him sitting at tables went up in a roar of good cheers. Lionel sighed and started filling mugs after refilling the drunk's first.

Ren lifted her brow and leaned towards Leon, "Did you hear that?"

Leon nodded and then glanced at the drunk. The man, who had been called Phineas by Lionel, was fair skinned and impossibly beautiful, even in his drunken state. His face was chiseled perfectly. His hair, though indeed greasy at the moment, was the perfect gold color and was long enough that it was currently pulled into a ponytail. His eyes shone bright blue like a cloudless sky on a summer morning.

Lionel caught Leon looking at Phin. When he was done filling that mug of ale, he walked over and leaned on the counter, making sure to lower his voice so that only Leon and Ren could hear him. "Poor bastard has been in a slump since that murder. Our Phineas, well, he's a bit of a scoundrel. Spends a lot of time at the brothel, understand?" Lionel shook his head, "Must have hit him hard. Might have even been sweet on the girl. Spends his days and nights drinking until he passes out; dead to the world."

Rennyn got up from her chair and stepped over towards Phineas. She slid up beside him and gave him a bright smile, her eyes shimmering brightly even in this lighting. "Hello there. Quite generous of you to buy the last round. Seems like you probably don't need another though."

"Listen to me handsome," Phin said as he turned those wonderful blue eyes towards her, "I'll keep drinking. If I'm drinking, then he can't do anything. Now mind your own-" he let out a disgusting burp that sounded like a stomach growling "- your own business."

Ren scowled and fanned her hand in front of her face. When she was certain none of his disgusting belch was under her nose, she placed a hand lightly on his arm and tilted her head to the side. She spoke in a motherly tone when she asked, "Who is he, darling?"

"He," Phineas replied, "Is me. I'm a cold blooded killer."

Lionel rushed over to stand in front of Phin across the bar counter, "Don't listen to that fool! He wouldn't hurt a fly. Now a thief? Yes, one of the best. And a dirty cheat, too. But violent? Never. I'd swear on that."

Ren ignored Lionel and continued to smile at Phin, "Phineas, why don't we go outside where it's a bit quieter? We could talk, you and I." She held out her hand "I'm a pretty good listener."

Phin finished off his mug and then nodded, "I have to piss anyway." He got up and headed out the back door. Lionel looked worried, but kept tending the bar. Leon followed after Ren who was already following Phin. She turned back and motioned for Leon to keep his distance for a bit. She wanted to see if she could get Phineas to talk more openly. Leon fell back but only a little. He was still alert and ready just in case things didn't go as Ren had hoped. Phin stumbled over to a bush once he threw the back door open and began to unlace his pants. Ren had slowly crept up behind him but not overly close. She wanted to make sure not to do anything to cause him to startle. Phineas let out a loud groan as a torrent of piss that watered the bush in front of him.

Ren leaned against a beam that held up a wooden awning that provided shade during the day, giving Phin some space while he did his business. "You seem like a pretty nice guy, Phineas. A tad bit drunk, but what else is there to do at an inn, right?" She smiled brightly, trying to make him feel more at ease. He didn't answer and kept letting it flow. He tiptoed a moment to squeeze out a quick fart and then rocked back on his feet. She walked closer to him, reaching out and putting a hand lightly on his arm, "Did you want to talk about the brothel? Do you know what happened that night?"

Phin sighed, "Figured it out, huh? I knew someone would sooner or later. Figured I was the monster and have come to put an end to me." He gave his trouser snake a shake and put himself away. He laced his pants again and turned to face her. Tears streamed from his eyes as he went on, "I deserve it" he said between sobs, "I killed that girl. I should have confessed and let them hang me, but I was so scared."

Ren furrowed her brow and stepped closer to him. "It's okay to be scared. I just want to figure out what happened that night." Phineas' head hung low and was now buried in his hands. She reached out and pulled his hands down, slowly, and then lifted his face. "You don't look like the kind of person who could do that much damage. That girl was brutally wounded." she looked him in the eyes. She wasn't sure if she wanted to urge him to do something. She couldn't believe that as he currently was, that he was capable of what he claimed to have done.

"The monster came. He always does." Phineas whispered, "I never know when. I could feel it when I was with her. I hoped it would stay at bay because when I stay busy, he usually doesn't come but not that night."

"What were you doing when he came, Phineas? Did she say something to make you angry? Upset?" Ren cocked her head to the side, "Did things not work the way you were expecting?" Something inside Ren wanted to make Phin mad. The more she thought on it the angrier she herself became at the seemingly senseless murder that happened. "Were you embarrassed because she refused you something?"

He laughed at her questions, knowing exactly what she was implying. The man was aware of how beautiful he was and what his looks could get him. Truth was he was rarely denied the company of a woman and any fool looking at him could easily see why. He stepped away from her and slowly unbuttoned his shirt. Once it was undone, he pulled it off and spread his arms wide. His body was lean and firm. It was just as perfect as his face. Across his chest were long terrible scars where he had once been mauled by something. He slowly turned around to show her that his back was even worse. It was painted with long scars and deep gouges. One particular patch looked like a bite mark.

He faced her again and dropped his arms to his sides. "I'm a wolf." Phineas said rather plainly.

"I'm not scared of you." Ren replied firmly. Her eyes burned into his.

Leon stepped in finally and placed a hand on her arm, "This fool is obviously toying with us, Ren. He thinks he's a wolf. This is silly."

Ren nodded and allowed herself to be pulled back from the would-be confrontation. "Sorry, Leon," she said, finally turning away from Phineas and looking at her new friend, "I was hoping to actually find a monster. I guess this is a trail that will lead us nowhere."

"I can prove it." Phineas said. Both Leon and Ren turned and gave him a look. Leon then looked at Ren to gauge her reaction.

Ren scoffed and broke away from Leon. She took steps towards Phineas, her voice getting bolder as she spoke, "Here's what I think. I think that the poor girl at the brothel turned you away. I think it made you angry and you were upset that someone with your looks was denied." Ren shrugged slightly, "But I don't think anything further happened. Maybe you were just too drunk to perform."

Phineas bent over and started twisting his body. Even while he contorted his face, he was still incredibly good looking. Leon quickly grabbed Ren and yanked her back towards him. Ran stumbled a bit, but she never took her eyes off Phineas. The beautiful man threw his hands up with his fingers spread and curled them as if they were claws. He growled and snarled at the pair. He took a step towards them, then another, then curiously, a step backwards. Ren raised a single brow as Phin stood up straight. His breathtaking eyes rolled up, causing his pupils to vanish underneath his eye lids and his body slowly leaned back. Just as slowly as it started, it ended fast. His body fell completely back making a thud as he hit the ground with his arms spread out. The man was blacked out.

Ren turned her gaze to Leon with a not so surprised look on her face. Leon only stared at the drunk for a moment before remarking, "I think he just fell in his own piss."

Ren let out a false laugh, "I don't think it was him, Leon." She looked at Phin once more, "I feel a strange energy from him, but I really don't believe it for a moment that he was the one."

"Maybe we'll learn something in the morning from Dwim." Leon replied softly. "Let's head in and go get some rest."

Ren agreed with a yawn, "Yes, maybe a good night's sleep will do us all some good."

Leon guided her inside and after another drink, they let Lionel know that Phin had passed out in the backyard. Lionel thanked them and told them both he would go out later and collect the poor bastard. They both said their goodnight to one another and headed to the room etched on their keys. They made themselves comfortable and climbed in their cozy beds. The rooms themselves were unremarkable. When they shut their eyes, sleep came to them both nearly immediately, allowing them only a moment or so to collect their thoughts before they drifted off to the dreams that awaited them.

CHAPTER 4

A few hours had passed and Leon, Ren, Dwim, and the Dwarf driver were all in their own rooms sleeping quietly. Dwim had come in not too long after Leon and Rennyn retired for the evening. Each of them dreamed of things other than burning homes and whore killing monsters in the night. The noise had settled down below at the bar around midnight when Lionel decided to close up shop and sent everyone out. He was even good enough to go out and drag Phin back inside, just as he said he would, and take him to his room.

Ren was sleeping rather deeply in her bed nude and covered in a thick blanket. The hour was nearing four in the morning when she felt a gentle shake trying to rouse her from her slumber. Her eyes did not open and she groaned softly, "It's not already time to depart is it?" She was shaken again. She opened her eyes now and glanced up at the window. When she saw that it was still dark, she began to fuss, "It's still dark out!" She sat up and looked at the figure standing next to her bed. She first assumed it was Leon and wondered why he had entered her room. Ren found it a brazen move coming from Leon, so she wiped at her eyes and looked again. "Phineas!" she yelped pulling the blanket up her chest more, though she wasn't bared to anyone to begin with. "What are you doing in my room?" Her voice was raised and accusing as she scooted her back against the headboard.

Phin stared down at her, even in the darkness she could see there was sadness on his face, "He's coming."

Her eyes scanned the bed side table for a weapon, "How did you get in here? Phineas you need to leave!" The last was said in a demanding tone.

Phin moved closer to the window as though he hadn't heard her command for him to leave. "I picked the lock" he said while he looked out. "I can tell he's coming because I can feel him clawing at my mind. The blood that flows within me is too hot. It longs for the hunt." Phin placed his hands on either side of the window and in a pained whine said, "I can hear it breathing loudly in my ears. I can feel its heart beating in my head," he cried out loudly now, "It's so loud!"

Rennyn eased herself out of the bed, dragging the blanket with her to keep herself covered. She moved to the door where her nightgown and cloak hung. She grabbed the gown and quickly swapped it for her blanket. Her change was fast and Phin saw nothing as he continued to stare out the window. "I don't hear anything, Phin." she said, doing her best to keep her voice from shaking, "Maybe you're still drunk." Her hand danced on the door knob, slowly turning it and hoping it would make no noise, "Maybe you should go back to your room to rest."

"I'm sorry." he mumbled. There was not much light in the room but the light that was there was light enough for Ren to clearly observe his body actually starting to twist shape. His arms and legs, accompanied with the sounds of bones snapping, grew shorter. His torso started to widen while thick gray hair grew upon his pale skin. As his body changed in front of her and its size grew, his clothes ripped and fell to the floor around him. It was no time at all that where a man once stood was now a wolf. Not just a wolf, but a dire wolf. A dire wolf nearly four feet tall on all fours with massive paws that showcased razor-like claws. It's mouth was filled with sharp, jagged teeth. It's eyes, the beautiful blue of Phineas' eyes, darted around at the scenery outside the window. The wolf's tail swung from side to side and smashed against the bed as well as the dresser. The wolf started to turn around slowly. Once it had done so, and realized that someone else was in the room, it began to snarl. Spit hung by a string from it's lip momentarily before hitting the wooden floor with a plop. It locked eyes with the red headed Elf in the corner near the door.. Ren, perhaps foolishly, never took her eyes away from the beast. Her heart pounded so heavily that she thought for a moment she might pass out. She held her hand out to the wolf and spoke in a whisper, "Phineas, it's okay. We can figure this out."

Phineas may have heard her words or at least some of them while the beast stood there. Ren had hoped that was the case at least for her own sake. The wolf stepped closer to her. It's massive paws thudded against the floor. It's tail was raised and it's fangs bared, lips drawn back as it let out a growl. Ren stepped towards him but only slightly. She whispered to him in a soft sing-song voice, "It's okay. I will help you." Her body started to shake slightly. She felt something inside her just like she did when she and Alastor were threatening each other in the caverns under North Normoon. Outside, the wind picked up, knocking tree branches against the window pane that would make terrible scratching noises that she hated possibly more than she hated the position she was currently in. "Phineas? Can you hear me?"

The wolf let out a bark that would scare the bravest of men and followed it up with an ear piercing howl. Ren let out a cry and jumped back into the corner. The gargantuan tongue licked over its chops and then hung limply out of its mouth. It took another step forward and then positioned itself into a hunting stance. It's lips drew back further from the large teeth. The door flung open, knocking Ren back against the wall and trapping her behind it. While she was trapped, the wind outside died down to a gentle breeze. Dwim rushed in with his sword ready and shield high, ready to do battle.

"C'mon ye' scoundrel-'" Dwim shouted just before his eyes saw the beast, "Oh shet" was all that he could mumble before Leon came rushing in as well with his bow. An arrow was already threaded and when his eyes spotted the wolf he pulled back and let the arrow loose. The wolf had no plans to allow itself to be preyed on and lunged forward at the group. Leon's arrow lodged itself in the wolf's hind leg. Dwim, upon seeing Leon's arrow land, moved from the door and thrusted his sturdy iron shield, crafted by the finest Dwarven blacksmiths, towards the monster's maw. Ren, who had been struggling against the door trying to push it away from her, finally broke free from it and watched as both Leon and Dwim did their best to fight the creature off. That strange feeling welled inside her once more and the wind outside picked up again. Instead of branches simply scratching against the window; a limb came bursting through sending glass shattering all over the bedroom floor. Oil lamps that rested on the nightstand and dresser also fell to the floor sending its glass to join the shards of the window. Leon threaded another arrow and aimed to fire when he noticed that something was pulling the wolf back towards the window. He took a look towards Dwim and noticed the Dwarf's beard also flowing out towards the window as though something were pulling. Leon glanced back at Ren now and found himself momentarily stunned. Ren's eyes did not seem her own as she stared at the wolf.

Whatever Ren was doing, it was working, but it did not stop the wolf for a moment from trying to attack. It bit at the air ferociously and then clawed out toward them. Blood lust was in those beautiful blue eyes. Dwim, not really paying attention to anything more than protecting the others, darted forward and bashed the creature on the nose with his shield but it only seemed to anger the beast more. Leon fired off another few arrows in rapid succession. Each landing its mark in the wolf's head, but nothing seemed to slow it down.

Leon turned to Ren and shouted, "I don't know how you're doing it but push it out the fucking window!"

The wind whipped around her and without understanding what she was doing, she thrusted her hands outwards, pushing Phineas closer and closer to the window. The beast left long claw marks etched into the wood as it scrambled to fight against the strange wind pulling at him. Ren, perhaps no longer her own, stepped out past Leon and then Dwim, closer and closer to the wolf. Her little feet walked over the shattered glass that littered the floor and left a trail of bloody footprints. She felt none of it. The tree branches that had broken the window seemed to now move on their own as if they were snakes. They bent and slithered in through the broken window, wrapping themselves around the direwolf. The wolf twisted it's head and tried to snap at whatever grabbed hold of him. It's spit flew all over the place now as its jaws snapped at the wooden limbs. The wolf was not successful however and was pulled further back until he was all but hanging out the window.

"Out the window, Ren!" Leon yelled out "If you don't let it go now people will get hurt!"

"Aye! We can track the bastard tomorrow! Out the window!" Dwim begged

Ren met the eyes of the wolf one last time before it was dragged completely out the window and thrown not too far away from the inn. It landed in the street and let out a whimper before immediately standing back up. It let out another ear piercing howl and darted off towards the wooded area in the distance on the edge of town. Just as Leon had predicted, people had begun to come outside to see what all the noise was about. Dressed in gowns, and few dressed in nothing, all stood there looking around aimlessly, having just missed the biggest wolf they no doubt would have ever seen in their lives.

Ren's eyes seemed to dull suddenly and the wind died down while the branches seemed to slowly slip back into place. She fell to her knees gasping for air while Leon and Dwim seemed to be momentarily frozen in place. That did not last though as Dwim had moved to her, dropping his sword and shield to the floor and placing a thick hand on her shoulder, "Are ye' alright, lass?" He gave her a moment to answer, but when she didn't, he spoke again in a soft gentle tone that belonged to a nursing mother speaking to the babe at her tit, "C'mon, stand up. I got ye'."

Ren, pale to begin with, was as white as a sheet. She shook hard in Dwim's large hands. Her head dipped into her quivering hands and her slender fingers dug into her hair and she let out a long hard sob, "I couldn't! I have never!" Her head shook from side to side, taking with it her hands as they clung to her head now. "I didn't want to hurt him! I promise!" She let her hands drop and looked into Dwim's face and even in the reflection of his own eyes she could see the confusion on her own face. "I could have killed him! Something was telling me to destroy him!" Blood ran down her feet and dripped to the wood forming puddles as she remained kneeling on the floor. She was unable to get up just yet. She felt drained and worst of all scared.

"Aye," Dwim said, trying to calm her down, "Ye' could have but ye' chose nay to kill, hm? That's commendable, that is.." Dwim looked back at Leon who was standing there with bow in hand and looking towards the window. "Lad, take her to yer' room and let her rest. Keep guard." Leon took a moment to acknowledge Dwim, but as he did, Dwim scooped Ren up into his arms and carried her to Leon. "I've got to talk to Zerrick about this." he passed Ren over to Leon who, though not nearly as strong as Dwim, took her into his arms with ease. Dwim turned and gathered his sword and his shield. Dwim's voice was filled with concern when he asked Leon, "It won't return, will it, lad?"

Leon shook his head confidently while making sure not to shake Ren around too much, "No. It will go off and lick its wounds and then find something to eat in the wild. We'll have no problem tracking the monster when it's light out." He stopped a moment to clear his throat to hide the fact his voice almost cracked, "I've never seen a wolf that size before, Dwim."

Dwim agreed with a silent nod. His eyes met Leon's. He drew in a deep breath and sighed, "Keep an eye out. Get her some rest." Dwim left the room first, towing his equipment with him, while his little white sleeping gown flowed behind him. Leon followed right after the Dwarf, carrying Ren back to his own room. He kicked the door which was already opened and it swung inward enough to carry her over the threshold.

"I'm going to lay you down in my bed and I'll return shortly." Leon said as he walked over, gently laid her down, and disappeared from the room. Ren lay there not truly understanding what was going on just yet. True to his word, Leon returned only a moment later with his bow. He laid it against the wall and then went to her side. "Don't move. I'm going to pick this glass out of your feet."

Rennyn lay quietly in the bed with her eyes wide open as she watched Leon at her feet. He carefully and meticulously pulled shards of glass from her skin; piece by piece. Now and again she'd draw in a breath like a hiss. He would glance up at her and mumble, "Sorry" before returning to his work, "You've got quite a bit stuck but not as bad as it could have been."

She did not hear him. Instead, she kept going over the whole thing in her head; replaying the events of what happened in her room. Every now and again a soft whisper left her mouth, "Maybe if-" and then she would stop. It would only be a moment later that she would start again, "What about-" and then let it go once more.

Leon finally finished pulling the glass from her feet and dug around to find some cloth wrappings he kept in his bags for injuries. He wrapped her wounds and apologized for not having some sort of ointment to help with healing and pain. Ren let him know that she could whip something up easily when she needed to and that she was grateful for his help. He offered her a smile and meant to tell her that it was no problem but saw that she was already sleeping . He stood and placed his bag on the floor, laid down next to the bed, and rested his head on the bag. He was used to sleeping on the hard ground and so the floor was nothing. He closed his eyes and drifted off to sleep himself.

Dwim returned at some point after the breaking of dawn. He headed upstairs and banged on Leon's door. Leon jolted awake and Ren let out a groan. The thick accented voice called from outside the door. "Get dressed, aye? We got work to do. I'll meet ye' both down stairs."

Leon sat up. He had never really fully undressed and so all he had to do was slip on his boots, which he did quickly. He then nodded at Ren "I'll just give you some privacy then." and exited the room.

Ren waited a moment after he was gone before she got out of the bed and crept across the hall to her own room. Her feet hurt, but she knew she couldn't just lay around. She was very careful to not step on any more glass as she collected her things and went back to Leon's room to dress. She removed her gown and slipped on one of the gowns she bought from the tailor. It was a soft gray blue and lined in a brown velvet. She fixed up her hair into a braided tangle on the top of her head and pinched her cheeks to bring a bit of color back to her face. Once she was done, she headed downstairs to find her traveling companions.

She found the both of them standing near the bar with a taller man wearing plate armor that looked identical to the armor Dwim was wearing. Leon noticed Ren coming down and signaled Dwim who then started with an introduction, "Ah! Here the lass is. Ren, this is Zerrick of the White. A Paladin of my order here in Karren's Call." Dwim stepped aside so that when Ren stepped up, her and Zerrick would be face to face, though he was at least a foot taller than she was.

Zerrick lowered his head covered in dirty blonde hair, "I hear you're having some wolf issues."

Ren gave him a little bow. There was something familiar about him though she couldn't quite put her finger on it. "It's a pleasure to meet you." Her lips pressed together in a thin line, "I think I tried to handle it. I am not quite sure to be honest. Either way, I was unsuccessful."

Leon snorted, "I wouldn't say that. She had the beast pushed back and out the damn window. Put a little meat on those arms and I dare say she could have upper cut the monster and put its lights out."

Zerrick offered a smile, "I believe it. However, our order has possession of a peculiar manuscript about people becoming wolves. They say the beasts can not handle the touch of silver. I just so happen to have a family sword made of pure silver." He stepped back and unsheathed a rapier and allowed it to rest in both hands. He held it out to the group, clearly proud of it.

Ren had a hint of blush on her face from Leon's kind words but kept quiet. She looked over the sword and found herself uninterested in it really, but feigned interest the best she could by raising her brow, doing her best to give a surprised look.

"I think the thing that attacked the girl at the brothel might be this wolf," Zerrick continued. He placed the sword back in its scabbard and nodded to Leon, "and with the legendary Leon Farharbor, we can track this monster down and we can end it. We can bring peace to this town."

Dwim nodded his approval, "Aye. We can do that." Dwim turned his gaze to Leon.

"Tracking it won't be a problem." Leon added and then looked to Ren. Rennyn returned his look and then found that his eyes weren't the only ones on her. Both Zerrick and Dwim were looking at her as well.

Ren cleared her throat, "I suppose I can take my leave then. It appears you gentlemen have everything under control here and I doubt that having an Elf tag along would be useful." She offered a fake smile, "I can go pack up my belongings and be on my way. I'm sure there is something in town that I could do to earn my keep for a bit." She dipped her head and turned to head back up the stairs to the rooms. When she turned away, she felt Leon's warm hand touch her shoulder and it gave her chills. She was then yanked back to the group.

"She's in." Leon said.

"What?" Ren asked in an unbelieving tone.

No one answered her. Zerrick smiled and headed towards the inn's front door. "Let's get to work then!"

Zerrick headed out the door and Leon, with his bow, headed out after him. Ren started to follow too but was grabbed by the wrist by a heavy hand. Dwim pulled her back a bit and lowered his voice, "Ye' remember the dream, lass?" he asked, staring up at her.

Ren looked confused for a moment and gave a bit of a shrug. "Some of it."

"In the dream, do ye' remember anything about a wolf?"

Ren thought hard but found that she didn't recall anything about a wolf. She shook her head and mumbled an apology.

"I nay know if this thing is as Zerrick says or if it's just a plain old fashioned wolf who's just big." Dwim whispered in a voice that sounded like gravel crushing under boots. "I'm nay a scholar, but if we are dealing with a man who can turn into a beast-"

Ren cut him off, "We are. I watched him transform before my very eyes."

Dwim's mouth hung open for a moment and then his voice raised, "And ye' nay thought that was important information to share?"

Ren shrunk back a little, "I'm sorry, Dwim" then she bit back at him, "I was busy being attacked!"

Dwim put his palms up in an apologetic manner, "Alright, alright" he exhaled and continued, "Well, now that we know it's a man, do ye' think our man wolf is the man that fights with himself? From the dream, I mean?"

Ren's mouth opened and then closed. Her brow furrowed and she spoke in a whisper, "Dwim, that's clever!"

"That dream, I think it said he had to come to peace with himself. I nay think that means he's s'posed to die. Ye' kin what I mean?" he asked.

Ren understood completely. "I do. I don't feel like he needs to die. I feel like I can help him if only I could get through to him."

Dwim nodded, "Aye, something bigger is at play here, lass. Something beyond our understanding. Zerrick is a good man and a fine Paladin, but he is very by the book. Understand?"

Ren nodded, "I do."

Dwim sighed and pressed on, "I hate to ask, but do ye' have a wee bit of something to er-" he frowned under his big mustache. He hated the idea but truly felt it was the right thing to do, "Anything to put him down for a moment? I nay want him injured, but a nice nap would be alright."

"I don't think I have anything," Ren said as she dug around in her satchel. A few vials of something, but there wasn't any more of Kalina's Mist or anything like it. She looked up and shook her head. On the way to Karren's Call she had opened her locked chest and removed several vials that she thought at a quick glance were potions with healing properties.

"Damn," Dwim hissed, "I do have a plan of sorts. I nay know if it'll work."

"What is it?" she asked genuinely curious.

He looked around to ensure they were alone, though when he drew the necklace from under his beard, it didn't seem to be anything worth hiding. It was a simple tied rope with a beautiful medallion depicting the symbol of the White, a circle with rays of light beaming from it. "A gift from my trainer when I was a wee lad. Pure silver. Zerrick says the wolf can't touch silver." Dwim licked his lips and continued excitedly, "What if the amulet can keep the wolf inside out of fear of being hurt by the silver?"

Ren beamed, "Dwim!" She grabbed his beard and yanked him forward, kissing his brow, "That's brilliant!" She released him and he stumbled back a bit with a chuckle. She looked at the medallion now resting on his braided beard; it was beautiful. She reached her hand out again, "May I?"

"Aye, of course." He removed the amulet from around his neck and handed it over to her gingerly. "I nay know if we can get this around the thing's neck or even how. We can think of that along the way. We best catch up with those two."

Ren agreed and held the amulet back out to Dwim after inspecting it. He shook his head, "I got this weird feeling ye' should be holding on to it."

Ren's fingers ran over the amulet mindlessly as they walked out and caught up with Zerrick and Leon. Ren hadn't noticed until now that a large greatsword was hooked to Zerrick's back. She then noticed the rapier was attached at the hip. Leon and Zerrick had been making small talk though Ren was unsure of what and when she looked at Dwim she saw that he seemed to be in deep thought.

"Maybe I should prepare a nice dinner this evening? I feel like I should make myself more useful and I'm sure Zerrick would appreciate a nice warm meal." she said, more to herself than anyone, not that it was loud enough to really be heard.

"If that's the way ye' would like to do it, sure" Dwim responded. "I nay want ye' to think that yer' just some woman expected to be in the kitchen," Ren looked at him as he carried on, "Yer' an accomplished apothecary; nay some handmaiden."

Ren awarded Dwim a smile that said she appreciated his words and almost bumped into Leon who was knelt down in the street. He pointed out some dried blood and spoke confidently, "There. My arrows didn't hurt the beast, but it bleeds like any other. We follow this and once we come to dirt or grass I guarantee we'll see tracks."

"Is it safe to be following him during the day?" Rennyn asked, peering over Leon's shoulder at the blood spot.

"Well," Leon stood up and dusted his pants off, "Out of the four of us, your eyes are the best to spot the devil. Besides, the dark is a prowler's friend. Best to have it out in the light with no surprises." He threw his arm out ahead of him, "This way."

They all followed Leon who seemed to know what he was doing (he did). He proved time and time again just how masterful of a hunter he truly was by pointing out small things that showed the wolf had come through the area. They walked for two hours following blood then tracks, and even droppings. They had finally made their way into the forest. More signs made it easier for Leon to track the creature. It wasn't even too far in when he started to creep upon a bush. The master hunter spread the shrub and peeked through. He smiled when his brown eyes fell on the target, "Got him!" Leon exclaimed in a hushed shout. He pointed through the bush and when the others had squeezed next to him and looked through they all saw the naked golden haired man with skin stained crimson laying in the grass. Next to him, torn apart, a large elk. Some of the poor thing had it's flesh devoured completely leaving only bones as evidence.

Ren still held on to the amulet while she looked sadly at Phineas, "How does this work, boys?" She looked at them now, "Anyone have a plan?"

Zerrick leaned forward to get a better look. His eyes, a shining blue like a cloudless sky in summer, squinted for a brief moment, "Phineas?"

Ren stood up and looked at Zerrick wearing a bewildered look, "Do you know him?"

Zerrick's face flushed scarlet and he stormed out of the brush. As soon as he reached the naked man, he delivered a swift steel boot to Phin's ribs, causing the man to wake with a yelp and gasp for air. Zerrick's speed was uncanny as the silver rapier was unsheathed and jabbed into Phin's neck. His skin encased the rapier as the point pressed into his neck.Zerrick glared angrily as he began to berate the blood stained man, "Just when I thought you were the worst of the worst, a king of scoundrels, you turn out to be a vile creature as well. It is by the good graces of the gods that our parents died when they did so they did not have to watch you become," he fought for a word and managed to spit something out, "filth!" Phineas of course said nothing and just stared up at Zerrick while holding his side where he was kicked..

Ren's mouth dropped open in shock and she looked over at Leon. Her brain could barely spit the words out, "I wasn't expecting this at all."

Dwim nodded in disbelief while Leon almost looked amused, "You know, now that they are together, you can tell they're related."

The others rushed from the bush and surrounded the two just as Zerrick spit on Phineas. "Lets see it then. Let's see if it's true." He then pushed the sword's point into Phin's neck. Phin grimaced as a trickle of blood pooled from the prick and slowly moved down onto the silver blade. As soon as the dark red liquid of life made contact, it smoked and let out a terrible hiss like water thrown into a flame. Zerrick looked angry, but Ren could tell there was also sadness there. He was a man devoted to the White and that meant he had to destroy the accursed; even if it was family. "You could have been so much more. What have you done to damn yourself so?" Phineas did not reply and only looked up at his brother. He was in no position to argue when he was on the pointy end of a sword.

Ren took a step forward and held out her hands, "Zerrick! Please!" The amulet dangled from one of her hands. "We may have a solution here!"

"Stay back, Elf!" he snapped at her, "I understand your people are peaceful but we do not worship the wild gods here. He is a creature now tainted with the stench of the terror lands. He is my brother and it is my duty as family and as a Paladin to eradicate the evil within him. His life has been nothing but sin." He looked at Phin and jabbed the rapier back against his neck, "This is the final sin." Tears were welling in his eyes and threatened to spill over. "Can your soul even be saved now?" he asked Phin, choking on grief and letting it out as a sob. "I know not. However, I can not let you taint other souls that are still pure."

Dwim wanted to step in and say something, but found that he couldn't. In most ways, he agreed with Zerrick. It was an oath they swore when they became Paladins. They swore to uphold the natural ways of their world and destroy the impure and wicked. Some of course took it far more seriously than others and wickedness was always up for interpretation. Dwim lowered his head feeling ashamed and disappointed in himself.

Ren looked over at Leon and then back at Phineas. She moved even closer to him and knelt near his head. "What if the wolf was no longer an issue?" She asked Zerrick while looking down at Phin's eyes while giving him a soft and reassuring smile. "You would have my word, my oath, that it would be at bay."

Zerrick, with the flick of his wrist, aimed the rapier's point at the Elf. He spit his words at her, "Your word means nothing if you protect a creature so vile. He is a beast of evil now. A merchant of sin."

Dwim and Leon rushed in closer now to stand with Rennyn. Dwim shouted out at Zerrick, "C'mon now, lad. She nay has anything to do with that. Lower yer' sword."

Zerrick's anger grew. He shouted at Dwim, never taking his eyes off Ren, "Have you forgotten your oath? Have you forgotten the light we've been shown?" Another flick of Zerrick's wrist sent the blade across Phin's chest with such unbelievable speed that Ren never saw it move. The blood dripped from the slice, not a deep one, and when the blade slashed back again, the blood steamed and hissed as it met the silver. "His blood is tainted! He is lost to the darkness! Don't you understand that?"

Ren threw herself in between the two brothers and laid her body over Phineas'. She covered him the best she could and cried out, "Please! Show him mercy! Deep down you know he did not mean to do the things he did. It was no different to him to hunt than for us to naturally take our next breath."

Zerrick stood at his full height as he threw the rapier to the ground. He reached over his shoulder and drew the greatsword. He held it in front of him and glared down at Ren, "Elf, you refuse to step aside and allow the White to complete its duty. You have taken the side of darkness. I will pray that your soul finds redemption." He began to raise the sword above him, fully prepared to cleave the little Elf in two.

Dwim yelled out, "Zerrick!" and rushed over, sword and shield drawn. Zerrick turned and swung the greatsword at Dwim. It banged against the shield and both men let out a growl as the hit vibrated through their arms. Leon dug through his leather hip satchel; for what, he wasn't sure. Finally he decided to thread his bow and just as he was pulling back to let it loose, Dwim caught his gaze and shouted out, "Put it away, lad! I'll handle it!"

Leon lowered his bow and relaxed the string. He slipped the arrow away with a shake of his head. He looked between everyone and threw his hands in the air, not sure what he should do now. Surely he couldn't stand there and watch the two Paladins fight each other. Ren stood up, allowing Phin to seize the opportunity to scramble away from the fight. Ren moved towards the two swinging blades at one another and shouted, "I won't let you hurt him when we have a chance to save him!" Her voice was high pitched as she screamed at Zerrick and as fast as she spit the words out she saw stars with a burning sensation on the right side of her face. She spun then fell to her hands and knees with a cry. Zerrick had back handed her with his plate gauntlet. Zerrick looked quite pleased with the hit but was caught off guard when Dwim yelled out in anger and bashed Zerrick with his shield. Zerrick stumbled back and almost lost his footing, nearly toppling over. Ren, hurt but unbroken, refused to give in. She dug in her own satchel and found one of the many vials she had found earlier. She squeezed it and in anger threw it at Zerrick as hard as she could.

The vial flew outwards from her hand and found itself caught between Zerrick's armor and Dwim's shield. The vial was smashed between another hit from Dwim's shield. It shattered and sent its contents, a mixture of black and red grit, into Zerrick's face. As soon as it made contact, each grain turned into a thick black plume of smoke and Zerrick let out a blood curdling scream. Dwim's eyes grew large and he stepped back as far as he could. Some of the mixture had latched onto his beard and went up in the plumes. Dwim was thankful it was only his beard as he looked down and saw that it ate away strands of hair. Even his shield had been scorched by the grit. Zerrick dropped his sword and fell to his knees screaming. The areas of the right side of his face where the mixture made contact seemed to melt right off. His hands clasped over his face as he fell to his back. Ren stood up and took a step back, absolutely horrified.

She looked from Zerrick to Dwim, "I'm sorry! I didn't know what I grabbed! I was trying to help!"

Leon ran towards Ren and then passed her. He cocked his right arm back and fell to his knees as he slugged Phineas in the face. The naked man fell back into the grass with blood pouring from his nostrils. Leon looked back at Ren, "Don't argue! Just run, dammit!" Leon lifted Phineas over his shoulder and started running off from the small clearing. Dwim stood there, wearing a look of shock on his face, as he watched Zerrick scream and roll around. He was helpless and knew not what to do for the poor man. "Move your ass, Dwarf!" Leon shouted out.

Ren got up and started to run. She turned her head and saw that Dwim was frozen with shock. She rushed back over to him and grabbed at his beard crying out at him, "Dwim! We need to run!" Another pull seemed to snap Dwim out of it and he started to run. Ren followed closely. Dwim looked back as they ran. He was torn on what he should be doing. Zerrick was a brother of the White and here he was leaving the man in what seemed like excruciating pain. Ren, though still running, struggled with what she had done. She had no intention of throwing Dragon Sand at him, at least not to injure him like that.

Dwim and Ren caught up with Leon or at least they were able to see him. The man was fast, even carrying another man over his shoulder. The Dwarf and Elf continued to glance back behind themselves towards Zerrick. The sound of his screams echoed in the wilds around them and It echoed in their heads as well. They ran further and further until the screams became but a quiet mumble. There was no doubt that Zerrick was still there, on the ground, in unimaginable pain, but as cruel as it sounds, at least they didn't have to hear it anymore. Leon decided they were far away enough that they could rest and he unceremoniously dropped Phineas from his shoulder letting him crash against the ground with a thud.

Leon drew in several deep breaths while hunched over with his hands on his knees. He glanced up at his companions and groaned out in huffs of breath, "That was terrible!"

Ren started to cry, "I swear I didn't do it on purpose! I didn't mean to! I wasn't looking at what I grabbed! I was trying to help!"

"No," Leon said, frowning at Ren, "When I picked him up," he pointed at Phineas, "his cock hit me on the mouth." Dwim dropped down to his rear and buried his hands in his face. Leon continued, "I feel gross now." He leaned against a tree and slid down it.

"I believe ye', lass." Dwim said quietly. He had ignored Leon's predicament.

Ren rushed to the Dwarf and dropped to her knees. She buried her face in his shoulder and let out more sobs, "Why was he so mad?" She had asked this between choked breaths of air.

"It is our sworn duty to destroy evil. That lad, like it or not, is cursed in some way. By my oath, I should have helped Zerrick end him. Our order was formed by High Priestess Ariel, a wonderful woman who used the magic of the holy realm of life and goodness. She, along with The Aegis, fought against darkness from the Terror Lands, which is the realm of death and its magic. In her name we fight the darkness." Dwim sighed, "The guiding light will forsake me."

"Surely we can explain what happened?" Ren asked hopefully.

Dwim shook his head. "I nay know, lass. I'm just a Dwarf. I nay understand the mysteries of our world. I believe in the guiding light but maybe nay as much as I did. Or maybe I just believe in the dream more at the moment." He put an arm around Ren and rubbed her back. "Ye' nay need to worry about me and my woes. We've got this knuckle head to attend to." He nodded towards Phineas.

Ren couldn't help but feel like ever since she appeared that these men had nothing but trouble. She got up and offered a hand out to Dwim. He took it and stood, giving her a small nod of thanks. Together, they walked over towards Phineas. Ren held out the silver amulet and asked glumly, "Would anyone like to do the honors?"

Both men shook their heads and Dwim piped up, "Ye' saved him, lass. Ye' do it."

She gave a slight nod and walked even closer to the naked man. She knelt down in the dirt beside him and carefully, very carefully, slipped the amulet around his neck. Once it was secured, she stood back up and rocked back on her heels. The three of them watched closely unsure of what to really expect. They waited for several minutes before Leon grew impatient and stepped forward where he delivered a kick to the blood covered man's ass. Phineas groaned out and fluttered his eyes. His nose was swollen from where Leon had punched him and the area around his eyes were already beginning to darken. "Where are we?" he asked in a low voice "Where is Zerrick?"

Ren squatted down and gave him a smile. She reached out, pushing his hair from his face, and spoke in a gentle voice, "We're in the forest. How do you feel right now?"

"Like I've been kicked in the face by a horse." He rubbed at his face and winced when he touched his nose. His hand was still stained red from the blood of the elk. He examined it for a moment before looking up at the Elf, "It happened again, didn't it?"

Ren took his hand softly in hers and held it tightly. Leon spoke up, "I think you owe us a story on how you came to be the wolf. We saved your ass. Well, Rennyn saved your ass. You owe us that much."

Phineas frowned, "I didn't ask to be saved. I don't deserve it. I'll tell you though; if you're really wanting to know."

Leon and dwim went off and gathered wood from the surrounding area. When they returned, the four created a small camp. Leon caught them some fresh meat and even though the sun was still high, they settled in for the day. The meat was cooked and passed around. Ren had given Phin her cloak to wear so that he wasn't sitting exposed to everyone. There was a long silence between them while they ate. They were all finished when Dwim finally said what Ren and Leon were thinking, "Time to tell ye' story, lad. All of it."

Phineas nodded. He thought for a long moment and threw the bones of whatever he ate, he didn't ask, into the fire. He cleared his throat, opened his mouth, closed it, and then opened it again, "My name is Phineas Lightfoot and my story is a bit long. It all started…"

CHAPTER 5

Phineas, a young handsome boy of no more than fourteen, laid on the soft couch inside the living room of his home. His parents, Morgan and Willameena Lightfoot, were scrambling about the house trying to finish their preparations for the trip they were going to take. They had hounded him a dozen or more times about his responsibilities to the family. He heard every word, but paid no heed to them. It was always the same thing. *Be more responsible* and *Your family comes first, not the scoundrels you hang around with*.

"Phineas, dear, are you paying attention?" Willameena asked, staring at him. Phin nodded. "Zerrick will be doing his training at the cathedral and can't be here the entire time so I need you to make sure Aven is taken care of." A little girl peeped out from behind her mother,hair as golden as Phin's, which they both got from Willameena. "Do you understand?"

Phin groaned out an answer and sat up. His parents finished their preparations, kissed Aven on the cheek and gave Phin a hard look. He took their meaning and gave them a nod. Standing, he and Aven escorted them to the front door. A carriage was waiting for them outside the manor, one of many that sat on a hill overlooking Karren's Call.

"Enjoy your trip to Morganna." Phin said, offering his best smile. Morgan knew it was a disguise and didn't bother replying. He had lost most of his faith in Phin after all the trouble he had gotten into over the last few years. It was a black mark on the family name to have his son arrested and thrown in the dungeon for days at a time for theft. Of all the things to be arrested for, when his family had more than enough to provide for him.

"I love you both!" Willameena exclaimed. She bent to kiss Aven all over her face and took Phineas into her arms kissing his cheek. "Don't-"

"-Be a disappointment. I know." Phin finished, eyes locked on his father.

"Zerrick will be back soon." She gave him one last kiss and a loving look before climbing into the carriage.

Phin and Aven, the little blue eyed doll, watched as their parents pulled off. As soon as they had cleared the tree line, Phin looked down at his sister. He offered her a smile and put his hand on her head. She was at least ten years younger than himself. "Come on inside, squirt. Before Zerrick comes home and sees you outside and I get blamed for a scraped knee or something." She smiled up at him, her front teeth missing. He brought her inside and once the door was closed, Aven ran off to go play.

The Lightfoots had a maid who did all the menial chores so that the precious nobles didn't have to. She was a dark skinned, middle aged woman with hazel eyes that seemed creamy. She had come in from washing and hanging laundry and while she always made sure to be prim and proper with the family, she let her guard down with Phin when they were alone. The boy was easy to talk to and made everyone, not just her, relaxed in his company. He was not a snob like the older boy and his parents. She thought that if Aven hung around him long enough, she might grow up to not be a bitch.

"Supper will be a bit late tonight, Master Phineas. I apologize and beg your forgiveness." she said, dropping the laundry basket down and starting to fold the garments inside it.

Phin, a bold boy and well aware of his good looks, gave her his best smile. "That's not a problem." He walked towards her and placed both hands on the arm of the couch that she sat on "Lona, when are we going to stop beating around the bush and get close to each other?"

Lona eyed him from the side with a look that made it clear not to play with her, but Phin saw the soft dimple of a smile. He gave her a wink and went to his room upstairs to continue lounging about. When the dinner bell rang later in the evening, he headed downstairs and joined Aven at the family table. She was always first to the table and made sure to let Lona know how delicious everything was, even if she didn't really like it. Aven's plate was placed in front of her, then Phin's was placed in front of him, and a third at the head of the table where no one sat.

"Where's Zerrick?" Phineas asked.

"Right here." replied a voice just before a body turned the corner into the dining room. Zerrick was four years older than Phineas and considered a man now. As his father wasn't home, it was his duty to sit at the head of the table and lord over the family affairs. He sat down and immediately began to eat.

"Lona, why don't you join us tonight?" Phin asked genuinely.

The plump maid smiled at his kind offer. "Master Phineas, I would love to" and she placed her plate down on the table and drew back a chair to sit.

"I don't think that's appropriate, Lona. Do you? What kind of example would we be setting for Aven?" Zerrick asked, not actually expecting a reply. He hadn't even looked up from his plate as he shoved food into his mouth.

"Yes, Master Zerrick." Lona replied in a monotone voice. She removed her plate from the table and went to sit in the small servant dining room out of view.

Phin glared at Zerrick, "You're a dick."

Zerrick finally looked up and placed his utensils down into his plate. He used the cloth to wipe his hands and swallowed the bit of food left in his mouth. "Phineas, you need to understand who we are. This family maintains its wealth and status by not fraternizing with the help. If they were good enough to eat at the table with us, they wouldn't be the help. You should work on being a better role model for Aven. Especially after your little stay in the dungeon."

"What does father's shit smell like?" Phin asked, glaring at Zerrick. Aven gasped at the naughty word and hid a giggle.

"What is that supposed to mean?" Zerrick asked.

"I'm just assuming you'd know since you have your nose shoved so far up his ass you clearly would be the first to know what his shit smells like. I bet you can tell what he had for lunch!" Phin called out. He was almost certain Lona was holding her laughter in while in the other room.

Zerrick slammed his fist down on the table. "That's enough! I'll be staying at the cathedral tonight. I want you to be on your best behavior. Do not leave this house. Do you understand me?"

Phin glared and nodded. Once Zerrick was satisfied with that he looked back down to his plate and before shoveling more food in, Phin mumbled out, "I bet you can tell exactly what father puts in his mouth because of how far your nose is up his ass."

Zerrick pushed the chair back and stood up. "That's it! Excuse yourself from this table and go to your room. You are a disgrace to this family!" Phin threw his cloth on the table and pushed away from it. He gave Zerrick one last glare before storming off to his room upstairs. Zerrick sat back down and calmed himself. He picked up his fork and before jabbing at the piece of meat, looked at Aven. "Sorry about all that, Aven. He should know better."

Aven smiled back at Zerrick, her little legs kicking under the table, "What does shit smell like?"

Zerrick sighed, "Don't say that." He shook his head and continued to eat.

Zerrick left after dinner and a few hours had passed since. The moon was hanging high outside of Phin's window bathing his bare chest in blue light. His hands rested underneath his head as he stared out. He almost startled when there was a knock at the door. Without a response, it opened and Lona stepped in with an oil lamp. She shut the door behind her and stepped forward.

"Dessert, Master Phineas." she said plainly.

Phineas looked at her and frowned, "No thank you, Lona. I'm not really in the mood for it. Sorry."

Lona sat the oil lamp on a table and spoke softly. "Not for you. For me." she stepped closer to him as she opened her gown. Phin swallowed hard as he saw for the first time a woman exposed to him. Her breasts were as large as they were round and hung, no longer perky like the breasts of the young. Still, he grew under his pants as he admired her. His eyes fell from her chest, down her pudgy stomach, and to the fluff of black hair between her fat thighs,

Phineas, always the charmer and suave, locked eyes with hers and simply said "I've never."

Lona nodded, dropping the gown to her feet. "Then let me teach you."

She walked to him, climbed upon his bed, and threw a leg over him. She straddled the young boy and leaned down, placing her plump lips against his. A soft gentle kiss first. Followed by a deeper, more lingering kiss. The next had their lips spread as they met where their tongues introduced themselves. He felt hot and found that she felt hotter. That night, Lona made Phineas a man. Using the fact that the young could continue to go for such a long time, over and over; she taught him his first lessons in love making and raw passion. She had no feelings for the boy other than natural lust. She admired his kindness and disposition towards her, true, but it wasn't love and nothing close to it. He made her feel good and she gave in to the desire. Through the night she let him explore every position he could dream up. She let him enjoy her body, even the places she had never had a man. He filled her over and over and only at the crack of dawn, just as the sun crept over the horizon as an orange ball of fire, did they finally give in to exhaustion. She lay against him, sticky and satisfied. They made pillow talk for a bit before she fell asleep against his chest. He dozed a moment after, a smile resting on his face.

"Harlot! Fiend!" Zerrick shouted at them. They both startled awake and cowered under his voice. Lona covered herself with a blanket and tried to climb out of the bed.

"Master Zerrick! I-" she fought to find words, "I'm sorry, sir! I-"

"Not another word, Lona. Gather your things and leave this manor. Your services are not required here and you are no longer welcomed in this home." Zerrick barked.

Phin shouted, "Calm down! You're overreacting!"

Zerrick rushed past Lona and grabbed Phineas by the hair and slung him out of the bed. Phin let out a yelp as he rolled across the floor. Lona's eyes grew wide and she apologized again before rushing out of the room. She had no intention of being the recipient of Zerrick's wrath. Phin stood up and took a swing at Zerrick. As his fist connected, Zerrick's head turned to the side but only a bit. He was already hardened from his training with the White. Zerrick grabbed Phin by the neck and pulled him in, bashing his skull against his own and knocking him down once more. Phin was relentless, even naked, he got up and charged back at Zerrick once more. This time he managed to take Zerrick down with him and the two rolled on the floor hitting each other. Phin was still smaller than Zerrick though and in the end, the older brother would win. One hard punch made Phin's vision hazy and he teetered on the verge of unconsciousness.

"Damn you, Phineas!" Zerrick yelled down as he climbed to his feet. "Why do you have to be this way? You break this family's heart!"

"Why?" he asked groggily, "Why? Because I want to be free of the chains that come with the family?" he rolled to his side and spit on the floor. His arms shook as he tried to hoist himself up. "Not once do any of you think that there is more to living than following rules? Can't you, or anyone in this family, live just to be alive? When's the last time you spoke to a stranger? Played cards with a drunk in the alley?" he stood to his feet now. His head marked red, mostly from the headbutt but also from the anger that was building. "I don't want to be cooped up here. Living as you and father do. I want to get out and experience the world, Zerrick. I want to have fun."

"Who said you couldn't have fun? " Zerrick asked.

"You do! You and father! I can't have my friends-"

"Friends, Phineas? You mean the same friends who helped you spend several nights in a dungeon while father had to use connections to get you out? Those friends?"

"Yes!" Phin shouted, "Those friends who were there living in the moment with me! Those who were living life with me!" His yelling turned to sobs, "I'll never be you, Zerrick. I'll never be my father either. Both of you walk around so rigid you'd think you had tree trunks up your asses. Why can't you both let me be who I am?"

Zerrick sneered, "Because, Phineas, you are turning into scum."

Phin wiped tears from his eyes and ran to his closet. He pulled out pants and a shirt and slipped them both on. Digging around more he found a traveling bag made of canvas and stuffed more clothes into it. He dropped the bag and sat on the floor to slip on boots that rested near the door.

"What do you think you're doing?" Zerrick asked, trying to lessen the hate he had in his voice though he still felt it.

"I'm leaving. If I'm going to put such a black spot on this house for being myself then I don't think I should be here."

"And where in the world do you plan on going, Phineas? What are you going to do? Live like some wild dog out in the streets begging for food?"

Phineas stood and grabbed his bag. He stared at Zerrick and spoke as calmly as he possibly could, "Better to live like a dog, wild and free, than to live in chains here. I love you, Zerrick. I wish you well." Tears had filled his eyes now and he turned and ran out of the room. Zerrick chased after him but Phin was faster; always had been.

Phin cleared out the front door and when Zerrick had reached it, he saw that Phin was already a good way down the path. Zerrick shouted out angrily, "You break this family's heart, Phineas! If you leave now you best never return! There won't be a family waiting to welcome you back!"

Phineas did not stay long in Karren's call. He ventured out on his own, leaving his life and family behind. He was determined to be as free as the wind and traveled where his feet took him. He robbed people on the road when he needed to and when in small hamlets he had no issues lifting food to feed himself. Days turned to weeks and weeks into months. The months turned to years and over those years he had not only become more skilled at theft but at his ability to talk to women. Almost from the first day he set out on his own he had taken many women. They ranged from older women with lots of experience to young virgin maids. He lied to each and every one of them. He made them fall head over heels for him before having them, swearing that he would be by their side forever. As soon as they drifted off to sleep from the vigorous love making, he would sneak off and set off on his own again. On occasion he even stole from them; robbing them of their jewelry to sell later.

Phineas had also become quite the cheat. He learned, from other scoundrels of course, how to rig games of chance so that he always came out on top. The risky ones were the ones where he lost on purpose a few games to allow the mark to become cocky and arrogant. Once they were feeling good about their chances, he would then bet it all. When he would win, he'd buy them all a round of beer, and they'd drink to sheer dumb luck. Even then, depending on how much money he figured they had, he might even rob them once they passed out drunk at the table. He always left after robbing the drunks. They were the violent ones and Phineas, as far as he knew himself, was a lover and not a fighter.

Time passed by fast for Phineas as he lived for the moment, especially the ones that made him feel alive. He loved no woman and he had no friends. He found himself across the ocean in the lands of Wuvemer. He had found work with a traveling circus doing labor. Hard work wasn't what kept him around though, it was the pretty girls he was laying to bed regularly. The group didn't mind sharing him and each had their turn with him when their chores or jobs were done. Between fortune tellers predicting he was going to cum harder than he had ever done before and others using clever job related lines, they would use him as much as they could making sure he had very little time to rest.. He was nearly twenty five now and life, he thought, could not get any better.

They had been traveling for a week or so deep into the thick forest made of trees that wore black bark and teal foliage. A mist hung low on the ground giving the place an eerie look; as if it were needed to look eerie to begin with. The group had kept to the road as instructed by those they came across on occasion. They were told the forest was a dark dangerous place to be and that Orillia, their destination, had high walls to keep the dangers outside. The wagon train stopped for a bit so that everyone could stretch their legs and eat a bit of food. Phin, never one to follow rules or instruction, walked off into the woods on his own for a bit of a stroll.

His golden hair was now long and hung down over his shoulders. The shirt he wore was little more than rags but that was okay. Even as he walked, the thick fog around him never seemed to dissipate. The sound of twigs snapping gave him pause and he stood frozen for a moment. His eyes darted around as he tried to see anything at all in the fog. He saw nothing and just as he nearly continued to walk forward, his heart dropped into his stomach at the feeling of fingers digging into his sides. He let out a yell and jumped forward a pace or two. The laughter of a young woman made him spin around and he let out a long sigh of relief.

"You nearly made me piss myself" he exclaimed with a smile on his face.

The young beauty with big dark eyes and raven hair laughed getting closer to him, "I didn't think you were such a little chicken!"

"Chicken?" he asked. He placed both hands on her hips and drew her in. "You know I'm the rooster in this hen house."

She laughed and reached down below his waist. She caressed his crotch which had already started to flex. "Oh, you are, aren't you?" she peered behind herself and then back to him, "Let me know if someone is coming." She started to unlace his trousers and dropped to her knees.

Phin's back was already turned to a tree and so he leaned against it. He closed his eyes and enjoyed her skill. He let out a soft groan of pleasure and didn't bother to open his eyes when he heard more twigs snapping. "C'mon! Unless you're wanting to join in on this, get out of here!" He got his reply, but not in the way he would have liked. There was a low growling that forced him to open his eyes. The girl freed herself of him and looked up at his face, seeing the concern she turned her head to see who was behind her.

The girl was barely able to scream as the paw of a massive wolf swiped across her face. Her scream was cut in half and replaced with a gurgling sound as her face split open. Phin looked down and upon seeing the mess that was once a beautiful girl, screamed as well. The wolf swiped at Phin next, tearing lines into his chest. The blood ran fast and hot and Phin was thrown to the ground by the force of the blow. He flipped on his stomach and tried crawling away. He moved as fast as he could until there was a moment that he felt the nails scratch into his back. The shirt ripped and then absorbed blood that left him so freely. He let out another scream of pain that reverberated through the woods. The wolf circled him several times, eyeing Phin, almost teasing him. Phin tried to crawl away again but the wolf came to him and placed one heavy paw down on his head and forced him to the forest floor. Phineas breathed in the smell of wet dirt and moss. The scent went into his nostrils so deeply that he was certain that after death he would still smell it. The wolf lowered its head and sank its gnarly teeth into Phin's back and pulled a chunk of flesh from his body. He screamed once more unsure now if he could be heard. The attack was very brief, but to him he felt as if he had been dying for an eternity now. The wolf lowered it's head to bite again, but a shout from a newcomer caused it to look up only to see a torch being smashed into its face.

The wolf jumped back and rubbed its face into the dirt before letting out a long howl. Once it rid itself of the burning sensation, the beast stared at the man who had come to the rescue. The man, thin and boney, held the torch out and jabbed it towards the wolf again. The wolf must have decided it wasn't worth it because it swiftly grabbed the dead raven haired beauty by the neck and dragged her off into the woods to make its retreat where it would have it's meal.

Phineas' vision blurred and he passed out. Now and again, he would open his eyes. On one occasion that he could remember, he realized he was being dragged through the foggy woods, then returned to unconsciousness. He would regain consciousness much later, unsure of how much time had passed, but knowing that he was in a room that he was unfamiliar with. He laid on his stomach and when he attempted to move he let out a cry of pain. A woman wearing a gown and apron came into the room.

"Just relax," she said, "I'll take a look at your wound and make sure it isn't infected."

"Where am I?" he asked. "What happened?"

"You're in Orillia. You were brought in by some of your friends with the circus. They say you and a girl were attacked by a wolf. I asked where she was and they said she didn't survive. I'm sorry to tell you that."

"The wolf, I remember it. It was huge."

"Yes, they get big around these parts."

"No, you don't understand. I've never seen one this size before."

"It's just shock. I'm going to pull your bandage back. It'll hurt," and as she did so he let out a howl of anguish, "It looks fine. It's understandable that you're in pain. Thing took a decent chunk from your back." The woman changed the bandage. "You're free to get up and walk around if you can manage it. I must insist, sir, that you thank Olm you're still alive."

Phin gave her an appreciative look and thanked her. She took a long moment to admire his face and tipped her head. She left the room with the bloody bandages in hand to properly clean them and use them some other time. Phin stayed there for a while longer to heal. At night, he had terrible dreams where he was the wolf that killed the girl. He would wake drenched in sweat and shivering. It was a while before the leader of the circus had come to ask if he would be leaving with them. Phin shook his head and apologized. The leader of the group dismissed it. He knew Phin was a free spirit and was never there to truly be a part of them. Later that day, the rest of the circus had come by to say goodbye to their friend. The girls would miss him most of all and they each kissed him before leaving.

One night, while sitting in a chair and doing absolutely nothing, Phin decided he had to get out and go for a walk. Sitting in the room alone was driving him mad and he could swear that he could hear his own heart beat pounding in his ears as well as his head. The night was cold and the hour late. Shops were closed, except for taverns and Inns, but he didn't feel much like drinking or gambling. He continued to walk alone; feeling that strange rhythmic beat in his head. Phin let out a cry as he dropped to his knees. His body ached like never before and he could feel his bones snapping. Before his very eyes, thick claws extended from a few fingers while his hands seemed to take another shape. Patches of gray hair started to push through his skin. With no one there to watch, Phineas Lightfoot changed forms for the first time.

Phineas did not remember what was done while he was the wolf. He rarely did. What he did know was that he woke up the next morning in the middle of the woods next to a horse that was half eaten. When he saw he was covered in blood, he began to panic. What was more alarming though was that upon further examination of himself, he found the wounds on his chest were no longer open but closed and scarred over. He wandered through the wilds until he found water and bathed himself clean of the blood. Phin returned to the city, but fled from Orillia as talks of a wolf loose in the city spread. While out in the wilds, the transformation happened several more times. It wasn't until much later that he understood that diving head first into parties, drinking, women, and whatever debauchery he could get into, kept the beast inside or at least kept him at bay for more than a few nights. There were times he could go months without the monster appearing.

Phineas found himself back in Karren's Call where he turned thirty. He had done much traveling, sleeping around, and thieving. He wasn't quite sure what brought him back to his hometown. He simply found himself boarding a ship in some harbor town across the sea and found himself here. As he left the ship with his bag slung over his shoulder, he breathed in deeply and took in that familiar aroma. His heart, at least in that moment, felt lighter. He walked the quiet and familiar streets of the bustling town, pointing out everything in his head that had changed. He thought about how eager he was to get back home to see his parents and his little sister. He even missed Zerrick regardless of how big of a shit he was. His feet carried him up the path to the hill where all the homes of nobles were built. Nobles, like his own family, stayed away on the outskirts of town far from the commoners. He found his house and a frown crossed his face. The place looked abandoned.

"Hello?" Phin crept closer to the door. He grabbed the door knob reluctantly and twisted it. The door opened with a long creak and he stepped inside. He shut the door behind him and looked around, dropping his bag to the floor. The place was covered in dust and most of the furniture was gone or broken. "Mother? Father?" He called out as he walked through the rooms. "Aven? Zerrick? Anyone?" There was no answer for him. He traveled up to his old room and peeked inside. Everything was gone. After a moment of standing in the empty room, he headed back downstairs and out the back door. His eyes searched the yard and saw that there, under the single oak tree, sat two gravestones. He crept over to them slowly; already knowing who they belonged to. As he came to them, he dropped to his knee and read out the names of his parents. The date etched into the stone was shortly after he had left so many years ago. A tear fell from his eye as his fingers traced their names. He stayed there for a while longer before getting up, heading inside to grab his bag. He slung it over his shoulder once more and left his childhood home to search for his brother and sister.

Phineas didn't know exactly where to look, but found himself heading towards the cathedral. He never intended to seek Zerrick out but, with his parents no longer living and the years having been so strange that he thought it would be good to reconnect with him. He tentatively walked up the stone steps of the majestic cathedral. He entered the large double doors and stopped in awe. It had been so terribly long since he had been there. He remembered the day Aven was blessed at the altar and how the stained glass behind it shone brightly on her face. There were always a handful of people in there at any given time, as far as he could remember anyway, saying their prayers or singing a hymn. As he looked over the seating he could see that they were knelt down with their hands clasped in silent worship. He approached a priest who was lighting some candles and spoke quietly.

"Is Zerrick here? Zerrick Lightfoot?" he asked, trying to be as respective as possible.

The priest spoke softly. "There is a Zerrick of the White. I am afraid I do not know the name he carried before that. Why?"

"I'm his brother. I'd like to see him if it's at all possible." Phin put on a smile for the priest as he mulled over the title Zerrick had for himself.

The priest nodded, "Follow me please." and he led Phineas down a torch lit stairwell that led into the lower chambers of the cathedral. These were reserved for the priests, priestesses, and paladins of the White. He was led down a few halls, each having to make a turn to another before they stopped at a door.

The priest knocked and the door opened slightly after a moment of silence. "Yes?" Zerrick's face appeared in the crack.

The priest bowed his head, "I'm sorry to bother you, brother. This man here says he is your-"

Zerrick cut him off, "Phineas." His voice trailed off as he opened the door wider. Zerrick wore humble linens. His face was clean shaven and his hair cut short. Nothing had changed much about the man other than he was wider and more muscled. "It's been fifteen years, Phineas."

Phin nodded "Sixteen, actually.. May I come in?"

Zerrick hesitated for a moment and gave a nod to the priest who promptly bowed his head and headed away. Zerrick moved to the side and allowed Phin into his room. As Phin stepped in he looked around and saw that the room was bare. Laying on a table, a polished greatsword and next to it, the family heirloom. A rapier made of pure silver with a hilt that was decorated with great detail. Zerrick moved to the table, clearing the swords from it and offered Phin a chair while he took the other. Phineas sat down across from him.

Phin cleared his throat, "You look well."

Zerrick said nothing for a long moment and then asked in a rather annoyed tone, "Why are you here, Phineas?"

"I just wanted to see you," he felt attacked, "to see mother and father."

"They're dead." Zerrick added quickly, "Shortly after you left."

Phin nodded and cleared his throat again, "I know. I went to the manor first. I saw their graves in the back. What happened?"

Zerrick frowned, "What happened? You ran off and mother couldn't handle that her little boy might be starving or freezing out there. It didn't help that father wasn't there for her because he was trying to keep himself busy to not feel guilty. He blamed himself for you running off. He blamed himself and me as well. Said we ruined you. So without you and father, mother simply gave up. She died. I think of a broken heart."

Phin looked down. He was already feeling terribly guilty, "And father?"

"Father hung himself that night when he came home and found mother dead."

Tears started to fall hard from Phin's eyes and roll down his cheeks, "I'm sorry, Zerrick. Where's Aven?"

"That's none of your concern." Zerrick said coldly.

Phin wiped at his face, "What? Why? I just want to see-"

"No." Zerrick stated. "She is married off and by Olm's protection will stay well hidden away from the likes of you."

Phineas opened his mouth to speak and then closed it again. He thought for a moment before he asked, "Why are you so angry to see me?"

"I'll tell you why," Zerrick said as his voice began to raise, "Because while Father blamed himself and I for you running off, I blame you. You are selfish and only think of yourself. Oh poor little Phineas, he didn't get to lounge around and act like a thug with his friends. The rest of us were being productive! You don't get to just do nothing Phineas! So I blame your selfish, lazy, no good outlook on life, for everything!" He slammed his hands on the table and stood up. His face had turned red. "You are the reason they are dead. You have done nothing but wrought pain and misery on this once happy family!"

"Zerrick, please." Phin pleaded.

"Enough! Phineas I never in my life want to see you again. Be thankful I have pledged my life to serving the guiding light of Olm or I'd thrash you good! Now leave me. Never return to face me again. You've already taken everything from me and I have nothing but resentment for you now."

"Zerrick, you don't mean that."

"I do," he replied. "Now go."

Phineas stood up and drew in a deep breath. With his bag slung over his shoulder he left the chamber without saying a word. He headed back to the manor where he would stay, living with memories of his family and the ghosts of his mistakes. While staying there he dedicated himself to fixing up the manor. By the time he was done, which was a year, Phin had completely renovated the place and made it look as good as new. In that time he transformed into the monster a lot. However, he was always lucky that the beast got into the wilds before anyone ever got hurt.

The last time he left the manor, he left whatever piece of him that remained a semi good person there with his parents. He never returned to the home even though he never left Karren's Call. Him and Zerrick, though seeing each other out in public on occasion, never spoke again either. Phin threw himself to the night. He loaded himself with heavy booze daily. He pleasured multiple women a night; sometimes two or three at a time. He gambled and cheated his way to fortune and would turn around and spend it all on whores. When he would spot a homeless person in darkened alleyways, he would empty whatever he had in his pocket and give it to them without thought. He stuck his fingers deftly into pockets and walked away with valuables. The people he met absolutely adored him even though behind their backs he robbed them blind.

A few months past his thirty second birthday, Phineas sat at a table with a bunch of unruly sailors at The Sleepy Sheep Inn. He had cheated every single hand so far and though they all accused him of doing it, they couldn't prove it. They continued to play until Phin said he had enough and boasted about how he felt bad for taking their money. He bought them all several drinks to calm their mood and when they were drunk ,he picked their pockets. It had been awhile since the beast had been let loose and he felt that thumping sound in his ears. It made his cheeks hot and he knew, at least tonight, he had to indulge to get it to go away.

"Lionel," Phin called out. "I'm going to head out and see what's going on outside. I'll be keeping my room."

Lionel nodded and replied, "You haven't left in nearly six months. Why would tonight be any different?"

Phin laughed as he headed out the front door into the cool spring air. Phineas Lightfoot was no longer just a petty thief. He had become so good that he dealt in things more valuable; secrets. Everyone had secrets. He had a secret. The baker had a secret. The maid at the cathedral liked to pleasure herself with candles. Even Lionel had a secret. Lionel of course had no idea that Phin knew he was sleeping with his nephew. Phin, in all honesty, could bring this entire town to its knees with the things he knew about people. He never did though. Live and let live is what he thought. As long as they weren't hurting anyone.

As he walked the streets, he waved to several women who begged him to come visit, which he declined because he had business to attend. His business of course was his favorite girl at the brothel. He turned down a street, trying to keep his mind off the feeling building inside himself. The pounding in his ears was starting to become too much. He stopped and took a deep breath. The pounding eased but he felt he had started to sweat. It faded in and out as he made his way through town slowly looking as though he was struggling with something. When he made it to the brothel his color had changed and he looked pale and sick. He tried to head inside but the madame had caught him just outside the door.

"Phineas my dear, back so soon?" she eyed him, "Wait a minute," she came out of the doorway and examined him. "You look terrible!" She was one to talk, a woman past her prime, still trying to take on clients even with her bad hip and terrible breath, "You finally caught a disease."

"I'm fine, just going to go in and get my fix and I'll be alright." he said, trying to push past her.

"Oh no you don't! I won't have you spoiling the goods! Go on! Get! Come back when that, whatever it is, has cleared up!" she hammered on, shooing him away from the brothel.

Phin nodded, "Alright. Alright. I'm going." he smiled and stepped away from the door with his hands up. He turned and headed down the street again when he was stopped.

"She might not let you in," said a young little whore, new to the business "But that don't look anything contagious to me. I've seen what a man looks like with the cock rot and that doesn't look like cock rot to me. Slip me the coin instead and I'll let you fuck me right here in the alley."

Phin thought for a moment and then smiled, "My name is Phineas, but you can call me delicious." She giggled and grabbed his wrist pulling him behind the brothel. There was an indent on the side of the building where a large pile of straw sat. She hiked her dress up and pulled her undergarments down. She turned and stuck her backside out.

"Go on. Get it. It's yours, for now." she said looking over her shoulder.

Phin pulled himself out of his trousers and spit on his hand. He stroked himself for a moment and when he felt it was sufficiently lubed, he jammed his dick inside her. He thought about nothing but his own pleasure. That is not to say that he didn't care to make others feel the pleasure he did, but right now it was just for him. "Let me out," a voice said to him, not from his mind but in his chest, "Let me out. You can't hold me forever."

"No." Phineas said, shaking his head and trying to get the voice to go. "No, please."

The girl looked at him, "No? You want a different position?"

Phin grabbed her head and turned it so that she faced it towards the wall, "Be quiet" he mumbled.

She bucked back against him, doing her best to get her client there. Afterall, it was her job. The voice called back out to Phin, "Let me free, damn you!" Phin ignored the voice. He thrusted faster inside her. Nearing his climax his vision started to blur. Only after a bit more of stroking inside her did he let out a howl as he released and that was all he would remember for the night.

Phineas' body began to twist and change while still inside the poor girl. The poor thing, doing all the dirty talk required of her, had no idea that behind her was a wolf of incredible size. Even if she had known, there would have been no time to react. The wolf brought it's maw down and snapped its jaws around her neck. Her throat was crushed and punctured immediately. It was a fast and painless kill with no effort. The wolf was pleased and began to tear the girl apart. He chewed off flesh and meant to devour it, but the wolf was disturbed by a voice calling.

"Hilda? You out back here? We got someone requesting you!" the madame called.

The wolf snarled and padded off away from the corpse and into the night. Once the wolf had made its way nearly out of the town it's ears perked at the sound of a fresh scream. The body had been found. The wolf lost itself in the night and continued its hunt. The clothes that belonged to Phineas still clung to the wolf but were later snagged on trees as the wolf prowled the darkness. In the morning, Phineas woke up next to an animal carcass and naked. He cleaned up, went back to the inn, and upon learning of the murder, he did his best to drink himself to death. It would be two weeks later when he would meet the group for the first time.

CHAPTER 6

The night had come and stayed with them well before Phineas finished his story. He didn't look at them while he told his tale. He did not want them to see the lack of tears in his eyes or emotion on his face. His story was filled with pain, but Phineas Lightfoot had finished crying long ago and simply couldn't do it anymore. Leon, Dwim, and Rennyn exchanged glances with one another. Each of them expressed sadness for the man's story.

"It wasn't your fault." Ren said, finally breaking the silence in the group. She was sitting cross legged on the ground near Leon, but crawled her way towards Phin to put a hand on his shoulder. "You deserve to be saved if possible. Everyone deserves a second chance."

"I'm a thief, you know, the best there is." Phin shook his head causing some of his golden locks, which were matted together with dried blood, to sway with the motion. "I've never wanted to kill anyone. I have no control when the monster calls. Even now," he reached up and touched the silver amulet, "I think this thing is working. I can hear the beast and he's angry, gods help me; he's so angry. Still, he can't come forward." He finally looked up at the group. "Thank you for that."

Dwim gave a soft nod. Leon sat there with his arms crossed while he mulled over the entire story. He felt that Phin's brother was right to some degree. Leon himself preferred to be wild and free, but he didn't go around breaking laws. There had to be order and Leon was finding that though the sad story might have worked on Ren and Dwim, he didn't think he could ever trust Phineas, much less respect him.

"What now?" Phin asked hoarsely, "What will you do with me?"

Ren looked over at the rest of the group. She bit her lip, unsure of what their thoughts were, but she couldn't see the harm in allowing him to travel with them for a bit. If he was as deft with his hands as he claimed, he might be good for something. Dwim stood and walked to the fire and held his meaty hands out to warm them.

"I think it important that I explain what I remember about the dream our dear Ren and I experienced." So Dwim did his best to recite the prophetic words of the Oracle and the visions that accompanied it. When Dwim got to the part about the man with two hearts, the three of them glanced towards Phineas who immediately turned red and lowered his head. Even Leon, who already didn't like Phin, had to admit to himself that Phin seemed to be who they were talking about. Dwim mentioned the baby and oath under the rose. Once he came to the part about the drunk crow, Leon jumped up to his feet.

"I think I know exactly who that's talking about!" He shouted out. His eyes were large and filled with excitement. Perhaps because this whole prophecy thing felt like a hunt and Leon loved the hunt.

Ren looked up at him wearing a look of surprised amusement, "Oh? Who?"

Leon turned to her, "You remember that hermit I was telling you about as we were leaving Whiterock?" He gave her no time to answer and continued on, "He wore an old banged up pointed hat. Frayed at the edges. Thing looked like it was going to fall apart at any moment."

Dwim chimed in, "So? Ye' nay think people wear pointed hats, lad?"

Leon looked back at Dwim, "They might, but this guy also had a strange little crow that followed him around. Trained, maybe?" He shook his head. He was focusing on the wrong details. "Anyway, standing near this guy, as friendly as he was, you could smell the booze coming off him." He looked around the group. Not seeing the same excitement he was feeling, he sat down again and did his best to keep his emotions under control. "He's just a hermit though. Why would he be important?"

Dwim shrugged "I'm nay sure, but it sounds to me like we know where to start looking at least."

Ren joined in. "That sounds fine to me. We should get some rest, but before we do, I'd like to head out into the woods for a while and try to gather some supplies. I might be able to find something out there that will allow me to make something useful for us. Just in case." She turned to Phin and cast a favorable gaze on him, "Our new friend here can join me. Would you help me?"

Phin raised a brow and looked at the others to gauge their reactions at the suggestion. "Sure?" he said, unsure if this was some sort of test, "If you think you can trust me."

Dwim stomped over to Phineas and jabbed a finger into Phin's chest. He continued to prod the man as he threatened the gorgeous man, "Lay a single finger on her, lad, and we'll kill ye' ourselves."

Phineas nodded. His bright sky blue eyes examined Dwim and Leon's face and could see very clearly they weren't lying; especially Leon who wore his distrust very clearly. "Understood."

Ren stood up and spoke very cheerfully, "He won't hurt me." She looked at Phin with friendly purple eyes and said,"I trust you." She did, however, walk over to Leon and lowered her voice to a whisper, "Do you have any extra weapons? You know, just in case?"

Leon grabbed the hunting knife that sat sheathed on his hip. He pulled it out and took hold of the blade so that the hilt was held out to her. She took the hilt and waited for him to remove his hand from the blade. Once he did, she looked the knife over and thanked him with a smile. Leon returned the smile and then continued to glare at Phineas.

"Let's go, Phineas!" she said starting off into the wilds. Phin stood up and followed. Wearing Ren's cloak wasn't helping much as it didn't cover very much and looked more like a little night gown on him. The two of them had been walking for a bit, making light conversation about nothing at all. Ren stopped for a moment and squinted her eyes. "Do you see that light? Is that a cabin?"

Phin stared ahead, "I don't see anything. Are you sure it's out there?"

Ren nodded, "Let's get closer. Maybe there is some clothing out on a line for you. We could leave some coin in its place so it wouldn't be stealing. Not really." She reached for his hand and dragged him along. Phineas was a wanted man in several cities and thought that no matter how much coin would be left behind, people simply did not like their property being taken. Her touch felt warm in his hand as they moved towards the light. Just as Ren had said, there was a cabin. Someone moved around inside casting silhouettes by candlelight. Ren released his hand and pointed to a clothes line where some clothes hung "There! I thought there might be something!"

Phin crept towards the line. Ren was astonished at how he made no sound when he walked over the mess of fallen twigs and brush on the ground. Even with her Elven ears, where she surely could have heard something, Phineas' footsteps though were silent. The handsome man with his deft hands made fast work of removing a shirt and pants. Ren dug out a couple of coins from her satchel and held them out. Phin slipped both the shirt and pants on rather swiftly and as he returned to Ren he plucked the coins from her hand and stashed it in his pocket. "Thank you." Is all he said and offered her a wink.

Ren gave him a motherly look, "Phineas...", but it would do nothing for him. His mother and father were basically saints and his brother, well they all knew about him now. No, Phineas was his own man and all the treasure in the world could never slick his lust for the thrill. It was never about money. Even now, he crept back towards the window to peek inside. Rennyn frowned and charged forward. She was not as silent, or even near it, as he was. She grabbed him by the collar of the shirt and dragged him away from the window. "Enough trouble for one night!" She hissed at him.

They headed back to the camp without gathering any ingredients. Ren found herself rather upset with Phineas who she felt like she stuck her neck out for. Halfway to the camp she even yanked the cloak back from him and covered herself. Phin half smiled, finding it funny how upset she was with him for doing what he told her he did. He made no sound as he walked behind her, not with his feet nor his mouth. It was something that aided in his ability to become such a cunning thief. He dug the coin from his new pocket and flipped it with his thumb, catching it in his hand, and over again.

When they reached camp Ren stopped on it's edge and her eyes searched for Leon. She watched him from a distance for a moment while he worked on something with his back to her. Phin returned to his spot and sat down quietly. Dwim acknowledged his presence and then searched for Ren. He relaxed when he saw her face.

"Ye' alright, lass?" He asked, stepping close to his sword so that he could grab it if she said no.

Leon turned around and saw her standing there watching him. Ren looked down as Leon spoke "About time you got back. I thought we were going to have to go looking for you."

A slight flush crossed her cheeks. She did her best to look at Dwim instead of Leon. "I'm alright. Didn't find any ingredients though. We did find Phineas some clothes; so his nakedness won't be an issue at least." She moved towards Leon and with the fire's light dancing in her eyes she held out the hunting knife, "Told you I'd be fine. I'm tougher than I look."

"No arguments there." He took the knife from her as slowly as he could while the two of them stared at each other. "Marrenval is quite far from here." He looked at Dwim now, "If we can get back to Karren's Call and get the carriage and horses, it'll shave off some time from the journey. Lilly Tree is on the southern side of the kingdom so there'll still be some distance to cover."

Dwim gave Leon's idea contemplation and then nodded his agreement. Rennyn hid a yawn behind her hand. It sounded to her like it was going to be an early morning. She looked around at the others, "Shall we take shifts for sleeping tonight?"

Phin piped up, "Because of me, right?"

"Oh," she stammered for words. It wasn't what she meant, but could see how he had taken it as such "I didn't mean to-"

"I'm not entirely convinced that the amulet will work, so yes." Leon said rather harshly as he laid down near the fire.

"Get some sleep, lass. I'll take the first shift." Dwim said. His eyes were also fixated on Phineas. Ren looked over at Leon for a brief moment and then removed her cloak. She laid it down on the ground and then herself upon it. She rested her head on her arm and continued to watch the rugged hunter. The fire was warm and the crackling of the wood was relaxing. It was not long before her eyes closed and she drifted off into a dream filled sleep.

Phineas, Leon, and Rennyn slept quite soundly. Dwim would wake Leon next when he was unable to keep his eyes open any longer. The Dwarf would lay down and Leon stood guard over the camp. After a few hours, Leon would wake Ren and have her take her turn. Ren sat quietly by the fire and watched it dance. The elements of the awesome machinery of nature always calmed her. She supposed it was because of what she was. Elves had always been so very close to nature. The fire light sucked her in and she was easily lost in it's beauty. She picked up a small stick and with the flick of her wrist flung it into the fire. She began to feel that weird feeling once more, the very same one when she and Alastor had argued, the very same where she pushed back the wolf somehow. Her eyes lost focus as if she were in a trance; hypnotized by the flame. The fire had become low and without realizing it, she commanded the fire to grow, not out loud but inside her head. It was to her shock that the fire shot upwards and changed from yellow and orange to a bright blue and back again.

Phineas, who slept as quietly as he moved, spoke up without opening his eyes, "You know magic is forbidden in Marrenval, right? You'll have the Hunters after you for that business. Even the small things."

The fire continued to grow. The flames shifted between their natural color and that wonderful blue. Embers flew up and floated down as the sun began to rise. Phineas opened his eyes now and watched. He said nothing, but his body was ready to jump and run should it get out of control. *An odd group* he thought to himself. *A cursed thief, a Dwarf, a master hunter, and an apothecary who seemed to be able to use magic.* For one reason or another Phineas thought of his sister and as he did so, the hymns once sung in the cathedral echoed in his mind. It gave him a chill, even in the warmth of the fire.

"They burned it down," she mumbled, "everything is gone." Her eyes flashed in anger as she stood up and stared into the woods around them, "It's all his fault that I have nothing left." The fire blazed upwards one more time before returning to normal as Ren dropped back down to a sitting position and slumped forward a bit.

Phineas sat up, realizing she was not going to let it go, and rubbed his eyes. He looked at the Elf. "Who did what?"

Ren snapped out and looked up at the golden haired man, "Alastor. It's his fault that I have nothing to my name."

"Who's that? Ex lover?" Phineas asked.

Ren looked towards Dwim. With anger in her face she muttered, "He let him get away. He just let him leave." Phin thought for a brief second she might attack the sleeping Dwarf. She seemed soft to him though and so he let her go on. She stood again and took a few steps towards the sleeping pair but stopped halfway to them. She turned, her bruised face easily seen now in the increasing sunlight before she placed her hands over it and sobbed, "I protected him and I lost everything."

Leon started to stir, roused by Dwim's awful snoring. Phineas was uncomfortable. It was not because of her anger or her use of magic, but because he was selfish and simply did not know how to handle a situation where feelings were involved. Had he been home, he'd simply have gotten up and left. He even thought about doing that now, but had no idea where they were and so he sat there. "Yeah. Losing things is bad."

Ren finally snapped and let out a frustrated yell. Dwim startled and called out in Dwarvish. Leon sat up and raised a brow watching Ren as she grabbed her cloak off the ground. She threw it around herself and stormed off into the woods. Leon looked at Phineas who promptly shrugged, "I didn't do anything" and then leaned over to let out a long winded fart. Leon grabbed a loose tree branch and threw it at Phineas. It pegged him in the head.

"You're an idiot!" he exclaimed while he got up to go look for Ren.

Ren found a moss covered tree and leaned against it for a moment before sinking down to the ground. She wrapped her arms around her knees and quietly sobbed, feeling so much confusion mixed with sadness. She only had a few moments to herself before Leon came around the tree.

"Did that moron say something to upset you?" he asked. He too leaned against a tree and crossed his arms over his chest.

Ren looked up at Leon and wiped her eyes. The Elf shook her head, "No. Just wallowing in self pity I suppose. I miss home."

"Ah. Well," he nodded and his messy hair blew gently in the morning breeze, "not having a home is alright. Never tied to one place. Get up and go whenever you like. See new things."

She plucked a blade of grass and fiddled with it nervously. It danced between her fingers as she spoke, "I suppose that's true, Leon. I guess I miss the people I knew. The routine of day to day life. This is also the first time I've-" she paused unsure of how to even explain herself.

"Used magic?" Leon asked.

Ren looked up at him. Until now she was unsure if the others had noticed it the night that Phin attacked her while he was the wolf. She nodded, "It's been a bit taxing on me. I don't know what I'm doing or how to control it."

Leon nodded "I understand," he pushed off the tree and walked a bit closer, "you'll need to get those emotions under control. Once we cross the border wall, they'll have Witch Hunters patrolling. If you use the slightest bit of that magic they'll know and they'll come for you. Witch Hunters, as dumb as that sounds, are outrageously skilled at finding, fighting, and taking prisoners. We don't want that kind of heat on us. Marrenval, home as it may be, can be very dangerous."

She let out a bitter laugh. "I feel like I'll be even more useless if I can't even help with whatever power I have. I'm not exactly experienced with a sword either."

"Aren't you Elves supposed to be good with the bow and arrow?" he asked, hoping she took no offense to it.

Rennyn suddenly looked embarrassed. "My mother thought it unnecessary for me to learn. She made sure I was at a work table reading and mixing up whatever I could.. Best to keep your head low in the Human cities when you're not a Human."

Leon nodded, "How about I teach you some time? It's my preferred weapon of choice. I'm damn good too." He mimed shooting an arrow at her and gave her a handsome wink and made a sound with his mouth indicating the target had been struck. "You'll be a dead eye shot in no time."

A pretty smile crossed her face, "I would love that." She stood up and hugged him.

He gave her a small squeeze and patted her on the back. He let go of her and looked back towards camp. "Dwim is probably losing beard hairs over us not helping pick up camp. Shall we go?"

Ren nodded and together they made their way back to the camp. They were both delighted to see that Dwim was chasing Phineas around the fire and smacking him in the back with a tree branch and fussing in Dwarvish while Phin cowered under it and fussed back. Ren giggled, "It seems like they have everything under control here." She looked up at Leon, thankful for his talk, and placed a hand on his arm. Leon looked back into her face and could have sworn that her eyes were sparkling. He smiled.

"Alright!" he clapped his hands together at Phin and Dwim. "I sure hope you're all in for some travel. This one is going to be long."

Dwim and Phin stopped their running around and Ren stood closer to Leon. She was happy again and spoke with cheer in her voice, "I'm looking forward to the adventure. I'm looking forward to getting things back to normal."

Leon chuckled, "Well, you, Dwim, and I? That was normal. This guy though?" he nodded to Phineas who now had his penis out and was flapping it at Dwim who in turn was threatening to rip it off. "Nothing is going to be normal with this guy."

Ren laughed, "Phineas! Leave Dwim alone!"

Leon shook his head and began to pick camp up. Phineas tucked himself away while still laughing. This was the beginning of their journey to Marrenval. The friendships between them grew deeper as they learned more about each other. Dwim and Leon were still wary of Phineas. The trip back to Karren's Call was long, but they made it after the midday sun sat in the sky casting no shadows. There was no fuss, at least that they found, about a missing paladin and so they gathered their things from The Sleepy Sheep Inn. Dwim found their Dwarven carriage driver and after a small discussion, the driver went off. He returned not long after with four horses, each equipped with a saddle. Dwim thanked him, wished him well, and watched the Dwarf climb back on the carriage. With a shake of the reins, the Dwarf driver headed off towards North Normoon and Whiterock. The four of them looked at each other once before climbing on their horses and heading out on the adventure to Marrenval.

CHAPTER 7

The wonderfully quiet town of Lilly Tree sat on the southern side of Marrenval not quite on the coast but close. Trees of large lily pad typed foliage, for which the town was named, covered a lot of the landscape making the town look more like a small hamlet. Lilly Tree got a lot of trade that came through though and the town itself was by no means hurting. The town had a single inn that boasted many rooms and tables which was good because most of the town would gather after a day of work. Further away, on the town's outskirts, was a large spacious manor that sat on a piece of empty land. This was the home of the local Hunters. Witch Hunters, as they were formally known, were highly skilled in combat and were tasked with bringing anyone who dared to use magic back to the guild; dead or alive.. Why it was outlawed here, people had no idea anymore. It had been so long now that it was more taboo than anything. To use magic would be to admit you were abnormal. Magic use, for the most part, had become extremely rare. The ones who did use it kept to themselves far away from the rest of the world. Elves did not venture into Human lands and Dwarves had no magic ability at all.

These days, Hunters were also tasked with bringing in wild animals that were becoming a problem. Each Hunter craved for the chance to hunt down some filthy magician though. For a Hunter to bring them to justice for the crown of Marrenval was still an honor and admirable by the locals. The Witch Hunters were funded by the crown and royal treasury; so their estate was royal property. That meant they were not taxed and the upkeep and maintenance was handled by the crown as well. The manor itself looked to be in good shape.

On this night, Rennyn, Dwim, Leon, and Phineas were already days into their journey to Marrenval. Under the light of the moon, a man leaned on the wooden fence post at the entrance to the Witch Hunter's Guild property. He was an old man and far beyond his prime in which a Hunter was useful. Many of his much younger fellow Hunters had just come back from a night of drinking and shenanigans. The old Hunter, Angus, smiled when he saw his favorite in the group walking up the path.

Jayda of the Hunt was left with the hunters as an orphan. Angus himself taught her to be a strong, fierce, and fearless Hunter. She was versatile with most conventional weapons, but there was one she excelled at more than the others. The whip spoke to her in ways that other weapons did not. She simply did not miss her mark with the whip and when it was at her side, she felt she was whole. After years of training she became a full fledged member of the Hunt and to celebrate, Angus gave her a special made leather whip whose braid was twined with the bones, set as studs for extra pain, of the first blood witch Jayda had slain. The hilt was adorned in the jeweled symbol of their order.

"Look at you," he said trying his best to hide the good nature in his ribbing, "out with this noisy lot? I thought you didn't like to have fun. You're all business."

Jayda stepped towards Angus, leaving the others who continued up the path to the manor. Her skin was tanned, but fair, and her hair as black as coal. She had emerald eyes that shined so brightly they almost glowed. "Lips loosen when drinking happens. Best time to find out the weaknesses of the new blood. Keep it stashed up here" she tapped on her temple, "In case I ever need to use it." Her hand, always lingering near or on the butt of the whip, tapped the coil of leather and bone absentmindedly. She wore a mixture of leathers and furs of various animals; most of it black with a few gray furs mixed in. Her boots were tall and worn with time and adventure. Her pants and shirts were leather. She preferred them tight so that her movement wasn't restricted. She was tall and lean. She was muscular and firm, but managed to maintain her femininity. She was by no means weak.

Angus let out a coughing laugh. He was the oldest living member of the Hunters. Under him, by nearly thirty years, was the Grand Master Jux of the Hunt; even he was getting up in years. Angus had quit counting how old he was a long time ago. He looked up at the twinkling stars, "Oh yes. Loose lips spill the beans and we love the beans, don't we, kid?" He looked back at her.

Jayda winked at him, "We sure do." She held out her arm to him. "How about we go in and I will get you some tea?" She lowered her voice to a playful whisper, "I learned that Izzy is terribly afraid of spiders."

He shook her grasp off "Bah. Maiden's got that onion soup going and it's burning my old eyes." He took in a deep, rattly breath, and sighed, "I yearn for a hunt, kid. These old bones though," he placed a thin trembling hand on her shoulder, "It's a younger person's thing now. Back when I was your age, business was booming. Spent decades chasing out everyone who even thought about magic. Now? Now we rarely see a case and it's usually just someone trying some simple trick."

"I understand, old man." She craved a fight too. Her muscles ached with the urge to release some pent up energy. Sure, training was fine, but she knew the yearning of a real hunt. "What will happen to us if the fiends who use magic cease to be?"

Angus shrugged, "I'll be dead by then, hopefully. I imagine the crown will keep paying to keep us around though. Might be less guild halls." He looked away up at the sky again and then back to her, giving her a fatherly smile. "I taught you well though. Even if they closed the manor, you'd find work doing something else. Maybe fighting in arenas?"

It saddened her to think there would be a day when he wouldn't be there anymore. She never said it out loud, as she did not want to seem weak to him, but she viewed him as her father and she loved him dearly. "I can't think of anyone better to have taught me." She smiled back at him. "Arenas might not be enough of a challenge though."

He chuckled, "Well, you'll certainly make more coin doing that then what we are doing now." Angus held his arm out now, allowing Jayda to take it and walk him up the path. She could feel his body tremble with every step. "I know Maiden tries but her soups," he made a retching sound, "gives me the runs every time. At my age though I guess I should be happy if anything happens." He laughed at his own joke as they carried on up to the manor under the moon's gaze.

Halfway up the path to the manor, an aquamarine blue light shone from the bracelets each had on their wrist. All Hunters wore them. They were small and in the center was a jewel who would shine bright light when magic use was detected. The jewel was round and would spin in a set ring showing the direction in which the magic was used. Both Angus and Jayda looked at their wrist. The manor door opened and Grand Master Jux of the Hunt came out. He was a tall and wide man. He squinted his wrinkled eyes and called out, "Angus, are you down there?"

Angus looked away from the bracelet and gave a weak wave, "Yes, Grand Master. Jayda too!" Jayda continued to walk Angus up the path.

Jux nodded. He waited, for a very long moment, until Jayda walked Angus up to the door. "Jayda, you're up. The rest of these fools are drunk. Find this fiend and bring them in alive."

Angus looked down at the bracelet, longing for the hunt, but knowing he was in no shape to even get down the path without help. "Go on, kid. One of us will at least get to taste the hunt."

Jayda looked at her bracelet once more. The ring began to turn, pointing to the direction of the magical source. She looked to Angus, sorry that he'd never get that last hunt, and her face grew serious. She looked at Jux and said, "Give me five minutes to get my things together and I will head out to catch whatever filth is out there hiding."

Angus clasped her on the shoulder proudly, "Yes, I know you will, kid. You always do." He reached out and latched on to Jux.

Jux helped Angus inside leaving Jayda alone as he said, "Let's get you some onion soup, hm?" to which Angus protested.

Jayda went inside up to her room and gathered her traveling satchel. She had everything else she needed. Her fingers danced along the handle of the whip. It felt good to know it would be used. She turned to leave, but before exiting, decided to grab her short sword. She picked up the scabbard and attached it to the belts that wrapped around her torso so that it hung on her back. "Just in case." she mumbled. She was confident but not stupid. Jayda headed down again, found Angus sitting at the dinner table with a few others, and kissed his forehead, "Behave yourself, old man. I'll be back soon enough."

Angus beamed at her, "Good hunting, kid!"

Jayda walked outside. The air was cool and crisp; not long off a cold winter. Her hands patted her body down making sure once again that she had everything. Her whip was there and ready, daggers were tucked into her belt, her satchel was filled with bandages and other things in case she got hurt as well as her sword which was polished and sharpened; it sat on her back. She had her fur cloak on to keep her warm. She nodded to no one, satisfied with her preparedness. She removed a leather strap from her bag, pulled her hair into a ponytail, and looked down at the bracelet. It had spun towards the south and east a bit. The only thing east of them was the coast. Without a second thought, she started off down the path, on her way to find her magician.

She spent the next few days tracking through marshland and woods, all the while following the bracelet's guiding jewel. She was traveling through one particular clearing when she felt that the bracelet began to move again. She lifted her wrist and found the jewel rotating in circles. This was a sign that she was nearly on top of the incident. Jayda examined the area and stepped in a bit further. Of all the trees there, she saw one that was black and sheared of it's bark as though struck by lightning. She walked around the tree and examined it for other signs. Behind the tree, a few yards away, she spotted the corpse of a wolf. Half of it was blackened and charred like the tree while the other half was rotting and covered in flies. Most of its insides had already been pilfered by the wildlife.

She returned to the tree and looked at the ground. The markings that her skilled eyes found showed signs of some sort of struggle between the wolf and another. This other was the one that survived of course. She continued to search the area and found another tree that looked like it had been bashed with a club. The earth at the base was disturbed and had a trail that led away from it looking as though something were dragged. She thought it was perhaps a tree limb. She walked the trail silently and found that it led out of the clearing and into the woods once more.

After an hour or so of losing and finding the trail off and on, Jayda stepped out of the wood onto a stony beach. The great ocean laid before her eyes and brought with each wave the strong smell of salt water. The waves crashed over the rocks, leaving small tide pools filled with crustaceans. The sky had grayed swiftly while she had been tracking the trail. She watched the blue ocean horizon as a storm, black clouds and lightning, threatened to spill over the water. That storm however would wait until the wind carried it above her before it would release its downpour.

Rolling thunder forced her to keep moving down the shoreline. She could see in the distance a small, crudely made, hut. It sat near the tree line and looked down over an especially rocky patch of beach with a natural stone pier leading out to the water. She walked closer, most curious about the pier, and saw that a little wooden row bow had been crushed and sunk by the waves. She looked up at the hut and swore quietly to herself. She should have gone there first and felt stupid for making such a mistake. She now had no idea if she had been seen or not. Her hand rested on her whip, ready to unleash it if she needed, as she crept towards the hut.

It started to rain. It was coupled with strong wind and it stung her exposed skin. Still, she moved to the hut and stood in the doorway. She was put off by the sound of snoring. Her eyes adjusted to the darkness in the hut and when they did, she immediately spotted a man sleeping on a straw bed. His hair was dulling blonde, nearly gray. His face was buried into a thin pillow. He wore a hand stitched overcoat of gray leather. A pointed hat, made of the same leather, sat on the hut floor. She noticed the brim was tattered and torn. Jayda spread her feet and got into a fighting stance. She was ready.

Thunder clapped again and sent vibrations through the hut. The man had stopped snoring and sat up with a groan. She unhooked the whip from her hip and let it uncoil to the ground where the tip sent up a puff of dirt. The man stared at Jayda with fierce green eyes. Jayda drew back a little, not expecting to see such cunning and dangerous eyes on a man who looked as if he hadn't bathed for weeks. The man scratched through his wild beard and with the other hand flapped his finger at something. She wondered if he was weaving a spell but followed the direction of his waving hand and to her right she saw a bottle of whiskey on the ground. The man continued to point and nod his head. Jayda slowly crept towards the bottle and pickled it up all the while making sure to keep her eyes on him. It was half empty. She raised a brow and tossed it to him.

The man caught the bottle without issue and bit the cork with his teeth. With a bit of a pull, the cork popped loose, and he spit it onto the ground. He raised the bottle to Jayda as though making a toast and then tipped it back to his lips. Every bit of what remained from the whiskey was chugged. Once the bottle was emptied, he dropped it on the ground and watched it roll away into another corner. Dark amber droplets dripped from his more than short but less than long, untamed, beard. He wiped at it with the sleeve of his overcoat. The man looked at Jayda once more and simply said, "Thank you." He laid back down on the straw bed and almost immediately began to snore again.

Jayda drew her arm up. She was going to attack. Even if she was wrong and this wasn't the correct target, she couldn't take a chance. Just as her muscles were releasing, the sound of flapping wings behind her caused her to spin on her heels. She let the whip lash out towards a crow, black as the void, and with two different colored eyes. A set of blue and yellow eyes fixated on Jayda and though she was fast, the bird was faster. The whip cracked in the air like thunder belonging to the storm that was Jayda of the Hunt. She snarled as the crow flew off and she turned to find that the man in bed was no longer there.

Had the man been in better shape, or perhaps finding himself tracked by a lesser Hunter, he may have gotten away. Jayda could easily see however the disturbed dirt around the bed's edge. It gave away the man that crawled under the bed. She narrowed her eyes and let out a huff, "What do you take me for, you drunk fool?"

"That depends," said the voice from under the bed followed by a wet burp, "What do you take me for?"

"A dead man!" She stated rather bluntly. She stomped over, grabbed the frame of the bed, and turned it roughly on its side. Her eyes flashed in anger and she drew her whip up once again.

The man laying on his back threw his hands up in protest, "Wait! Wait! Wait! Wait!" The end of the whip's braid snapped an inch by his head, the sound bit into his ear and caused a ringing. This was a warning shot, not a mistake, and he knew it. He flinched and then slowly got to his feet. Their eyes locked and he decided then and there to make an attempt to run past her. He started his run and shouldered the woman as he went by her. Jayda, hardly moved at all, spun around in place and grabbed him by the collar of his coat. With a growl she yanked him back hard. As he stumbled backwards, she kicked at his leg. She immediately jumped on him as soon as he fell. Her fist balled and she stuck him several times in the face as hard as she possibly could, not meaning to simply strike him but strike through him.

"I'm tired of your games already!" She said, spit flying from her mouth and into his face just before her fist did again.

"Yeah," he said, blood running from his nose and lips, "I'm tired of this game too. Why are we playing it?"

"Don't pretend you don't know why I'm here!" She looked down at him with her fist drawn back and poised to strike again. For a sliver of a moment, she wondered why he was making this so easy on her, "What's wrong? Too drunk to use your power?" She taunted, "This has got to be the easiest capture I've ever had."

He groaned, "A Hunter? I should have known. I know not what power you speak of, madam," she wasn't sure if he was insulting her just then, "but I can assure you I am too drunk to do most anything!" He shook his head. "Let me try that again. I am anything too drunk to do anything." He shook his head once more. "Sorry, my thinking is a bit fuzzy on account of being repeatedly struck in the face. What I mean to say is that I can assure you that I am both powerless and drunk and that they have nothing to do with one another. Even if I could be powerful and sober, why in the world would I do it here? Do you think I enjoy being beaten up? This isn't some sort of sexual fantasy for you, is it?"

Jayda struck him in the face a few more times. Each hit sounded as though she were punching a cut of meat at the butchers. His blood spilled more freely now. She climbed off of him and grabbed his coat lapel. She yanked him up to his feet. She threw him out of the hut and onto the rocky beach. He landed face first on the rocks. They cut his face and he let out a hard groan. He got to his hands and knees slowly as she marched up behind him.

He turned his head to try and look at her, "You know, I've met quite a few people in my travels who like this sort of thing. Let me go and I'll point you in their direction." He was still mocking her, even as he was spitting out a mouthful of blood. It washed away immediately in the hard rain.

"That is not my. . . I'm not . . ." she frowned and delivered a hard kick to his stomach. The man rolled down the rocky beach even further. He let out a cry of pain as he laid there in the rain, now soaked in water and blood.

He held a hand up and continued to poke at the angry Hunter, "No, no of course not. Wouldn't dream of making that implication. You're much classier than that. This isn't a sexual assault you're dishing out. This is a high class beating! Very refined!" He struggled to his feet, nearly falling once more as he stepped on a rock, "Let me assure you that your dignity is lost on me. I am beneath you. Allow this poor scum to crawl from the sole of your boot back to the pools of creation from whence I came. You've got better things to do." Jayda started down the beach towards him. He raised his arms and then dropped them to his sides exasperated, "Are you sure this isn't a sex thing? There's no need to be ashamed. I mean it's not my idea of a good time, but I try not to judge."

Jayda raised her arm up and back which in turn raised the whip. It seemed to vanish, only briefly, before she reached out and in a snap the leather whip kissed his cheek. The man spilled back with another cry of pain and fell once again. The back of his head hit a rock in the water and it wasn't but a moment later that the salt water began to turn red as he laid there too weak to even move now. Jayda wasn't having any of it though and as she got to him, she stomped down on his testicles. This caused him to somehow find the strength to turn over on his side. He cried out and tears began to fall from his eyes. He fought for air as hard as he fought the urge to vomit. She took another step and kicked him hard in the face next. He turned over on his other side now. She bent down and wrapped her whip around his neck. She forced him on his stomach and then placed her boot on his back. She pulled on the ends of the whip and choked the man. When she was sure he wasn't going to put up a fight, she removed her boot from his back and dragged him, whip still around his neck, up the beach towards the hut. She dragged him inside and then finally removed the whip from around his neck.

The man gasped for air as the blue in his face slowly turned to red and glared at her. His face was cut and swollen. He noticed the bracelet on her arm and said, "That's a lovely little thing." He waved his fingers around for a brief moment that was followed by a loud popping sound. The bracelet immediately began to glow and spin. "Oh wow, it does work."

"Why you filthy little. . . " she drew a dagger from her belt and slashed at him. He knew he had gone too far this time and as the blade crossed his face into his beard, the man put his hands up again, "I'll come quietly!"

Jayda pushed her foot against his chest and forced him down to the ground. She dug in her bag pulling out some rope. She bent over and bound his hands together. "Up!" She ordered him, yanking on the rope. "I hope you're just as snarky when they hang you."

"Please, a request from a doomed man then." He nodded over to his hat. "My hat, please, I don;t go anywhere without it." Jayda grabbed the hat and looked at it carefully. Finding nothing out of the ordinary to her, she jammed it on his head. "Thank you. Inside my pillow is something I refuse to leave without. Get it for me and I'll not be troublesome anymore."

"What is it?" she asked, eyeing him carefully.

"A ring on a silver necklace. My wife's ring." If the man was drunk before, he was completely sober now. His eyes never changed though. They looked as dangerous as ever. "I won't leave without it."

Jayda reached in carefully and extracted the silver chain. She went to hand it over to him and then thought better of it. She slid it into her pocket, tucking it down safely. "I imagine this will help ensure that you come along willingly."

The thunder rolled. His brow, swollen and beaten, furrowed. In this moment, for the first time in the encounter, he truly hated the woman. He said nothing though because she was right. He'd torch the world for that ring if he were capable of doing so. She yanked him to his feet and pushed him into the rain. He started walking while she kept a hold of the rope.

"You sure you don't have something better to do than drag some old hermit to his death?" He spoke rather matter of factly. "That's what they'll do with me, isn't it? Kill me because of some spell I may or may not have cast? I confess nothing."

"I just do my job." She said and shoved him forward and he almost tripped over another rock as he walked. There was no sign of emotion on her face. "Just keep walking. We have a long trip ahead of us."

He nodded as he continued to walk just as she commanded. Jayda passed him and tugged on the rope forcing him to walk faster as she led the way. "Ah, just the minion." He mumbled. "All brawn and no brain. Makes sense. I wish I had myself a puppet too. Must be nice to have someone do as they are told without question."

She gave another hard pull on the rope that forced him forward. As he stumbled, nearly falling to his knees, she threw her elbow back against his nose. They both heard the break and he cried out while more blood spilled down his face and onto his coat. She then yanked the rope again to force him to keep walking. "I am no one's slave. I am the best Hunter in our guild. Do not tempt me to anger my Grand Master by killing you myself."

He called out, "Amun! My old friend!" The crow with different colored eyes came flapping to him and landed on his shoulder. Jayda turned around and held the dagger out to the bird who cawed loudly at her. "Just a bird!" The man said in a panic. Jayda eyed him and slipped her dagger in her belt.

"If it attacks me I'll kill the thing and eat it in front of you." She was in a foul mood now.

"We head to the noose! If this is the end then I suppose it's the end. Can't live a quiet life, can we Amun?" The man asked. The bird cawed it's reply. Jayda shuddered but kept her mouth closed. Crows were never good omens. They didn't even make a decent meal.

They traveled for a few days, having to move slower than she normally would now that she had her prisoner. Night was coming upon them and she needed to build a camp. Like the nights before, she tied him up completely and sat him against a fallen log. He watched her as she made the fire. Once done, she went out to the wilds and came back an hour later with a small rabbit. She skinned and cooked it for them. Once it was done, she untied him so that he could eat and threatened him with another beating if he tried to run. He believed her.

"Do you know who I am?" the man asked, "I assume you do since you decided to give me such a beating when you found me."

She shook her head as she tore into the rabbit. The juice ran down her chin. "No. It doesn't matter either. I'm only with you until I turn you over to the Grand Master and then our paths will never cross again."

He raised a brow, "And your bracelet is how you found me?" Jayda nodded. The man laughed. Amun joined in by cawing. "You use magic to hunt magic? The hypocrisy!" He pulled off a piece of meat and Amun snapped it out of his hands. "What's your name, girl?"

Jayda looked at the bracelet and then to the man narrowing her eyes. She wasn't used to so much chatter. She thought it would have been better if she could have just taken him out. "Jayda."

"Single name. I like it. Very intimidating. I'll give it a try. I'm Oberic. My feathered friend here is Amun. Say hello, Amun." The crow cawed. "What is it you think I am, Jayda?"

She licked the grease off her fingers and looked away, "Some type of magician. Now shut up before I make you continue to walk through the night." She learned on the first night that Oberic knew how to push buttons to the point that it caused great rage inside her.

"What kind of magician? Am I a simple conjurer of cheap tricks? Am I master of the arcane, twirling squalls of fire around me? Does that *magic* bracelet of yours tell you any of that? If you hunt those who use magic, what did you do to the one who enchanted your bracelet?"

Jayda ignored him for as long as she possibly could before she lost her cool and uncoiled the whip and snapped it at him. The whip bit into his neck and he fell over on his side holding his throat. 'Enough!" She yelled, her eyes flashing in anger, "I don't care what kind of magic you do! All magic is evil!" she wrapped her hand around her wrist tightly. "This bracelet is the only magic we are allowed and it's used purely to find and destroy those like *you*!" Jayda coiled her whip, satisfied that he was in pain, and laced it back to her hip. She laid down near the fire and closed her eyes.

Amun remained silent as he walked along the log glaring at Jayda. It wouldn't even make it an hour before Oberic piped up again. "How do you know magic is bad? I've never hurt anyone, much less with magic. Again, I confess nothing." Amun cawed and at this point Jayda was certain the damn bird was mocking her. "And if you don't know what kind of magic I do, which I don't, but if I did, how do you know you even really have me captured? Maybe I'm merely a figment of your imagination. Maybe the *real* magician is my friend, Amun." Amun cawed. "Who knows? Who knows?" Oberic shrugged his shoulders.

She sat up and stormed over to Oberic putting her nose against his broken one. Their eyes, both green and full of fire, stared into one another's. His eyes scared her, but she would never admit that to him. When she spoke, she hissed her words and her spit hit his face, "Because magic killed my mother!" She grabbed Oberic by the neck and slammed his head into the log, "Now shut your mouth and I swear, I *swear*, if I hear one more peep out of that fucking bird I'll gut the little shit and make a soup with him!"

Amun flew from the log as if he understood her words. "Well," Oberic mused, "You've gone and hurt his feelings."

Jayda had reached her threshold and grabbed Oberic's hair, lifting his head from the log and then slamming it back into it. She did this over and over until a new wound spilled fresh blood onto the log and he was unconscious. She breathed in and out rapidly. She stepped away from Oberic and looked to the black sky and yelled out "You're next you winged shit!" Her words echoed in the darkness and she could hear birds take flight somewhere in the distance. Jayda laid back down and closed her eyes. She tried to sleep but was far too angry now to even come close to it.

Another hour passed and Jayda was relieved to not have seen or heard the crow since. She rolled over and saw that Oberic was once again awake and staring at her through swollen, blackened eyes. "I'm sorry about your mother." He croaked out. "There are those who wield terrible magic, but that isn't me. You're taking an innocent man to his grave." His voice was sincere in his apology. He never met his mother. He was sold as a baby. It was a story he wouldn't share until some time much later, but for now he thought about his childhood which led him to think about his wife and how he would never see her again. Finally, for once in the last few days, Oberic fell truly quiet with no wise cracks.

"Go to sleep or I'll tie you up again." Jayda said, rolling on to her back.

Oberic laid down and sighed. He stared up at the night sky, at least what he could see through the treetops, and furrowed his brow. "Do you see that, Amun?" The crow cawed and Jayda jumped up.

"That's it!" she dived for the crow who promptly flew off. She growled at Oberic "When did that damn thing come back?" He didn't answer and only continued to stare at the sky. "What in the world are you looking at?" She turned her gaze up and looked "What? It's just the sky."

"You hunt magic and do not understand the power of the stars?" He asked, almost insulted, "Care to be educated or am I not allowed to?"

Jayda rolled her eyes and muttered "Go on." She sat back down.

Oberic motioned to the portion of sky he was looking at. "See that purple light?"

Jayda looked up again and saw it. "Yeah? So?"

"We shouldn't be seeing that star right now. That's called a black star, Death's Eye. It has many names, but the point is I have studied the star charts and I know their passages. They show up naturally of course but not now." They both continued to stare at the purple light; a star that sparkled more brightly than the others in the galaxy painted sky.

"What's your point?" She asked.

"It's a terrible omen." The crow cawed as if to emphasize the statement. "Certain stars look favorably on certain types of magic. The black star, as you might guess, gives power to the magics associated with death." Amun cawed once more.

Jayda thought for a moment "Would this black star help you?"

He thought for a moment. He considered lying and saying no star would help him but why bother? She wouldn't believe him regardless nor would she let him go. "Me? No. Blue stars, yes. "

"What type of magic do you use?" she asked, unsure of why she was making conversation.

"I deal in illusions and enchantments. I of course can do destructive things but I have no desire to."

For a tiny moment, sadness rested on her face. If he was being honest, and for some reason she believed he was, she truly was leading a man who did nothing wrong to his death. Just as quickly as it came though it vanished and she laid back down now feeling tired once more. "Go to sleep," she mumbled "Long day tomorrow."

Jayda lay there quietly for at least an hour to make sure Oberic was sleeping. When she thought it was finally safe, she stood up and quietly paced a bit, contemplating the situation to herself. The woods were filled with the noises of animals, both prey and predator. Owls hooted in the distance as a fog set in that gave the woods a terribly eerie look. As she paced, her black hair nearly becoming one with the night, her bracelet came to life with that bright light. The jewel rotated once more and as she looked at it, it settled in the direction of Lilly Tree. Jayda scooped a handful of dirt and threw it on the fire. Unsatisfied with it's death, she scooped another handful and dumped them on the embers. She swiftly moved to Oberic and kicked him in the ribs. He let out a groan as he woke and glared at her.

"What did I do now?" He grunted, cradling his ribs.

"Get up. We have to move now. I don't want to have to tie you up as it'll slow us down, but if I have to I will. I need you to move your ass." Her voice was harsh and her words delivered like whip lashes.

"Not only do I get to be executed, but I also get to rush to it. Fun." Oberic mumbled as he got to his feet, really not looking forward to the beating he was sure to get if he didn't. He was groggy and rubbed at his beard when he felt his ribs were okay. "What happened to getting a good rest?" Amun flew and landed on his shoulder. Oberic, in the dead fire light, saw that her bracelet was shining again. "I didn't do it, I swear!"

"Shut up and follow!" She commanded him

"Lead the way," he gestured with his hands and then followed her into the darkness. Jayda seemed to be in a rush and Oberic was having a hard time keeping up. Now and again she barked at him to move faster or she'd drag him by his hair. "Is something wrong?" He asked as he did his best to keep up. His body was still a wreck from the fight, not so much a fight as it was a brutal beating, and it caused him pain to move as fast as she did. "I did mention I was an illusionist, yes?"

"I don't care! Run!" she yelled back at him.

"I'm just saying that I can see things. Things you might not. If you're in trouble, I can help you. If I see something strange, I'll let you know. I'm not deceiving you." He was being honest though he knew she would not believe him. One facet of his speciality in illusionary magics was that he could see the unseen and it mostly came in handy while other times it was useless. He pushed himself and did his best to keep up with the raven haired Hunter. She was far too fast for him in this condition and she left him behind.

CHAPTER 8

Angus had only just had his twelfth birthday when the incident happened. He had returned to Lilly Tree from visiting an aunt who lived in another town and upon his return had learned that his father was being held in the dungeons for murder. The magistrate that passed along the sad news hesitated at first but upon further prodding from Angus told him the full grim story of the death of his mother. Angus did not cry and insisted he be taken to his father at once. The guards didn't think it was wise to allow Angus down there to speak with his father but the magistrate allowed it. The boy seemed mentally capable of handling the news so far.. The boy, just a few years shy of being a man, was already quite adult like in his demeanor. Angus was led by guards, who did so reluctantly, to the cell where his father sat, chained to a wall with both hands bound tightly in iron gloves meant to keep witches from weaving magic. Angus crept close to the bars and looked at his father without emotion on his face.

"Why?" he whispered, "Why did you kill mother?"

Angus's father, James Blackhave III, looked up at his son with sunken eyes. "You've not been in love yet, boy. You wouldn't understand."

"You're right. I don't understand why you would kill mother if you loved her so." Angus' reply was bitter and curt. He had not cried yet but would later when he was alone.

"Your mother was sleeping with another man," James said coolly. "So I killed her lover and then her. I tried to bury her, to lay her at rest, but I loved your mother so much, Angus. When you love a woman as much as I loved her, you never let her go. Our family has secrets. I used those secrets."

"What sort of secrets?"

"Dark ones."

"And you'll take them to the grave now."

"Our family has always dealt in the darkest of magics, son. Necromancy. I raised your mother from her grave because I could not bear to be without her. Of course it was stupid. I knew in my heart that the Hunters would come for me. They of course caught me dancing with your mother in our living room. I loved your mother, son. I still love her."

Angus swallowed. It was hard to picture any of that taking place, "I'll never forgive you."

"You don't need to. I request one thing from you son. Just one. If there is ever a night where a star twinkles in the sky, a black one, visit your old mother's grave, hm?"

Angus did not reply, but instead got up and left his father. James was hanged the following day and all of the family's possessions including the estate were left to Angus. He would visit his mother's grave often and would recite the strange little poem etched into her gravestone. Angus would later that year join the Hunters and vow to end every single magician that he possibly could. His career with them was quite successful and he relished in the idea that he was avenging his mother and spitting in the face of his family name. The name of course would be dropped, as all Hunters did to show that they only had loyalty for the order.

Angus, the aged Hunter and father figure to Jayda, sat outside enjoying his pipe. He had tried eating Maiden's miserable potato soup and couldn't stomach it. He was thinking of Jayda and wondering how her hunt was going. He laughed to himself because he knew exactly how it was going. Jayda was out there giving the poor soul who cast that magic a terrible time. He laughed even harder when he thought of the proud look on her face when she'd return with the culprit. He was proud of her, his daughter be it by blood or not, was going to be Grand Master of the guild some day. He was sad to think he'd never see that happen and it turned his laughter silent. He looked up at the night sky and sighed. His eyes traced the patterns in the sky, admiring the beautiful stars that he could actually see, and found that out of all of them, the purple light was the most beautiful one.

For some odd reason, one that Angus could not even begin to explain, he decided he needed to visit his mother's grave. He grabbed his cane and hoisted himself up. He shook terribly as he walked and it took him quite a while to reach the cemetery where his mother had rested for so long. His chocolate hand reached out and stroked the stone. His wrinkled lips read out the odd little poem as he had so many times before.

Revered soul
Bound to none
Bathed in black light

Your hour has come
Souls are collected
For death to hold
Vessels left behind
Forgotten and cold
The eternal night
Prevents the dawn
Heavenly light
Forever gone

The wind blew hard and nearly knocked the old man over. Angus, kneeled over the grave and looked around to see what had caused such a gale as there had been no signs of that sort of wind all day. His ears, though old, were sharp and he could hear something shifting but was unsure of where it came from.. He looked down and saw that his bracelet was spinning in circles and glowing it's blue light. He stared at it confused, knowing that when it spun as such he was at the center of it.

"Show yourself!" He yelled out, "I may be old, but I can still take you on, you best understand that now!"

A hand, devoid of flesh completely, reached out from the grave and wrapped it's bony fingers around his shirt. It pulled him downwards slowly as if mocking him and his struggle to break free. Angus's nose was nearly in the dirt when a skull, his mother's skull, emerged, "Hello, boy! Mommy missed you! Give me a kiss!"

Angus cried out in horror. It was his mother's voice and he had no issue remembering it. He was released by the hand and he attempted to crawl backwards, but his frail body wouldn't allow it. The skeleton continued to crawl out of the dirt, all the while calling out to Angus. The skeleton reached for him and he attempted to swat at it with his cane. The cane fell from his hand however as the other hand clutched at his chest. Angus watched his mother's bones crawl from the grave, easily too, and in those last moments of life before his heart gave out he begged Olm's forgiveness.

Angus collapsed back. Even before he hit the ground, death had come to collect him and ferry him on. The skeleton however went nowhere. It stood over Angus and then collapsed on top of him as a purple wisp of light left the bones and dove into Angus instead. The old, now dead, eyes opened and briefly caught the vision of a remarkably tall and gray skinned woman whose face looked quite skeletal itself. She had long black hair, so pitch that it reflected no light. She wore a long black cloak, as black as her hair, that she opened up to him. Inside was not a body but instead a sky filled with stars and galaxies and what could be assumed all of creation. The corpse of Angus sneered, "Not today. Not ever."

The woman closed her cloak and glided away from him, vanishing into nothingness. Angus stood up without the use of the cane. He did not need it anymore. He looked down at the pile of bones at his feet and frowned. "Time to get to work." Angus, not the real Angus, headed away from the cemetery. The thing inside could access all of the memories this vessel once held and decided to start at the church. Angus walked inside. There was no one there but it did not matter. Chaos had to start somewhere. Angus called out to death herself as he grabbed a candle stick and began to light the curtains ablaze. "I hope you're hungry, bitch! It's feeding time!" He cackled madly as the flames grew around him. It was no time at all that the fire took the church. The old wood used was thirsty for the flame and even the furniture went up quickly. He stepped outside and spotted a few men running in his direction.

"Angus! Are you alright? What happened?" They asked in frantic voices.

Angus stuck out a thin, trembling finger, and pointed at the church. "Children inside! Help them!" and both men nodded, running into the burning church to search for the poor kids. Angus walked behind them, no longer trembling, and shut the wooden doors on them. The men were too busy calling out for the children to notice right away, but when they did they ran to the door and began to beat on it. Timber fell from the rafters and after a bit of screaming, the banging on the door stopped.

Angus carried on that night setting more fire and trapping people inside. Those who escaped found themselves being slaughtered by a man who could barely walk the night before. Men, women, and children; they all died gruesome and horrible deaths and Angus continued to prance around the town. The Hunters were the easiest to kill. They trusted him fully and as soon as they turned their heads he ended them. He then made his way to the Hunters manor and continued the carnage throughout the night and next day.

Oberic and Jayda traveled for hours more and both of them were out of breath. Jayda continued to push on though and on occasion would have to grab Oberic by his coat and drag him along. They were both exhausted by the time the sun was preparing to set in the evening. Jayda's fears had come true. The bracelet guided them right back to Lilly Tree where she saw smoke billowing above the trees. She found new vigor as she rushed off towards the town. Oberic looked around for a moment and saw that she had left him alone here. He looked behind him and knew that he could easily make a run for it now. She was too caught up in whatever was happening in that town and none of it had to do with him. He took a few steps back into the woods, intending fully to escape and then he stopped. There was something terribly wrong and he knew it. The black star had appeared before them earlier and now this.

"Jayda, wait!" He yelled out as he chased back after her. "Something isn't right-" Oberic tripped over a vine and ran face first into a tree. His wounds opened up once more and for a moment he was unconscious again.

Jayda broke free of the woods only to find her home of Lilly Tree burning to the ground. Most buildings were already rubble and ash while others continued to blaze. She nearly vomited as she came across the first corpse. She composed herself and screamed out for her mentor, "Angus!" She knew he was old and that he would soon die but she did not wish for him to die like this. Her gut told her he was already dead but she fought it. She ran through the street and was barely able to take in the death that lay around her. Her boots pounded on the pavement as she ran towards the only home she had ever known. She never looked behind her once; Oberic had been all but forgotten.

Oberic came to and only took a few seconds to remember what was going on. Amun cawed loudly for him to get up. He grabbed his hat, made sure to pull it down, and got up to run. He ran as fast as he could towards the burning town. He saw the same mess that Jayda had and did his best to not look at the bodies. Most of them were burnt while others were completely dismembered. There were some who hung from nooses while a few had their heads sitting nicely in flower pots. Oberic spotted Jayda quite a ways ahead heading towards a large building on an empty plot of land. Amun lifted from Oberic's person and circled the area. The building itself was on fire and he ran towards it, hoping to get to Jayda in time.

Jayda reached the manor and kicked the front door open. The smoke stung her eyes immediately but she suffered through it. "Angus!" she screamed out. Her friends and her teachers, people she had grown up with, they were all dead, burnt, and scattered around the manor. She attempted to run upstairs, but the fire that burned there was high and hot. Blue flames licked her skin as she shielded her face from it. She spotted Angus standing on the second floor looking over the railing. "Angus!" She cried out, "I'm coming!"

Oberic charged through the doorway and tackled her before she could even attempt to climb to the second floor. "We need to get out of here, you're going to get yourself killed!"

She threw her elbow back and busted Oberic's nose once more, "I need to get to Angus, damn you! I have to save him!" She reached into her pocket and pulled out the silver chain with the ring. She threw it at him with force and yelled at him, "Go! Consider this your lucky day!" Oberic caught the ring and without thought stashed it into his coat. He watched her with wide eyes, or at least as wide as his swollen eyes would allow. She scrambled to her feet and ran to the wall. She was truly majestic as she leapt at the wall and kicked her leg out to thrust herself away from it. She pushed off the wall like a nimble acrobatic. When she was air bound she reached out to grab the second story flooring. Her fingertips grazed it but could not make purchase and she fell back to the floor below.

Angus looked over the railing and laughed, "Well look at that! You're still alive!" He threw one leg over the railing, then the other, and promptly leapt off. He landed on the floor with a thud. He was a crumpled mess on the floor, but he stood up straight and tall with ease and smiled at her. Jayda didn't even process the feat he had just accomplished. She was far too happy to see that he was alright and she scrambled to her feet once more and ran into his open arms.

She cried into Angus's chest without hesitation, "I'm so thankful you're alive! What happened, Angus? What happened here?"

"No need to fret, child. This is a good thing." Angus said while he smiled a terrible smile. He opened his mouth once more, but was interrupted by Oberic, who had picked up a piece of timber and struck Angus in the head with it. The old man crumbled to the ground again.

Jayda's mouth opened in shock. Her hand, without command, went down to her hip and unleashed the finely crafted whip. She cracked it out towards him and the bone fragments bit into his skin. The leather wrapped around his wrist and provided to the sarcastic magician a painful bite that only the Hunter could appreciate. Oberic let out a cry at the lock of the whip against his skin. Blood squeezed through the tight twine of the leather and dripped from it. She yanked the whip back and pulled a dagger from her belt. When the foolish man came stumbling forward, she stuck her blade in Oberic's left shoulder adjacent to his breast. He let out another moan of anguish. "I'll end you!" She screamed out.

Oberic threw his free hand up, "I can see him! I can see things, remember? Please," he begged her now, "believe in me!" His eyes stared into hers but not for long. His eyes eventually fell upon Angus who had stood up again behind the angry Hunter.

"That wasn't very nice. Kill him, girl. Spill his blood. Do it for dear old dad." Angus said, his voice low and calm.

Jayda turned slowly with a look of unease on her face. She wasn't sure how he could have survived a hit like that at his age, but to call himself her father made her more unsettled. They had never said such a thing to one another though she knew in her heart they both felt it. Oberic pulled the dagger from his shoulder and cried out as he threw it on the floor. Jayda still held on to the whip and gave it a quick yank to make sure Oberic knew there was no escaping. "Angus, why did you say this was a good thing?"

"Because you have the magician who did this in your hands! Look at him!" Angus commanded. Jayda turned her head and looked at Oberic who was sitting on the floor now looking rather pathetic. "They're all dead because of him!" Angus's finger shot out and when Jayda turned back to face him, saw that it was completely snapped in half and hanging downward. "We need to end them all."

Oberic breathed as calmly as he possibly could. He did his best to use a sincere voice when he spoke, "I can see him." Oberic explained, "I don't know who he was to you, Jayda, but that man is gone. Please, let me help you!"

"Kill him, Jayda! Make me proud! Avenge your fallen brothers and sisters!" Angus shouted now, no longer in his own voice.

Jayda flicked her wrist forcing the whip to loosen from Oberic. She stared at Angus for a long moment. "Make you proud?" she asked. Angus had always been proud of her and she knew it. He had said it many times and never once demanded that she make him so.

"It's not him!" Oberic shouted.

"Silence, worm!" Angus shouted back.

Oberic said his next words as calmly as he could, "Jayda, you can't see him like I can, I know, but look around you. Look carefully."

Jayda looked around herself and saw nothing but destruction. She looked over the bodies of her friends and shook with anger. Oberic was distracting her and she would kill him for it now. Then she saw something unsettling; something that made her feel as though she were falling. One of the burnt corpses was staring at her. She looked at another and found it was doing the same. Her head moved swiftly to find each corpse with her eyes and she saw that they were in fact all staring directly at her. Chills ran down her spine. She dropped her whip as fear and grief took over. Her hands dug into her dark locks and pulled. She believed she was going insane and there was nothing to be done about it. The heat from the flames was overwhelming and the taunting voice of Angus was too much. She thought to herself *that wasn't Angus though, was it? Not that last time at least*. She was sure the voice was different. It didn't matter. She looked at Oberic and drew the sword from her back. "It is my duty, Oberic."

"Yes!" Angus said, but it wasn't just Angus. It was each and every single corpse in the room. A blue light caught Jayda's eye. She looked down and saw that her bracelet was spinning. She looked at Angus's bracelet and noticed it was spinning even faster. "Kill him! It is your sworn duty. End him. Kill him. Bathe in his blood. Let us devour his soul together!"

In a moment quicker than she ever realized was possible, she closed her eyes and swung her sword out. "I'm so sorry!" She sobbed out as the blade bit into Angus's neck. The blade went clean through and only the sound of a wet thud signaled that it was done. Jayda dropped to her knees and cried loudly.

Oberic had stood now and rushed to Jayda's side. He squatted down and grabbed her arm, "We're not out of this yet!" He dragged her to her feet though she resisted as much as she could. The house was starting to fall down around them. The flames had surrounded them and there didn't seem to be a way out. Dread filled the both of them as Angus's laughter filled the room. They turned to see the detached head smiling at them "You'll never be out of it. The black light has released me. I am reborn from the black fields. You know nothing of the terror that shall be wrought upon you!"

Oberic ran over to the talking head and lifted his leg until his knee nearly touched his chest. When he dropped it, his boot went through and crushed the abomination. Even though Jayda could not see with her eyes what was happening afterwards, Oberic could; and the look on his face, one of absolute horror, would have been an indication to her that something was wrong. Oberic's eyes followed the purple wisp as it lifted from the head and drifted off into the fire.

He didn't know what it was. A spirit? A soul? He did know though that whatever it might be, it was terrible.

Jayda did her best to not look at Angus's body but she found it was unavoidable. She rushed to his decapitated form and dropped beside it resting her head on his chest. So many things rushed through her head. Why did this happen? Why did she have to lose everything? Her friends? Her home? Most importantly, why did she have to lose her father? Angus had cared for her since she was a child and he helped her grow to be who she was. What terrible poetry it was that she was the one responsible for his death. "What did I do? Angus, I'm sorry! I'm so sorry," she cried harder, "I love you! Please, forgive me! Please!"

Oberic grabbed her arm again and tried to pull her away. When she pulled her arm away from him he knelt down beside her, "Jayda, I don't think you killed him. I can't say it for sure, but I think he has been dead since the black star appeared." She tried to push him away from her again. He pushed her hand away and grabbed her. He shook her hard until she met his eyes, "I'm going to get us out of here. When you see the chance, run. Do you understand me?" Jayda hesitated for a moment and then nodded. She looked back down at Angus's body and trembled.

Oberic's hands weaved and danced in such a strange fashion, that of which Jayda in all her time as a Hunter, had not seen. The fire blocking the front door seemed to move out of the way. She raised her brow watching the flames creep towards Oberic and swirl around him creating a squall of fire light. The edges of his coat and hat began to smoke as the flames bit them. "Go!" He yelled out while the pillar of fire grew around him "Now is your only chance!"

She gave him a nod and ran for the door. She leaped over the door that had fallen off its hinges and obstructed the path. She hit the ground and rolled a few times before forcing herself to stop. She wasn't even off her hands and knees yet when she yelled out from the safety of the cool spring air, "Oberic! I need you to come with me!" The words spilled from her mouth before she even realized what she was saying.

Oberic heard her shout his name but didn't hear anything beyond that. He had to let the fire go or it would consume him. He looked around for a moment and saw Jayda's whip laying on the floor. He drew in a deep breath and released the fire. The flames returned to their original spots in what seemed like an explosion. Oberic dived for the whip. When his hand wrapped around it he shoved it into his coat and stood up. He adjusted his hat and made a run for the door. As he drew closer to the door, the house began to crumble around him. Jayda could see his form through the smoke and flame but he was lost to her when one of the manor's support beams crashed down in front of the door. More of the manor began to collapse in on itself and Jayda stood there frozen in fear. She wasn't sure why she wanted him to make it out alive; she barely knew the man.

Jayda waited for a few minutes that felt like hours. Her chest rose and fell with deep breaths. Amun landed beside her and flapped his black wings in a frenzy. She saw something glimmer in the fire raging at the door. She tried to call out but her voice had left her for the moment. She watched though, with interest and amazement, as Oberic climbed over the door covered in sheets of ice. The man had a blue appearance under the thick ice. Her mouth hung open and she didn't even notice her bracelet spinning like crazy, but she did notice that the ice was melting away rather fast. He walked stiffly, a living ice sculpture, while chunks of frost fell off of him and crashed into smaller bits as it hit the ground. When he was clear of the fire and it's rage, he let the spell go. The ice melted away fast leaving him drenched. Even the chunks on the ground seemed to turn to water just as fast. He collapsed to his knees and let out a nagging cough. He put his arm in front of his mouth as he coughed. Blood splattered his coat sleeve as the cough came from those deep places in the lungs. He examined the blood on his sleeve and would have initially thought it was from Internal injuries if Jayda hadn't been beating the hell out of him the last few days.

Jayda moved closer to the man, nearly stepping on Amun who let out an angry caw. She was a little scared by his blatant use of magic and a bit in awe that he somehow managed to escape. Oberic dug in his coat and brought out her whip. He looked at it for a moment and threw it to her feet. "I swear if you hit me with that damn thing one more time-" Jayda rushed in and threw her arms around the wet hermit. The unexpected hug nearly knocked him over.

She squeezed him tight and spoke in his ear, "You saved my life. I brought you here to be killed and you saved me." She pulled away from him now, "I don't understand. Why?"

He looked in her eyes with his own, still as dangerous as ever, and smiled "I really don't have an answer for that."

Jayda stood and held out her hand to him to help him up. "I am grateful for it. Whatever the reason may be,"

He took her hand and stood up. Once he was to his feet Jayda bent down and picked up the whip; the only thing left of the only life she knew. She brought the leather to her lips and kissed it. "Goodbye, Angus." She stared watery eyed at the burning manor as she attached the whip to her hip. She sighed and turned to see Oberic walking around the yard with his palms open and in the air as if feeling around for something. Amun had flown back to his shoulder and followed his hands with his strange colored eyes.

"What was that? What. . . was that?" He mumbled. He tried breathing through his nose forcing a whistling sound, compliments of Jayda, "Necrotic, yes I can feel that. I'm not seeing it though" He walked around in circles, turning now and again to face the manor, "No doors either." He stood still and scratched at his blood soaked beard.

"What are you doing?" she asked, genuinely curious and mostly perplexed by the behavior.

"Magic leaves traces. I'm trying to get an idea of what that thing was."

Jayda looked down and then held her arm up, "Would this help?" The bracelet on her wrist was still spinning. Oberic thought for a moment and then shook his head. Jayda dropped her arm to her side.

"I need to get to my books. What's the nearest town?" he asked, taking a stance near her as they watched the burning building.

"Faron is up north a bit. Real tiny. Shouldn't be more than a day and a half." she Replied.

"I guess this is farewell?" Oberic said as he turned to face her.

"Maybe I'll join you-" she cleared her throat, "At least until your face looks better. It's the least I could do." Oberic snorted (whistled) and nodded. Jayda looked back at the fire one last time and turned to leave town motioning for Oberic to follow her. "You're really bad at fighting. Did you know?"

CHAPTER 9

They had walked north from Lilly Tree for an hour when a wagon rode up behind them. Jayda looked behind herself and groaned, "More Hunters. Keep your mouth shut," she narrowed her eyes at Amun, "the bird too!" Oberic mimed locking his lips and throwing the key away then gave the crow a nod. When they pulled up a handful of the Hunters leaned over the side of the wagon.

"Hold it right there! You've just come from Lilly Tree, haven't you?" The shortest of the group asked. Jayda nodded. "What happened back there? The whole fucking town is gone!"

Jayda shrugged, "I wish I knew. My whole guild hall has been slaughtered." the tears in her eyes were quite genuine, "If I weren't out hunting this one down I might have been killed too. I'm heading to Faron to report with them."

The other Hunters looked over at Oberic. "Why isn't he bound?"

Jayda thumbed towards his face. "Does it look like I need to tie him up?"

"And the bird?"

"No idea. Likely fed by this idiot at some point and just follows him around."

The group eyed Oberic closer and gave Jayda an approving nod. "Alright, alright. What kind of magic?"

Jayda sighed "Obviously not very useful magic as it didn't save his ass. Are you going to give us a ride or not? I want this clown hanging as soon as possible."

They invited her and Oberic to get on. While they were on friendly terms with Jayda, they continually poked fun at Oberic, mocking his oncoming execution. They even went as far to fuss with Amun who finally had enough of their taunting and flew away, but kept close enough that he could follow. Oberic of course was okay to play along as he pretended to brood to catch a bit of sleep.

It was the evening of the next day when they arrived at their destination and Jayda thanked them for the help. Amun returned to Oberic's shoulder once the others had left. The bird let out an annoyed caw and nipped at Oberic's beard. They journeyed into town and the duo, still looking quite terrible, made for the small inn. They purchased their room for the night and Oberic requested the use of a bathing basin to clean himself up.

The innkeeper was happy to oblige the request, but insisted on knowing what happened to Oberic's face to which the magician simply replied, "I'm not quite sure what you're talking about."

Unfortunately, the two of them would have to share a room. Jayda went up to the room and Oberic disappeared to clean himself. He appeared quite a while later. His face was still swollen and bruised, his nose still broken, but at least he wasn't bleeding all over the place. Jayda watched him come in and frowned. She felt increasingly more guilty about how she treated him. She sighed, stood up, and walked towards him. He had just dropped his coat and hat near the door and found himself frozen in place when she placed both hands upon his scruffy face. "I'm sorry," It was all she said before she used her thumbs to forcefully realign his nose. There was a nasty crunch and Oberic doubled over in pain while holding his hands to his face. He initially opened his mouth to curse at her, but as he breathed in he found there was no longer a whistling sound. "Better?" She asked, a smirk on her face.

"Actually, yes," he said, talking through his hands, "I mean besides the pain, that was quite nice. Thank you." He grabbed his hat while he was bent over and moved to the little table and chair in the corner of the quite small room. "I've spent a good portion of my life studying other worldly occurrences." He chuckled to himself, "My wife hated it." He stuck his hand inside the hat, whose brim was now not only worn and ripped, but burnt as well. First his hand vanished inside the hat and then all the way up to his forearm, which Jayda figured made sense because the hat was after all pointed, but her mouth hung agape as he pushed in shoulder deep. When he pulled his arm back, he drew out a large tome which he promptly dropped on the table and opened. It looked old but otherwise well taken care of. The Hunter watched this, knowing some kind of magic was involved, never once thinking to look at her bracelet which was not spinning as it should be. "Now, I don't know much about necrotic magic personally, but I have many old books. Maybe I can learn something from these about what we've encountered." Amun, who had gone to and from the bath with Oberic, perched down on the table and examined the book as if he were quite interested in it himself.

Jayda let herself fall back onto the bed. She put her head on the pillow and found it remarkably comfortable. She was trying to get some sort of an idea of what happened and what she had done. She was no stranger to having blood on her hands but Angus' blood hit her on a different level. She was actually connected to him emotionally. She loved the man like a father. Oberic continued to blather on about his books and when he turned to her and saw her lying there, looking as if she were in deep contemplation, he frowned. He cleared his throat and did his best to put on an appropriate tone, "I'm sorry for your loss." His words were sincere and he was happy to hear that they came out that way. "I don't know what the loss you're feeling feels like, but if you'll allow me to, I'd like to figure out what happened to your friend. I believe he was possessed by a spirit. What sort of spirit I can't say for sure just yet." Jayda listened to him, but didn't really hear anything he was saying. "I know you feel terrible about what you did, but try to remember you very likely did him a favor by putting him to rest for good so as to not be allowed to be tormented by some foul creature any more than he was."

She looked at him and met his green eyes, "My mother wasn't even there for me. I don't remember much about her other than her constant urge to be manipulated with magic. She became addicted to the way it made her feel. She lost sight of the real world and eventually my father left us and she went crazy."

Oberic listened to her and understood the situation or at least understood it at its core, "Magic corrupts the mind. Makes life too easy. Makes you feel unstoppable. I understand that feeling." Amun cawed as if to say that he also understood.

Jayda took that into consideration as she went on, "She chose magic over me. I was found wandering around the streets one evening when the Hunters had come. Couldn't have been more than five, I'm sure." She swallowed hard, "I was starving, cold, and alone. Then Angus found me. He took me in and trained me to be what I am today. He was my father for a lack of a better term. He cared for me when no one else did." Her hands clasped one another tightly as tears dripped from her emerald eyes. She wiped them away, "It was then that I knew I needed to be the best Hunter I could be so that the things that happened to my mother would never happen again. I associated magic with evil things."

Oberic nodded, "It can be," he agreed, "magic can do some terrible things." He lifted his rear and dragged the chair closer to her now. When he was situated closer to the bed, he dropped himself back down in the chair and went on, "It can also do good things."

Jayda nodded, "Good things like you saving me?"

Oberic didn't really know how to answer that. He still didn't see that he saved her. He just couldn't in good conscience allow her to be hurt. There was a silence between them and Oberic thought it best if he tried to relate to the girl, "When I was born, my parents were poor farmers. I showed some signs that I might have the blood of the High Men and I was sold to some recruits from Maer'lyn."

She lifted a brow, "Where?"

He waved his hands to dismiss it, "It doesn't matter. Point I'm making is that I was brought there as a baby and all my life has been books and learning. I can't pretend to know what it's like to lose a parent since I've never known either of mine. I know what it's like to lose someone though. It's never any easier. We just learn to cope."

She was not to be sidetracked and brought the conversation back to her rescue, "Why did you save me after everything I put you through? You could have left me there and let Angus do whatever he wanted to me."

Oberic still had no answer for that and he leaned forward, stretched out his hand, gripped her shoulder, and smiled, "You are who you are. I am who I am. Just because we were at odds then doesn't mean I should let you suffer. Get some rest, huh? There are other Hunter guilds as you say and when word gets out about what happened in that town, they'll be looking to pin it on someone. I don't think you'll be able to get us out of that one. I'd rather be on our way sooner rather than later."

Jayda nodded with agreement, "That's a good idea." She closed her eyes and fell asleep nearly instantly. Oberic fought back a laugh at how fast she dozed off. He grabbed the blanket and slid it over her and then blew out all the candles except for one. He took it, and the chair, back to the small table. He placed the candle just above his tome and spent the night reading. Even Amun managed to be polite enough to not caw while the Hunter slept.

Jayda woke up the next morning to a bright light that casted itself through the window by the rising sun. She sat up and looked at Oberic who had his head laying between some pages of his massive book. Next to the book was a candle which had melted completely and spilled its wax all over the base of the candlestick as well as the table area surrounding it. Upon further inspection of the sleeping man, she noticed that at his feet was an empty bottle laying on its side. She wasn't sure what it was or how strong it might have been, but he obviously had left at some point in the night to get himself a drink. She threw her legs over the bed and found that her entire body was sore. Considering how the last few days went she was at least able to admit that she exerted herself beyond her ability. She considered waking him but decided to let him get a bit more shut eye. She slipped on her fur cloak and headed downstairs to get some bread and drinks.

While downstairs she had taken a glance towards the window and saw Amun perched on the window sill. Jayda assumed Oberic must have let the crow out at some point in the night. She walked to the inn's door and swung it open, "Come on, bird." Amun flapped his way past Jayda. "I still don't like you." She mumbled as the bird perched itself on the stair railing. She ordered their breakfast and drinks. When her order was finished, it was placed in front of her. She dropped some coins on the counter and carried the wooden tray back up the stairs. When she opened the door to their room, Amun flapped past her again and immediately landed on the table where Oberic slept. The crow picked at Oberic's beard. The magician's hand twitched at his side but never let go of the necklace with the ring on it.

Jayda ripped a small chunk of warm bread from the loaf and held it out to the crow, "Peace offering?"

Amun eyed her closely then fluttered over and nipped the bread from her hand. After devouring the offering he let out a loud caw which startled Oberic awake. "Another whiskery, please," he said as he lifted his head. He blinked, looked around a moment, then turned in the chair to look at Jayda, "We don't have whiskey, do we?"

Jayda afforded him a slight smile and lifted a mug from the wooden tray towards him, "I thought you might need a little pick me up." She looked down at the bottle at his feet and then back to him. She placed the mug down when he didn't take it and then ripped the loaf in half. She placed it near his mug. She sat down on the bed and crossed her legs. She pulled off another bit of bread and held it out to Amun, "Maybe I can convince this thing to tolerate me?"

"Doubt it," Oberic said as he grabbed the mug and lifted it to his lips, "he's a bit of an asshole." He took a sip from the mug and made a face as though he was drinking the sweat from an Orc's ass. It wasn't whiskey and he was disappointed, "What is this?"

Jayda took a sip of her own and placed it down, "Hot milk and honey."

"It's delicious." He put the mug down. Amun charged at Jayda and plucked the bread from her hands again. Oberic watched the interaction between the two and shrugged, "He may warm up to you quicker. I tried to eat him when we first met. Took him a while to come around again."

Jayda grinned, watching the crow eat the bread swiftly and then politely wait for more, "Food works wonders." She nodded to the large book on the table, "That's a lot of information there." She shoved more bread into her mouth.

He raised a brow and looked down to his book, "Ah! Yes," he looked back at her, "just one of my books on necrotic magic. I didn't find what I was looking for though. I'd look in some of the others, but I can't read them." Amun let out a caw, "You can't read them either." Amun cawed again, causing Oberic to roll his eyes. He grabbed the tome, slipped it carefully back into his hat, and shook it to ensure nothing would come out. Once satisfied, he slipped the hat back on his head. "I am afraid, as of now, I am completely stumped."

Jayda briefly wondered if Oberic and the bird could understand each other, but pushed it out of her head; she couldn't handle such nonsense at the moment. "What do you suggest we do?" she asked.

"Well. . . " He stood and went to the window. He stared out at the beautiful day. He had to squint his swollen eyes to shield himself from the enormous amount of light pouring through the glass pane, "We could go to Maer'lyn, but I am not fond of that idea." He rubbed at his beard. Amun fluttered to his shoulder. "We certainly need to get out of Marrenval though."

"I'll join you for a time if you could handle having a Hunter lingering around." She drained her mug and wiped her mouth. She grabbed her black hair and pulled it into a tight ponytail. She hooked her whip to her side and held out the last piece of bread to Amun who promptly left Oberic's shoulder and took the bread from her again, cawing his pleasure.

"If I'm right, there's a harbor town to the north, correct?"

Jayda nodded, "Sirentide."

"We can head there. We'll see what our options are once we get there." he walked to the door and bent down grabbing his overcoat. He slipped the ragged thing on and looked gravely towards the Hunter. "I aim to find what I saw last night. If you want vengeance for your friend, I'll be grateful for your company."

"It's the least I can do after what you've done for me."

"For Angus."

She smiled sweetly at him, "For Angus."

"Shall we?"

They headed down together and Jayda cleared their tab. Oberic stepped outside the inn first with Amun on his shoulder. He lowered his voice and mumbled to the crow "I need some coin, old friend. Go and get us some. Find me when you're done." Amun cawed and flew from Oberic's shoulder. Jayda stepped outside and breathed in the warming spring day. "Look!" Oberic pointed to a carriage nearby. "We may be able to travel in comfort."

Oberic walked rather casually to the carriage and slapped a hand on the carriage, "Good morning, friend. I don't suppose you could get us to Sirentide, could you?"

The carriage driver looked down at Oberic's tattered, burnt, and bloody clothes and spit on his coat. Oberic looked down at the spit and frowned, mumbling something about being rude. The carriage driver barked out at Oberic, "No carriage for you, ya bum!" Jayda stepped up next to Oberic and glared at the driver who in turn quickly changed his tune, "Ah but for a Hunter," he climbed down the carriage and bowed his head, "Yes I can make that trip for you."

Jayda smiled and swayed to the carriage with a cocky swing of her hips. She turned and leaned her back against it. There were absolutely some perks of being a Hunter in Marrenval and she enjoyed them greatly. The carriage driver smiled his best smile and then looked back at Oberic where he promptly dropped the smile. "Still a long trip. You got gold?" Oberic held out an empty palm. The carriage driver snickered and Jayda furrowed her brow wondering just what in the world he was doing. The snicker nearly turned into an out right gut busting laugh until a coin purse dropped from the sky into his hand. Amun landed on his shoulder and Oberic smiled a most self indulgent shit eating grin. He tossed the coin purse to the driver who caught it, nearly dropped it, and peeked inside.

"Take what you need for the cost and keep the rest as a tip. We want to get there fast." he said.

The driver nodded and stammered, "Yes sir! He then removed his hat and bowed to Jayda, "Madam." He held the carriage door open for them.

Oberic stood to the side, "After you?"

Jayda shook her head. His cheekiness wasn't so funny when she was hunting him down, but she had to admit she found it funny at the moment. She climbed in and made herself comfortable. Oberic climbed in after her. Amun chose to stay outside and flew off. He would follow them.

It was another few days' journey, traveling as fast as the driver could push the horses, before they arrived in Sirentide. They exited the carriage, Oberic insisted Jayda go first, to a bustling harbor city. The buildings were old and worn by salt water and gusts of the wind from the ocean. Large trade ships sat in the harbor being loaded and unloaded with freight. She watched as people went on with their day to day lives and found that she was angry at them for it. Her day to day ended days ago and she figured she'd never know a normal routine again. Oberic stood at her side, oblivious to her emotions, and looked around almost cheerily. "Well. We're here. Now what?" He asked. Amun flew and propped himself on Oberic's shoulder.

Jayda glared at him, "I'll find us a place to stay." She stomped off into the crowd. Oberic raised a brow wondering why she was suddenly upset with him and decided it best to not ask and simply followed her.

It didn't take long at all for Jayda to spot the sign for a place for them to rest. "The Rusted Anchor," she mumbled, "very original." She was in a terrible mood now and the crow cawing on Oberic's shoulder was grating her nerves once more. The Rusted Anchor was a run down but decent sized inn. It was the type of place you could keep a low profile because everyone was trying to keep a low profile and while Jayda, a Hunter, would be okay here, it worked out more for the odd and occasionally annoying Oberic.

They slipped inside and found the smell of the sea to be stronger inside than outside. The inn was filled to near max capacity with large men and women who made their livelihood on the water. A table near the center of the room was especially loud as a high risk game of cards was in progress. The men and women at the table each looked as though they would shank you if you looked at them wrong; all of them except one man who had such a perfect face and the most beautiful golden hair. That perfect man was also the only one winning any hands and making sure everyone knew it. Behind him at another table sat a graying Dwarf, a small gorgeous Elf, and a rough and rugged, but handsome, Human. The three of them watched the golden haired one with such disgust they might as well have spit on him.

Oberic, who now more so than Jayda blended in with the crowd, went to the bar and ordered a few drinks. No one gave him any trouble about the crow on his shoulder who simply sat there quietly while it's head darted around the room. Jayda had silently joined him. When the drinks were brought to him, both intended for himself, Jayda grabbed one and downed it swiftly. She slammed the glass back on the bar top and then glared at Oberic as if daring him to say something about it; he did not. He raised his hand and simply called for another and then drank the first. There was a loud uproar from the card table and several threats were made before the golden haired man calmed them down.

"One room or two, Oberic?" Jayda asked before realizing how it must have sounded and blurted out, "I didn't mean it like that. Don't go getting any ideas either or I'll break your nose again." Amun flapped his wings and glared at her.

Oberic raised a brow and when his drink was brought to him he downed it. "Whatever you're comfortable with."

Jayda looked back to the innkeeper, an older woman without teeth and a missing eye, and did her best to remain calm. He hadn't really answered the question. The innkeeper opened her mouth to speak revealing black gums. "Doesn't matter if they are sea dogs or fancy lords, dear. They're all idiots." The innkeeper walked away after Jayda let out a bit of a laugh.

"I'd recognize that damn crow anywhere!" A voice said while grabbing Oberic's free shoulder and spinning him around. "Oberic!"

Oberic flinched a bit expecting to be punched but then smiled, "I remember you! Leonard, right?"

"Leon," the rugged man from the back table exclaimed, "but close enough!"

Oberic nodded and shook Leon's hand vigorously, "I apologize my good man Leon! Good to see you!"

Leon placed both hands on his hips after the magician released it from the handshake, "Oberic, you dirty bastard," he looked over Oberic and the smile faltered, "and I mean dirty. Look at you man! You look terrible! What happened?"

Oberic thumbed over his shoulder to Jayda who glared at Leon daring him to say something stupid. "That happened."

Jayda's glare focused on Oberic with a strong desire to punch him in the back. Leon nodded a hello to Jayda who then put on a fake mocking smile. Leon leaned in and whispered, "Nice pull."

"I didn't do the pulling." Oberic replied rather stone faced.

Leon nodded, "Alright." There was a long silence before Leon spoke again, "Well, you've managed to make this whole thing awkward which I suppose is nothing new from you."

"I aim to please." Oberic retorted.

Leon wasn't sure at this point if Oberic was toying with him or not and nearly let out a laugh, "It's quite the coincidence we've run into you here."

The innkeeper returned with two keys and Jayda shook her head and held up a single finger. The innkeeper looked at Oberic and then back to Jayda, "You're too pretty for that one." Jayda snatched the key from her hand and threw the appropriate coin on the table.

"It isn't like that." she mumbled. She turned and held the key out to Oberic, who looked at it then looked back at Jayda. She blinked a moment before rolling her eyes and stashing it in her cloak. "Not even five minutes and you've already made a friend."

"Acquaintance, mostly. We've met once before." Oberic explained

Leon reached out beyond Oberic to shake Jayda's hand, "Leon Farharbor."

Jayda took his hand and gave it a squeeze and one hard shake. "Jayda of the Hunt."

Leon nodded, "I could tell by the get up. I'm from Black Moss myself." He thumbed to Oberic. "He's being modest by the way. We shared many bottles of wine over a few days like a couple of lovers." Leon looked between the two of them and then followed up "Don't worry. Nothing weird happened."

Jayda's mouth hung open, not liking one bit of what he was implying, "There's nothing going on between him and I, you moron!"

Oberic looked at her with a look of insult worn on his beaten face. Amun let out a caw. Oberic shook his head slowly and looked back at Leon who couldn't hold his laughter back. He waved his hand to the group he was with at the table to invite the over. After a moment a Dwarf and Elf had made their way through the crowd to join him.

"Allow me to introduce everyone," Leon exclaimed, "this is Dwim of the White."

The Dwarf stuck out his hand and shook both Oberic and Jayda's. "Nay for much longer I'd wager. Dwim Frothfire will do. Pleased to meet ye'." He said in a rather glum tone.

Leon continued on with the introduction, "And this beautiful lady is Rennyn A'sun'al. Guys this is Oberic Wintersong and Jayda of the Hunt." Amun let out an angry flapping of his wings having been skipped on introductions.

Rennyn froze a bit having already heard stories of the Hunters in Marrenval. She tipped her head to them and mumbled her greeting, "Nice to meet you both. It's nice to see another pretty face around here." Jayda offered a smile to Ren but her gut told her to instantly distrust the Elf. Elves, afterall, were known to be wielders of magic.

The golden haired man got up from the table of angry card players and bombarded the group with his arms draped around both Ren and Leon, "Thank you. I am indeed a pretty face and the next round is on me!" He pulled away from the pair and threw some gold coins on the bar table. Leon did his best to smile through the annoyance.

Leon lowered his voice and leaned in to speak to Oberic directly, "I am surprised you are with a Hunter, Oberic. We came to Marrenval specifically to find you."

Oberic nodded his understanding about the Hunter, "She knows," he pointed up to his face, "her handy work. What were you trying to find me for?"

Leon's voice remained low, "We have an issue with a curse. We're curious if you could lift it."

Jayda had heard enough. It was taxing on her to remain neutral when she suddenly found herself surrounded by people she would have previously been paid to hunt down. Her hand fell to her whip out of habit and she groaned. "I need some air." she said before she turned from the group and headed outside.

Leon raised his brow, "She okay?"

Oberic watched Jayda leave, "She's had a rough week."

Ren, having felt the coldness in Jayda's body language, spoke up, "Maybe we should take this conversation somewhere more private? I have a room where we can all talk more openly." Phineas had returned to the group and had been trying to stick his finger in Amun's mouth who promptly snapped at him. Phineas drew his hand back and swore. Oberic agreed to go with Ren, Leon, and Dwim up to the room. Phineas was not invited and was left there at the bar.

"I didn't want to talk to you either." He was bothered by their lack of acknowledgement. They had learned on their travels so far that Phineas needed attention like a man in the desert needed water. He headed outside and saw the dark haired beauty that was with the ugly guy. He walked over, as casually as the egomaniac could, and stretched his arms above his head. "Hunter, huh?" Jayda stared at him but did not reply. "Dead give away."

Jayda glanced at the man whose golden hair was illuminated in the sun. "Tiny dick, right? Dead give away." Her fingers danced along the whip again.

"Ha! Not a chance." he moved to stand in front of her. "So how did a Hunter end up traveling with a wizard or whatever he is? Are you planning on bringing him into the local guild?" He was talking to her but looked over his shoulder now and again to watch a merchant ship that was at port being unloaded with freight.

"Do you know where the local guild is?" She relished at the idea that she could report in and return to some sort of normal life.

"Big manor around here somewhere. I don't make it here often. All the women look like men." he looked back at her. "Not you though. Janice was it?"

Jayda narrowed her eyes, "Jayda. And you? Are you with those others? Why didn't they introduce you?"

"Phineas. They didn't introduce me because they can't stomach me, but they won't let me out of their sight." He turned around again to face the dock, still watching the merchant ship.

"And why won't they let you out of their sight?"

"Too damn good looking I guess. It's a curse." He stood on the toes of his boots, craning his neck as if trying to spot someone. "Please excuse me, I've got to have a chat with my friend there on the ship."

She watched him run off and shrugged. She knew there would be a guild hall here. She was happy to have another option laid out for her. Jayda had no idea she was being watched by plum purple eyes from one of the third floor windows at the inn. Ren stood there looking down with her arms folded across her chest. "She's not the friendliest person, is she? I can tell she already doesn't like us."

"Jayda? No, she's an absolute peach." Oberic said, drawing a chair from the desk and sitting. Ren looked at Oberic and like the others, wasn't able to tell if he was kidding or not. She looked back out the window deciding it might have been his swollen face throwing them off. "Poor girl watched her father die. She's a Hunter and I think she's coming to terms with the fact that not all magic is terrible."

Ren turned to look at Oberic a little excited, "So it's true? You really are a wizard?"

"I'm not a wizard." Oberic said plainly. Amun promptly flew from his shoulder and landed on the window sill. The crow stared out; no one was sure at what.

Ren frowned; the disappointment was etched on her face. "Sorry, Leon made it sound as though you were. I apologize."

Leon chirped, "He is!"

"I'm not." Oberic replied.

Leon laughed out loud. "You're going to sit there with a straight face and tell us you don't deal in magic/"

"I didn't say that. I said I'm not a wizard." Oberic looked at the group. He removed his hat, letting greasy hair fall to his shoulders.

Ren rubbed at her head, "This is giving me a headache." Amun looked back and cawed.

Dwim interrupted them, "This is all well and fun, but can we get back to the matter at hand?"

Oberic nodded, "I'm not good with curses. It's not my area of expertise. Even if it were, there's a chance it can not be removed. Curses, by my accounts, are strange magics."

Leon started again, "So you are a wizard?"

"I am not a wizard," Oberic groaned out.

"But you said you deal in magic!" Ren shouted now, finding the whole thing to be frustrating. Dwim flopped down on the bed and covered his face with his hands.

Oberic sighed, "I am not a wizard, but I deal in magic."

Leon shouted now as well, "Then what are you?"

"A sorcerer." The words left his mouth as casually as could be.

"What's the difference?" Dwim cried out through fat fingers.

"A wizard uses words of power to cast their spells, a warlock is gifted their ability from a higher power, and a sorcerer has the ability to wield magic within them naturally." Oberic stated this in such a matter of fact tone that the other stared at him. He didn't realize he was going to be giving out lessons and was annoyed by their questions.

Leon's mouth hung open for a moment before asking, "Why didn't you just say that from the beginning?"

"You didn't ask." Oberic said and the three, Dwim sitting up at this point, just stared at him. "As for your curse, you could perhaps try getting some help in Maer'lyn. I'm not keen about going there myself. Bad memories."

Leon headed over to the window and joined Ren. Amun looked up at the both of them, let out a soft caw, and looked back out the window. It was his turn to look out the window at the golden haired man. "Maer'lyn, as in the tower on the ocean?" He looked back at Oberic who nodded.

Ren frowned, "Tower on the ocean? How are we supposed to get there?"

"Well," Oberic said, rubbing his beard, "there is a storm that surrounds the tower city of Maer'lyn. Rages on continually to keep visitors out. There is a spell they use to provide safe passage through. I happen to know it."

"So you'll help us?" Ren asked.

"I don't know if I can. I have business of my own to attend to." Oberic offered an apologetic smile and then looked at Dwim, "Tell me about this curse."

Ren, Leon, and Dwim shared the story about Phineas and how each of them came to be a part of it. Oberic listened with great interest, slowly finding himself desiring to help them the best he could. When they had finished, Oberic sat back in the chair and stroked his beard mulling over the whole story.

Jayda had watched this Phineas character walk to some grizzled old sailor and strike up a conversation. At some point Jayda thought the sailor looked green in the face and decided to see what was going on. She strolled up to Phineas who was just finishing the conversation. Phineas looked at Jayda and offered a terribly charming smile. "Decided to try out your sea legs?" He asked as the sailor walked off swearing loudly.

"I get the impression you and trouble go hand in hand." She said, folding her arms.

"Trouble is just one of my names. I did manage to score us a free ride here on the lovely MOIRA, if we need it." He gestured to the merchant ship where MOIRA had been painted on the side.

She examined the ship from the dock, "Do I even want to know how you managed to do that?"

He stretched again and breathed in deeply. The silver amulet around his neck glistened in the sun. "You deal in ass kickings and I deal in secrets. Everyone has them and they are usually very willing to give you anything you want if you find the *right* secret. That sailor I was talking to? Actually the captain of this fine, sea worthy, vessel and *his* secret is that most of his cargo happen to be children. When I let it slip that I happened to know that, he was very eager to give us free passage and even make some cabin accommodations for us. Which is great if the brains of this operation could decide what we're going to do." Phineas grinned, looking quite pleased with himself. "You never said how you ended up with the wizard."

"It wasn't intentional," she noted, giving him a smile. She had the feeling that they would be good friends. "I was bringing him back to Lilly Tree to have him killed." Her face turned sour, "The rest is kind of messy."

"Fucking around with wizards usually is. Arrogant fools, all of them. Just because they can make things float and make fire? If you're going to be arrogant you need to be good looking, like myself." His charming smile returned and he offered a wink to let her know that he was well aware of what he just said.

"Well I'd say that's rather arrogant of you." She replied and the two shared a small laugh.

Phineas dropped his arms and looked at her, "Say, how's your back? I could use some help lifting something."

"It's not a body, is it?" She asked, only half joking.

"It is, actually. Follow me." he started off down the pier. Jayda's face went pale. She thought that he surely must be joking. She followed him to a large cargo crate. He gave it a light tap with his boot. "You ready to be loaded?" he asked the crate as he leaned on it.

For a long moment there was no reply and Jayda thought that he was playing a joke on her. Then a voice replied roughly, "If you ruin this for me, Human. I'll rip out your innards!"

Phineas nodded, not really paying attention to the voice's threat. "Yeah, that's good. Glad to hear it. Listen, we're going to move you into place. Consider our deal done. Got it?" Phin waited for a moment and took the silence as agreement. He nodded to Jayda, "Alright. We're going to lift and take the crate down near the ship. Captain thinks it's our luggage. Good?"

"Good? No! Is there someone in there?" She was rather shocked by the whole idea.

"No, it's a fucking magical box with the ability to think and speak." he replied. He squatted down and started to lift "Come on! Help me out here! Lift with your knees!"

Jayda, for one reason or another, decided to go along with it and squatted down lifting her end of the crate. "You're going to have to tell me how this deal happened." She thought it humorous for a moment then looked quite sternly at him "Are they imprisoned? Enslaved?"

The voice from the box roared out, "I am no one's slave!"

Phineas nodded, "See? Magic box says it's fine." He could see on her face that it wasn't good enough. "You know what you don't see every day in towns? Orcs. This fellow thought he could sneak into town unnoticed. Now while the town itself wouldn't pay much attention; these docks are heavily guarded at night. Especially with the recent pirate sightings. So I approached him and ask him a few questions-"

"You harassed me and threatened to call the guards!" The voice called out.

Jayda grunted out, "You're supposed to be a box. Shut up."

"Point is, I found out what he wanted and we cut a deal." He groaned as they reached the drop spot and let the box hit the ground. The crate growled and Phin banged on top of it "Sorry."

Jayda dropped her end causing the magic to swear and stared at Phineas. "So what I'm hearing is that I really don't ever want to cross you or have to owe you a favor. Seems like you'd be a wicked enemy to have."

"Wickedly good looking, sure." He wiped sweat from his brow.

"What was the deal you got out of him?" She asked curious as to what he could get from an Orc, something she wasn't entirely sure she believed. It spoke too well to be an Orc.

Phin shook his head, "This one is free."

"Why?" She asked, raising a brow. He didn't seem the type to do favors out of the kindness of his heart.

"Because he wants to save the kids. Seems like a good idea to me so I helped." In truth, Phineas thought about his sister when he made the deal. To him, she would always be the four year old he left behind. "I'm mostly harmless. Unless you're into mindless animalist night romps." He wiggled his eyebrows at her. She rolled her eyes. "Otherwise, I'm just a guy who likes winning more than he likes losing and getting some kids out of a terrible situation seems like winning to me." Phin lifted a hand and waved at two sailors who were walking down the gangplank. "Afternoon, gents! I've got this crate for you. Your captain has a room for us. This is our luggage." The sailors nodded and moved to the crate where they easily hoisted it up and carried it up to the ship. "Wow. I'm kind of embarrassed how easy they made that look."

"Maybe we should get back. You can share the good news with them." She brushed off her hands and pulled a stray strand of black hair from her face."

"Yeah," he looked up at the sky, "Dwim and Leon don't like me being away from them too long. Bunch of mother hens." Phin and Jayda started to walk side by side towards The Rusted Anchor and made small talk as they did. Phin had put her in a better mood and she was sure now that she could at least fake being polite to the others. They had made their way up to the room and opened the door finding the others sitting there silently. Ren looked at Jayda and wrinkled her nose. She didn't feel confident in their safety with her around. She moved from the window and tried to make herself look taller and more intimidating than she was.

"Where have you two been?" She asked, doing her best impression of someone who might have been in charge, "We were discussing important things here." Amun flew from the window sill and landed on Oberic's shoulder.

What good mirth Jayda may have had coming in was immediately gone. She found that, even more than Oberic, she wanted to hit that Elf. Phin spoke up, "Our new friend and I were securing passage on the merchant ship, MOIRA. They'll be leaving at dusk if we decide to go."

"Where's it headed, lad?" Dwim asked. Phineas shrugged. "Well how much did ye' pay?" The Dwarf then asked in a very accusing tone, "How did ye' pay?"

Phin shook his head, "We helped them move some crates. It's that easy." Phineas wove lies like an expert tailor weaving fabric.

Jayda agreed, "Yep. Just a bit of heavy lifting." She moved near Oberic and leaned on the desk. Her hands removed her ponytail and she shook her head letting her hair fall. She ran fingers through it, "What's our plan, Oberic?"

Oberic sighed, "Well, since both our tasks are having to do with dark magics I would agree that we could turn to Maer'lyn, but it would be an overly giant pain in the ass to not only get in, but to even talk a ship into sailing that direction. That leads me to the next idea, Hadryn, which I am not overly fond of as well."

Dwim's eyes widened, "The White City? Are you familiar with the White, Oberic?"

Oberic nodded, "Intimately." He cleared his throat and his hand slipped into his pocket where he fiddled with the ring on the necklace. "If our friend here says we have a ride though, we can see where it's headed. If it isn't going to Hadryn, surely we can find something else."

Jayda picked at her fingers, "I don't know what kind of upside down mess I have gotten myself into but I'm in for the adventure. Who'd have ever thought I'd end up with a group like yours?" Jayda smiled as she said it, but Ren saw it for what it was and looked angry.

"You know," Ren started, "no one is forcing you to stay. I doubt any of us would miss a Hunter hanging around." She pointed a finger at Oberic, "I bet you were the one who did that to him! Do you get some sort of sick pleasure out of torturing people?"

Oberic cracked a smile and commented, "You know I asked the same thing?"

Jayda's eyebrows raised, "*Excuse* me, Elf?"

"It's clear you hate this group! You've been acting like a bitch since you've arrived! If you want to go, then just go!" Ren was red in the face, but wasn't backing down, not even after Jayda pushed herself off the desk and stepped closer to her. The Hunter's hand resting on the whip.

"How about I drag your tiny ass into the local guild hall and let them string you up by your toes, you filthy little-"

"Ladies! Ladies!" Phineas interjected, "If you're going to fight," he flexed, "The winner gets to have me!"

Jayda turned her head and yelled at Phineas, "Sit down, asshole!"

"Everyone!" Oberic stood up and tried to go between Ren and Jayda. "Let's just relax-" Jayda had placed a hand on Oberic's face and shoved him back. He hit the desk and knocked the chair over. Amun cawed and Jayda shot him a murderous look. The crow decided to not make a peep for the rest of the encounter.

Ren stood nose to nose with Jayda, having to look up at her only a little. "You think you're so tough but you're just a bully! A terrible bully! If this is who you are I feel sorry for your parents-" she had barely gotten the word out when Jayda slugged her in the mouth. Ren, not used to physical altercations, fell to the floor. Her eyes immediately coated in tears, but it did not stop her from getting to her feet and screaming out as she charged Jayda. Jayda stumbled back as Rennyn barreled into her but not much. She grabbed the Elf by the hair and forced her to stand. When the Elf was upright, she struck her in the face again. Ren yelled out and swung her hands out. Her nails dug into Jayda's face. Jayda cried out, but was determined to not lose to some underweight Elf. Ren's hands dug into Jayda's hair and ripped a handful of black threads. Leon ran up behind Jayda and grabbed her around the waist, lifting to try and pull them apart.

Ren smiled thinking she had the last laugh on this. Jayda made sure to let her know how mistaken she was. When Leon lifted, Jayda threw her legs up and kicked Ren in the chest. Ren hit the wall and slid down. She fought to catch her breath. The Hunter wasn't done either. Jayda threw an elbow back and busted Leon in the ear. He dropped her and fell away from the fight. Dwim looked to Oberic and shook his head. Oberic shook his head in agreement. Neither of them were going to get involved. Ren stood finally and clawed at Jayda once more. She even managed to swing a fist that busted Jayda's lip wide open.

Jayda spit blood at Ren, "I've killed monsters who have dropped logs of shit bigger than you!" She delivered a right hook that rocked Rennyn. She stumbled as her vision blurred. Though she could not see, anyone who was looking into her eyes could see there was a change. The wind outside picked up causing the signs of shops to swing violently. Jayda's bracelet began to glow and the jewel began to spin its track quickly. She growled and made to hit Ren once more but as she made her move, intending to knock the little bitche's lights out, the window behind Ren shattered and a gust of wind blew in. It lifted Jayda off her feet and slammed her into the wall behind her. The wind, something Leon, Dwim, and even Phineas in another form, were all familiar with, sounded like a hurricane in their ears. Each dived to the floor. Dwim reached up and grabbed Oberic, pulling him down. His hat flew from his head and he watched it get caught up in the winds and it slapped against Jayda's face.

Jayda did her best to reach up and grab the hat. The squall was so strong that she nearly couldn't do it. She pulled the hat away by its brim and let her arm be forced down; the hat was dropped to the floor. The wind shifted back and let Jayda down. Jayda instinctively grabbed her whip and lashed out at Ren. Unfortunately for the Hunter, the wind picked up once more and not only caused the whip to jump back and bite her in the face; it slammed her against the wall again. The boards splintered and sent small debris into the gale. The forceful wind pushed behind Jayda and within a moment the Hunter found herself being thrown outside the window three stories down. Her body hit the rundown road and she rolled until she nearly laid on the wooden docks across from The Rusted Anchor. Amun flew out the window and perched himself on top of Jayda.

Rennyn had calmed herself enough to let the winds return to the sky. She looked around, almost apologetic, and then looked out the window. The others rushed to her and looked out as well.

"Seems like windows are your thing." Leon mumbled as he looked out in shock.

Oberic did not waste time at the window. He grabbed his hat, slammed it on his head and spoke loudly, "We need to go, now!"

Ren snapped back, "She started it!"

Oberic went to her and grabbed her arm, "You do not understand. Her bracelet picked up your magic! If hers did, so did every other Hunter in the area! There is a massive guild hall in this town and I can promise you they will come looking, especially after one of their own has just been flung out a window!"

Ren frowned and looked back outside. People had started to gather around Jayda who lay on the dock still. Amun pecked at anyone who came to close.The harbor bell began to ring signaling a ship departure. Phineas spoke up, "That might be our ride trying to ditch us by leaving earlier than expected. Now or never."

Oberic swore, "Why did this have to go sideways so fast? Come on!" He opened the door and ran out. Phin did not wait for the others as he followed Oberic. Dwim and Leon grabbed Ren and ran out with her. Oberic was already out in the street with Amun having already flown to his shoulder. He rushed over to the group of people surrounding Jayda. "Excuse me! Excuse me! Just here to collect my friend. Bit of a bar fight. She'll be okay though."

"Bar fight?" One man asked in disbelief. "From the third floor?"

"Yes. First floor was too crowded and the second floor too small. The third floor had the perfect amount of space for a brawl and as you can see worked out perfectly. You should see the art they have hanging. Beautiful." He reached down and flung Jayda's arm around his shoulder and lifted. She was out cold. "And look! She's fine!"

"She's unconscious!" Exclaimed a dock worker.

"She was just thrown out of a window in a drunken bar brawl of course she's unconscious. Goodness, have you never been in a fight?" Oberic asked. The dock worker looked at Oberic's beaten face, assumed he was also a brawler, and stepped away. Phin had caught up with Oberic and Jayda and slung her other arm around himself. Together they walked Jayda down the pier, her boots dragging the entire way, to the gangplank leading up the MOIRA. Leon, Dwim, and Ren chased after them, busting their way through the crowd that watched the other three (two men dragging an unconscious woman) go down the pier to the merchant ship.

The captain was standing at the railing frowning, "I had hoped you'd miss the tide." he grumbled upon Phineas's arrival.

"If I had, I would have at least been able to warn the orphanages around the area." Phin said, giving the old captain a smile.

The captain hushed him and scowled, "This way to your quarters."

Phin and Oberic followed the captain, dragging Jayda along. Amun flew from Oberic to the highest mast and perched himself there so that he loomed over all. The captain showed them to their rooms. Ren, Leon, and Dwim had caught up and as soon as they were met by the captain, they were shown to their own rooms as well. Unfortunately, the captain was only able to spare four rooms. They had to choose who would be their bunk mate for the voyage.

"Ren and I can share a room; or Jayda and I. Either one is fine by me." Phineas said.

"Uh, no." Leon said. "You're with me."

"I'll bunk with Ren, if it's alright with her." Dwim said. Rennyn nodded. She would enjoy the Dwarf's company.

Oberic and Phin dragged Jayda to a cabin, laid her in bed, and left. They shut the door quietly. "I guess that last room is mine then." Oberic said. "Let me take the smaller of them so you all will have more space." They agreed to that decision. They picked their rooms and decided to settle in. Just as Rennyn turned to follow Dwim, Oberic placed a hand on her shoulder. "Can we talk?" Ren turned and looked at Oberic questioningly. She took a moment and then nodded. He offered her a smile and offered her to enter his cabin. She did so, not finding any reason to not trust the man. Oberic followed after her and shut the door behind them.

CHAPTER 10

Oberic had no luggage to carry in unlike the others who at least had knapsacks and satchels that they were wise enough to bring with them when they rushed from the inn. He motioned to the chair for Rennyn to sit. Ren did so and looked at Oberic. Her purple eyes scanned him up and down, taking note of his greasy hair, dirt and blood covered burnt coat and how swollen his face was. She thought he looked more like a homeless man than some sort of great sorcerer. He sat down on the bed and stared at her with eyes that Rennyn found unsettling and without knowing why, they made her feel like she was in danger.

"What sort of magic do you know, Oberic?" She asked, trying to start a conversation to ease her nerves.

"My specialty is illusion and enchantment." He replied. "May I ask you something?"

Renyn nodded "Of course, sir."

"Forgive my bluntness, but your power is untrained and you allow your emotion to control it. That, as we have seen today, is dangerous. You know that, don't you?" He asked, doing his best to not sound as if he was scolding her.

Ren's face bunched together, "She started it!"

Oberic raised a hand. "I'm not yelling at you. Merely one caster to another having a conversation about our abilities." Ren's face eased once he recognized her as a caster. It made her feel good. "I am very familiar with your people-"

"How familiar?" she asked, not sure that she believed him. He replied to her question in the language of the forest Elves. "Familiar enough I suppose." She was sad to admit that should not speak the language of her own people and so she didn't.

"I know that they train their young to harness and control that power. Why weren't you?" He asked, a genuine curiosity resting on his face.

Rennyn looked down feeling somewhat attacked, "It's a long story."

"We're on a ship for a few months. I think we have time." He said staring blankly at her, possibly waiting for her to give another excuse. Ren drew a deep breath and decided to tell Oberic her story.

"I'll name her, Rennyn." the thin and pale, plum eyed, Elven woman said in the tongue of her people as the baby was placed in her arms. She cradled the crying thing and looked lovingly at it. "My shining star. The sun that lights my night." She ran a thin finger over the baby's cheek. "I have waited a long time for you, little one."

The nurse maid who handed her the baby stood by beaming. She was using a cloth to dab at the woman's forehead, pushing strands of nearly silver hair out of her face. "That one nearly killed you, Aunei."

"Death serves life and life serves death. I would have accepted this glady if it meant Rennyn would be born into this world. Thank the waters of creation that my life was not needed for her to come." Aunei looked at the nurse maid, "Any word from my husband?"

The nurse maid shook her head, "No, lady. They've not returned. The relations with the Desruc of the Mahir have grown weak. You know this."

Aunei did know and she was fearful he would not return. They had left in full battle armor for this peace talk. She continued to look down at the baby. The bundle of joy laid there with her eyes closed resting after the strenuous birthing. "He will return if only to see this miracle." She lowered her head to the baby and whispered, "You are loved, Rennyn A'sun'al." Aunei had, over her life of more than three hundred years, tried to have children with no success. There were many pregnancies which did not make it to life and it had nearly broken the woman. The entire time she carried Rennyn she feared that death would come to her as well. You can imagine now the joy she felt when Rennyn kicked at her insides until she came into the world screaming.

"Your house will be very proud of the new addition, lady." The nurse maid said. A horn blew signaling an approach to the gates. Aunei looked up at the nurse maid. She understood that Aunei was expecting her husband to have returned. The nurse excused herself and headed out of the room.

Aunei continued to adore the resting baby. She was curious who the girl would take after more. Her narrow pointed nose rubbed against the baby's red skin and she kissed a pointed ear. "Who will you grow to be? You will be wonderful regardless. I know it." The auburn haired nurse maid returned into the room and fidgeted with something in her hands. Aunei looked up and asked "Any word?"

The younger Elf cleared her throat and stepped up to Aunei's bedside and laid upon it a ring of wood, finely crafted to look like trees twisted together. In it's crevices sat emeralds. Aunei looked at the ring and then to her newborn. "It seems death was required for life afterall."

A few years had passed and Rennyn was, for the most part, an average Elven girl. She played with her friends and learned their people's history, but was never allowed to train in the ways of the elements or pick up any sort of weapons like the others. Elves, exceptional creatures, started these things early in life. Those activities were replaced by the study of the properties of minerals and herbs. She was very skilled at this and excelled in the subject, but she felt she was missing out on so much, especially the friendships she thought she might be losing.

One night, as Rennyn laid in bed, her brightly colored red hair spread over the pillow, she overheard her mother and grandfather having a heated discussion. She had never known her grandfather, or her mother really, to raise their voices. She crept from her bed and opened the door to her room. She peeked her little pale face out and listened.

"Aunei, you are being most unwise, my child! I am begging you to listen to reason!" her grandfather pleaded. "You can not do this! Our kind belong here, in the wilds! Where the natural order is still respected!"

"I have made my decision, father. I will not be swayed." Aunei replied.

"How can you do this to our house? You will take away the only grandchild we know!"

"I am doing what I must to protect her!"

"You think doing this will protect her? She is far more safe here with us than she will be out there with them! At least here she will learn to commune with the world."

"And pick up a sword and bow? No. I have seen what your lessons do, father. I know the pain they bring. Has my beloved, my one heart's true love, not paid the final price for knowing these lessons? Your communion with nature? Your sword and bow?"

"His passing was regrettable and it pains us all, Aunei, but he died for our people's survival. You know he would not want you to leave with this child."

"He is not here, father. He is not here to watch my light grow; to see that flower bloom. I am sorry, I truly am sorry, but this is best for Rennyn."

"And you think they do not have war in the lands of the Human? They have war and plague and famine! Rennyn will miss out on her heritage!"

"At least in those lands she will not be forced to learn the arts that could end her life so early. So needlessly."

"Aunei, please-"

"Enough! My father, how I love you and wish I could adhere to your plea, but Rennyn will grow up without a father as it is. Must she grow up to die the same way? I have already made arrangements. I have hired a guard to travel with me across the ocean. We will find a new life there. I hope someday you can forgive me and accept what I feel must be done."

"If you want to turn your back on your people then so be it. Rennyn will be prayed for. Goodbye, Aunei. May the wild gods watch over you both."

Rennyn popped her head back into her room and shut the door as softly as possible. She slowly crept back into bed and laid there staring up. She had no feelings about what she heard. She would not miss anyone except for her grandparents. She had no friends, not really. She turned over and closed her plum colored eyes rimmed in gold and fell asleep.

Rennyn stood in the living room of the small house in North Normoon. It had been several years since they had come here and she was on the verge of becoming a young woman. Her mother spent their gold purchasing this little home and it didn't buy much. It was the same home she would later run her apothecary business out of. The girl had become quite skilled at mixing and had started making easy concoctions to sell to local children. They were silly and fun things. Potions that made one extra gassy or perhaps feel like their head was floating. Her mother, upon arrival into this new world, threw herself and Rennyn into learning the culture. It wasn't long after that they both spoke the common tongue of the Humans with ease and no longer used their own language, even at home. They wore Human clothing and not the beautiful gowns of their people. Aunei even avoided the small population of Elves that did live in the city just to further escape that life. So Rennyn grew, her most formative years, with a different people from her own and eventually could not even remember how to speak her native tongue.

It was when her mother grew ill and frail that Ren, that is what she called herself now, noticed that when she became emotional the world would react as though it could feel everything she was. She could have sworn she made it rain one day as her mother laid in bed, too ill to move. She sat out in front of the home praying to Olm that her mother would not pass. The more and more she thought about it the cloudier and darker it became until there was rain falling down on what was otherwise a bright and sunny day. In that time, Ren threw herself into studying alchemy, all with the hope that she could find some strange cure for her mother's unknown sickness. She became so skilled, even at that age, she could have rivaled the best apothecaries in the city. She even had the idea she would like to go work in one of the shops but her mother forbade it. Her mother insisted they would have her create terrible things to hurt and cause harm and that Rennyn was better than that. She of course listened to her mother and years later decided to start her own business from inside the home.

Rennyn sat at her mother's side several years later on a dark winter night. There was a blizzard in the mountain range and the streets had been covered completely within minutes. The wind howled outside the windows and Ren had pulled the rocking chair to the fireplace and grabbed a heavy blanket for Aunei to stay warm. She cooked a hot soup for them and hunkered down next to her, feeding her, and making small talk. Aunei was frail and weak at this point. Her frame so tiny that her bones jutted out making her look angular as opposed to her once astounding visage.

"Ren," Aunei said quietly, "do you remember why we came here?"

Ren nodded, "I do, mother. You did not want me to suffer the same fate as father; wild gods watch over him."

Aunei nodded. She reached out and shakily brushed strands of rusted hair from Ren's face, "Do you resent me for it?"

Rennyn shook her head, "Of course not, mother. We have a good life here and we have each other."

Aunei's plum eyes filled with water on the verge of breaking and streaming down her sunken bony face. "We do. We have come to accept the ways of these Humans, but I want you to know that does not mean our ways don't hold true."

"I don't understand what you mean, mother."

The wind outside screamed out as though to punctuate this moment. "I think the wild gods are calling me, Rennyn."

"You know I do not like it when you talk like that, mother. You're going to be fine. I swear it. I will find something to make you strong once more."

"Life serves death and death serves life. It is the ebb and flow of the natural world, my light. We can not avoid that. No matter how much we try."

"Mother-"

"Hush, my guiding star. I have robbed you of your heritage thinking this life would be better, but I realize now I can control that no more than I can control my own mortality." She dropped her long slender fingers and held her out hand. "Take my hand, my love. My sweet Rennyn; my only child blessed to me by the waters of life."

Ren took her hand and lifted it, placing her lips against her mother's cold skin. "Mother. . ."

"The wild gods have granted me a vision, I think." Aunei looked into the fireplace and watched the flames dance. Ren could see their reflection in her mothers large purple orbs. "There will be a day in the years to come where you shall give birth to a precious gift of your own. This child will not be only of our kind but of another as well. She will grow beautiful like her mother and be as untamed as her father. She will find her own way back to the wild gods who will embrace her. They have shown me. They are pleased." She swallowed, "Ren, go to my nightstand and remove from it a book bound in fine leather. It will be heavy for it has much to say."

Rennyn did as her mother requested and went to the nightstand. She dug around in it for a bit before finding exactly what her mother described. She traced her fingers over the letters etched into the leather by a delicate and skilled hand long ago. She went back to her mother and kneeled before her holding out the book. "What is it? What does it say on the cover?"

Aunei did not take the book from Rennyn. She was far too weak now. She felt sorrow that her daughter could not read her native language that was etched into the cover. "It is your name, Rennyn A'sun'al, in Elvish." Rennyn looked over the book once more and back up to her mother.

"What would you like me to do with it, mother?"

"It is yours, Rennyn. Inside, written in both Elvish and the Common tongue of man, is the history of your family name. I have written over the years our traditions and customs and the ways of our culture. Everything I have stolen from you lies within those pages. Take it, as my final gift to you, Rennyn A'sun'al. Take it and know that I still believe a great destiny awaits you."

"Mother please, don't-"

"Hush now, child. I hear the flutes singing their dirge. The Wild Gods call."

"Mother, no please! I can't live without you! We will make you better! I swear it! I will cure you!"

"We will meet in the clearing, my guiding light." She looked at Ren and smiled, saying her last words in Elvish. Ren's eyes watered knowing the phrase meant "I love you." The light that once sparkled in Aunei's eyes vanished. She had gone to the great clearing to join her ancestors to be with the spirits of the wilds. Ren placed her hands upon her mother's skin after setting the book down. She was cold. Rennyn buried her face into her mother's bosom one last time and cried. One last comfort from a mother to her child.

Rennyn wiped the tears from her face as she finished her story. She looked up at Oberic with watery purple eyes that were bright and beautiful. She saw that Oberic's eyes were also glossy and she felt comfortable with him again, finding he wasn't anything like the Hunter. She cleared her throat, "That's why I do not know how to control it, Oberic."

Oberic said nothing for a while and leaned forward, taking her hand into his. He rubbed and warmed her hand in his and when he finally spoke, it was soft and gentle, "I'm sorry. Truly."

Ren nodded and whispered a very soft, "Thank you."

"Do you want to control it?" He asked. Rennyn looked up at him confused.

"I'm sorry?"

"Do you want to learn to control it? To harness the elements around you? Your people are natural sorcerers. It is inside you. It is your birthright to communicate with the natural order and with it's blessing manipulate it. I can help you, if you so desire."

"What if I can't?"

"You never will if you do not believe you can. The power is there. I've seen it. You just have to learn to command it."

Rennyn nodded, "I would like that, Oberic. Thank you." She offered him a smile.

CHAPTER 11

The rocking of the ship in the rough waters of the ocean caused Jayda to stir. She sat up and looked around the cabin. She was not familiar with this room and wondered what had happened. She rubbed her face and then hissed as she ran over the wound caused by her own whip. It started to come back to her now and she found herself getting angry all over again. "I'll end the little bitch!" She stood up just as the ship rocked and she stumbled into the wall. It only made her more angry and she swung the door open; the door knob slammed into the wall. She stepped outside into the hall and yelled, "Where are you?"

Phineas was leaning against the wall near his and Leon's room. He grinned and blew her a kiss, "I'm right here, doll face. You needing some special company? Little bit of action to help you get your sea legs?"

Jayda glared at him, "You couldn't keep up."

"We could find out together!" He said, pushing himself off the wall.

"Come near me and I swear that you'll be eating your own worm before I throw your ass into the grave." Her eyes relayed that she was not kidding and Phin leaned back against the wall once more. "Where is she?"

"Where is who?" He asked. He was flipping a coin into the air with his thumb.

"The Elf!" Jayda was only up for a few minutes and was already fed up with this.

Phineas shrugged. "No idea." Dwim popped out of the door that Phin's room shared a wall with.

"What sort of trouble are ye' starting out here, lad?" He spotted Jayda and smiled "Oh good, yer' awake. I'm glad to see yer' alright."

Jayda drew in a deep breath and then released it. She calmed herself enough to be civil with the Dwarf. "I'm alright. Thank you."

Dwim stepped out and continued to talk with her. "Aye. I've known a few Hunters in my younger days. You'll be an asset to this team, lass."

Leon popped out of his room as well and pointed at Phineas who he assumed was the reason for the raised voices. "You keep that amulet on, you understand me?"

Phin had grown annoyed now and shoved off the wall to meet Leon face to face. "I don't like the beast either. Now back off." He shoved past Leon and went into their room and slammed the door. Jayda threw her shoulders up in confusion.

"What was that about?" She asked.

Dwim explained the curse to Jayda since she missed the story at the Rusted Anchor. When he was done, Jayda pinched the bridge of her nose.

"Fuck me. I'm surrounded by this shit." She turned and looked down the hall. "I need fresh air." She found her way up to the deck and spotted Ren leaning over the railing of the ship looking out at the horizon. She played out a scenario in her head where she would run over and toss the Elf into the ocean. She looked around herself to see if anyone was looking, fully prepared to do it, and found Oberic's dangerous eyes resting on her. He stood there in his burnt coat and hat wearing a charming smile. Jayda wondered if that smile was the same one he used on his wife.

"You're awake. That's good." he said as he walked over to her. "I think we got onboard just in time. I'm certain the docks were swarming with Hunters as the ship made birth. "Ever been across the ocean?"

Jayda's anger seemed to vanish and she smiled, "No. I've never traveled outside of Marrenval. You?"

He nodded "Oh yes. A time or two. Several, really."

"I'm sorry, Oberic. For my actions before. I really was just doing what I had always been raised to do." She cast a glance up at him with bright emerald eyes. "Do you think you can forgive me and put it in the past? Fresh start going forward?"

Oberic thought it over. "I'm sure Ren feels the same way."

Jayda's smile faltered. "I didn't mean that incident. I'm still considering throwing her overboard. I meant you and I. I've treated you horribly and you've done nothing but be kind to me. I'd like us to start fresh." She held her hand out to him. Oberic looked at it and grasped it, giving it a shake.

"No worries. I don't hold grudges. Well, I hold one grudge, but that's neither here nor there. I'm glad to be out of Hunter country. If they had managed to come down on us we would be in some serious trouble."

Jayda didn't hesitate a moment with her next words. "I would protect you." Her eyes opened wide, shocked that the words left her mouth. She forced the conversation ahead to not linger on the awkward comment. "What now? We're just on this ship? For how long?

Oberic removed his hat and dug elbow deep inside it. " Few months at least if the waters are fair." He removed from the hat a full bottle of whiskey. Jayda seemed perplexed by the hat and yanked it from his hands. She looked inside.

"Where are you getting these things you pull from this thing? I don't see anything! It's just a hat!" She thrust the hat back at him. He grabbed it and tugged it down upon his crown.

"It's not *just* a hat, Jayda," he winked at her, "It's *my* hat." He popped the cork out of the bottle and took a long drink. He swallowed and held the bottle out to Jayda who laughed at the strange hermit. She yanked the bottle from him and took a generous drink from the neck. She passed it back to Oberic who took it and tipped it back once more. His other hand rested in his pocket and stroked the silver wedding ring.

Leon had come up a bit after Jayda and Oberic had started sharing the bottle and conversing about nothing in particular. He spotted Ren standing alone near the railing and over to join her. He removed a pipe from his satchel and lit it, flinging the match into the waters below. Ren smiled up at him, "How well do you know Oberic? Can we trust him?"

Leon let out a plume of smoke and shrugged his shoulders. "I don't know him well at all. We met once and he was kind enough to offer me a meal and a drink. Then we had several drinks. Talked for a good long time. He showed me his personal library. Not much more to our meeting than that. I was hunting when I came across his hut." Leon chuckled "I know the man looks like a loon but he's sharp and quick in the mind." Leon shrugged again. "Or maybe he used to be. He does seem to be absent now again when you speak with him." He took another pull from the pipe.

"And the Hunter?" Ren asked. She glanced behind her and saw how friendly her and Oberic were getting. "I've got a bad feeling about her, Leon." In truth, she had gotten used to their little group and felt uncomfortable adding new members to it.

"I'm not worried about the Hunter." Leon said calmly. "Little more out in the waters and we won't be in Marrenval. There's no guild halls across the ocean for her to bring anyone to and if it's Maer'lyn that we end up going to; well she won't want to make it known that she's a Hunter."

She sighed and nodded, "I trust you, Leon." She still didn't like the idea of the Hunter being with them. She smoothed her dress out and continued to look out on Sirentide as it became smaller and smaller. "Have you been to Hadryn?"

Leon nodded and pulled from his pipe once more. "I have. It's a breathtaking sight. Also home of Dwim's holy order. The people there are far too religious for me but the city is wonderful nonetheless. I would still prefer to go to Maer'lyn. The fact that Oberic would be able to get us in is that much more appealing."

"I'll travel whatever path you do," Ren smiled at him, "If you don't mind the company, I mean."

Leon smiled back at her, "I wouldn't mind at all."

"I've never traveled anywhere. Not really." She looked back out to the sea, finding that Sirentide could no longer be seen, "I'm still a bit scared if I'm being honest."

"I think when it is all said and done you're going to have the time of your life." Leon said. He placed a hand on her shoulder giving it a reassuring massage and then removed it. The sway of the ship was taking a toll on most of the group. Leon was fine mostly due to his natural love for travel. The others handled it pretty well. They may have felt moments of sickness come upon them but then it would pass. Dwim was not so lucky. He had burst from the cabins under deck and ran to the railing. He hung his head over and deposited his last meal into the ocean below.

151

"We nay meant to be above ground, much less the damn ocean!" He shouted at no one in particular. He leaned over and lurched again. Jayda and Oberic had finished talking and sharing their bottle. Jayda spotted the Dwarf and walked over near him. She leaned on the railing.

"Phineas is offering sea legs or something if you're interested." She grinned at the Dwarf who looked at her with a rather pale face. "You'll get used to it." she added.

"This is absolute madness! A Dwarf sailing the tides. . ." He turned, not having anything left to spit overboard, and slid down to his rear. "Got yer'self caught in our little adventure, aye?"

"It would appear so." Jayda said rather monotone like. She still wasn't sure she wanted to be there. She sat down next to the Dwarf. She took a moment to think about it and then spoke again. "It's not that I don't want to be here, I mean to say I don't hate any of you" she looked at Ren, "I don't hate most of you. This is just outside of what I've known my whole life." She pointed at Oberic who was finishing the bottle of whiskey off himself. "It was my duty, much like I'm sure you have your own as a Paladin, to bring in those who dare to use magic." She then glanced at Ren. "And here I am, on a ship traveling with one I decided not to hand over and another who used magic to throw me around a fucking room!" She felt her anger boiling up again. "And then, to make things worse, I find out I'm traveling with some asshole with a hard on who is apparently cursed and turns into a dog."

"Dire wolf, lass" Dwim interjected.

"As if it matters!" she kicked her boot out at nothing. "Point being they were my enemies before this. Now I'm here rubbing elbows with them and fighting everything in me to not tie them up." She glared at Ren again. "She threw me out of a fucking window!" Jayda made to get up but found herself grabbed by Dwim.

"Can't let ye' do it, lass." He released her once he was sure she wasn't going to get up again.

She crossed her arms and huffed "I suppose the whole experience is a bit more humbling than I care for."

Dwim attempted to stand. His legs shook beneath him at first but he managed. "Ye' and Ren have more in common than ye' think, I'd say, but I also know nay about anything other than a mountain's stony depths and snow-covered peaks. It'll be alright, lass. Ye' will see that soon." He headed off below the deck to get some more rest leaving Jayda to sit and watch the sky. She sat there lost in her thoughts for hours until the sky began to turn to darkness. Her heart bid farewell to her home.

There was a common area on the merchant ship where crew members could do a bit of relaxing in their free time. There were several tables in there, each surrounded by chairs, and upon one Ren found a deck of cards. She went to the others trying to get them all to play a hand or two. She managed to track Phineas down and was trying to convince him to wager a bit of coin.

"Listen, sweetcheeks," Phin started, "I don't lose. Luck is too good. If you're wanting to gamble you better be ready to wager a bit more than some coin. Like spending a night with yours truly." He lifted a finger and twirled a strand of her rust colored hair around it. "Now that's a gamble I'm willing to play for."

Ren slapped his hand away, "Don't be gross. Come on. I've got a bit of coin. You wouldn't take all a pretty girl's money, would you?"

Phin laughed, "I've done worse."

Jayda appeared near him almost silently, "I'll take that bet." Jayda held out a small coin purse. Ren looked at her not quite knowing how to handle this. They were going to be traveling together now and she knew there was still bad blood between them.

Ren forced a smile, "Yes, join us. It'll be a lovely game."

Phineas looked at Jayda, "Hey now! Better idea, hear me out, the three of us slip away for a bit of priv-" He was interrupted by the captain yelling out.

"I want all night shift crew out on the deck! I'm going to get some shut eye." the rough voice called.

Phineas looked alarmed "Is it dark out already?"

Jayda and Ren both nodded, each giving their own version of "It's nightfall".

"Get back to your rooms, now! Unless you want to get strung up by a bunch of sailors!" and in those words he departed back to his room and slammed the door. Jayda and Ren were left looking at one another. They said nothing, but went to their rooms as instructed.

Dwim looked at Ren "In for the night, lass?"

"I suppose I am. Phineas was acting strange just now." Ren said, climbing on the bunked bed above Dwim.

"Just now?" Dwim asked, "As if he ever stopped?"

Ren let out a laugh but was drowned out by a bell ringing madly. Both Dwim and Ren looked at each other. A voice shouted out after the bell silenced "MURDER! MURDER!" Dwim and Ren's eyes grew.

"What in Olm's name has that fool done?" Dwim groaned out.

It wasn't long after Phineas had entered his shared room with Leon when the bells and shouting happened. Leon sat up and looked at Phin, "What have you done?"

Phin shook his head. "It wasn't me."

There were bangings at all their doors. The group, each in their rooms, stood and answered and were promptly dragged out by angry sailors. They were each slung against the wall with swords held to their throats.

"Which one of you shits killed the captain?" asked a round man wearing a bloodied tricorn hat that belonged to the captain. "Eh? Which of you swine slit his throat? Hands out!" The group all extended their hands. The new captain examined them. He sneered, not seeing a drop of blood. "Cleaned your hands, did you? This entire crew has worked with the captain. Not a soul on board MOIRA would harm a hair on his head. Then he picks you lot up and what happens? Murdered in his own cabin. I'm not a thinking man, but I've got the impression the only change here is you."

Leon spoke as calmly as he could, "We have been in our rooms away from the captain's quarters. Keeping to ourselves."

The new captain eyed Leon for a moment then pointed at Phineas, "Grab that one!"

The sailors grabbed Phineas and yanked him from the wall and held his arms tightly so that he couldn't fight back. "Oh come on," Phin cried out, "I didn't do anything!"

"Bring him on deck! I don't want blood down here!" the new captain commanded. The sailors dragged Phineas upstairs and the group followed behind him. The sailors surrounded Phin and were shoving him around in a circle taunting him and making threats.

Leon grabbed Ren's arm and whispered in her ear, "Keep calm. We may yet be able to salvage this situation." Ren nodded. After her talk with Oberic she was hopeful that she would soon be better able to control it.

Phin was pushed around until one sailor threw a punch. Phin collapsed to the floor on his hands and knees. His hand landed in a puddle of blood and he looked up at the mob. "You son of a bitch, you broke my nose!" he shouted. They all stared at him.

Rennyn called out, "You're not bleeding!"

Phin dabbed at his face with his other hand. She was right. There was no blood from his face. He looked at his other hand and then looked around him. The blood puddle led nowhere. He slowly lifted his head to the sky. As he did, a drop of blood splattered on his brow. They all looked up now and saw the body of the old captain hanging from the sails, completely devoid of skin. Jayda unleashed the whip at her side and cracked it. "Boys," she called out. They all turned their heads to look at her. "He was with me the entire time. I lost a sexy bet and he was cashing in."

The group of sailors started laughing. The new captain entered the circle. "They was fucking she says," they all laughed. "Hear that? She thinks that a bunch of men on a ship for long periods at a time can't smell that oh so sweet aroma!" They all laughed again. "Listen to her sing her lies to us like a siren at sea. I don't see no harp. They have the nerve to not only kill the captain, but they strung his body up to taunt and mock us!" He pointed up at the body.

Oberic cleared his throat, "Where did you find the captain's body?"

The new captain looked annoyed that he was interrupted but answered, "In his quarters and you know that!"

"And then you came to collect us. Correct?" he asked. The question was followed by a burp. The sorcerer reeked of booze again.

"That's right. Because you're guilty!" The new captain retorted. The sailors cheered.

"If his body was found in his quarters and you immediately apprehended us, finding us all in our rooms, then may I ask how exactly the body was strung up?"Oberic stared at the new captain with the dangerous green eyes Jayda had seen before. No one on deck knew how close he was to spewing everywhere. He pushed himself to the center of the circle. The entire group could smell the booze on Oberic now and it even made Dwim's stomach turn again. Oberic's question seemed to have stomped the new captain who then looked around at the other sailors. Jayda cracked the whip again.

"Let our friend go," she said as calmly as she possibly could, "Before I have to get mean."

The new captain grinned a smile filled with broken and black teeth. "You might be good with that whip, woman; you might even take a few of us out, but you can't take us all out."

Oberic had started to lean forward and almost fell over. He pointed up at the corpse, "If you look carefully you can see that the way he was skinned is a method used by Orcs. Very crude but it gets the job done-" Oberic turned green in the face as the ship raised and dropped as another big wave went under the hull. He looked as though he were going to fall and then puked. It shot from his mouth and splattered down the chest of the new captain.

"You're as drunk as they come!" The new captain said and lunged forward. He pushed his fist into Oberic's already swollen face. Oberic toppled to the side and hit the deck. His nearly empty (what a waste) bottle of whiskey rolled away and off into the ocean. Dwim grabbed Oberic's arm and tried to persuade him to stay down.

Leon stepped up, "Gentleman, the guy simply could not have done it. Now I know you're all upset with the loss of your captain, I get it, but hurting an innocent man is going too far."

"String up the pretty boy first, then this one!" the new captain shouted as Oberic's sick dripped off him. The sailors all started to cheer. They grabbed hold of Phineas who did his best to fight them all off. Phineas, who had been in several brawls that he himself started, was no push over, but to fight against so many was useless. Jayda had just reeled her arm back meant to start attacking when a voice, no one but Dwim and Ren would recognize, spoke up.

"I am the one you seek," the voice was rough and husky, "it was at my hand that your captain died and it is at my hand that all of you will share his fate." A gray skinned half Orc had come out of hiding; from where, no one could be certain. "Taste my ax!" The Orc, with amazing agility, flung a new hand ax at the acting captain. The blade wedged itself into his head. New captain said nothing as he stumbled back a step or two and dropped to his knees. Another moment longer and he tipped over on his side. The fight had begun.

Jayda rushed to help Oberic up. He was mumbling about his whiskey and Jayda responded with annoyance clear in her voice, "Stand up, you drunk! We'll find you a new bottle, but we need to make sure you don't end up dead first!" She turned her head and watched the Orc. Was she sure it was an Orc? She thought he was too small to be a full blooded one at least. It was just one more insane thing she had to accept. The Orc wasted no time yanking his ax from dead captain number two and attacking other sailors.

Rennyn stared at the Orc with her mouth open. She knew damn well who it was and screamed at him, "Alastor!" She rushed towards him, but found herself pulled back by Leon.

"Not now, Ren!" Leon said as he too watched the Orc cleave sailors left and right. The Orc'oth was in his element which is to say carnage and blood. The Orc rage was inside him and he made the killing look easy. Phin had crawled away from the group and stood up with the others watching the gray skinned thing that he himself helped sneak on board. Oberic made it to his feet completely, with Jayda's assistance, and balled his hands into fists. Jayda watched the fighting Orc and had a strange chill touch her bare skin. She glanced down and saw that Oberic's hands were covered in thick ice.

"I wasn't finished with that bottle!" Oberic screamed and broke free of the group. He charged in and with the block of ice surrounding his hand, slugged one of the sailors who lost a tooth immediately. The sailor stumbled back and after he regained his composure, slugged Oberic in return. Oberic hit the deck once more.

Jayda shook her head. She cracked her whip and licked her lips, "No way you're having all the fun!" She ran in and threw the whip out. It lashed and wrapped around the neck of the sailor who hit Oberic. It bit into his skin and Jayda could already see blood oozing from underneath. She gave it a hard yank and the sailor fell to the deck. A flick of her wrist unraveled the whip and she reeled back to attack another.

Dwim looked at Leon and Ren and smirked, "Aye, if a drunk can fight, ye' better believe that I'm going to get some as well!" Leon laughed. Ren, however, was still fixated on Alastor.

Dwim charged in and grabbed one of the sailors. Leon followed, giving a fast uppercut to a sailor who was not paying attention. Even Phineas was back in the middle of the brawl doing his best to help.

"Everything is gone because of you. . ." Ren whispered. Her eyes flashed in anger as she watched Alastor. She was familiar with his handy work already. It was of course because of him that she was in any of this to begin with. It was clear to her that the Orc simply relished in chaos. She took a moment and looked at the others who were all fighting now. She realized she was the only one standing there doing nothing. Even Jayda, the only other woman, was in there getting her hands dirty. "I'm not weak!" she shouted to no one. She closed her eyes and much like before the wind began to listen to her emotion; it was however, not the only element to respond.

The fight raged on for what felt like forever. One by one the sailor's dropped to the deck, either slain or knocked out. Oberic had been knocked out a few times already. He was simply too drunk to fight. No one on board noticed the increase in wind and how violently the ship began to rock. Waves from what were once mostly calm waters, began to splash up over the railing sending a spray of foam over their feet. A few, including Phineas and Leon, lost their footing and fell, even sliding a bit as the ship started to tip. The water that washed on board seemed to be flooding towards Ren. It pulled around her forcing the smell of salt up her thin nose. The water swirled up around her thighs and then rushed in a mini tidal wave towards Alastor who was washed off his feet. The Orc'oth landed on his back and started to hack at one sailor's legs. He seemed to be unphased by the small wave.The water rolled back towards Ren once more and began to swirl again. The sails ripped from the masts as the wind gusted and continued to increase. There was no storm and yet they all found themselves in stormy weather. Ren would have done far more damage if the sound of cannon fire had not disturbed her. She looked around to see who fired the cannon. She saw nothing but the explosion of wood on the starboard bow.

"Fucking pirates!" one of the sailors shouted. He left the fight immediately. The others stopped fighting and glared at one another before they all ran to their stations. Leon and Dwim even took orders from the living sailors. They could all kill each other some other time. Right now though they agreed that they had to survive. Jayda looked around and did her best to count each group member.

"Can you get an eye on the colors?" one sailor called out. There was no answer except another firing of the cannon. This one missed the ship but just barely. "Well?" Another shot was fired and the projectile took out one of the masts. It snapped right through it and it came crashing to the deck. Ren let out a scream as it landed in front of her. The ship swayed, tipping once more, and the mast slid on the deck towards the railing where it crashed through, having been thrown off into the sea. Jayda ran and tackled Ren as splintered timber caught in the wind began to fly around like miniature projectiles. She covered Ren's head while she looked around for the others. Most of them were hanging on the best they could to the ship.

"We're taking on water!" Another voice shouted out. The ship shuddered and groaned as if to emphasize the comment. "What about the cargo?" Another sailor asked. The first replied "Let the little bastards drown! Save your own ne-" Alastor's ax cleaved into his flesh and he spoke no more. Once the man fell, Alastor retrieved his ax and ran, disappearing below deck. Phineas darted after him.

Jayda watched them run down below and then spotted Oberic walking around the deck rather calmly and looking as though he were examining the ship. "Where are they going?" She called out to him. He didn't answer. She looked in the direction of the firing ship and saw that it was nearing. Sailors had started jumping overboard. Jayda stood up, grabbed Ren's hand, and dragged her along towards Oberic. "Oberic! What do we do?"

Oberic scratched his chin, "No sailing her now, I don't think." He looked around almost as if he were amused by the situation. Over the thunderous sounds of waves and the wind now dying, they could hear children crying. Every one of them stopped and listened. Their hearts filled with dread, "What's that? Where's it coming from?" Oberic shouted out.

Children began to swarm the deck from below, each wearing a look of fear. Phineas and Alastor came up behind them arguing. "You weren't supposed to kill the guy the first night!" Phineas shouted.

"The young ones needed to be freed. I was not going to let them remain in chains for an entire voyage!" Alastor growled back.

Rennyn gasped as the children surrounded her. She knelt down as more than a few clung to her. She gathered them in her arms and looked at Leon as he approached. "Look at them all!"

One had run to Jaya and wrapped its arms around her thigh and pushed their face into her. She, as they would find out now, was not the motherly type. "What am I supposed to do with this?"

Phineas made his way through the crowd of children towards Leon, "I snuck the Orc on board because he was going to help the kids! I didn't think it would go down like this." Rennyn stood up as she caught a glimpse of Alastor again.

Leon gave Phin a respectful nod, "You're still disgusting, but I can respect what you tried to do." He then turned to Oberic, "Well, wizard? What are we going to do?"

Oberic looked back at him, giving him a stare that made Leon feel uncomfortable. "I'm not a wizard."

Ren huffed, "Oh don't start that again!" She charged past Leon and through the children to come face to face with Alastor, "You!"

Alastor looked Ren over and finally seemed to recognize the little Elf. "It is you, Rennyn. How strange that our paths meet again."

"Oh very strange seeing as how you ditched me!" she yelled. She slugged Alastor in the shoulder.

Leon shouted out again to get Oberic's attention, "Wizard!"

Oberic nonchalantly answered, "Not a wizard."

"I don't give a flying shit what you are right now, Oberic! Can't you do something? This ship is sinking and in case you haven't noticed we're all going down with it. Me, them, these kids, and you." Leon gestured around himself.

"What would you suggest I do?" Oberic asked.

Leon threw his arms up in the air, finding Oberic's lack of action to be pissing him off. Jayda stepped towards Oberic and spoke to him. "Please, Oberic, I know that you are capable of saving them. If not all of us, the children at least. They deserve that chance."

"Someone needs to do something!" Ren shouted as she turned away from Alastor for a moment.

Another cannon was fired. The rudder exploded sending splinters everywhere. The children all screamed and fussed, clinging to whomever they could. Oberic thought for a long moment. "I might have an idea." He pointed to Alastor "You! Orc! Take the idiot with you and prepare some cargo crates to be lifted. Dwim, Leon, and Jayda. You'll help me with these ropes and we'll pull them up when I open the cargo hatch!" Phin and Alastor ran off below deck again and did as they were told. Oberic unlatched the cargo hatch. He was unable to lift it and instead waved his hands about. The hatch lifted and then flung itself over snapping from the ship completely. "I over did that, sorry!" Oberic peered down into the hole. "How's it looking down there?"

Alastor shouted up from below deck, "We have the first crate ready to go. Hurry, we are taking on more water down here."

Oberic nodded and grabbed his rope, "On three!" He shouted to the others. "One. Two. Three!" They each pulled the rope and the empty cargo crate was lifted. They then angled it so that it could be lowered on deck. Leon rushed forward and unhooked the crate. Together they lowered it back down into the hatch."Hook up another!" Oberic shouted down to them. "Ren, start loading as many of the children as you can into the crate."

"What?" She asked, unsure of his request, "You're mad!"

"Just do it!" He shouted back at her and Ren leaped back, unprepared for the tone he gave her.

"Come on children. Into the box!" She said lifting them and placing them in where they huddled near each other. They were scared, all of them, for their future looked bleak and even if they didn't understand what was happening they understood that they were in danger.

Oberic peered down into the hole once more, "Good?"

"Pull her up!" Phin yelled.

Again, the four of them pulled the crate and moved it to the side. Ren was told to do the same for that crate and so she did, placing as many children as she could into it. "One more should do it!" She yelled to Oberic.

"One more!" Oberic shouted into the hole, "Once it's hooked head back up!"

There was a long pause interrupted by another cannon. This one ripped through the hull and they could all hear Phin and Alastor let out a yell. Oberic peered down the hole again trying to spot them, "Are you okay? Answer me!"

"This one is hooked, boss," Phin shouted, "Haul her up!"

Dwim, Leon, Jayda, and Oberic all began to pull the ropes for the last time. Phin and Alastor made it back up and though Phineas was fine; Alastor looked to be injured. They ran over and assisted with the crate. Once it was placed down Ren began to load more children. The three large cargo crates were now filled with all the children and Ren returned to the small group. "They're all packed in, Oberic. Now what?"

"No one is going to like this," he said sternly "but I need two of you to get in each crate with the kids. I'll seal you in and get you to the firing ship." They erupted into protest. Oberic closed his eyes and when he opened them he raised his voice. "Silence! Do as you're told!"

"It's not just us," Ren pleaded. "It's the children too, Oberic. You can't send them over there."

"Take a chance with them or they can all drown here." He retorted. Dwim and Alastor climbed into a box. The kids shifted around them. Oberic placed the lid on it and did his best to hammer in the pegs. Phin and Leon were next. The children and Oberic each did their job to settle the crate.

Jayda faced Ren and pulled a dagger from her belt. She held it out to Ren. "Take it. Whenever we are let out, come out fighting."

Ren, looking fearful, took the dagger from Jayda and nodded her understanding. "I'll be right back!" The Elf darted away and down to her room as fast as she could. She grabbed her little wooden chest, kissed it, and ran back up. When she rejoined Jayda, the two of them climbed into the crate and the kids shifted around to make room. As Oberic was lowering the lid Jayda grabbed his coat, "What are you going to do?" Oberic said nothing and instead offered her that same smile she found charming. He lowered the lid and beat down on it to make sure it was shut tight.

"You'll probably feel sick," he called out, "Nothing I can do about that!"Oberic stood back and took a deep breath. He drew his hands forward and began to move them about in such a fashion that seemed as though they were dancing. His magic was no small conjuration or trick. Had they been able to see what was happening, they'd be amazed by the spire of water rising from the ocean. It came down upon the crates, sounding like thunder to those inside, and soon enveloped them completely. Oberic moved his hands again and when he did the water lifted all three crates and surfed them across the water towards the other ship. All the while the crates moved over the ocean, the group along with the children could only hear the hard rush of water and in the midst of that another cannon shot. That was followed by an explosion and lastly the screams of men and women. They had a terrible sensation of suddenly being dropped and when the crates landed they smashed open. Children spilled out screaming and crying once more while the adults all stood ready for a fight. Jayda was the first to her feet. Her whip was already loose and cracking into the air.

"Stay back or I put an end to the first asshole I lay eyes on!" She shouted. They were all surrounded by hardened sailors. A woman in a decorated coat and hat, with a plume in it, came down the steps.

"What in the world was that bullshit?" She asked Jaydan, "And what are you doing with those kids?" Ren spread her arms out to protect the children as the others came forward ready to defend them.

Jayda looked at the others to see if she was the only one appalled that the woman had the nerve to ask such a question. "You attacked our ship, you looney bit-"

"I'm attacking that ship-," she cut Jayda off and came nose to nose with her, "because it has constantly stolen from me and my boss! Now why are there children?"

Jayda breathed in and out trying to collect her thoughts, "They were held captive by that crew. We saved them."

"I saved them." Alastor chimed in

The captain nodded, seeming to find that answer acceptable, "Alright you lazy good for nothings! We have extra souls on board! Rationing starts now! Get these kids some supper and find them a place to rest. If I hear of one hair on their heads being harmed I'll lash every damn one of you and let the vultures have at you while you're still breathing! Are we clear?" The crew answered back with a thunderous Aye and then the woman turned to the adults. "I'll get you to the closest port I can. I won't be able to return you to Marrenval as we are wanted there. Hadryn will have to do. You can sort out your own affairs once we arrive. I expect you all to help out on this ship." The party nodded and were thankful they wouldn't have to fight anyone anymore.

Leon leaned forward and whispered to Phineas, "You really need to behave." Phineas nodded.

"Where's Oberic?" Jayda asked.

Dwim raised a brow "I nay think he could cast his magic while stuck in a box, lass. He stayed behind to make sure we were all safe."

Jayda looked back at the ship they had come from and drew in a sharp breath. The ship was engulfed in flame and sinking faster. She turned and yelled at the captain. "I need to get back to that ship!"

"You what? We hit the powder keg with that last shot. That thing is as good as sunk. There's nothing you can do." She replied.

Jayda looked back out towards the ship. It was indeed sinking quite fast. She even debated if she could swim the distance. Jayda looked back at the captain, "Please!"

"If someone was left on board they are gone!" the captain snapped her fingers "Drop her a row boat." The sailors nodded and prepared the small craft. Jayda climbed into it and sat down.

Dwim came up to her, "Lass, I hate to say it but I think he might be gone."

Jayda frowned, "No, I have to go look for him. He would do that for me or any of you."

"How could ye' know that?" Dwim asked.

"I just do." She replied; and she did know. She felt it within her bones.

Leon, Phin, Alastor, and Ren joined Dwim and Jayda. Ren was the first to ask. "What's going on?"

"I'm going to look for Oberic." Jayda said and gave the nod to the sailors to have her lowered.

"I can't swim." Phineas lied and walked away from the group.

Leon eyed Phineas and sighed. He returned his attention to Jayda, "Don't stay too long, Jayda. You're looking for a needle in a haystack out there."

Jayda did not reply. She waited as patiently as she could until the little boat met the water. She grabbed the oars and rowed herself towards the wreckage. The waters were rough, but she eventually made it close enough that she could feel the heat from the fire that roared before her. "Oberic!" She called out hoping to hear some reply. Sadly, she heard nothing but the crackling of the fire. "Oberic! Can you hear me?" She tried again. Her emerald eyes scanned the wreckage while she slowly lost hope. Then, like music to her ears, she heard a caw. "Amun! Amun, where's Oberic!?"

Amun was standing a flaming piece of wood. He hopped around the board for a moment after she asked where his old friend was and then flew off from the wreckage. He circled a few times and then landed on another piece of wood. He cawed repeatedly at her. Jayda rowed the boat as close as she could. Amun fluttered from one bit of wood to several others before landing on one close to the sinking ship. Trapped under a set of sails was Oberic half clinging to a bit of wood. His face turned up to the sky and a large gash across his brow. Jayda got in closer, risking the burns she might suffer from the fire, and used an oar to shift the sails off of him enough that she could drag the wood towards her. Amun cawed more and Jayda found that nothing was helping. She stood up, removed her cloak, whip, and her sword and then dived into the water.

She swam up to Oberic, who was dangerously close to being taken under with the ship, and fought with the sails. They were far too heavy for her to move like this. "Stay with me, Oberic!" She grabbed the lapel of his coat and shoved the bit of wood he was somewhat hanging on away. He sunk further into the water, but she continued to hold on to him. There was a hard whine of wood creaking and groaning and the terrible feeling of being pulled under as more of the ship sank beneath the waves.

She held her breath as she was pulled under, along with Oberic, by the force of the sinking ship. It dragged them down quite a bit. She kicked her feet trying to propel up. Oberic was heavy, even in the water, and she desperately needed the air. Her chest was hurting now. The fire on the ocean became brighter as she neared the surface. Her face was turning blue as she fought to keep the air in. Her vision began to fade and she let Oberic go. Jayda broke the surface and gasped for air taking long and panicked breaths. She drew in another deep breath and dove back down. Oberic hadn't sunk very much further when she grabbed him and filled with new strength she managed to make it top side once more; this time getting Oberic's head above the water.

She knew she wouldn't be able to lift him in from the water and so she took his arms and flung them over the side of the boat. It tipped threatening to capsize but at least he was hanging on and not sinking again. Jayda swam to the other side and used Oberic's weight as leverage to pull herself up and climb in. As she managed to roll into the boat, it tipped from side to side and loosened Oberic's hold on the boat. Just as he began to slip back into the water, Jayda grabbed the back of his coat and planted her feet on the side of the craft. She pulled with everything she had and finally won the day when Oberic collapsed into the boat.

Jayda rolled him on his back and hovered over him. She slapped his face. "Oberic! Oberic!" There was no response. She began to beat on his chest. She had no idea what else to do and so she leaned down, locked her lips to his and gave him the breath from her lungs. She sat up and hammered on him once more. Oberic let out a long gasp for air, rolled over, and puked up a stream of water and then passed out once more. Jayda sat there, thankful the man was breathing again. She grabbed the oars and called "Amun! He's okay!"

Amun came flying into sight holding Oberic's hat in his beak. He soared over them and dropped it. The soaked leather hat landed on Jayda's head perfectly. Amun perched on the bow of the row boat and cawed in victory. Jayda pulled the hat down to make sure it was snug and found that Oberic had quite a large head. She rowed them back to the ship. She called out as she neared where the boat was originally dropped, "I found him! Someone help!" Sailors looked over the railing and lowered down ropes with hooks attached. She connected them and let them know they were ready. The boat was hoisted up and when it reached the top Leon and Alastor helped pull Oberic over. Dwim helped Jayda out. Amun fluttered about the group cawing loudly at the sailors. He was losing feathers over the whole thing.

"It'll be okay, Amun. He's safe now." She looked to the others, "We need to get him to a bed and get him warm." Leon and Alastor lifted Oberic and carried him off. As he was lifted, a ring with a silver chain strung through it fell from his coat. Amun landed on Jayda's shoulder and cawed. Ren joined Jayda and watched them carry Oberic off.

"I can take a look at the gash. He'll be fine, Jayda." Ren said. She swallowed hard and added, "I was wrong about you. I'm sorry."

Jayda looked at Ren surprised and found herself apologizing too, "I'm sorry as well. Fresh start?" Ren nodded with a smile and then followed Alastor and Leon. Dwim bent over and picked up the ring.

"What's this, lass?" He asked, looking inside the ring.

"That belongs to Oberic." She said. Jayda had seen the ring quite a bit already.

"*Eve,*" he mumbled with curiosity and then showed it to Jayda, "See it? Inscribed on the inside."

Jayda took the ring and looked at it. "That must have been his wife's name. I'll give it to him when he's awake." She stashed it away and turned to get her things out of the row boat. Dwim nodded and heeded below deck with the others. When Jayda was sure that she was alone she pulled the ring out again and examined the name inscribed on the inside once more, "Eve. . ."

CHAPTER 12

"Time for bed, little girl!" Said a plump and tired mother to her daughter who was running around in circles in front of the fireplace. The little girl with blonde curls and brown eyes looked up at her mother.

"Do I have to?" Her bottom lip jutted out in an overly dramatic pout.

"That works on your pa, not me. Come on. Get your doll and let's go," the mother replied while leading the way to the bedroom.

She followed her mother while pulling at the doll's hairs made of yarn. She had been rough with it over the time she had it, but it was her favorite and she refused to go anywhere without it. Her mother lifted her up and placed her in bed. The little sweetheart kicked her legs until they were covered by the blanket. Her mother made sure to lift the blankets over her the rest of the way. She tucked them under her which caused the little girl to giggle. She kissed her forehead and smiled. When she grabbed the candle to take it with her the little girl called out.

"Wait! Ma!"

The woman turned around and smiled, "What excuse do you have now?"

"I'm scared."

"Of what, my dear?"

"Marie said she saw a dead man coming out of the cemetary a few days ago and that he was going to eat us!"

The mother rolled her eyes and sat on the bed, "Now you know that's absolute nonsense. The dead do not come back to life. Even if they did, why would they eat anyone?" The little girl shrugged. "I think they would see a girl as pretty as you, and would not dare to eat you because it would be such a crime against nature to harm something so beautiful and precious." The little girl grinned again. "Now go to sleep."

The mother stood and walked out of the bedroom, giving her daughter a loving smile before shutting the door. The child laid there quietly staring up at the ceiling. The wind outside had been blowing hard all day; still she startled as the tree's branches scraped against the window. She watched the shadows cast by it dance in the blue moon light that filtered through. "There's no such thing. There's no such thing. There's no such thing," she muttered to herself. The sound of scratching was terrifying her regardless of her mantra and she gulped.

The sound of something falling in the closet forced her to sit up straight. She found she was far too scared to scream. She uncovered herself and threw her little legs over the edge of the bed. The wood floor, though covered in a rug, was cold to her feet. She inched slowly to the door and reached out with a trembling tiny hand. Once her hand touched the knob, she found in herself a strange sense of courage and twisted it. She heard the latch click and yanked the door open. Some of her toys spilled out in front of her and she was at this point able to find her voice. Her scream could have shattered glass. The bedroom door swung open and her mother stepped in.

"What are you- " she spotted the toys on the floor and shook her head. "you've gone and put it in your head that there's some monster." She held the candle out and pointed, "It's your toys!"

The little girl looked up at her mother with tears, "I'm sorry, ma! I don't want the dead man to get me!"

She was lifted by her mother once again and placed back in the bed. The routine of covering her up and tucking her in commenced once more. Her mother sat on the bed one more time. "Now, do you think we would ever let a dead man come and take you?" The little girl shook her head. "And you know your pa is a town guard, don't you?" The girl nodded. "And you know he's big and strong and more than anything in this world, he loves you most. You know that too?" The little girl smiled and nodded.

"I'm his favorite!" she said with another giggle. She seemed to calm down a bit.

"Your pa, nor me, would let anything get you. I promise you that."

"Double promise?"

"I double promise!"

"Promise to dolly?" She held out her ragged doll.

"I promise you, dolly, that nothing will harm this little fawn of mine." She leaned down and kissed her child once more. "Now go to bed. No more of this nonsense." She stood, grabbed the candle, and left the room once more.

She laid there with her doll tucked close to her. The noise at the window was still bugging her. She glanced over to the window and froze when she thought she saw something move. The window, thanks to a gust of wind, pushed open. She got up out of the bed again and walked to the window slowly. When she neared it, she reached out and slammed it shut. She latched it close with the hook and took a few steps back. This would not be a night that she got much sleep.

She turned and took tiny steps back towards the bed when she had a dreadful thought. "It's under the bed. . . " she whispered to herself. She slowly got to her knees and then her hands. She swallowed hard and told herself, "I'm a big girl! I can't be scared!" and then lowered her head to peek under.

Her body felt icy as her heart stopped beating for a moment. Fright overcame her as her eyes locked onto another set of eyes. These eyes were terrible eyes. They were the most terrible eyes she had ever seen and she had seen a lot of eyes because she knew at least thirteen people who had them and by all accounts that is enough eyes to have been seen to know that there was something wrong with this pair. She could not scream. When she was able to look away from the eyes she noticed the rest of the body and felt sick. It was the grossest thing she had ever seen. It looked old and in her mind she couldn't really explain what rotting was, but if she could she'd have put that description.

"Are you the dead man?" she asked in a whisper again. The corpse under her bed nodded, never taking it's eyes off her. "Are you going to eat me?"

The voice that replied sounded friendly enough, "No. I do not eat children. I am dead and therefore I can not eat. Where did you get such an idea?"

She laid on her stomach now. She was intrigued now that a dead man was so friendly and talking to her, "Marie said so!"

"I don't think Marie knows what she is talking about."

"Marie lies a lot. Pa says Marie's pa is worthless and that's why she lies."

"And what makes Pa so knowledgeable?"

'He's a guard! He protects everyone and has to arrest Marie's Pa from time to time."

"I don't think he can protect everyone."

"You're wrong! Pa is strong! Hey mister, what are you doing under my bed?"

"Waiting of course."

"Waiting for what?"

'To eat you."

"I thought you said you didn't eat children!"

"I lied."

A hand reached out from under the bed and in the moonlight she could see bone was exposed from where flesh should have been. She wanted to scream but the hand of the dead man grasped around her face and she was dragged under the bed with him along with poor dolly.

The bedroom door creaked open slowly. Ma had turned her head and looked down the hall, "You better not be out of bed again!" She went back to scrubbing a pot and humming to herself. What was she going to do with this girl? She was just as stubborn as he Pa and that alone made her smile.

"Ma. . . " the little girl called out. Ma jumped but did not turn around. She was not going to play into her daughter's trap of staying up late.

"What is it, little one? I thought I told you not to get out of bed again."

"It's the dead man, Ma."

"There is no dead man running around town."

"There is though! He isn't running around town. He is here!"

Ma sighed and placed the pot down, "And what is he doing here?"

"You said he wouldn't hurt me, Ma. You said you wouldn't allow it. Then he ate me and I'm dead."

Ma turned around and screamed such a wretched scream. She slid down the counter to her rear. Her daughter stood in front of her but where brown eyes used to be were dark sockets that cried blood. Ma's fingers reached into her hair, pulling out graying black threads as her eyes left her daughter's non-existent ones and traveled down to the open cavity of her chest. Where there should have been a heart, there was only empty space.

"You said you would protect me and you lied. He ate me. He ate my eyes first and then he cut me open real slow. He touched my heart while it still beat, Ma! He squeezed it and pulled it out and then he ate it while I died!" The little girl walked closer and pulled a meat cleaver off the counter that was used to remove the heads from chickens earlier in the day. "He's going to eat you too, Ma!" She reached out and grabbed her mother's hair and with unbelievable strength that did not belong to her she dragged her mother to the fireplace. Ma kicked and screamed the entire way. The little girl lifted the cleaver and with no eyes to see, managed to hit her mark. The cleaver dug into Ma's shoulder. She screamed out in agony. "Why didn't you save me, Ma? I said there was a dead man! You should have believed me!" The cleaver lifted from the shoulder and came down again; this time nearly severing the arm.

Ma called out for help. She pleaded with Olm to send her some sort of guided light. Some sort of savior. There was no answer; not tonight. She looked at her daughter, begging that there was something left of her, and as if being able to read those thoughts, she shook her head of blonde curls. She grabbed her mother's arm and ripped what remained from her torso. The arm was thrown into the fire and Ma watched it be engulfed and listened to the sound of the skin blistering and popping. The girl grabbed her mother's hair and held it tightly.

"He ate me, Ma. It's your fault. It's okay though! Dying isn't that bad and you get to die with me!" She slowly pushed her mother's face into the flames. There was a new, more terrible scream as Ma's face ws being broiled. Her skin blistered, popped, melted, and then charred. Her eyes liquified in their sockets and dripped onto the burning wood. When her nerves had been burned away and there was no pain, she was cleaved in the back of the skull. Ma dropped face first into the fire with the cleaver dug into her. She was dead.

The morning light broke over the horizon as dawn had come. Pa made his way down to his meager little cottage to greet his wife and favorite girl. The night had been an easy night and he was in a great mood. When he opened the front door he called, "I'm home, ladies!" He removed his helmet and placed his sword and shield down by the door. He was a simple town guard and didn't have the luxury of hardened metal armor and instead had to use thick leathers, but nothing ever happened in the sleepy little town of Oakember. He took a deep inhale and slapped his stomach. "Do I smell pork? It smells wonderful! Is that what we're having for breakfast?" There was no response and he narrowed his eyes. "Girls?"

"We are in our little girl's room, Pa," Ma had called out. "Your child has been awfully naughty."

Pa walked down the hall and entered the room. "How naughty?" His words fell flat as he saw on the bed, dolly's yarn body with his little girls' head sewn to it. His little girl's body, what remained, was on the floor in pieces. Blood had already soaked into the wood and stained it red. He screamed the pain of a father losing his child.

"She killed me. That's so naughty!" Ma said. Pa turned around and gasped as he came face to face with his wife. Her arm was gone and her face was nothing more than blackened bone. Her hair had mostly been burnt away. She reached up with her remaining limb, pulled the cleaver from her skull and planted it into Pa's face. Pa stood there only for a moment before falling back, bouncing off the bed, and landing on the floor face first. The cleaver dug in deeper. His blood ran down the cleaver like watered sap from a tree until it pooled on the floor where he lay. One small and happy family murdered and joined together once more in the cold embrace of death and the beyond.

CHAPTER 13

Jayda was brought to Oberic's room after inquiring where he had been taken. She knocked softly and opened the door to find Dwim, Leon, and Ren already inside watching over him. He was covered in blankets and furs. Rennyn sat beside him in a chair mixing up a small vial of something. Jayda did not suspect it was anything to cause harm and so she did not bother inquiring about it.

Leon had noticed Jayda was soaked from head to foot as well and he got up, grabbed a blanket, and waited for Amun to hop from her shoulder before throwing it over her. She wrapped herself tightly with it and offered Leon a smile. Amun fluttered to the table where Ren sat and let out a caw. "He'll be okay, Amun." Jayda said. She hoped she was right.

The door swung open and Phineas peeked in, "Oh good! You found him."

"Get out, ye' coward!" Dwim growled.

Phin rolled his eyes and spoke as though none of this was a big deal, "The wizard is going to be fine."

The other four replied in unison, "He's not a wizard." and then laughed.

"We should let him rest," Ren said as she stood up, "We all had a long day. We should all rest."

"I'll stay with him." Jayda said softly and when everyone looked at her she felt as if she needed to defend herself. "Just to make sure he doesn't die."

Ren held out the vial and smiled, "His heart beats strong. I believe he'll be okay. Give him this if he runs a fever."

Jayda took the vial and examined it before giving a solid nod to Ren, "Amun and I will keep watch. I'll come find you all if I need to." She ushered them out of the room and closed the door. She sat down in the chair Ren had been occupying and watched silently as the blankets and furs over Oberic moved up and down with every breath he took.

It may have been hours or even days that passed. Jayda thought it all blended together. In that time, Oberic cracked an eye open and let out a low groan. Amun let out a series of furious caws as he flapped around the room. "Keep it quiet, Amun. This hang over is murder." Oberic mumbled. Amun flew and landed on his chest. His head rolled and saw Jayda sitting there with her head on the table sleeping. She had stayed with him the entire time, having turned down invitations to dinner to stay by his side. He did his best to sit up and not wake her. He rubbed at his pounding head and let out another groan as he ran a hand over the gash. "Not a hangover. Just actual pain. That's certainly-" he paused, "Well it's something." Amun flew to Jayda and started pecking at her ear and cawing loudly.

Jayda startled awake, disoriented for the moment, "Amun? Is he-" she blinked, bringing herself to the present moment and then she met Oberic's eyes. "You're awake!" She stood, bombarding him with questions, "How do you feel? Does anything hurt? Are you hungry? Thirsty?"

"I'm fine," he said, trying to calm her, "I'm fine. Could use an ale if you have one handy." He offered her a weak smile. "What happened? Last thing I remember was accepting my fate of going down with the ship. I accepted it and was ready and then just a loud noise and, well, nothing."

She smiled, "Let me go get you something to drink and I'll come back." She left the room and decided then the best thing to do was find the others. She wandered around the ship for a bit before finding them all in the galley. She explained that Oberic had finally woken and they all decided, excluding the Orc who had not been seen since they arrived, to join Jayda in bringing him a refreshment. They opened the door to his room after getting him a few mugs of ale to find Alastor sitting in the chair and speaking with Oberic.

"We have not met. My mother named me Alsator. You may call me that if you wish. My Orc kin call me Orc'oth. You have earned my respect and my loyalty for saving the children and your friends. I have a gift." Alastor held out a tiny leather pouch. Oberic took it and looked inside.

"It looks like some dried nuts." Oberic said, looking up at Alastor with a curious grin.

"That is correct. It is the slaver captain's testicles. I removed them while he still lived and kept them as a trophy. I give them to you now. Consider me your brother."

Oberic grimaced, "Well, I wasn't completely wrong. Thank you."

Alastor extended his arm out. Oberic reached out to shake it but Alastor grabbed his forearm instead and shook. Alastor turned his yellow eyes towards the group, "It seems you have visitors. I will let you be with them now. Be well, brother." He stood and moved through the group without saying anything. Ren's face turned red and she excused herself so that she could follow Alastor out of the room.

Once the door shut behind her she hissed at Alastor, "How dare you? How dare you leave without saying a word?" Her voice had raised halfway through the question as she beat against him with her tiny fists.

The Orc did not move from his place nor did his expression change. He stared at her with us ugly face and grunted, "You seek the friendship of a monster, girl. I did you a favor and left you in the care of men of holy words. You do not wish for the company of monsters."

Ren shouted now, "You're only half Orc!"

"I may be half Human, but they too can be monsters. Cruelty sleeps within us all. Mine is just more primal. Be angry with me if you wish, but at least now you stand amongst friends."

"No! You don't get to tell me what to be thankful for! You did me no favors! You have taken everything from me! I have nothing left! No home! No job! Nothing!"

Alastor placed a hand on her shoulder, "I am sorry for what I have cost you. I admit I am guilty of not thinking ahead. I accept your blame for what is gone. Does that make you feel better?"

Ren went silent for a moment and spoke softly, "No. No it doesn't."

"I did not think it would. We can not change the past, girl. We can only look and work for a better future. I'll leave you now." Alastor removed his hand and walked away. He would vanish for another several days before reappearing again. Ren collected herself the best she could. She did not want to enter the room again looking upset. She took several deep breaths, fanned her face, and then forced a smile. She turned and went back inside to join the others.

"We're glad to see you made it out alive." Phin had finished saying as Ren entered and shut the door behind her. "I think we were all worried. Not so much myself but the rest were. Especially her." Phin nodded to Jayda.

Jayda's cheeks went red and she stammered, "I feel like it's my fault that you're on this journey. She wrapped her arms around herself, "I couldn't let something bad happen to you. Not after what you did." Ren stood beside Leon and gazed up at him with a knowing smile. Leon returned it with more of a smirk than a smile. Jayda held out a mug and made sure his hands had a grip before she let go. He drew it to his lips and drank.

"That's not hot milk and honey." he said as he pulled the mug from his lips with a smile.

"Not this time," Jayda chuckled, "today it's ale."

The others tried to give him food, but he denied them and continued to drink the ale. Dwim spoke quietly, "How ye' feeling, lad?"

Oberic shrugged, "Bit of a headache. I had a good nurse though it seems." He lifted fierce green eyes to Jayda's own emeralds.

Phin clapped his hands together, "Wow. This got weird. Glad you're alive." Phin made a clicking noise with his mouth as he gave an exaggerated wink to Obeirc and then turned and left the room.

Jayda turned away from his gaze and placed the other mug on his table, "I need to stretch my legs. I'll return later with some dinner for you." She did not wait for a reply as she took the tray and exited just as fast as Phineas had.

Oberic watched her go with a confused look. He looked at Dwim and Leon, "Did I do something?" Amun dipped his beak into the full mug.

Leon laughed, "No. Just women being women."

Dwim chimed, "Dwarven women just punch ye' in the face. Why when my late wife asked me to marry her. . . " he looked up dreamily, "She uppercut me. Gave me a blackened eye." He sighed and wiped a fat tear from his eye and sniffled, "I miss ye', sweetheart."

Jayda found herself on deck. She spotted Phineas leaning over the railing and joined him. Phin looked at her, "Not watching the old guy?"

"Needed a break." she mumbled. She uncoiled her whip and lashed out at the air, having decided to get a bit of practice in to clear her mind.

"Sure. Feel free to lie because hey, why not?" He moved away from her a bit, as did sailors in the area, to ensure they were not struck by the whip and it's bits of bone. "Got the hots for the guy, huh?"

She fumbled on her strike and the whip cracked back and bit her in the leg. She drew in breath with a hiss, "I was just worried about him. Nothing more."

"Listen," he unlaced his trousers and hung himself out to urinate overboard, "I've broken many hearts so forgive me when I say it's written all over your face. Don't worry though. I won't say anything and he's too dumb to realize it." He must have been full because the stream was long and ongoing. "Guy looks so much older than you though. That bug you?" He didn't give her a chance to answer. "I've had older women. Good times."

She didn't seem bothered by his crudeness having just pulled himself out in front of her. "Age doesn't bother me. I *suppose* I enjoy his company. Strange as that is for me to admit. I think he enjoys mine as well." She waited until he started to shake himself and then snapped the whip at his feet to make him jump.

Phineas jumped and dripped a bit on his boot. "Aw!" He put himself away and laced up again. "Well it doesn't matter. Guy doesn't even realize you're a woman. He isn't a wild animal like myself." He faced her now, "You sure you don't want to ride this wagon before the wheels fall off?" He proceeded to model himself in front of her.

Jayda grinned and stepped in closer to him. She ran the soft part of her whip around one of his wrists and then the other. She leaned in close, her chest pressed softly against his, and stepped up on tiptoes. She whispered softly, her breath against his skin, "Tempting. . . " her lips nearly pressed against his ear, "however the idea of fleas doesn't appeal to me." She gave him a playful kiss on the cheek and pulled her whip away from him, coiled it back on her hip, and walked off with a laugh.

"I like it!" he called out with a laugh, "Just make sure you don't give the old man a heart attack if you do end up getting your claws in him!"

Jayda passed by Leon as she was heading back below deck. He gave her a nod as he pulled from his pipe, "He's in there by himself again. Ren made sure he was comfortable."

Jayda stopped and gave him a sincere smile, "I appreciate that you've accepted me so easily into the group, Leon. You and Dwim. You've been kind. I'm sorry if I've been any trouble."

"This whole group is a bunch of misfits. He saved a bunch of lives and then you saved him. As far as I'm concerned you're both one of us now." His eyes trailed back up the stairs, "Still not sold on that one out there though."

Jayda looked back behind her up the stairs as well, "I like him. He's funny." They could both hear Phineas harassing some female sailor.

"Captain is going to put us to work soon. You ready for that?" Leon asked.

"Don't really have a choice." She patted his shoulder. "I'm going to get back to the room in case Oberic wakes up." She said her goodnight and made her way to the room once more.

She entered the room and shut the door softly. She looked at Oberic who was laying on the bed with an arm outstretched and hanging over the bed. She sat down on the chair and tried to make herself comfortable. She pulled the ring on the silver necklace from her cloak and ran her thumb over it softly before she decided it was best to give it back. She held out and dropped the ring into Oberic's hand. His fist grasped around it tightly though he never woke. Jayda leaned back in the chair and dozed off.

Jayda had no idea how long she had been asleep when she heard his voice. "Don't you have anything better to do than sit around watching me?"

She replied without opening her eyes, "I was enjoying the quiet until you woke up."She cracked one eye open and then the other, "Are you hungry?"

He shook his head "No." His fingers fidgeted with the ring before he slid the necklace over his head and the ring down his shirt. Amun had been a quiet and well behaved bird and even now only cawed softly. "We're even, you know? I helped you out. You helped me out. There's no need to keep an eye on me. I dare say I'm relatively safe if Amun still considers me a friend." Amun flew up and perched himself on Jayda's shoulder. "Seems he has taken a liking to you."

Jayda looked away not wanting Oberic to see her emotions on her face. What was it? Anger? Sadness? She wasn't sure herself. She reached up and stroked Amun's head. "I wasn't aware we were keeping score. Besides, I wasn't watching you. I was just resting away from everyone else." Her eyes fixated on the crow and her next words were soft and let more of her emotion show than her face did, "If I am being a bother, please let me know. I will go and see if Phineas is busy."

"I'm glad it's you," he said, "ee watch out for each other, you and I. I don't know them any better but for some reason, I trust you. Do you trust me?"

Jayda looked back at Oberic and locked eyes with him. "I trust you with my life now, Oberic."

"Well," he offered her that charming smile once more and Jayda felt her chest tighten a bit, "I dare say we're two peas in a pod at the moment." Amun cawed. "Sorry, three peas."

"Even if we didn't trust each other," she gave the crow a scratch under the wing and grinned, "I think Amun and I have become friends so you won't be able to get rid of me that easily anyway."

"I wouldn't dream of it." He closed his eyes and got comfortable in bed. Oberic Not A Wizard Wintersong dozed off once again.

CHAPTER 14

The captain made good on her word and put every single one of them to work. They were all given laborious jobs except Rennyn and Oberic who were tasked with putting more wind in the sails. Oberic was only in bed for another week under Jayda's care and from there, Oberic worked with Ren closely, teaching her how to feel for the elements around her. He would then work with her to learn how to dictate what she wanted those natural elements to do. It was a rough start, but at the end of the first month she was able to control the air so long as she kept it small and simple. She was in awe with Oberic who made it look so easy. He would create large squalls, but then would nearly collapse at the end of it. He would always then remind her that magic drained and exhausted you.

The group had grown together. They all enjoyed one another's company. Even Alastor, who did not come around often, was friendlier, but not by much. Phineas, however, continued to annoy everyone and only seemed to get along with Jayda. She was sitting there on the upper deck with her legs thrown across his as she soaked in the sun seemingly lost in thought. She was looking over at the horizon when she thought she saw it.

"Is that-" she was cut off by a sailor in the crow's nest calling out.

"Land! Land ahead!"

Jayda got up and walked to the railing with Phineas joining her not a moment later. There on the horizon just barely visible was a city of white spiraling towers gleaming in the sunlight. Leon, Dwim, Ren, Alastor, and Oberic all joined the two.

Leon smiled, "Hadryn! The white city!"

"It's beautiful!" Ren declared in absolute awe.

"Bout time. I'm ready to get my boots on land!" Jayda said. She was over the Ocean and hoped they'd never set foot on a ship again for a while.

Ren looked at Oberic who looked quite ill in the face, "You alright?"

Oberic nodded, "Fine."

"The way Leon and Dwim talk about this place it doesn't seem like we're going to have much fun. I bet there aren't any brothels. I bet they serve watered down ale. I bet this-" Phin was cut off by Dwim.

"Aye! All that and ye' best watch your tongue, lad!" Dwim's voice was stern.

Jayda gave Phin a playful kick, "Poor thing! How will you ever survive?"

Phin shrugged his shoulders, "No idea."

Alastor had nothing to say on the matter. Ren elbowed him, "It is quite beautiful, isn't it?" Alastor did not answer. Not satisfied with that she turned to Leon, "You were right! It's stunning!"

Leon nodded, "You will all want to mind yourselves here. The High Priestess is not one to allow things to go unpunished." They all turned their heads, including Amun, and looked at Phin.

Jayda said what everyone was thinking, "Do you hear that, mutt? Behave yourself."

"Not much happens there though," Leon continued, "this city is inhabited by devoted followers of Olm."

The captain showed up behind them without the group noticing and when she spoke nearly all of them jumped, except Alastor; the Orc was incapable of being startled as far as the group could tell. "Well. I wish I could say that I'll miss you all, but the truth is you're absolutely shit sailors and the work you did was terrible at best. I'll be glad to see the backs of you. I'm only docking here to get you and those kids off my ship." She then stood in front of Phineas, "And you, you'll be staying won't you? For me?"

Phin drew in a breath, "Beautiful, you know I'm crazy about you. You made those lonely nights out at sea very special. My heart belongs to the land though, just like yours belongs to the tides."

"You said you loved me!" the captain exclaimed, her face turning red from both anger and embarrassment.

"Oh, I did say that, didn't I?" he questioned, the look on his face making it quite clear he had forgotten. They all stared at the two for a long moment. "Well, you'll always be in my heart." The captain's nostrils flared and she slapped Phineas and stormed off.

Leon shook his head watching Phin rub his cheek, "You're lucky she didn't flog you or something."

"No, flogging was the other night."

Within the next few hours the ship pulled into the harbor. The captain checked in with the harbor master and after explaining the situation was given the pass to allow them to unboard. The group was escorted off the ship after the children were. When they inquired what would happen to the children they were told they had been brought to the orphanage. As they were talking to the harbormaster they had all noticed that there was no citizen there who was not properly dressed. There were no beggars nor homeless. Even rough sailors were dressed well and mindful of their manners.

When they were released and free to roam the city they made note of how clean and well kept the streets were. Cathedral bells rang all around them. Several stood in the city but one in particular stood higher than every building in the vast city. Dwim seemed to be in a dream, "Look at this! The cathedrals alone are so breathtaking!"

The others agreed. Even Alastor grunted a comment about how lovely it all looked. Jayda dropped back to a slow walk with Oberic who seemed to be lagging behind everyone on purpose, "You okay? You look a bit, I don't know, worried?"

Oberic glanced over and caught sight of her emeralds staring at him. He then looked back ahead at the palace that sat at the center of the city, "Yes. I'll be fine. We should find some lodging." Amun sat on Jayda's shoulder and looked around at his new surroundings.

"I know just the place!" Leon said. Ren had been holding on to his arm, making endless chatter about the beauty of the city.

"It's so clean! Look at all the flowers! I could never imagine such a place!" Pure joy radiated from her face as she continued to point things out. Leon, having been there before, was more than happy to point out other eye-catching scenery to her. Jayda looked away from Oberic. She didn't believe his words, but thought it best to not push the subject.

As they passed people in the street they were greeted with "Olm be with you." and "Olm's light upon you." as well as other similar blessings. Leon found an inn quite near the palace and when they stepped inside they found that it was also very clean and well taken care of. It was made of white stone and healthy green ivy climbed up the sides creating a beautiful contrast of civilization and nature. Phin offered to pay for everyone's rooms with gold he had earned from cheating sailors while on the ship. No one argued against this. When they were given their keys, they each wished each other a pleasant rest and went to their rooms. Amun seemed to be unsure of who he wanted to go with, but ultimately decided just as Oberic was entering his room that he should go with him and so he flew from Jayda's shoulder to join his old friend.

They all slept through the night without any disturbance. Dwim, happy more than any of them that he wasn't constantly rocking from side to side. It was a bit into the morning, not quite close to noon, when Oberic knocked on each of their doors. "I've taken the liberty of arranging an appointment with the local tailor for you all. Please go and see them when you can."

They all got dressed in the same clothes they had been wearing for an entire journey across the ocean, which is all they had since their bags sank with MOIRA. After waiting for Oberic for nearly thirty minutes, they decided to go on without him. It was easy enough to find the place. When they came in, the tailor knew exactly who they were; they of course stuck out like sore thumbs in this city. "Please," The black haired woman said, "Olm's love be with you. Pick out any garment you like. Your friend has taken care of the payment already." They were all curious where Oberic got the money to cover such a cost.

Dwim found a few shirts and trousers, but had to have one of the tailor's assistants take it in and make adjustments. The others would find it much easier to find clothing their size. Alastor, who rarely wore any shirt at all, was having trouble finding one that felt comfortable and finally settled on a simple linen colored much like a sack of wheat. He also grabbed a pair of linen pants and a new pair of traveling boots.

Ren had found a lovely soft blue dress and let her hair hang loose. It was long and ran down her back. She even managed to wrangle Jayda into a dress, much to Jayda's objections. The dress was simple and dark green. Ren then forced Jayda down into a chair and grabbed her inky black hair and began to braid it into delicate tangles around her head. Her bright purple eyes stared into the mirror at angry emerald ones. "Isn't it refreshing to get cleaned and dressed up?"

Jayda's cheeks were bright red and she scowled, "I look like a girl."

Leon and Phineas dressed much like Alastor did. Leon wore it best. Phin would have worn it better had he not decided to make sure his chest was exposed. His hair was pulled back into a ponytail and tied off with a large blue ribbon much like some young noble youth; it fit him. When Dwim was finished getting his outfit adjusted, each met up in the center of the shop and complemented how great they all looked.

They all made their way back to the inn in quite the cheerful mood; new sets of clothing can do that and they each had a few new sets now. They were thankful to no longer have to wear the same thing over and over. When they entered they all stopped and stared at a man they had known but had not seen quite like such. Oberic stood there in a clean (for once) blue overcoat with brown trousers and a white linen shirt. His hair wasn't greasy and instead brushed. It was still long but well managed. His beard was also trimmed. His face had healed over the ship ride and though not an overly handsome man, he cleaned up quite nicely. He even had a blue pointed hat, banded with gold, sitting on the counter next to him.

Ren stepped forward, "Oberic!" she cried out, "Look at you!"

Jayda had seen Oberic and felt she was looking at him too long. She felt around at her hip and feigned concern over something else. "There's nowhere to put my whip on this silly get up!" She looked uncomfortable, but had any of the men in the room been asked, by all accounts she was beautiful.

Oberic had not responded to the adoration from Rennyn. Instead he seemed to be preoccupied with whatever was outside the window facing the palace. Several guards dressed in polished silver armor and draped in white cloaks came into the inn. Amun flew in above their heads and landed on Oberic's shoulder. "Whose bird?" the guards asked.

"Excellent!" Oberic said. He walked to the counter and grabbed his hat. He slipped it on his head and smiled, "She got my message."

The guard seemed annoyed with the notion but nodded, "Yes. The High Priestess will see all of you. Especially the wolf."

Phineas looked extremely annoyed, "Really? You had to bring me into it?"

"It's what we're here for ye' idiot!" Dwim growled out. "Quit crying and get moving. The High Priestess must nay be kept waiting!"

"You heard the Dwarf." Leon said and waited for the guard to turn and leave. He followed them and each of them filed out behind.

Oberic walked behind Jayda and as he did he leaned in and said, "Green looks good on you."

Jayda blushed and looked at him, "Thank you. Rennyn said it would be better if I didn't dress less like myself." She looked to Amun who then promptly leapt from Oberic's shoulder to hers. She felt better with her new feathered friend close, "This High Priestess, have you met her before? What's she like?"

Oberic nodded, but didn't answer her first question, "She likes order. Probably why she doesn't like me very much." The two of them walked side by side at the end of the guard led procession. The people of the city they passed by once again gave them praise and prayer. They climbed the steps of the beautiful palace crafted of white stone just like every other building in the city. The guard held open the front door and ushered them in.

As they all entered, they could not miss how grand and at the same time humble the palace was. In the center of what they assumed was the throne room was no throne but a simple chair. A woman draped in a humble white cloak sat on it and looked out at the group. She lifted her hands out to them, "Welcome! Welcome to Hadryn, travelers!"

Dwim, finding her voice to be like a beautiful song in his ears, dropped to his knees. "High Priestess Evelyn of the White! Such an honor to meet ye'!"

Ren dropped down into a courtesy and then nudged Jayda in the ribs. She let out a soft grunt and followed suit. The others joined them and knelt. None more than Dwim though whose nose was nearly touching the floor. Oberic was the only one who hadn't and after a long moment they all seemed to turn to face him to see why he hadn't.

Oberic smiled awkwardly and called out to the woman on the chair, "Hello, sweetheart. It's been a long time."

The woman stood up and stepped into the light cast down by stained glass windows painting her a number of colors, all of them made her look like a painting come to life. Then she stepped out of them, returning to her normal color. Her pink cheeks were easily noticeable with her fair complexion. Her hair shimmered like gold and she looked to Oberic with crystal blue eyes before giving him a soft smile, "You've gained weight."

Jayda tried her best to hide the shock she was experiencing. Did she hear him correctly? Did he call her sweetheart? She glanced over at the others who seemed to be wondering the same thing. She was glad she wasn't the only one wearing the confused expression on her face. She watched Oberic walk forward and stand before the woman who stood at the edge of the small lift of stairs so that she towered above him. Amun left her shoulder and flew to him with a caw.

"It's been a little over twenty years. You've done well for yourself." he said in a voice that seemed softer and far more kind than any of them had ever heard him use.

The High Priestess dipped her head and then lifted it, "And you're still. . .``She paused for a moment, "You. Have you done nothing in all these years, Oberic?"

"I wouldn't say I've done nothing." Oberic said, attempting to be suave, "I thought of you every night."

Evelyn shook her head, "Not the time, Oberic." She looked at the others in the group. "Please rise, I am no queen and I do not require your praise. I am High Priestess Evelyn Locke-" Oberic mumbled under his breath something about her dropping his name and stared at the floor. "- of the White. You are guests here and I welcome you to stay in the palace while you are here. It is my understanding you have a problem with a curse."

Oberic looked at the floor still. Almost any bit of confidence the man had ever shown seemed to be sapped in Evelyn's presence. Jayda found she couldn't bring herself to look at Oberic. Rennyn stepped forward and spoke on behalf of everyone. "Our friend here," she pointed to Phineas, "has a small problem."

Phineas scoffed, "No woman has ever said that about me."

Dwim cast a glare at Phineas and stomped on his foot. Phin swore and Dwim did it again. After that had settled, Dwim and Rennyn took turns explaining Phineas' curse to Evelyn who listened with great interest. When they were done she took a moment to think about the situation.

"I will do my best to assist you. We can research this curse and see what we may learn of it, but please know that my resources are spread thin at this moment. Hadryn has problems of its own and I must see to the safety of these people. They are my first priority." She looked to Phineas, "I am sorry."

Phin shrugged, "I've learned to live with it."

Dwim scowled, "Show some respect, lad! Ye' stand in front of a holy woman!"

Evelyn smiled, "It is more than alright, Master Dwarf." She then addressed them all, "Please. My guard will show you to your rooms. The palace is open to you. Roam as you like."

As the guard approached they all bowed one last time, except Oberic who just stood there staring down at the intricate carved stone tiles. Ren slipped to Jayda's side and lowered her voice to a whisper, "Are you alright?" She watched her new friend, once an enemy of sorts, with concern in her purple eyes. Jayda nodded silently. Ren decided to let her be. They all followed the guard to their rooms and each slipped into their humble but nice rooms.

Jayda seemed to rush into her room and as she closed the door she locked it swiftly and threw her back against the heavy wooden door. Her hand covered her mouth and she let out a soft muffled sob. She had just assumed that Oberic's wife was gone. That perhaps the ring was nothing more than a memento. She had, not once, thought to ask more details about her. She shook her head and tried to clear her mind. "It's fine," she said softly and then followed it with, "I'm fine."

There was a knock at the door that startled her and she rubbed at her face hoping that she erased any evidence that she was upset. "Hey! It's Phineas!" He knocked again. "I know you're in there." He knocked another time, more obnoxiously. "You up for a little trouble?"

Jayda turned and opened the door staring out at him with red puffy eyes, "What kind of trouble are you thinking?"

"Guards are gone. Everyone is in their rooms." Phin grabbed her wrist and dragged her along through the halls. They took a few turns here and there until they eventually came to a simple looking door at the end of the hallway with no other rooms. "Make a bet that's her room?"

Jayda grinned at him, "I'll take that bet. I'll keep watch?"

Phineas picked the lock with such ease and expertise that it was a little surprising. Despite his attitude and lack of care, he was absolutely skilled when it came to theft. He opened the door and revealed a simple and modest bedroom. Phineas took a deep breath in "Yep. This is her room. Has her smell." He walked in; pulling Jadya in with him. Once she was inside he closed the door behind her. "Now a lady like this *has* to have secrets!" Phin started to immediately go through her things.

Jayda stared at him in shock that he would be so brazen. She hissed at him softly, "Phineas! Don't make a mess!" Though she did not want Phin to do much digging, her curiosity got the best of her and she joined his side as he rifled through her drawers. Her eyes fell upon some jewelry sitting upon the dressing table Phin was going through. "This would go for a bit of coin, wouldn't it?" She picked up a delicate necklace with a single large diamond hanging from it. "We're just looking for secrets right? No stealing."

"No," Phin muttered, "Unfortunately, no stealing. A woman like this has a stick up her ass and she'll know when things are out of place or missing." He was digging through another drawer where he found letters. He read through them swiftly, but seemed displeased with the information. "Nothing yet."

Jayda watched him work, "What are you looking for specifically?" She kept glancing at the door, unsure if she had heard footsteps.

"Anything I can use for blackmail. Do you know the kind of information you can get when you have a leader in your pocket?" Phin rubbed his hands together furiously, "The possibilities!"

Jayda had not heard anything he had said. She was certain she could hear Evelyn coming down the hall arguing with someone, "Phin!" She grabbed his arm, "She's out there! We have to hide!" She immediately dropped down and rolled under the bed and made sure to leave room for Phineas. Phin put the papers back in the drawer, shut it, and slid under the bed. He had made it under the bed just in time it seemed.

The door swung open and Evelyn stopped in followed by a pair of men's boots, "Oberic, we have nothing to discuss."

Oberic shut the door behind her and pleaded, "Eve, please."

"No. You have not been my husband for twenty years. I have gone my own way and I had hoped you would as well."

"I'd have followed you, Eve, you know that. I would have done whatever it is you wanted me to do."

Amun flew from Oberic's shoulder and landed on the floor. His strange colored eyes fixated on Jayda and Phineas, both of whom were wide eyed with worry. The crow let out a single caw and Phineas silently waved a hand at the bird who promptly flew into the air and landed back on Oberic's shoulder.

"And that's the problem, Oberic." She moved to him and touched his face, "I fell in love with a man who could have easily moved the stars. The power you possess," she looked up at him and peered into his eyes, which did not look dangerous at all to her, "others would scour the world for such power."

Jayda felt Phin's hand wandering down her back and she drove an elbow into his side and glowered at him.

"I didn't want power, Evelyn!" Eve moved from Oberic and sat in a nearby chair. He stepped towards her to close the distance again, "I wanted you! Some of us don't need to have high aspirations. I enjoyed my work as a librarian in Maer'lyn. Why was that so hard for you to accept?"

"Because you could have changed the world if you wanted to, Oberic!" She stood from the chair and continued but with anger in her voice, "You could have made such promising changes. I do not want power either, but I have it and I chose to use it to help others!"

"Is that why you left me? Not even a goodbye? Just a neatly written letter?"

"I regret doing it in that manner, Oberic, I do. I still stand behind my decision to leave."

Oberic was silent for a moment, "But why?" His voice was low and soft.

"Because I can not be with a man who refuses to be all that they can be. I am sorry, Oberic. I do love you, I do. I will always cherish you, but you are not the man I thought you were when we married."

Oberic drew in a deep breath, "You know what the worst part of it was, Evelyn? It was going to sleep one night knowing that your heart belonged to me and only me. It was that I slept soundly without fear knowing you would be there when I woke. Then I opened my eyes and found you were gone. Your indent still in our bed. Reading your note and wondering when you had decided to leave? Surely you didn't lay there in the night and decide to pack up and go. It was that you gave me no signs that your heart was changing. You let me believe that everything was okay." Oberic reached into his coat, "I understand. I'm just here to get his curse business taken care of." He pulled out the ring on the silver necklace and tossed it to her. Evelyn caught it and looked at it. She recognized it immediately as the ring she removed from her finger and left beside her goodbye note. "I can't hold onto that anymore. If I am to make a new life, then I need to let your ghost go." She turned the ring over in her fingers, almost tempted to slide it on. Tears formed in her eyes as she looked back up at Oberic. She was touched that he held onto it and saddened to know she had hurt him so badly. Oberic then removed his own ring and placed it on the vanity. "It was good seeing you, Evelyn. Let me know if you need assistance with the research." Oberic turned and left the room. Once the door was shut Evelyn let out a quiet sob but composed herself just as fast. She had other matters to attend to. She fixed her cloak, left the ring on the vanity next to his, and exited the room as well.

Jayda laid there quietly, unable to bring herself to move. She felt sick to her stomach having intruded on such a private and emotional moment. Phineas snorted, "I guess she's single." and he scooted from under the bed. He crept to the door, opened it and peeked out, "Looks like we're all clear. You gonna stay under there?"

She slid out from under the bed looking quite pale. "Phin, let me go get changed and then let's go find somewhere to get a drink." She needed an escape from the events that were unfolding. Phin nodded and left the room. Jayda stepped forward, stopped, looked at the rings on the vanity for a long moment, and then left the room as well.

Phineas waited outside her door for her to get changed. When she exited, she looked more herself wearing the same Hunter gear she had when she met Oberic. She walked out and felt reassured as she felt the whip on her hip. "Let's get drunk." They left the palace together not really saying anything to one another. The setting sun cast an orange hue over the clean city. She pointed to a tavern, "Let's get into some trouble."

"I don't know how much trouble we can really get into. This place seems too uptight." Phineas said not knowing that he was absolutely correct.

"Come on. We'll go in, I'll distract the bar keep, you grab a few bottles."

"Aye aye!" was his reply as he gave a salute. As they approached the tavern Phin took a peek through the window. "Oh, actually, I have a better idea." He grabbed Jayda and pulled her inside the tavern and led her to a table. He pulled her so hard that she had no choice but to sit in the chair. The color that had once returned to her had drained again as she saw Oberic sitting at the table staring down into an empty glass. "I'll go get us some drinks!" Phin said as he left the two alone.

"They've got wine but it's watered down." Oberic muttered.

Jayda glared at Phineas. When she turned her gaze to Oberic she softened, "Is everything okay, Oberic?" She wouldn't let him know that she heard the conversation.

"Actually, yes." He looked at the finger that once wore a ring for more than twenty years. "Surprisingly." He looked up from his empty glass. "Evelyn and I were married. So I'm just letting the past finally rest where it belongs." He sighed and sniffed. He had been crying a bit before they arrived and she could tell. He blinked at her, "You changed. Shame. You looked good in that dress."

Phin returned to the table with a large bottle of wine. "It's cheap only because they water it down I'm sure. Also, all they have is wine! Don't these people know how to let loose?"

She wanted to comfort him. She wanted to tell him he was better off without her. She wanted to say there were others out there. Maybe he needed to find another girl. A girl like her perhaps. She looked at Phin and then back to

Oberic, "Phineas and I were going for a walk and I thought it better to change so that I didn't get it dirty. You know Rennyn would have my neck for that."

Oberic shrugged, "If either of you are planning on getting into a mess, make sure you get yourselves out. I don't need what's left of my good name to be tarnished. Or do. I don't care." He grabbed the bottle from Phin who was struggling with the cork. He popped it with no issue and poured his glass to the top. "I wonder what issues she's having with the city. This place looks like it's run very smoothly."

Phin took a long swig from the bottle and then passed it to Jayda who took a much longer drink. Oberic bolted up straight and slammed his fists down on the table. Jayda startled and spilled red wine down her outfit and then glared at Oberic. "I bet she has a mirror!" Oberic exclaimed.

Phin asked, "So? Every woman has a mirror. Except maybe her." He nodded to Jayda who then glared at him instead.

"Hey! Watch it!" She punched Phineas in the arm.

"Oh, I'm sorry. You walk around acting *so* lady-like all the time. Now Ren, that's a gal that has a mirror." Phineas said, giving a hard nod at his assessment of the two.

Oberic stared with amusement at Phineas, "You're somewhat stupid, aren't you?"

Jayda did her best to ignore Phineas now after he insulted her. "A mirror? What kind of mirror?"

"Evelyn calls herself High Priestess, and that she is, but she fails to mention that she is also a wizard, or a witch if you prefer that term. You'd be wrong in that statement but that is neither here nor there. Nearly everyone from Maer'lyn has a special mirror. It's old and ancient magic used to communicate with other wizards."

Jayda didn't pretend to understand what he was going on about. She was still getting used to the fact that she wasn't hunting anyone down for even talking about it. "Do you think that has something to do with the issues she's having?"

"I'm thinking, if she has the right size, it may be a gate to Maer'lyn. Her issues in Hadryn are her own. I doubt she needs our help for it." Oberic said before taking a drink from his glass. The wine spilled over it's edge and onto the table.

Jayda took another long drink from the bottle of wine. Oberic was right, it was watered down. "Do you need access to that mirror? I bet Phin and I could acquire it for you."

Oberic shook his head, "I don't need it, but even if I did, I doubt she'd deny me that." He lifted the glass to take another drink and then stopped, "How would you two even know where to go?"

Jayda and Phineas shared a look and they both looked back at him. Phineas spoke up first, "I'm sure it wouldn't be hard to find."

Oberic shrugged, "Maybe not." and stood up. He placed the hat back on his head and tugged it down. "I'm going to the cathedral, the big one, if either of you care to join me."

"I'll join you," Jayda said. She stood up and pulled her hair over her shoulder. She looked at Phin and offered an apologetic smile. Their adventure to find trouble was done for now.

"I don't want to tempt any ladies of the cloth so I'll stay behind or head back to the palace. This place is kind of boring." Phin tipped the bottle back and finished the rest. Oberic rolled his eyes and he and Jayda left the tavern together.

They were both quiet as they walked down the streets lit now by lanterns. Oberic apologized, "I am sorry if I ruined a night you and Phineas were sharing. I did not think anyone would be going to a tavern but me. If you'd rather stay with him I would not be offended."

Jayda glanced at him, "No, it's fine. It wasn't that kind of a thing."

"I'm sorry," Oberic replied, "I didn't mean to imply anything."

"I'm sure we would have gotten into some sort of trouble. Dwim made it very clear that we should behave, so I am. Besides," she looked at Oberic again, her eyes sparkling in the dim light, "I am happy to see more of the city with you."

She nudged his arm softly with her elbow. "No Amun tonight? Has he decided to give your ears a break?"

"I've actually got him doing me a favor."

"Oberic," she stopped him in the street, "Is Amun, you know, a normal bird?"

Oberic shrugged. "I've often wondered that myself. If there's anything magical about him, I can't sense it." They continued to walk again.

"What do you have him doing?"

"I asked him to survey the city from the sky. Just curious what the issue might be. He hasn't returned yet though so I'm going to the cathedral bell tower to take a look myself."

They turned down a few streets here and there until they arrived at the base of the cathedral. They both looked up in awe. The steps leading up into the cathedral were bare. "All the way to the top?" Jayda asked. Oberic nodded. Together, they climbed the massive steps leading up to the equally massive doors that were held open by large wooden beams in front of them acting as door stops. As soon as they entered, their ears were filled with a choir of beautiful voices singing softly, one of the many hymns of Olm. There were many people, even at this time of night, who knelt and prayed. Candles filled the cathedral giving off a beautiful glow. Moonlight shone through the stained glass windows each of which portrayed Olm in one way or another. Oberic said nothing, but his eyes watered a bit at the chilling feeling the choir of voices sent into him. It was not that the hymn was profound in any way but the absolute dedication and devotion in the voices of those who sung it from their lips; it made him wish he had that much faith in anything at all.

Jayda did not feel chills, but instead a warmth both physically and emotionally. She remanded quiet as she stood close to him, reaching out now and again, to rest a hand on his shoulder. Her emerald eyes darted around trying to take in the absolute majesty of her surroundings. They traveled down the aisle slowly and when they nearly reached the altar Oberic pointed to the right corner, "Door. Probably a staircase leading up to the bell tower." They moved to the door and as they opened it they found he was quite incorrect. The door led to a dimly lit library. At the end of the library however they would find another door that would lead up to the bell tower. They climbed it together. Jayda walked side by side with him, unsure of what to say or even if she should say anything at all. In that silence, the tapping of their feet on the stone was the only thing to be heard. The climb seemed to last forever, but when they finally did make it they both seemed taken away by the view they had while under the cathedral's bell. "Now isn't that a sight?" he asked as he moved to the railing and looked over the city.

"It's beautiful." she added, as she joined him at the railing. The city was lit by thousands of oil lamps and torches. "Oberic, where are you from?"

"You mean where was I born?"

Jayda nodded, "Is that okay to ask?"

"I don't know where I was born. Just that it was a farm. My parents were supposedly too poor to raise a child."

"Do you not fear magic at all? Are you not angry about it being the reason you were torn from your family?"

"I'm more fearful of the hearts of people. Hateful hearts can and will hurt others regardless if they can weave magic or not." Oberic turned to look at Jayda and saw that she was crying, "Jayda, what's wrong?"

"I'm sorry," she wiped her eyes, "I was thinking about Angus and that terrible thing that had him. Then I started thinking about my parents and I just. . ." she sniffed and cleared her throat.

"Tell me about your family." Oberic said and placed a hand on her back.

'No. You don't want to hear about it."

"I'd like to understand what caused you to distrust magic so much that you distrust me."

She turned and looked at him. Her wet emeralds glimmered in moonlight, "I don't distrust you, Oberic."

"Then trust in me now. Share your story. Might help to get it off your chest." Oberic said. Jayda nodded, wiped her eyes again, and sighed. Where to begin? She thought for a long moment and then decided she knew exactly where to start.

CHAPTER 15

It was no secret in Lilly Tree that Desmond LaReux, a good looking miner with coal colored hair and emerald eyes, was having relations with other women outside of his marriage to Sylvia. Not once had he ever really tried to hide it. After a long day in the mines, chiseling away at rock and ore, he liked to relax at the tavern with the other miners and a few ladies of the night. He could have very well been home and spending time with his wife and their only child; still, every night, it was beers, dancing, and drunk sex in one of the whore's rooms.

Sylvia, the fool of a woman, would spend those nights watching out the window and wishing that for once he would come home to her instead. Sylvia was not blind and was very aware of what was happening; not that it was absolutely behind her back. Desmond and Sylvia had met each other years and years before when they were younger. Her hair was ink black and her eyes emerald as well and the two seemed to naturally pull towards each other and so it would stand to reason that their daughter, now five, had raven colored hair and emeralds of her own.

How many nights had their daughter Jayda, so named after Sylvia's favorite story of The Aegis and The Lady, asked when daddy was going to come home? Sylvia knew that even one night was far too many. She took in a deep sigh and continued to watch out the window. The woman had once been plump, but had wasted away to thin skin and angular facial features. She did not eat nor did she sleep much at all; only when her body simply could not be awake any longer.

When Desmond would come home, a rarity, it was never pleasant and on occasion violent. Jayda would sit on the floor and play with her wooden toys while Desmond berated and yelled at Sylvia over nothing at all. On increasing occasions, he would hit her and Jayda would get up and leave the room. Even then, Jayda not fully understanding the situation, knew that wasn't supposed to be happening. On those nights she would go and pretend she couldn't hear him yelling or hear her crying.

Desmond, the worthless man he was, did take care of the finances and made sure food was available to them. Sylvia learned to no longer cook for him which helped. They learned to eat heated soups from the day before. When Desmond wasn't home, Jayda and Sylvia had a mostly good peaceful time together. They played and sang children's songs to each other. Sylvia would share stories and fairy tales from when she was a child and always shared the story of The Aegis and The Lady, who as mentioned before was also named Jayda, every other week or so. This was routine until Desmond grew far too bold and began to enjoy the misery he caused his wife.

Even now, Jayda could remember the night so very clearly. Desmond had come home from the tavern while she was playing on the floor. Her mother had asked her to go to bed several times already but did nothing to enforce it. Sylvia stood up, genuinely happy to see her husband return, as she always was. Desmond grabbed her by the arm and pulled her from in front of himself to the side as he escorted another woman into their home. Sylvia looked at Desmond with a mixture of shock and hatred. It was more insulting that the woman he brought with him did not even compare in beauty to what Sylvia in her best years looked like.

"Jayda, go to bed." Slyvia said in a low and stern tone.

"But mama, I don't-" Jayda started

"Now Jayda or I'll tear your hide!" Sylvia shouted. Jayda jumped up and ran to her room. She was not used to being yelled at by her mother. Once Sylvia heard the door shut she continued, "Desmond, who is this woman and what is she doing in *our* home?"

"Calm down, Sylvia," Desmond started. The girl was hanging all over him and Sylvia could feel her blood boiling, "She's just a friend."

"A good friend," the girl added. She giggled and ran her fingers through his hair.

"I am not stupid, Desmond!" She was screaming at him now. "I know what you do at night! I know who you see! There is not a passing day where I can't hear their whispers about our marriage out in town! I take all that in stride and do my best to make something of this work, but you will *not* bring another woman into this house!"

Desmond stepped towards Sylvia and then lashed out. He slapped her across the face and threw her to the wooden floor. She would have cried if she could have gotten past the shock that he had actually hit her. This was not the first occasion upon which she was struck, but each time it happened she reacted as if it were the first. She knew things were bad, but never dreamed once that Desmond would ever strike her. Even after the last time, she never dreamed it would happen, but it always did. Desmond wasn't finished though. He made sure to add insult to injury and he unclothed the whore he had brought home and he had her right in front of Sylvia.

The next morning Desmond left for the mines. He left the whore in the bed he and his wife were supposed to be sharing while Sylvia slept in the front room. Once he was gone, she got up and woke the whore by hitting her with a broom. She screamed and cried. She called her a homewrecker and then grabbed her clothes and threw them out the front door. The whore rushed and grabbed them, taking off to the tavern once more.

Once that commotion was done, Sylvia sat by the window and bit at her fingertips as she looked out. Jayda had come into the room with big eyes and laid her head on her mother's lap. Sylvia twitched, a bit startled, and then stroked Jayda's head. There had to be a fix. There had to be something she could do to remedy the situation. She sat there for a long moment and then finally, something popped into her head.

She fed Jayda and got them both dressed. They left the house and began walking down the streets heading towards the outskirts of town. Though the mark on her face had cleared a while after he struck her, the sting was there. It bit into her heart and everytime she thought of it she nearly collapsed.

"Where are we going, mama?" Jayda asked, gripping her mother's hand tightly.

"We are going to meet someone. Mind your manners." Sylvia replied.

There was no lie there. She was indeed going to meet someone. Sylvia had no desire for revenge. She was a good woman and never wanted to hurt Desmond the way he hurt her. This person they were going to see was rumored, never proven, to be a witch. Sylvia knew about the Hunters and their special bracelets that detected magic use and so a part of her told her that this old hag could not be a witch for surely they would have found her already. Magic was forbidden and punishable by death. Still, something about this old woman screamed to Sylvia that she could help her.

What was once a sunny start to the day seemed to change as they neared the old woman's run down shack. As they neared closer, Sylvia stopped, knelt down in front of Jayda, and placed her hands on her cheeks. "I'm going to go inside and speak with the old woman. Stay right here and don't run off. I'll be out soon. Do you understand?" Jayda nodded and did just as she was told. Sylvia moved to the front door slowly. A certain unease penetrated her bones and she thought about turning away and leaving. Her hand raised to knock and then lowered. She took a step back. She decided she had changed her mind.

"Don't make an old woman wait." a voice from inside the shack called out. The door seemed to have opened on it's own. "Come in."

Sylvia looked back at Jayda who was doing just as she was told. She smiled at the beautiful little girl and then headed inside the shack. The shack was dirty and the smell of mold and piss filled Sylvia's nose. There was no flooring under her feet but soft wet ground. There was not much in this shack to observe. There was a small fireplace big enough to put a small pot in. There was a tiny table covered in bottles of strange liquids that bubbled. One bottle Sylvia was certain had an eye in it.

An old woman sat on a raggedy bed that seemed to barely be held together. Her ragged gown was short and showed off bony legs with loose skin. They were covered in spots of dark coloring and varied in size. They were also just as bushy as her eyebrows which hunger over big orbs colored onyx or at least it seemed to be that color in the light. The old woman barely had any hair on her head and when she opened her mouth she could see that there were no teeth at all.

"I'm well aware that I don't look very appealing, miss. No need to gawk at me. Sit." She jabbed a long hooked finger at the chair by the table. Sylvia did as she was told. "Now, what have you come for?"

Sylvia remained silent for a minute before she was able to gather her courage. "My husband-"

The old woman cut her off. "Yes, your husband Desmond has been fucking every girl he can get. The whole town knows about that. I'm not looking for a history lesson, girl. I want to know what you *want*." Sylvia thought for a moment. Her mouth opened but no words came out. She didn't want to hurt Desmond. She wasn't even sure what this woman could do. She clasped her lips together and stared blankly. "Ah," the old hag said as she got to her feet, "I know what you want." Her knees knocked together repeatedly as she stood there. She made her way, very slowly, across the one room shack and grabbed something from a shelf. She looked at the object, mumbling something to herself, and then hobbled to Sylvia when she found that she was satisfied with it. She laid it on the table in front of Sylvia.

Sylvia looked down on the table and saw the petrified ear of some animal or creature. She let out a scream and then covered her mouth in fear that the old woman would be insulted. The old hag was not offended and in fact seemed quite happy to have caused such a fright. "What is it?" Sylvia asked while her emerald eyes examined the long and pointed ear.

"The ear of an Elf." She said plainly. "Enchanted to help you forget your woes."

"How can I be sure it works? If you did magic the Hunters would be coming for you, wouldn't they?"

"Those cheap bracelets? Who do you think enchants them here, girl. Do not let the crown of Marrenval deceive you into thinking there is no magic here still; there are ways to fool them. All you have to do is hold it up to your head and think of the memory you want to forget and just like that, it'll be gone. Lost to you forever."

Sylvia reached down to pick the petrified ear up. Her hand shook as her fingers nearly grazed it. The hag reached out fast though and grabbed her wrist so tightly that Sylvia let out a whimper.

"Payment first, girl!"

"I have coin. How much?"

The old woman sneered, "I know you've heard tales about my kind, girl. You think we deal in the arts to place our hands upon riches and treasures? No. I require something more precious."

"Such as?" Sylvia asked, unsure of what she meant.

The old woman's eyes rolled back in their sockets showing nothing now other than cream colored and moist whites. Jayda, who had been sitting outside patiently, turned her head to look at the shack. She had a strange idea she was being watched. "A blood price must be paid! The first of hers offered to the goddess Malluscena!"

Sylvia had no idea what the old woman was talking about and nodded her agreement. "Yes! If that is what you need so long as Jayda and I are safe!" The old woman released her grip and her eyes rolled back down and gazed at Sylvia.

"Oh, precious little Jayda will be okay." A string of spit hung between her lips. "Go on, now. Our dealing is done. Remember, think of the memory and place it upon your brow."

Sylvia grabbed the ear and nearly tipped the chair back as she got up. She exited the shack fast, leaving the old hag to cackle madly. She grabbed Jayda's hand, who was quite thankful to be leaving, and they both rushed away from the terrible feeling that the shack put inside them both.

When they arrived home and Sylvia had time to calm her nerves she looked at the petrified ear. Had she been played a fool? She wondered if the old woman really could fool the bracelets of the Hunters. The memory of Desmond striking her in the face and having the woman right in front of her popped up in her head and without thinking she placed the petrified ear against her brow. The ear barely touched her skin when the memory was gone. She sat there quietly wondering why she had the creepy thing pressed against her head. She removed it and looked it over. She remembered that the old woman said it could remove memories, but she had no idea what memory she wanted erased so badly. So it became a regular occurence that anytime Desmond hurt Sylvia, she would place the petrified ear against her brow and forget the pain and sorrow.

Sylvia had become happier. She started to play with Jayda more and even gained a bit of weight as she ate and slept better than ever. Desmond's behavior never changed. If anything, he pushed the line as far as he could. Bringing women home just about every night and forcing her to take part in their night time activities. In the morning she would hold the ear to her brow and it would be gone.

Jayda of course was aware of the gross ear that her mother continued to push against her forehead. She didn't seem to mind though as every time her mother did it, she was in a better mood. Time went on for them all. Desmond continually being terrible, her mother continually using the ear, and Jayda continually being happy when her mother was happy. Anyone who seriously dealt in the arcane arts could have told Sylvia that using magic, even that of an enchanted item, corrupted the soul. It was a lesson she would learn but never understand that it was such.

It was not long after Desmond decided to leave his wife and child behind. Perhaps he had grown bored with the night to night torture he had given Sylvia or maybe he didn't even care about Jayda enough to stay. He didn't even leave them a note. He packed his belongings and said nothing. He would never return. He wouldn't even send money for them to live on. Sylvia had taken to erasing memories of Desmond all together and when Jayda would ask when papa was coming home she would laugh and ask "Who are you talking about?" and then go about her business.

Food began to run short and Sylvia, for the life of her, could not understand why money was becoming an issue. For as long as she could remember she had always done well enough to provide for Jayda and herself and always had time to be around and take care of the home. She just couldn't remember what it was that she did for a living. She did know that she needed money though and when she couldn't think of any of the skills she used to take care of them she began to sell her body.

The ear was used more and more as night after night she was used by men for only a few coins at time. That rapidly progressed into using it anytime she felt unhappy at all. Eventually, Jayda who was now a year older, would come inside their home that was starting to fall apart and find her mother sitting in her chair. Drool hung from her lip and ran down her chin. Her eyes were glossy and she would never be aware again. She had used the ear so much to erase anything unpleasant that she at some point removed everything she ever knew. She only sat there staring at the wall and soiling herself. Jayda tried to rouse her mother but after hours of trying, she accepted that she could not.

Jayda found herself living on the streets of Lilly Tree, taking food from strangers when it was offered and smart enough to run away from men who asked if she wanted to come home with them. Her mother passed away in the chair. The smell of death eventually caused enough issues that the home went to be inspected. Jayda of course had stuck around the area for it was the only home she knew. Even the ones that they called Hunters had appeared to investigate. They had found the petrified Elf ear and destroyed it. A tall black man had stepped outside the home and spotted Jayda staring at him. He moved towards her and knelt down in front of her.

"You must be Jayda." He said, doing his best to offer her a smile. Jayda nodded. "I'm sorry to tell you, but your mother has passed on, girl." Jayda looked down and shed a few tears, but did not cry as one would expect a girl of her age to do. In her heart, her mother died long before. The man, who looked to be getting on in years, grabbed her shoulders, "Jayda, do you know what killed your mother?"

Jayda spoke softly, "It was the ear, wasn't it?"

The man nodded, "Jayda, it was enchanted with dark magic. You know what Hunters do?" Jayda nodded. "Good. Jayda, I am a Hunter," he showed off the bracelet, "I want to stop whoever did this to her, but I need your help. Will you help me?" Jayda nodded once more. "Can you tell me where she got it?"

It wasn't more than two hours later that the Hunters had dragged the old woman from her shack and beat her mercilessly in the streets. Jayda stood there with the Hunter who had spoken to her and watched as the old woman cackled loudly just before she was beheaded. The shack, with ease, was torn down and it's debris destroyed. When it was all done, the old man knelt down in front of Jayda again.

"Do you have anywhere else to go, Jayda?"

"No." She admitted.

"Will you come with us? The Hunters I mean. Most of us are orphans too. We can take care of you and you'll be safe with us. I swear that to you."

Jayda thought for a moment and then examined him with emerald eyes, "Will I become a Hunter? I want to help."

The man nodded, "I can train you. You'll learn to fight against the very thing that tore your family apart."

'What's your name?" She asked.

"Angus." He replied, smiling at the innocence of a child who would now have to learn to grow very quickly.

Oberic watched her wipe at her eyes again. She had never told the story to anyone before and it felt good to get it out of her. Oberic did not want to impede on her space nor was he much at comforting anyone as he had not been doing well at comforting himself over the last twenty years. When he spoke, it was soft and apologetic, "I'm sorry. That is a terrible fate."

Jayda shook her head, "No need to apologize. Nothing could have been done. I know that." The voices of the choir singing a new song below them made her feel at ease and she found some sort of peace standing there with him under the bell. She had shared her story and would never do so again. She found herself being thankful Oberic was the one to hear it. "What about you, Oberic? There has to be more to your story."

Oberic shook his head. He didn't believe there was. Nothing really defined the person he would be other than a genuine curiosity about the world and the books he studied. "I'm afraid not."

"And you and Evelyn?" she asked, not sure if she really wanted to hear that story or not.

"Look," Oberic pointed outwards towards the city wall where a faint white glow pulsated. He was eager to change the subject. "She's cast some sort of barrier around the city." He squinted, "I can't see what she's trying to keep out though."

She picked up his ruse and nodded, deciding to drop the subject. "Sounds like we have something to look into while we're here."

"I wouldn't suggest it," Evelyn said from behind them. They both jumped and turned to face the woman. "Something dark has appeared in the forest there. Something I've never seen before." Oberic turned around to face out towards the city again.

"Well, you're not us." Oberic said. Jayda raised her eyebrow and looked away from Evelyn. "Jayda and I are professionals."

Jayda looked back to Evelyn, feeling somewhat protective over Oberic. She stood tall and her fingers ran against the whip at her side. "I'm not worried about darkness in the trees."

Evelyn didn't seem to be bothered by the look, "You should be. The dead walk there." She stepped to the other side of Oberic and looked out across the city. "I know you have some books on necromancy, Oberic, but I think this is far beyond that. I've sent my Paladins in to investigate, but only a few have returned."

Jayda didn't like being ignored by the High Priestess, "I don't think you understand. Neither of us fear what may be in the wilds," she puffed her chest out, "and you don't give Oberic enough credit!"

Evelyn raised a single brow. If she was bothered or shocked, she did not show it. "He does like the fiery ones," her crystal eyes fell upon Jayda's face, "at least save yourself the trouble and go during the day. Skilled as you may be, an army failed out there." She looked back to Oberic. "Oberic, speak reason to this girl."

Oberc shrugged, "She's right. We'll handle it just fine."

Her feet were planted firmly in a powerful stance. She was a Hunter and the attitude and confidence that came with it started to bleed through. "Perhaps it is best we find accommodations elsewhere. I would hate for my unreasonable temper and small amount of patience to be tested"

Evelyn gasped, "I am not your enemy, girl! I am simply trying to save your neck!"

"Keep calm, Eve." Oberic said, turning to her, "Jayda has quite the punch."

Eve looked at Oberic, quite stunned by the comment or perhaps it was meant as a threat. She drew in a sharp breath, "I am not saying that you can't handle the issue! I would just feel better if you didn't go at night!"

Jayda said her last to Eve for the evening in such a cold tone that even Oberic seemed to be frozen by it, "You forfeited the right to care for him when you left him without a word!"

The color drained from Evelyn's face. Even Oberic looked at Jayda quite stunned by the comment. Eve's eyes locked on to Oberic as she growled out her words, "Is that what you do now, Oberic Wintersong? Do you tell every woman you meet about how you were left behind?" Eve did not give him time to respond. She turned and stormed off down the staircase into the cathedral.

Oberic watched her go and then looked at Jayda, "I haven't seen her that mad since we were kids." Jayda smirked as Oberic turned and faced the city again. "I didn't tell you that though. How did you know?"

Jayda's smirk vanished and was replaced by a look of guilt. Oberic, had he looked at her, would have thought she looked like a child who was caught stealing candy. He wouldn't look though, not right now, not when the subject matter was so sensitive to him. "Well, Phineas convinced me it would be a good idea to go see if we could dig up any secrets on Evelyn," she wrung the grip of the whip in her hand, "but then we heard her coming so we hid under the bed. We may have overheard some, no, we heard all of it." She placed a hand on Oberic's shoulder. "I didn't mean to intrude on such a personal matter, Oberic. I swear it."

Oberic looked down for a while not saying anything, maybe embarrassed by his vulnerability. Jayda hung her head low feeling ashamed. She was on the verge of telling him that she'd leave him alone when he spoke. "I've tried to drink away her memory for many years and not once had it ever worked. Even my dreams were plagued by that woman. Seeing her today," he shook his head, "letting go of those rings; I feel free now. I think she was right about one thing."

Jayda looked at him again, "And what's that?"

"I don't think I'm living to my full potential. I don't know what I'm doing at all, really. Maybe I could be doing better though."

Jayda shook her head quickly, reaching out and taking his hand in hers. "No! Never think that. You, who was willing to give up your own life to save a ship full of children and us, people you hardly knew," She pulled her hand from his and lifted it to touch his face. His skin felt hot under her palm as she forced him to look into her eyes "you saved me even after I treated you terribly. You are wonderful the way you are."

They stared at one another. Jayda studied his face and found that he seemed to look at her as if truly seeing her for the first time. Oberic leaned in slowly, meaning to kiss a woman for the first time in over twenty years. Jayda closed her eyes and leaned up and into the kiss. "Caw!" Amun had fluttered in between them just before their lips touched.

Oberic straightened up and cleared his throat, "Sorry."

Jayda's chest rose and fell as he moved away from her. She glared at the crow for ruining the moment. She wanted to grab Oberic, the fool that he was, and shake him until he kissed her like she needed him to. Amun opened his mouth and dropped a finger onto the railing. Oberic and Jayda, who was still catching her breath, examined the finger. It was rotting but they didn't find that the most disturbing part. What disturbed them most is that it was still moving.

"You and I have a different idea of a good dinner, my friend." Oberic said as he looked over it.

"Oberic! It's still moving!" She gasped. Oberic nodded. Jayda looked at Amun, forgiving his intrusion for the moment, and spoke to the bird as if she expected it to answer her back, "Where did you find it?" Amun cawed and Jayda shook her head wondering why she even bothered to ask.

Oberic looked out over the city again, "Probably from behind the barrier. Amun, take the finger back beyond the wall. Can't risk spreading anything here in the city; whatever it may be." Amun cawed again, picked up the finger, and flew off. Oberic looked at Jayda and asked, "Now or morning?"

Jayda stepped to him and placed her hands on his shoulders, leaning in to kiss him, "Now. . ."

Oberic took her hands and held them but did not lean in, "I mean when should we leave to investigate?"

Jayda looked at Oberic, a mix of hurt and insult on her face. Her cheeks became scarlet and she reached up and slapped him across the cheek before she stormed off down the staircase. Oberic called out to her, but she did not respond. He stood there for a long time wondering why he didn't kiss her. He had no reason at the moment, but felt that he would regret not doing so. Scared of being hurt again perhaps? "Fine mess you're making, Oberic. Fine mess indeed." Amun returned and perched on Oberic's shoulder.

The cathedral's bell ringer appeared at the top of the staircase and shouted, "Might want to head down sir. These bells will make you go deaf."

Oberic nodded, "I'll do that. Thank you."

"What'd you say?" The man asked, poking his head out to hear him a bit more clearly.

Oberic smiled, patted the man on the shoulder, and headed down the staircase. He left the cathedral and it's beautiful singing voices. He walked slowly back to the palace where the guard let him in. The halls were empty and dark, but he found his way to his room without an issue. He stopped for a moment just outside Jayda's door and raised a hand to knock. He paused and just as fast as the idea had come, it was gone. He entered his own room and shut the door. Amun flew from his shoulder and made himself comfortable on the bed. Oberic joined him by throwing himself on the bed. Once he was comfortable, he let out a long sigh, "Fine mess."

CHAPTER 16

The morning came quicker than Jayda had hoped. She had gone through so many emotions in one night and this morning was no better. She considered running to Oberic's room to tell him if he needed time that she would wait. Then she got mad at herself for even thinking about it. It's not like she was in love with the man. Even as she thought it, a voice inside her demanded she at least be honest with herself and admit that she loved him. She refused.

She fixed her hair and tried to force her Hunter attitude back into her mind. She was tough and strong and she didn't need the geezer to want her. She was ready to leave and she swung the door open with such vigor that it threatened to come off the hinges. Yet, she found herself walking to Oberic's door. She stood there staring at it. Before she could stop herself she lifted her hand and knocked. She silently swore at herself and yet did not move a foot. She waited and when she got no answer she opened the door. Oberic was nowhere to be seen. She wondered if he had even returned at all. Surely Oberic wouldn't have left without saying anything to her, or them, but mostly her. She walked down the halls and found the group, excluding Oberic, in the throne room with Evelyn.

They were all hunched over a table where Evelyn was showing them a map that included the forest where Amun had found the rotting and still alive finger. Eve cast a cold glare to Jayda, but remained as polite as she could possibly be. "You're just in time. Your friends are discussing a plan to venture into the forest to investigate."

"And Oberic? Where is he?" Jayda asked.

"Gone," Ren said casually, "Left before dawn."

Jayda's heart sank. She never thought he would but she was wrong. She lashed out at Ren, "And you just let him leave?"

They all looked at her. Jayda could have sworn she saw a flicker of a smile on Eve's face. Dwim's face was twisted with bewilderment and he raised a brow, "Said he had to do some thinking and that he'd return when he was ready, lass. Ye' okay?"

Jayda felt foolish immediately and she lowered her voice, "Any idea where he may have gone?"

Alastor looked up at Jayda and spoke in that harsh husky voice, "Just that he thought the choir might help him think. Do you have any-" She did not wait to hear his question. She exited the palace and left each of them looking at her, and then each other, in bewilderment. Once she was clear of the palace steps and in the street she took off at a full sprint towards the cathedral. She raced up the steps and when she entered, she looked around hoping to see his stupid pointed hat sticking out of the crowd that had gathered for prayer this morning. She walked, taking a glance in every direction, hoping to pick him out of the crowd, but she did not see him. Something in her stomach told her to head up the staircase to the bell tower. She listened to her gut as she used to do and climbed the steps beyond the library as fast as she could. When she reached the top she took a moment to breathe. What was she doing? What was she going to say? She had no idea. She also had no idea what she was going to do when he rejected her but, she knew that she had to say something to him. Anything at all would be better than nothing.

She climbed a bit more and when her head broke the horizon of the tower floor she saw him. His back was turned to her and he wasn't wearing either his coat or his hat. "Oberic. . ." her voice carried his name on an air of relief. She stepped towards him quickly. Oberic turned around and looked at her; Amun did the same. For a brief moment she almost stopped, but she knew in her heart she had to say something. She reached him and began to blurt everything out at him, "I was too forward and if you need more time-"

Oberic took his hands and placed it against the sides of her face. He brought her beautiful visage closer to himself and leaned in. The sorcerer placed his lips against hers. Her body was not her own as her arms betrayed her and wrapped themselves around his neck. First it was only their lips mashing together, but it soon gave way to their tongues dancing with one another in a heated moment of passion filled with desire and need. Both of them tangled their hands in the other's hair and when they broke away from each other; they gazed into each other's eyes. She knew at that moment that Oberic Wintersong belonged to her and she to him.

"Why didn't you kiss me last night?" She asked him.

"Because I'm a fool. I have no other excuse than that." he said to her, being quite sincere. She buried her face against his chest and they held each other for a while. They needed no other words. Both of them knew that it was the start of something between them and a fresh start seemed to be all that either of them wanted. How nice it would be for them to do so together.

The two of them, and Amun of course, returned together sometime past noon. When they entered the palace, the others turned to look at them. They joined the group and Jayda leaned up and kissed Oberic on the cheek. She then turned her emerald eyes to Evelyn. She didn't seem to have anything to say on the matter, but her gaze was just as cold as earlier. "How lovely of you to finally join your friends, Oberic." Evelyn remarked. She seemed to have been annoyed that he was not there earlier. Rennyn elbowed Leon and nodded towards Oberic and Jayda with a child-like grin on her face. "We are discussing how the dead walk in those woods. Risen from our own graveyards outside the city. I have tried many spells, but nothing is putting a stop to the issue. The barrier keeps them out and that's all.

"Between the seven of us, I think we stand a pretty good chance." Ren said. Amun cawed in agreement. Ren did not mean to sound cocky, but the High Priestess took it that way. After all, she had lost many well trained Paladins who spent their lives dedicated to fighting such terrible things and they had failed.

"If you fail, we will not be able to retrieve your corpses. If the circumstances were different at all-" Evelyn was saying when Phineas cut her off.

"We'll be fine." He waved a hand at her. Evelyn had started to become angry.

Alastor grunted his approval, "Living or dead. They shall fall."

Evelyn sighed, "Do you need weapons? Armor?"

Dwim nodded, "We lost everything when our ship sank."

Evelyn understood and had an answer, "I'll get our blacksmiths to fit you and make you top priority for smithing. You will be equipped well before you head into the darkness."

Each of them lost their gear except Jayda who never let the whip leave her side and Ren who carried her satchel with her wooden chest everywhere she went. Oberic mumbled something about having a staff. Ren looked at Phin and asked, "How well do you think you could control the wolf?"

Jayda looked up and shook her head, "Hold on a second, Ren. . ."

"Just hear me out," Ren said as she continued to push the subject, "I have faith that he could control it if he took off the amulet."

Phineas's fingers reached up and touched the silver amulet of the White. Evelyn was thankfully sane enough to shoot the idea down immediately, "I will not allow that curse to run loose in my lands. If the wolf comes out, we slay it. Are we clear?"

Jayda uncoiled the whip and snapped it on the floor, "Anyone who lays a hand on Phineas will lose it shortly after. That includes you, High Priestess." The guards in the palace immediately drew their swords and stepped in to surround the group. Evelyn held her hand up.

"Calm down, everyone," Evelyn glared at Jayda, "She isn't *that* stupid. Besides, she wouldn't want to hurt Oberic."

"Aye," Dwim made sure his voice was loud enough for everyone, "While Oberic's ego is being stroked, I'd like to say that I nay think releasing the wolf is a good idea. It almost got Ren once, already." Dwim looked at Ren and gave her an apologetic nod. "No offense, lass."

"No," Ren said, placing a hand on Dwim's shoulder, "you're right. The risk would be too great. I shouldn't have suggested it."

"I didn't think it was a great idea either. I don't want to hurt any of you." Phineas trailed off.

"I'll take the lead on this excursion if that's alright with all of you. I can sense magic. Evelyn can too, but I'm assuming you're not coming. Are you?" Oberic looked at Evelyn who had been glaring at Jayda still.

"No. I have a city to look after." Eve replied.

"That's it then. Go get fitted. Get your hands on some weapons. We'll leave first thing in the morning." Oberic said in a commanding voice. Jayda wondered if he was doing this to show off in front of Evelyn in some strange attempt to win her back. The truth was much more simple than that. Oberic Wintersong now had a purpose.

The rest of the day was filled with getting their armors and weapons sorted. The blacksmiths and leather workers were doing their best to make sure the group would be well protected. Dwim picked out a new shiny sword and shield to go with his armor of the White. Alastor picked up two new axes. Ren and Leon both chose a bow. Leon had been training her on their travels and she was getting rather confident with it. Jayda had no need for weapons as she still had her whip, sword, and daggers. Phineas picked out a rapier and dagger. Oberic chose nothing.

They were all fitted for either new armor or leathers. Even Jayda accepted the new leathers so long as she didn't have to get rid of her fur cloak. Leon, Ren, Oberic, and Phin all decided they'd rather be left to their linens to allow more movement. Alastor let them know he would be removing his pants and shirt when it came time so that he could battle in the Orc way. They all made sure that he would at least wear some kind of loincloth.

Things remained a bit awkward between Oberic and Jayda. They walked side by side nearly everywhere as Amun jumped from one to the other. They had not shared a kiss since that morning and neither was sure if going in for another was the right thing to do. They both figured they would fall into a routine at some point though. They both, without saying so, decided to continue to let it be fresh and new.

The others were not blind to their affection. They watched as the two of them carried on, making sure to point out every sweet gesture one made for the other and giggling like school children about it. Alastor had joined Oberic's side to talk with him about a strategy for when they were entering the wilds. Phin took this time to grab Jayda's wrist and pull her back to his side.

"Alright, pal. Details. You got your geezer. How was the sex?" Phin asked, staring at the back of Oberic, "I can't imagine it's very good."

Jayda rolled her eyes, but couldn't help the flush that flooded her cheeks. "Shut up. Nothing like that happened. Just a kiss. A simple kiss." It wasn't simple at all. She knew in her gut that both of them felt something there more magical than anything Oberic could have conjured up. "Mind your business."

"You were my business until you went and got hooked by the old man. What do you see in the guy anyway?"

"I don't know." She said, being completely honest. She knew that she saw something in him when he saved her from the creature that took over Angus. She knew she felt it more when he saved everyone but himself. "Maybe because I know Oberic would always put others before himself." She blushed even harder, "That he'll put me before himself."

"Yikes, you're going to make me puke. Enough. I'm sorry I asked." He said, giving an exaggerated gag. Jayda elbowed him and they shared a laugh.

They would share a dinner that night in the palace. Ren, Jayda, and Dwim were the first to appear at the table where Evelyn was already seated. Jayda watched one of the Paladins on duty speak to the High Priestess and for a brief moment she could have sworn Oberic was in that armor parading around in a disguise. The guard left just as Oberic was entering. He sat down next to Jayda and gave her a smile. Phin, Alastor, and Leon came soon after. When they were all seated, Evelyn asked everyone to bow their heads. When they did, she recited a blessing for the meal and ended it with "Praise be to Olm." Dwim repeated the line.

They mostly ate in silence except for Phineas who was talking loudly about all the "sweet ass" he had seen in the city that day. He then proceeded to tell Evelyn why a brothel would make a great addition to the city. Finally Dwim could no longer take it.

"How dare ye' talk that way in the presence of the High Priestess of the White! The holy mother, Ariel herself, must be rolling around in her grave! Have ye' no shame, lad?" Dwim's face was red and quite the contrast to his graying hair.

"I don't know what shame feels like." Phineas said simply and continued to shovel food into his face.

When dinner was done, and Dwim was finished patting his stomach to showcase his enjoyment, they decided it was best to retreat to their rooms to get a good night's rest. They would be setting out on foot in the morning. They all said their goodnights and entered their rooms except for Jayda and Oberic who stood there looking at one another longingly. Jayda finally rolled her eyes and fussed at him, "Get over here and kiss me, Oberic. Be a fool once more and you might end up hurt." He laughed and came to her. Her heart swelled and she knew then, like she knew earlier, that he would come to her anytime she called for him. They placed their lips to each other once more before she pushed him away and winked at him, "Good night, handsome."

The morning had come and Oberic was up before any of them. He knocked on their doors and pleaded with them to get up. When he knocked on Jayda's door, she opened it and pulled him in and gave him a hard deep kiss before pushing him out. She slammed the door and told him she needed to dress. Oberic liked it ,but hoped none of the others would greet him in the same manner.

They all came down around the same time to find Oberic and Evelyn standing outside the palace. Amun, as always, sat on Oberic's shoulder. She was adjusting his hat and coat for him. Jayda immediately grew ill tempered. Evelyn looked to the palace door and when she saw everyone, mostly Jayda, she offered a smile, "I'll walk you all to the city gates." Jayda went down the steps and wrapped her arm around Oberic's and threw her nose up as they started off. Evelyn walked on the other side of Oberic and the others followed behind. Rennyn made a face that Leon picked up on, both were thinking at some point Jayda and Evelyn were going to have it out.

As they made their way down the streets, people dropped to their hands and knees for the High Priestess. Blessings of Olm and praises were shouted at them. When they finally reached the gates, Evelyn lowered her head and said a prayer for the group. She spoke words that none but Oberic might have understood. "I have placed upon your weapons an enchantment of holy wrath. They are blessed and should you battle, may they guide your hand and allow your strikes to be true." Dwim lowered his head and thanked her in Dwarvish. "Open the gates!" She yelled out.

The gates opened and Oberic stood there looking out into the green wilds. He looked at his longtime friend and smiled, "You stay behind, Amun. We'll catch up again soon." Amun cawed and flew from Oberic's shoulder. The bird took to the sky above to become a black speck in the bluest of skies. The sorcerer removed his hat and pushed his arm inside shoulder deep and pulled from it a long sturdy staff topped by a strange crystal with no color. The clear crystal was held in place by wooden fingers that reached up and encased it. He slipped his hat back on and called out, "Dwim, you'll go in front. Jayda and Alastor will go behind him. I'll be in the middle. Ren and Leon will take up the rear making sure to pick off anything that comes up on us from behind. Phineas," Oberic looked at the scoundrel and shook his head, "you just stay close to me." He took a deep breath and looked at his friends. They were a strange collection of souls heading out to face darkness and he found that he wouldn't change that for anything, "If we die, it's been a pleasure." With those words, the group set out on the adventure to investigate the dead walking amid the living world.

They had stuck to the original formation like Oberic detailed for nearly two hours, but eventually broke it when nothing of any consequence was seen. Dwim still led the group in his new armor looking quite pleased to be in the service of the White again. Ren chatted to any and everyone who was willing to listen. Oberic hadn't said anything at all since they started out. Though he was the first to notice that the foliage, bright and green when they started, was now turning brown and looked to be dying; Alastor was the first to mention it. "The earth here is poisoned," it came out sounding more like a series of grunts, "whatever is in these wilds has begun to drain the life of these woods."

Ren looked around and did find that the trees, though fully grown, looked to be completely rotted. Even the sky above them was covered by dark clouds. There was a chill wind blowing dead leaves across the small path they walked as though setting the mood for what might lay ahead.

"There should be a town soon," Leon said, "Evelyn pointed it out on the map." Just as Leon had said it, they came across a sign that read "Oakember". They walked along the path further. Each could tell that at some point, as they neared the town, that the area up until very recently was quite lively. Wooden fences stood along the road and despite the dying scenery, they themselves were well crafted and taken care of. Lamp posts lined the road every few yards. At one point they provided light to travelers in the dark of night but had not been lit for a while. They finally came to the first house on the outskirts of town. They stopped and each looked at it for a moment. The house itself was in great shape and much like the fence, had been crafted by skillful hands that clearly had a passion for the craft. Stil, the feeling they got inside gave them chills. The creaking of a sign that swung in the wind from a nearby shop finally made Phineas speak.

"Spooky." was all he could manage to get out. The others nodded in agreement. They stepped away from the house and passed another, just as abandoned as the first, then one more, and when they reached the shop with the swinging sign they came to a stop all together again.

"I have a bad feeling about this." Rennyn said as she shuddered. She walked towards the shop and peered in through the clear window. "It's empty," she turned and looked at the group, "It's full of stuff though. It's like the people just vanished."

"They did not leave." Alastor said. The others turned to him and found that he was looking up at the trees that grew tall around them. They looked up as well. Ren let out a gasp and covered her mouth while Dwim whispered a prayer. Above them, tangled in the trees, hung the bodies of the villagers; upside down, tied by their ankles. The bodies were rotted and some even began to show bone.

"That's certainly not a good sign. Unless I'm just bad at reading these sorts of things." Leon said, trying to add a bit of humor to the ghastly situation but none laughed and rightfully so.

Ren looked at Oberic and asked, hoping he would have the answer, "Who could have done this? Why?" Jayda had uncoiled her whip and looked around.

"We know where the villagers went," Oberic started, "let's each take a house or shop and investigate inside. I'll stay outside and keep an eye out." He wanted to stay outside because he could feel the necrotic energy around him. It caressed his skin, it whispered in his ear, he felt it deep in his bones. His eyes were able to see the hidden things as he once told Jayda. Secrets not meant to be seen by anyone. It was a part of his speciality in illusion magic.

They all picked a house and entered cautiously. Phineas chose the shop Ren had been looking in. He walked inside and rubbed his hands together. Something had to be of value here. He walked to the shop counter and leaned over it to see what lay behind. As he did he was met by a strange wooden doll who stood as tall as he did once it was completely up on its feet. The candles in the shop lit around him and they seemed to burn brighter than Phin would imagine they could. The wooden thing had a stupid smile painted on it's face and wore a strange wig that looked as though a child had made it. He jumped back, shocked by this things sudden appearance

"The fuck you come from?" Phineas asked as he placed a hand over his chest. "Nearly made me shit my pants."

"Good evening sir," the wooden shopkeeper said, not once moving it's painted on lips, "what interests you today? We got a wide variety of ladies."

Phineas raised his brow. He liked what he was hearing already. "Ladies? Well, let's see them!" His interest had peaked. As he leaned on the counter five women came from the back room. Each of them was completely naked. A light, seemingly from nowhere, shined down on the first. She was thin and did not have much in the way of a shape. She was nearly flat, but her breasts were small and perky.

"This is Vivian! She loves rain storms and having a good time!" The wooden thing said. "Up next," the light moved to the next girl. She was tall and muscular with brown and wild hair, "Vivian! She loves rain storms and having a good time!" The light moved to the next. She was a short and thick woman with large breasts accented by two perfect dark nipples. Her skin was a creamy chocolate color and matched her big eyes perfectly. "This is Vivian! She loves rain storms and having a good time!"

"Vivian! I choose Vivian!" Phin said as he admired the dark skinned beauty. The other four girls smiled as they slowly sank back below the counter. Phin leaned and looked over the counter. "How are you doing that? Trap door or something?" He turned his head to face the wooden salesperson but he had vanished. Vivian had come around the corner and placed a soft hand against his face.

"Are you ready for the best mouth you've ever had your cock in?" Vivian bit her lip as she looked up at him. Phineas turned his head to look out the window and saw no one but Oberic who was simply staring up at the trees.

Phin looked back to Vivian and nodded eagerly, "Yeah, let's do this. It's been a long day!" He unlaced his trousers and pulled an already erect penis out. Vivian dropped to her knees and took him into her mouth. Phin closed his eyes and relaxed.

"I'm going to suck it off!" Vivian mumbled with a full mouth.

"Yeah you are!" Phin said, rather liking her style of dirty talk.

"I'm going to bite it off. I'm going to mash it between my teeth and I'm going to swallow the only thing you hold precious." She said in a sultry tone.

Phineas opened his eyes and frowned. It started out great, but he thought that had to have been the worst dirty talk he had ever heard. He looked down and his member immediately deflated. It was trapped between the teeth of a decomposing corpse. She looked up at him with dead eyes and smiled as a maggot crawled out of her nose. She gripped Phineas's manhood tightly in her cold hands. Phineas let out a scream and jerked away from the corpse.

Oberic, who had been standing outside, saw none of that through the window. He was far too busy trying to keep the voice out of his head. It whispered to him as if standing just beside him, "I could play tricks on you, Oberic Wintersong. You would fall for them just as the others would, but why miss this chance to talk when we're alone?"

"You're the thing that took Angus, aren't you? You hurt Jayda. You'll pay for that. I promise you that much."

"Oh and you're a man of your word, aren't you, Oberic Wintersong?'

"I am. Do I get the displeasure of knowing your name?"

"What makes you think I have one?"

"Just because no soul loves you enough to say your name doesn't mean you don't have one."

The voice laughed, "If you are the song of winter; then I shall declare myself it's death. Not to the season, but to the years. I am sorrow and pain and all your years shall be as cold and dead as the winter. You can call me Wintergrave."

"Well that's annoyingly on the nose."

The voice cackled, not just one, but in many voices, "I like you, boy. What fuels your nightmares I wonder? You aren't scared of the normal things, are you? No creepy crawlers, no monsters hiding under your bed? No, none of those things strike fear in you. You're a hard man, I'll give you that."

"Then you've got nothing on me. I'm glad you've realized that. Now show yourself so we can be done with this business."

"Oh I said none of the ordinary things frighten you, sorcerer, I didn't say you didn't have fears. Why didn't you kiss that beautiful girl the first time?"

Oberic frowned, "You can read minds. Cute."

"Oh I can do so much more, Oberic. I can even tell you why you didn't."

"Which is?"

"Rejected by love for so long. Tsk tsk. What if she broke your heart? Could you handle that again? Here's a secret, boy. She will."

Oberic shut his eyes. The bastard had been right. He had hesitated that night for the exact reason. He did his best to act like it wasn't, "You're wrong."

"Why would she have you?" the voice asked as ghostly visions of Jayda appeared hanging on to Leon and Phineas. "She could have both of them if she wanted. She's far too spirited for you. You're older than her. You don't have the fire that burns like she does."

Oberic dropped to his knees and shut his eyes tightly. Already he wondered if he had been a fool. What if this terrible thing could also see the future? What if it knew Jayda's heart better than he did. Oberic could hear the sound of glass breaking and the cry of Phineas as he hit the ground and rolled. The others rushed out of the houses they were investigating to see Oberic on his knees and Phineas getting to his feet. They looked at the glass on the ground and then to the shop window where the once lovely but now dead Vivian was crawling out. Her skin caught on shards of glass and ripped like paper as she made her exit.

The air filled with laughter; not just one voice but many voices. Dwim looked back up to the trees and froze. "Any of ye' seeing these poor souls laughing?"

Leon looked up and nodded, "Yeah, I see them."

Jayda lashed out and her whip wrapped around the torso of one of the laughing corpses. She gave a hard yank and the body tore in half. It's black innards spilled to the ground along with the other half of the body and landed with a sickening crunch. She had hoped it would cease it's laughter but she found that she was wrong; in fact it seemed to laugh harder now. They all covered their noses at the awful smell that came from the rottings guts.The thing had landed on its back and though it never stopped laughing, it did take the time to roll over on it's chest and start it's crawl towards them. Its bony fingers dug into the dirt and pulled itself along leaving a trail of black behind them.

The thing stopped laughing and said, "More bodies to claim." Then they all stopped laughing as they chanted, "More for us. More for us. More for us. More for us." They had begun to let themselves down from the ropes. Each fell with a sickening crunch as bones broke.

Rennyn screamed out and jumped in front of Leon, "Something touched my boot!" She looked down where she was standing and saw a hand, no longer attached to a body, pulling itself across the dirt towards her foot again. Phineas, who was still living in the horror of what happened to him, darted forward and kicked it towards a house. It made a thud as it slapped against the wood. When it landed in the grass, it flipped itself and started in their direction again.

The voices called out to them now, "I am your doom from the other side! I will devour you!"

Dwim drew his sword and held his shield in front of himself. He shouted out at them with his heavy accent "Nay without a fight ye' coward! Show yer'self!" The bodies that could stand, did; the others simply continued crawling to them. A man in what appeared to be a guard's outfit stepped out from a house. A cleaver was buried deep into his skull; the handle nearly obscuring the vision of one of his eyes.

The man called out to them, "There is no saving yourselves from yourselves." Everyone seemed to experience a vision issue. Each of them blinked their eyes and shook their heads as a strange fog seemed to take over them. They all felt the world spin under their feet and as they stumbled, eventually falling to their hands and knees where they found themselves alone.

Jayda's hands felt around the ground. Her hands grasped wet leaves and clumps of dirt. She looked up hoping to spot the others. Unfortunately, no one was there. She crawled to a tree and used it to pull herself up. It was not dark, but it did seem that she herself was the source of light. Her visibility only went for twenty feet or so; beyond that was pitch. Once her feet felt like they could hold her, she stood up tall and began to wander towards the darkness. As she approached, she could see more but looking back revealed that the darkness had engulfed what she left behind. She called out, "Oberic?" but got no reply.

Rennyn found herself sitting at her home in North Normoon in the same rocking chair that her mother passed away in. She opened her eyes wide and looked around herself. Everything was just as she remembered. The fire that roared in the fireplace warmed her skin and she leaned back in the chair. She furrowed her brow and questioned herself, "Did I dream all of that? Everything?" She stood up slowly and hoped the floor wouldn't give way. When she didn't fall through it, she walked to the front door carefully, and reached out to grab the knob. She closed her eyes and turned the knob, whispering, "Please let me be home.". When she opened the door she was greeted by flame licking at the bodies of guards who had been burnt to charred remains. She cried out and fell back landing on her rear.

Dwim stood in the palace of Hadryn with his hands bound together in chains. Before him stood a jury of Paladins. Evelyn called out and her voice echoed deep in his ears, "Dwim Frothfire of the White! You stand accused of treason against the holy order!" Dwim tried to defend himself, but found that though his mouth moved, his voice was gone. "Zerrick Lightfoot, is this the man who did this to you?"

Zerrick stepped from behind Dwim with his face burnt and scarred nearly to a point of not being recognized, "Yes, High Priestess. Dwim had the chance to stop the Elf who did this. He chose to let his brother in holy arms suffer. He even sided with the impure creature that is my brother. Even when they heard me scream, they did nothing."

Dwim looked around in a panic. The other Paladins there began to chant in unison, "Guilty! Execution! Guilty!"

Phineas stood on the corner of the brothel in Karren's Call. His ears detected a girl moaning out in a tone so fake that even he would have lost interest. When he went down the alley to investigate he saw the wolf, that is to say himself, mounted on the girl. Once the girl and the wolf realized he was there, the girl shrugged her shoulders and spoke rather plainly, "Guess it's time to die now. I've had a good life." When she had made her morbid declaration, the wolf leaned down and bit into the girl's neck. Phineas could taste her blood in his own mouth and tried to spit it out. As he opened his mouth a long howl left his lips. He grabbed at his throat trying to stop the sound. He felt the heart of the wolf beat inside his chest along with his own and they were out of sync.

Leon stood next to a grave where the grave digger was shoveling dirt on top of a body. Leon peered into the grave and saw himself. He startled and stepped back. A priest stepped up and shook his head at the grave digger. "Poor soul had no one come to pay their final respects. Not even a name to go on the gravestone. No one knows who he is. I doubt he left any impact at all on the living world. Just a man who existed and then didn't. Why even bother with a box? No, go on and let the earth reclaim him. Might be more useful that way." Leon jumped into the grave and started digging at the dirt, throwing it back out of the grave, but no matter how much he threw out, the pile became bigger and bigger.

Alastor found himself sitting in a cleared grove on an oak tree stump. He felt peaceful and drew in a deep breath. The sound of laughing children filled his ears and he stood up. He felt no anger, but he could feel it boiling inside his blood; that wild urge to kill. Without him telling his arms to do so, they drew his axes. His feet disobeyed as he ordered them to not walk; they ran right toward the sound of the children. His yellow eyes found the group of younglings playing a game together. Alastor fought hard to stop himself, but his strength was none compared to whatever compelled him. He leapt into the air and cleaved one of the children in half. The others stood around and asked him over and over why he was such a monster.

"Jayda," Angus called out to her, "why did you let him kill me?" As she walked, she found Angus's head smashed beneathe Oberic's boot. Oberic stood there in a heroic pose laughing. "You let him kill me and now you want to lay with him? Where are your priorities you stupid child? You're evil and a disappointment to Hunters, but most importantly you're a disappointment to me!" Jayda reached out for Angus, crying heavily.

Ren backed away from the door for a moment and when she gathered her courage she stood up trembling. She grabbed the door and slammed it shut with all her might. When she turned around she saw her mother, Aunei, sitting in the rocking chair. "My dear Rennyn, guiding light of my life, you are worthless. You got those people killed by hiding the Orc. You let them be slaughtered. You are so worthless. You promised you'd save me. You said you'd cure me but you didn't. Now I am dead. Know what else? The wild gods have forsaken you. We will never meet in the clearing. I still know the ways of our people but you never will. You'll always be some stupid girl in a world where none want her. Alone forever with nothing but your stupid potions to keep you company." Ren dropped to her knees again and sobbed. "Runned out from your Human home and our kind will never accept you. You are lost to the void and you deserve it. You deserve everything that happens to you." Ren covered her ears and screamed until her voice gave out. She lay on the floor and curled up. The flames ate away at the house, surrounding Ren in an infernal, and she accepted her fate.

"Dwim Frothfire, you are hereby relieved of your title as a Paladin of the White! You are not fit to bear the holy word of Olm! You are exiled from this order and by decree of Olm, this life!" The Paladins surrounded Dwim and raised their swords. He watched them with dread as their weapons began to shine a brilliant and blinding light. He was yanked down so that his nose smashed against the floor. "No need to make it quick for the traitor!" Evelyn called out.

Phineas rushed forward to kick the wolf away from the girl who hung limply in its mouth. He yelled out in anger and threw his leg out. His boot met the fur of the beast but instead of hitting it, he went through the creature. Phin looked on in confusion before understanding he was being absorbed into the wolf. He scratched and clawed, having fallen as it slowly sucked him into its body. He lost the fight and when he next opened his eyes he watched through the eyes of the wolf as it tore open the girl. He smelt the blood. He felt her blood dampen his fur. He screamed, begging it to stop and got no reply.

Leon had made no progress in his attempt to unbury himself. His face had become covered and as he tried to remove the dirt, he felt himself choking on it. He held his hands to his throat and tried to spit it out and though the dirt fell from his lips, it felt neverending. He was going to suffocate.

Alastor had made quick work of the children. They laid there around him in beautiful and shining crimson pools. His blades glistened and from their sharp edges dripped ruby. "You're not done," he heard himself say though he did not think he was talking. "Now you have others to kill. It is your blood. It is your nature. You are an Orc. Show them you are true to yourself!" Alastor shook his head. The visions of the children vanished.

Alastor's yellow eyes fell on Leon and Phineas who were near each other. Leon laid on the ground clawing mounds of dirt towards himself then shoveling it into his mouth and swallowing it. He coughed as he started to choke but did not quit trying to shove more in. Phineas knelt there clawing at himself and howled. Alastor narrowed his eyes. "This one first." he said to himself. He would take care of Leon next.

Jayda lay on the ground, "I'm so sorry Angus. I love you. You were my father and I loved you," she climbed to her knees and then her feet, "but Oberic saved me that night. I feel horrible that your life ended the way it did, but you're gone and I'm not going to pretend you aren't." She reached out towards nothingness, "This isn't real. It can't be real!" Jayda closed her emerald eyes and screamed to the top of her lungs, "This isn't real and I'm sick of your shit!" The world seemed to melt before her eyes. The darkness faded and when her head felt clear, she saw each of her friends struggling. Ren laid on the ground crying while Leon was stuffing dirt in his mouth. Oberic seemed lost and in a strange depression. Dwim was slowly dragging his sword against his own neck, cutting into his flesh. Alastor stood over Phineas with his ax raised and poised to strike.

Jayda lashed out with the whip. It coiled around Alastor's wrist as it did so many others before. The bone chunks bit into his flesh and drew blood immediately.. She yanked back on it and Alastor was dragged along like a helpless dog collared by a cruel master. His ax fell from his hand and scraped down his back. He let out a pain filled yell as the sharpened edge dragged down his body, splitting his skin like curtains being drawn to allow the sunlight in. Jayda wasted no time reminding him there was no sunshine though. She tipped herself over and threw out her boot. Alastor's already mashed face connected with her kick and he crashed down to the ground. He tried to get up but Jayda was already in full swing with another kick. Her boot met his chin and she could hear the sound of teeth hitting one another. Alastor laid there, knocked out with his blood streaming from the corners of his mouth. Jayda loosened the whip around Alastor's wrist and ran to help Dwim next.

Dwim laid there silently in the palace as each Paladin took a turn cutting at his neck. The beheading was going to be slow and painful and he knew he deserved every bit of it. Perhaps if he allowed this to happen, Olm would forgive his transgressions and he could go to the beyond with a clean slate. Evelyn watched with crystal blue eyes, enjoying the sentencing and it's execution. Dwim watched her and realized she was rippling like a lake with a stone thrown in. Jayda walked though Evelyn as if she were a dream. She reached down and grabbed him.

"Snap out of it, Dwim!" she said as she yanked something back. He felt the swords leave his neck and let out a sigh of relief. The world started to melt before his eyes and when it vanished he saw that he held his own sword that was covered in his blood. He dropped the sword and reached up to touch his neck. He let out a hiss as his fingers grazed the wound. The cuts were there but thankfully not deep at all. Whatever happened to him that caused him to do such to himself helped him understand the thing was going to make sure it was a long and painful process.

"Lass," his head was groggy, "What in the name of Olm is going on?"

Jayda was going to answer him, but saw that Alastor had gotten up. "Dwim, go help Leon! The others too if you can! I've got a feeling I'm going to have to beat this Orc's ass!" She charged off from Dwim towards Alastor. The Orc seemed ready for her and as soon as she got there he let out a terrible roar.

Dwim got to his feet and rushed to Leon and used his big hands to grab Leon's so that he could force them down.

Jayda showed no fear. Alastor's battle cry was finished as she neared him and he took a swing at her. She leaned back from his punch and felt the wind from the swing brush her face. He swung at her again with the other arm. She threw her arm up, blocked the punch, and in turn delivered several of her own to his ribs. Her punches were unrelenting. She delivered blow after blow to his ribs and stomach until the Orc finally had enough and grabbed her head. She could feel his claw like nails digging into her head before he banged it against his own. Jayda's head pounded as she stumbled back, temporarily stunned by the hit.

"Come on, lad," Dwim said as he flipped Leon over and started banging meaty hands against his back. "Spit it out, stupid!" Leon started to cough up dirt and a bit of blood as he gasped for air. The man was nearly purple in the face.

Alastor grabbed the Hunter again. He lifted her, with ease she realized, and threw her against the column of a porch. She cried out as her spine took most of the hit and she crumpled to the ground. She let out a groan, beaten but not broken, and climbed to her feet as fast as she could. Alastor charged at her again and Jayda stepped aside, placed her hand on the back of his head, and used his own momentum to shove his face into the column she had been thrown against. The wood cracked and Alsator fell down with his hands over his face. Blood poured freely from his mouth and nose.

The spirit of the Hunter burned inside her and she could not help but get cocky as she looked at Alastor laying on the ground. She sniffed, cleared her sinuses, and spit on the Orc, "Get up, bitch!" She stomped on his stomach and when his hands left his face to cover his abdomen, she stomped on his face next. Alastor covered his face once more. Jayda stepped over him, dropped to her knees to straddled him and began to rain down blow after blow to the sides of his head. "When I hit you, you just stay down! Understand?"

Alastor removed his hands from his face and reached out in an attempt to strangle her. Once he placed them against her slender neck, he began to squeeze tight and his thumbs pressed into the small of her throat. Her hands abandoned their barrage against his bald dome and grabbed at his hands instead to pry them away from her neck. He squeezed tighter. He started to sit up which pushed her back until their positions had nearly reversed. She was pressed against the column fighting for air while her face began to change color. Her vision had started to blur and one Orc became two. She was going to lose this fight. Her emerald eyes stared into Alastor's yellow orbs and a memory popped into her oxygen deprived brain. Her and Angus were out in the yard after training. He was teaching her to use her whip and she asked him what would happen if they couldn't use their weapons in a fight and Angus laughed quite hard. The old man, meant as both a literal and metaphorical phrase, placed a hand on her shoulder and looked her in the face, "Then you fight dirty. They use magic and will always have the advantage. Fight dirty and hard. Without honor if you have to. So long as you come out on top, kid."

Her cheeks were blue as she trembled under Alastor's hands. She removed her hands from his and reached down. She searched for a moment and grinned when she finally grabbed a hold of his testicles. She thought it was curious that he didn't seem concerned with the threat but it did not matter. The Hunter was going to fight dirty, so she squeezed them fully intending to pop them if she could. Alastor released her nearly immediately and howled out. Orc or not, he was a man, and a man's weakness was always the same. She caught her breath and thrusted her head forward. His chin met the crown of her head and he tipped back. Jayda slid from underneath him and stood. He rocked forward and she took no chances. She grabbed his head and repeatedly bashed his face into her knee. Alastor was stunned for a moment. Jayda picked up a nearby rock that was painted with images of a serene lake surrounded by pine trees, and bashed it against Alastor's head. The half Orc dropped and let out a hard snore through his beaten nose. She stood over the Orc who called himself Orc'oth with a look of victory on her face. She examined the rock and let out a single laugh at how the painting on the rock was a stark contrast of the current environment. She dropped the rock to her side after making sure it would not land on Alastor.

Now that she was catching her breath and looking around, Jayda heard the most terrible cries of pain she had ever heard. They grabbed at her heart and tugged on her emotions. Her eyes found Ren and she rushed to her side after picking up her whip. She grabbed Ren and shook her, "Rennyn! It isn't real! None of it is real!"

Ren laid on the floor of the house. The flames had surrounded her now. Still, her mother had been fussing all the while at her about being weak and useless. Ren laid there accepting the fate of burning with the house when she saw Jayda's face in the fire. Jayda called out to her telling her none of it was real. "Jayda? How are you here?" Ren asked, pushing herself up from the floor. "You weren't here!" Ren looked around. As it slowly dawned on her. The more she understood, the more the burning home melted from her and her head cleared. She shook her head and mumbled, "None of this is real." When it was completely gone and she was back in the real world, she threw herself into Jayda's arm. They hugged each other tightly. "What's going on?" Ren asked in tears.

"I don't know! Right now you need to get Phin to come back to us! I'll go help Oberic!"Jayda said in a commanding tone. She let go of Ren and ran to Oberic who had not moved since the whole thing started. As she knelt in front of him she saw there was no emotion on his face other than absolute sadness and despair. She placed her hands on his shoulders and shook him, "Oberic! Snap out of it!"

Phineas had been eating the girl's entrails when Ren's face appeared on the dead woman's head, "Phineas! It isn't real! None of it is real!" Ren said to him. He looked at Ren for a long moment.

"I'm the wolf! Go away before you get hurt!" Phin said to her in between chomps of whore meat.

"You can't be the wolf, Phineas! You have the amulet on!" she called out to him.

"Then how?" Phin looked around himself. How was he the wolf if the amulet had been on him. He hadn't turned once since he wore it. The back alley and the girl melted away. When his head was clear he looked at Ren and smiled, "Oh man! You're a way better sight than a dead whore!"

"I'll take it as a compliment for now," Ren huffed, 'Now get up!"

"Oberic! We need you to snap out of this!" Jayda said as she shook him.

"Why bother?" he asked, "You'll leave me like she did and I'll be alone again. Forever."

"I haven't gone anywhere, you idiot!" she continued to shake him until she felt a cold hand grasp her forearm. She looked down and saw the half of the body she pulled down earlier. "Not now!" She grabbed the dead torso's arms and stood. The corpse tried to bite at her. Jayda paid no mind and turned her body and used the force to fling the corpse off in the distance, away from herself. She knelt back down, "Oberic!"

Leon had coughed up all the dirt he could and was able to breath just fine now. Ren let out a scream as one of the bodies grabbed hold of her. Phineas grabbed at it's hair and tried to pull it away but pulled nothing but it's scalp back. Ren looked at it in horror. Another corpse fell from above and landed on Phineas' back. It clasped it's arms around his neck and as he struggled to break free from it, the silver amulet broke from his neck. Ren watched it fall to the ground in slow motion. Her purple, gold rimmed, globes followed the precious thing until it hit the dirt. She watched it lay there, free of its master, before she looked up at Phin again. The terribly perfect man was already shifting forms.

She stood and started to move away from Phineas; once a man, now a beastly dire wolf. The monster sized wolf gave one shake of it's coat when it was done with the transformation. The sky blue eyes spotted the Elf and charged wildly towards her. Ren threw her arms up and screamed thinking she was about to be done in by the beast, but when she felt the wolf breeze by her, she dropped her arms. She dared to open her eyes and saw no Phineas. She turned around to see that the wolf had run past her and had gone after the other crawling corpses nearing Jayda and Oberic. It snapped one in its jaws and thrashed it about like a stuffed doll. When he was done, he would fling his head to the side and send its heavily chewed body flying into a bush. Phineas howled and turned to face them. It made eye contact with Jayda, barked at her, and started to pad towards her.

Jayda pulled her eyes away from the wolf, sighed, and placed her forehead against Oberic's, "Please, I need you."

Oberic grabbed her shoulders tight. His eyes darted around until they locked onto hers and when she looked at him she could see the danger she had once seen twinkling in his eyes. He spoke so calmly to her that it unnerved her, "Keep me grounded? If I ever get out of control with it, I mean. Will you be there to save me from myself?"

Jayda nodded, "One way or another, Oberic. I won't let you become something you're not. I'll do whatever I can to make sure you're the man who saved me."

He let go of her and stood fully now. He turned and faced the wolf. Jayda tried to stand by his side, but he grabbed her arm and flung her behind himself. Jayda nearly fell as she was slung and even thought to comment until she saw Oberic weaving his hands about. He extended his arms and opened his palms towards one another. Between them grew a brilliant orb of light that shimmered. His eyes fixed upon a group of the undead and bolts of light flew from the orb into the air. They danced and swirled amongst each other before shooting downward and striking the undead. Some were flung back while others exploded in a mess of gore. More of the missiles of light floated from the orb of energy and each flung itself down upon a target. One by one, the undead were either pushed back or destroyed. Even Phineas' dire wolf form was hit by several of the sparks of magic and though he was not overly injured, it was enough to force him to retreat. The wolf howled again and turned, taking off in the other direction. He disappeared into the wilds leaving only the echoes of another howl.

Jayda watched for only a moment as the wolf ran off. She decided now was the time to go and check on the others. They all seemed to be fine. The undead behind Oberic were not safe from his barrage of power as they too were struck by the spell. Ren searched around and spotted the silver Amulet on the ground. She bent and grabbed it. She lifted it close to her face, examined it for a moment, and tied it around her neck for safe keeping. She then went to the spot where Phineas had changed. Upon the mess of torn clothes, she found his dagger and rapier. She picked them up as well. She thought he would no doubt want them later. She turned to the others and tried to ask if they were alright. Her voice cracked and she rubbed at her throat realizing how sore it was.

Dwim and Leon went and checked in on Alastor who was still laid out in the dirt where Jayda had left him. The area seemed clear of undead thanks to Oberic who was still letting those threads of light flow from the energy between his hands. Jayda headed back towards Oberic as he dropped his hands to his side. The blinding orb of light vanished along with its projectiles. Oberic swayed from side to side for a moment before falling to a knee. The magic had worn him out. Jayda put her arms around him and held him close to her body afraid to let him go now, "Rest, Oberic. You've done it."

"No he hasn't." said a voice. The man with the cleaver in his skull stepped out from another house. The creature, Oberic assumed the one who called himself Wintergrave, had hid while everyone battled. Jayda stood and drew her whip back; the Hunter prepared to strike at the corpse, whose skin had become blackened by the aging of death. The dead man's eyes fell on her, "Angus didn't even put up a fight. He died of fright. Some Hunter he turned out to be." The man laughed, but it was not with one voice but several coming from the same throat. Jayda's whip was lightning incarnate. The leather wrapped itself around the man's neck. Jayda pulled the whip, dragging the corpse towards her and even though it was choked by the whip, his black tongue hanging from his mouth wiggling madly, the creature showed no fear.

When the thing was in reach, Jayda pulled a dagger from her belt and thrust it into the creature's chest. It looked down and in the voice of a little girl cried out "Why?" The man sobbed in the little girl's voice for a moment before it turned to laughter. He grabbed his head and twisted so that his face looked behind him. There was an awful sound of his neck snapping. The man collapsed to the ground and spoke his final words. "You are powerless here. Even in my weakened power you nearly fell. How do you think you'll manage when all the dead are at my command? Doors will open. It is only a matter of time." There was no more from the corpse and Oberic watched as the purple wisp lifted from the body and fled off into the wilds.

Leon brushed his hair back and stared off, "What the fuck is going on around here?" Dwim was standing with shield and sword in hand; spinning and looking for whatever may come out after them. Jayda bent and pulled the dagger from the dead man and loosened the whip from it's neck. She turned to Oberic wearing a brave face.

"We need to keep moving. We have to find Phineas." She squatted in front of Oberic who had cold sweat forming on his head, "Come on, we can't stop now."

Oberic nodded. The man knew much, seen a good deal more, but never once had to watch a creature end itself like that. It was unnerving but quite a powerful play. The monster calling itself Wintergrave had shown them that it had nothing to lose. The group had gone and collected Alastor. When they woke him and explained what happened, he congratulated Jayda on besting him in combat. She offered an apology but found she did not really mean it.

The six of them continued into the dark forest leaving Oakember. They walked for hours and the day turned to dusk. When they found living fauna again, the night had come upon them. Owls hooted alerting the darkness of their presence. Things moved in the trees that could not be seen. This territory was no man's land; it belonged to the night or at least it did right now. Oberic, now and again, could swear he heard whispers. There were none of course, but the events of the day had him paranoid. Ren scanned the area as they walked, trying her best to see anything at all and jumping at any noise that came from the darkness. Jayda walked quietly beside Oberic. Her hand never left her whip. Leon walked the entire time with an arrow notched and ready to fire. There had been no signs of Phineas at all. The forest ground had become too dense and even Leon was unable to track him. It might have been possible if he were of a more sound mind but that hour had come and gone. The group was far too tired and drained. All of them were as useless as a burnt out lantern in the dark.

CHAPTER 17

None of them knew just where they were. Alastor had been quiet the entire walk and kept his head low. Leon finally spoke up and broke the silence, "No one is going to want to hear this, but I can't keep going. I don't have it in me."

Dwim nodded and let out a croak, "Aye, lad. I'm done for."

"Let's make camp then." Oberic said. "Keep it on the path though. No wandering off deep into the woods."

"We can sleep in shifts," Ren suggested, "two of us should stay awake. I'll take a spot on the first watch." She looked at Leon and then Jayda "I think you two need to rest most. Anyone else willing to stay up with me?"

Alastor spoke up with a voice that was soft and low, "I will keep watch with you."

Dwim elbowed Leon and Oberic, "C''mon, lads. We'll need wood. Can't be in this kind of darkness without it." Both nodded and headed out with Dwim. It wasn't long before they came back with a bundle of dry wood in their arms. They set up the sticks and with a bit of simple magic got the fire going.

They all stared quietly into the fire before Dwim yawned and laid down. Leon followed suit and placed his hands behind his head. Jayda removed her cloak and laid down covering herself with it. She looked at Oberic who seemed to be lost in thought as he stared into the fire. "Oberic," her words were gentle and light, "You need to get some rest too." Oberic did nothing for a long moment and then he sighed. He laid down and pulled his hat over his eyes. All that were left were Ren and Alastor. Both of them looked off into the night over the flickering fire light.

Ren kept her gaze forward and sighed, "This is far different than I ever expected the story of my life to be." She glanced over at Alastor with a half smile, "I'm sorry I was so angry with you."

Alastor grunted and spoke low to not wake the others. His ugly face did not show much emotion but his words were sincere, "I had every intention to kill you that night we met. I was rash and did not think much. I have cost you your life and safety. I am a savage, but I forget my mother's blood too often."

"I assume your mother was Human?" Ren asked, hoping she didn't sound rude.

Alastor nodded, "Her name was Aria Maudit."

"What happened to her?"

Alastor growled out at her, "Are you expecting my life story, girl?"

"If it helps you," Ren answered honestly, "If it's something you need to say; to feel closer to your other half."

Alastor looked away from the Elf. There was silence between them for a long time. He grabbed one of the many sticks the others had brought back and poked at the fire with it. "She was raped," his yellow eyes looked up to Ren, "by an Orc raiding party. They passed her around and when they finished they left her for dead. She was found by a hunting party and brought back to the city. How or why she was out in the wilds to have run into such a situation I do not know. She was already an older woman when it happened. Supposedly, beyond her birthing years. Then she had me." Ren sat silently listening to Alastor speak. "She said the day I was born was the happiest day of her life." He snorted through his busted nose, courtesy of Jayda. "Hard to believe anyone could ever be happy to give birth to a monster." He looked up at Ren again. His yellow eyes twinkled with tears and Ren felt her heart twist. It was the first emotion she had really seen from the Orc, no, not the orc, from the man. "She did not make me feel like a monster. She named me Alastor after her own father who in my experience was a ruthless cold blooded man. If either of us was the true monster, it was him."

Alastor had grown up in a large mansion in the city of Wild River in the kingdom of Palan which lay south of Marrenval. He was a happy child. His mother, daughter of a noble and very rich man, had returned to the family after she was taken by the Orcs and Alastor took care of her and the child. This was no act of kindness for them of course. He simply could not have word getting around that she had decided to keep the child. Even when the grotesque thing slid from his mother's womb, Alastor demanded the thing be drowned in the city well. Aria made sure to let her father know that if the baby was disposed of, she would join him. Instead, they were kept under lock and key. Aria realized very early on he was no average boy. He had the blood and the senses of an Orc in him too. He enjoyed games of hide and seek where he pounced out at her. She made sure to feign fright everytime he let out a growl at her, but found it to truly

234

be the most darling thing she had ever seen. The boy never grew hair. His teeth came in fast. They were sharp and tore through raw meat like a knife through butter. He preferred the flavor of bloody meat rather than something cooked and seasoned. He was strong too and would often break things by accident. His mother, never once, disciplined him for such accidents.

There was a time though where a rabbit had been out in the garden darting between the shrubbery. Alastor had managed to catch the thing and bit into it. He ripped the leg off the prey while it was still alive. His mother spoke harshly to him and explained that she understood the nature of his being, but that he had to understand the nature of his own. "Maybe you can't control it, Alastor, but you will put it out of its misery fast. If you have to kill, you do it with kindness in your heart. That creature does not need to know such pain."

Alastor wouldn't understand what that meant until much later in life. The boy was not treated so kindly by the rest of the family. His grandfather, who made the boy call him Master Maudit, would often beat him for the simplest mistakes; never around Aria of course. Even then, the Orc'oth had too much pride to run and tell his mother. He slowly learned to hate his grandfather.

Aria did her best to teach the boy to read and write. He could speak well enough, even if his words were short and direct. There was no elegance in his speech. He was unable to master reading and writing though and his mother, never saying this to him, assumed it was his Orc intelligence that was stopping him. Even before she was raped, she knew the beasts were extraordinarily dim witted and functioned mostly on primal instincts. The boy might have been something more if he had known more love from more Humans than just his mother, but that would never be the case.

Alastor was able to recall the hour his mother died. It was just after eight in the evening when the sun was setting over the horizon behind the garden. She was tending to a flower bed when she collapsed and never woke. He never learned what caused her death, if anything at all other than it just being her time to leave this world for the next. He held her in his arms and while he had a simple mind, he understood one thing for certain. Any kindness he had known had died with her and even in that moment he understood he was more Orc now than Human.

How fast it happened or even when it happened was a blur for Alastor. He only knew that he was beaten by whips while still holding his mother in his arms. The scars from those lashings would remain on his chest and back forever. He had an iron collar, with tiny nails on the inside, placed around his neck and he was dragged to the basement of the mansion where he was chained there like an animal. Master Maudit could not let him go because the secret would be out and he couldn't kill the thing because he knew Aria's spirit would never forgive him. So he begrudgingly kept him locked away in the basement. He was fed and watered, but just barely. They didn't want the Orc'oth to be strong. They just wanted him alive. He was never allowed to bathe himself at all and when servants went down to provide him his provisions, they wore clothes pins on their noses.

For years, the boy was kept in those chains and for years he was beaten by his grandfather for simply existing. He was mocked and ridiculed for being a simple minded monster. Alastor however, was not as dense as they all believed him to be. For years he would piss on the same spot of the chain. It would rust more and more over the years until one night when a storm raged on, he grabbed the chain, placed a foot against the wall, and let out a roar as he struggled to pull the chain free.

Thunder rolled just as the link broke as if signifying the turning of the tides of war. He landed on his back and rolled on the floor. He was free. He looked up the wall hoping to find a key. There was none. The door to the basement opened and he scampered into a dark corner and hid. His yellow eyes watched them coming down the stairs. It was one of the guards that the family hired to keep watch on him. He was one of the crueler ones and Alastor knew he would enjoy killing him.

The man reached the bottom of the stairs. Alastor's blood felt hot and the lust for carnage pumped from his heart to every limb. His face grew hot and he licked his twisted lips. The guard turned the corner and froze, "Where? Shit! Master Maudit he esca-" Alastor had rushed from the darkness and tackled the guard from behind. He wasted no time at all in grabbing the man's greasy hair and slamming his face into the stone floor over and over until the skull was caved in and it was no thicker than a runny pudding.

Alastor searched the corpse. He found a few keys and tried them all on the spiked collar. He was becoming frustrated when none of them were working and then the fifth unlocked the torture device with a light turn of the key. The collar dropped to the floor and slowly lifted his hands and felt his neck. There were more cuts and scars he would live with for the rest of his life. He thought he might weep, but that emotion was gone, never to return. Instead, he picked up the collar and chain and looked up the stairs. Each step was heavy footed and filled with one objective; he was going to kill Alastor Maudit.

He broke free from the basement and just as he stepped into a hall he had not seen in so long he was spotted by a maid who dropped a tray of tea cups. She screamed for the last time before Alastor thrusted his thumbs into her eyes and then broke her neck with a quick twist. He dropped her body and moved on. Each step, every single heartbeat, drove him to his target. There was another unlucky soul who came across him that night. It was a cook he had never met before but had no problem slaughtering. Alastor grabbed the man's ears and pulled them until the flesh tore and they came off his head. The man dropped to his knees and screamed out in pain. Alastor walked behind him, pulled his head back by his hair, and hammered his fist into the man's face until there was gurgling noise and the occasional spray of blood. Once the body dropped to the floor, Alastor lifted a foot and stomped on the head until it matched the first guard he killed.

The screams had not gone unnoticed. Guards came rushing around the corner and though Alastor was half Orc, he was simply too weak to fight all of them. They tackled him and shackled him again. After they beat him mercilessly, they brought him to his grandfather's study. He was thrown on the floor in front of Alastor Maudit. The old man looked down at him with absolute disgust, "My sweet child gave birth to an abomination. I will abide you no longer, boy. I've sold you to a mining company. You will live out your entire life in chains. You might end up dead at the end of some dark tunnel. I don't really care. You have been a burden to me for far too long." The Orc roared at him in anger and fought to break free but could not. Alastor Maudit shook his head. "Take him away."

Alastor would be sold as his grandfather had told him he would be. He spent years doing slave labor down in dark mines. Fed enough to keep him alive. Others, some of his kind but mostly Humans, would beg another to kill them. Some would oblige and those that did were tortured by the company until they also died.

Alastor threw the stick into the campfire. "I never killed Master Maudit. I wanted to, but I wasn't able to break free from the mining company."

"How did you get away?" Ren asked.

"Orc raiding party came across the camp at night. Murdered everyone but the Orc'oths. They put us in their own chains and used us for slave labor until they got what they needed out of us. Then we were forced to fight each other to the death. I won. When I was no use to them at all they strung me up and left me for the vultures. I was freed by someone who thought I was a corpse of some Human. They did it as a kindness and as payment I killed them." Alastor sighed, "I am a monster, girl," he looked at her now, "but I am trying to be better. To remember and follow the lesson of the rabbit that my mother taught me. I try to live her patience as she must have struggled while raising me. I try not to forget that she lives on within me."

Ren's eyes had started to water, "I'm sorry, Alastor." She didn't know what else to say other than that. Then, whether it was in good taste or not after his story, she said "I guess though that you setting my life on this path has caused me to meet some new friends and learn things about myself that I may not have learned before."

He said nothing for a moment longer. He did not like the feeling of opening up and would not ever admit it, but telling her the small bit of his story did help him a bit. "Orc'kin do not believe in Gods. They believe in strength and savagery. There is nothing more to life than food, procreation, cruelty, and survival. My mother taught me much about the Gods of her kind. I am aware of this Olm and his meaning to people. I know much about many of them. She once told me the Gods would watch over and protect me. I did not believe her then and I do not believe her now." Ren felt sorry for his lack of faith in something. She herself followed the Gods that Humans did, not really knowing much of the Wild Gods. "Maybe though they decided to put people in my path who may understand me; even just a little. I am not treated well being a half breed, but you," he nodded to her and then to the others asleep, "them, have been kind to me. I am grateful."

Ren stood and walked closer to him. She placed a hand on his shoulder and smiled, "You are among friends now." She sat down beside him for the rest of their shift. Jayda had begun to mumble in her sleep, fueled by nightmares of the horrors they saw earlier. She was sleeping poorly and the whimpers grew louder as she screamed in her dreams. Now and again, a muffled scream passed her lips as she tossed and turned.

"Their dreams haunt them. Fear has taken hold. I do not think fear holds me the same as it does the rest of you. That fear of losing my fight with the Orc'kin rage is a daily battle. Even the Dwarf, stout and strong as he may be, is losing the fight. You can see it on his face. Your man though," he nodded to Leon, "I think he is the most held together of them."

Rennyn blinked and looked over at Leon's sleeping form. *Her man,* she thought and she turned red. It sounded nice to her. "He is very brave and if anyone will make it through this alive, I believe it will be him." She looked back to Alastor, "Oberic and Jayda will be fine if they can rely on each other. I think I might be the weak link here. Under-trained and not very strong physically." She got up and moved to Jayda and sat down next to her running her hand over her inky hair. "Shh, it will be okay." she whispered to the whimpering girl. Jayda fell quiet again as she slipped into a deeper sleep. There was another howl deep in the woods and they both looked up, both thinking it might be Phineas.

"The wolf man," Alastor said, "I would like to do battle with him. I have never seen such a thing before." He ran his thumb along the sharp edge of his ax. Blood seeped from the wound, but it did not seem to bother him. "What do you think happens from here?"

"We continue on, of course." She was confident in her words. "If there is one thing I have learned is that no one in this group quits."

Alastor snorted, "This one," he pointed to Oberic, "Is filled with doubt. He will be the first to fall." Owls hooted as if to mark his words.

Ren looked over at Oberic and then back to Jayda. "I hope for her sake that it doesn't come to pass."

"She is strong. She could carry on. That man was broken before her and is broken still," Alastor let out a yawn, "maybe it is time to wake others. We too need rest."

Rennyn yawned as well and agreed, "I think maybe Jayda and Oberic need more sleep. I'll wake Leon and Dwim." She got up and headed towards the pair. She bent down and eased them awake, calling softly to them both. They both got up slowly but did so without a fuss. When Alastor saw they were prepared to take their shifts, he laid down in Dwim's place while Ren took Leon's.

Leon and Dwim said nothing to one another. They shared glances now and again. Leon, at one point of the shift, fired an arrow off into the wilds when he heard a rustling but snared nothing. The sky was turning from pitch to a faint light as the moon was vanishing behind the trees. The next shift belonged to Jayda and Oberic. Leon was kinder in waking Jayda up than Dwim was waking Oberic. He gave Oberic a not so gentle kick. Oberic sat up immediately and told Dwim to get some sleep. He stood up, stretched, and cracked his back. Jayda awoke with a start and pulled a dagger from her belt and held it out to Leon. Leon backed away with his hands up.

She blinked, realizing she was staring at Leon, and apologized. "I'm sorry."

Leon lowered his hands and smiled. "It's alright. I'm sure we're all on edge." He stretched his hand out and offered to help her up.

Jayda grasped his hand and pulled herself up, "Thank you, Leon." She gave him a pat on the shoulder and walked over to the dying fire. Leon took her spot and closed his eyes. Jayda smiled at Oberic as she moved closer to the fire. "Just you and me this round, huh?"

Oberic returned her smile. "I'm sure you could have better company." He nodded to the snoring Alastor, "You could be up with chatterbox there."

"I prefer this company," she said as she scooted closer to him and laid her head on his shoulder. Oberic slipped an arm around her and thought of this feeling of having someone who wanted to be near him. It seemed new after twenty years and he was unsure how to handle it. In their short time of knowing each other, he found that he trusted her more than anyone. He thought she was strong and not someone he had to watch over; he only had to care about her and that was just fine for him.

"I know Angus gave you the whip. Where did the bone come from though?" It was a question born of genuine curiosity.

Jayda looked down at her hands, unsure of how he would react to it. "My first kill," she lifted her head and looked at Oberic, "but that's not who I am anymore. I don't want you to think of me like that."

Oberic shook his head, "You did not know any better then and I can't be upset about that, especially now that I know how it is you became a Hunter. If I'm being honest, some of them were justified I'm sure. There are some who use their power for terrible things." Oberic took her hand and squeezed it as he looked into her eyes, "If I think anything of you it is that you're strong. I think you're cunning and amazing. I think you're absolutely beautiful and I know that you are loyal. You, I'm certain, will always be that person. We all change, but that was always you at the core. That will never change."

Jayda blushed a deep crimson and laid her head back on his shoulder. They enjoyed the silence and watched the fire flicker together. It was a long time before she cleared her throat and looked up at him once more, "Oberic? Could I ask a favor?"

He gave her a nod and looked at her, "Anything that I have power over, yes."

The request left her lips as a whisper that was as light as the wind itself, "Can you make me forget?" Her emerald eyes rippled with tears that threatened to spill over her eyelids and down her cheeks. "Everytime I close my eyes I see them. Angus, the bodies, the nightmares; all of it. I see your body hanging over a piece of that sunken ship in the water. I hear Rennyn's screams." The words had flooded from her mouth like a raging river and she squeezed his hands tighter. She dropped to her knees in front of him, "Just a little, please? I just want it to go away for a while."

His face, soft and comforting, gave way to something far more grave. His eyes, as always, appeared dangerous to Jayda and she shrunk back just a little. "That is dangerous magic, Jayda. You could lose yourself to false memories. I would never dream of putting you under a spell that forced you to forget. It is slavery and I'll have no part in it."

Jayda took his hands and placed them on her face. Her tears broke free of their prison and streamed down her cheeks and over his thumbs. "Oberic, please," her words but a whisper now, "it hurts to see it. It hurts to hear it." She had seen many awful things as a Hunter and that included dead bodies. However, none of them belonged to anyone she cared about. That is what troubled her the most.

Oberic Wintersong, a man who at most times could be cold and calculating, realized one simple fact about Jayda. He knew that, in this very moment, she had power over him like no other had. Not even Evelyn, who held his heart for twenty years, could ever convince him to do such a thing. Yet, here knelt Jayda, a woman he knew that he'd end worlds for if she only asked him to do so. "Jayda, please, think this over. Are you absolutely certain this is what you want?"

Her tears had run down the backside of his hands. She looked up at him, more vulnerable in this moment than she had ever been with him; even more so than when she shared her story. She was letting go of her fears of magic, only with him, knowing in her heart he would not be cruel to her. She trusted him completely. "Please, Oberic. Just once."

He took a deep breath and found that he wouldn't say no to her; likely never. He closed his eyes, resigning to the fact that she had complete power over him in just a matter of a few nights together. "Think hard of those events you wish to replace. You're going to feel hazy," he placed his fingers against her temples, "when you do, think of a memory you wish to put in its place. It does not matter what it is. Do not concoct some outrageous fantasy for those are the easiest to break." He leaned forward and kissed her forehead. His fingers left her temple and danced near them, weaving the unseen magic that only a sorcerer could feel and manipulate in the world. She did as he asked of her. She thought of the terrible things she had seen and just as he said she would, she felt hazy and light headed. There was a moment she thought she might pass out. She started to think of herself and Oberic escaping that night under the bell to the little library. It was a base thought and she let her mind fill in the blanks to replace everything that fueled the panic she felt. The haze thickened in her mind. Things that once were, were no longer and those that never happened suddenly did. There are so very few moments in existence, this reality or any other, where things are ever real. Her memories of what had happened were pushed back and locked away, camouflaged by the dreams that, before this, were nothing more than just that. They themselves were becoming the reality, but only for the dreamer. The void of memory was filled. The false memories would shatter at some point and of this he had no doubt. He thought she may very well in the end hate him for having done it and she had every right to; he hated himself for doing it. The truth of what had happened was nothing to hide from, no matter how dark, cruel, and frightening they were.

When he was done he pulled his fingers away from her. Jayda wore a blissful look on her face. Oberic already felt terrible guilt and knew nothing good would come of it. Not even a few days into, whatever was between them, and he already wronged her. "I had such a nice rest, Oberic!" Jayda said as she opened her eyes. "I dreamt of our time in the library that night!" She smiled playfully, "Do you remember?"

Oberic leaned forward and kissed her head once more, "I am glad you dreamed such sweet dreams."

She laid her head on his lap and smiled. The group was on a lovely adventure together and she was happy to have been able to spend more time with Oberic. The morning came quickly after the fire had died completely and the others began to wake. Ren had just sat up and stretched when Jayda bombarded her with pleasantries, "Good morning, Ren! I hope you slept well. We better get ready for the day." Jayda grabbed her fur lined cloak from the ground and threw it over herself. Ren watched Jayda with a concerned look and then looked at Oberic who wore his guilt on his face clearly.

Ren walked towards Oberic and dropped her voice, "Oberic, what's happened?"

Oberic stood and readied himself by adjusting his overcoat, "A mistake." He looked at Ren with rather grim eyes. He glanced at Jayda to ensure she would not hear and then he whispered back to Ren, "She asked me to alter her memories and like a damn fool I did it because," he drew in a breath and sighed, "it does not matter why. As far as she knows, at least for a while, nothing terrible has happened. The undead, Angus; I've helped her replace it with a false memory." Oberic bent and grabbed his hat and slammed it down on his head. "I was a fool before and a fool now." Oberic stomped off and barked at the others to wake up. The man was rarely in his life ever angry, but could not help but be irritated at his own actions. He absolutely knew better and because she, that breath taking girl he had not truly seen until the other night, had asked him to.

Rennyn sighed and muttered to herself, "Not a fool, Oberic. Just a man in love." She stole a quick glance at Leon and then gathered her stuff. She placed her bow on her back and spoke up so that Oberic could hear her this time. "Continuing our journey? Looking for Phineas as well?"

"We've already headed further in than I intended looking for that boy," Oberic scratched his beard, "I don't even know if we'll find him now."

Ren lowered her voice, "Maybe we should let the others know about what you've done. That way no one triggers any sort of relapse in memory." Her eyes darted to Jayda who was clearing up camp with the others.

Oberic nodded and sighed again, "Do that for me? Let the others know the grave mistake I've made. I don't think I can handle any more judgment than I've already passed on myself."

Ren smiled at him sweetly. She wasn't sure if the others could see what she saw between Oberic and Jayda. She reached out and took one of his hands into both of hers and squeezed, "It's never a mistake to take care of someone." She released his hand and went to inform Leon, Dwim, and Alastor of what had happened. Each of them gave Oberic a glare that he didn't much care for. He lowered his head. He was angry with himself but what was done was done.

"We're a day and a half out from Hadryn," Oberic called out, trying to reclaim some sense of leadership, "I'm sure at this point Evelyn has declared us dead. We can either head back and hope Phineas finds us somehow or we can push forward and hope we find him." He threw his arms up, "I leave it up to you."

Ren looked around and decided to be the first to speak. "I think we should push forward. We've already learned what we needed to, right?" She looked to Jayda hoping she wasn't triggering a memory, "I'm sure Phineas would want us to look for him. He would for us."

Nearly the rest of the party disagreed with her logic. Nearly all of them believed Phineas would tuck tail and leave them alone. That being made clear, they did it agree that looking for him was the right thing to do. They each agreed that they should push on. The journey continued. Oberic kept to himself mostly that day and Jayda could not understand why. The morning turned to midday and with it returned all the lush and beautiful foliage that the wilds should have always been. They stopped to make a quick fire to eat. Leon would of course provide the meal, but he also took Ren along so that he could help her track and even make her first kill. Ren danced back to the camp excited that she had improved so much that she had been able to bring food back to the group.

"Should have seen it," Leon said as he dragged the deer back to the group, "She did just as she was instructed. Good clean kill." Ren beamed with happiness and Jayda congratulated her. Leon and Alastor made quick work of skinning and preparing the deer meat for cooking. Dwim had traveled out and found a small source of water for them. They each took a sip and it was gone as fast as that. When they were done and spirits were a bit higher from having been fed, they continued onward. They unfortunately had to leave a lot of the meat behind. Leon wished they had come across something smaller.

They had gone for quite awhile longer. The beautiful sky of blue started to turn purple and the light had grown low. Oberic was going to push the group until nightfall again. Just as he opened his mouth to tell the group that, a finely crafted arrow lodged itself into Alastor's thigh. The Orc snarled and pulled his axes out and snapped the wood between his blades. He then let out a terrible roar while he tried to pull the arrowhead from his thigh. Ren and Leon both pulled their own bows and notched an arrow. They aimed out into the wilds but saw nothing.

Jayda's hand was on her whip and ready to lash out. Dwim drew his sword and Oberic simply leaned on his staff.

Several tall and beautiful Elven archers dropped from the trees in front of them. Alastor growled and charged towards them, but Oberic stopped him by holding out his staff. The Elves spoke in their native tongue. None of them, except Oberic, knew what they had said, but Oberic would say nothing. Better to leave the enemy clueless. When the Elves got no response they spoke again in the common language shared by most people. "You trespass on our land and we do not take kindly to trespassers." The Elf speaking was the tallest. He had pink eyes and snow white hair that hung far past his shoulders.

Rennyn stepped forward from the group. Her purple eyes met his and he eased seeing she was one of his kind. "We do not mean to trespass," her voice was soft, "ee have been sent to investigate the woods and we have lost our friend on the way."

The Elf's head tilted a bit, "You come from the dead wood? Beyond?" The Elf asked in a rather upset tone, "From where have you come?"

"We've been tasked by the High Priestess of Hadyrn to look into the town that I assume you're calling the dead wood."

"Hadryn? The city of zealots? How did you survive the dead wood?"

Jayda leaned into Leon, "What in the world is this Elf going on about?"

Leon remembered Jayda had her memories tampered with and fought to find an excuse. He ended up shrugging and said, "Elf stuff, I guess."

The head Elf called out, "If you're creatures of undeath we will put you down!" Each Elf raised their bow again and pulled their arrows back for an attack.

Ren held her hands up in front of her. The wind briefly picked up as her sudden defensive stance provoked it. It died down as she tried to remember the things Oberic had taught her so far. "We aren't the enemy."

The manipulation of the wind did not seem to phase the Elve. "Would you betray your kin?"

Ren didn't know how to say she wasn't really raised around her kind and so she simply thumbed behind herself, "These are my kin. I am no traitor to them nor are we any danger to you."

The strings on their bows tightened and nearly let loose to fire upon them. Her answers were no good to their ears. "Be still," said a beautiful voice, "they are no enemy of ours." A beautiful but short Elven woman with white hair much like the head archer's, stepped out from the group. Her eyes were teal and her skin was nearly as white as her hair which was braided down her back. "They are weary travelers. Isn't that right?"

Rennyn lowered her hands slowly and nodded, "Yes. Just weary travelers not meaning any harm or offense."

The Elven woman opened her arms to the group. She was draped in a sheer cloth that was very clearly translucent making her body exposed to them. Jayda elbowed Oberic and gave him a look that demanded he keep his eyes off of the woman. "Welcome to Laru'el N'stir; what you would call in the common tongue the Lake of the Forest."

Ren dipped her head, "Thank you." She turned to her friends and smiled "Someplace safe for a little while?"

They all looked to one another, except Oberic who understood Jayda's glare and was looking up examining the growing dark. The woman had a strange glow about her as she spoke to them, "My guard will lead you to our home. Rest easy knowing that rest and peace are ahead of you." Her form dimmed and seemed to shimmer before she vanished before their eyes.

"Come," said the head archer, "The Lady has vouched for you. I hope you have enough sense to mind yourselves and understand you are guests in our home and not the other way around." He turned and began to head down the path. Jayda didn't care for the tone that was used and narrowed her eyes. She looked at Oberic and let out a laugh, "Oh stop before you break your neck!" She placed an arm around his and they walked behind Ren who was leading her group now and finding a small boost of confidence.

"Boy," Dwim said amongst their group low enough for the Elves to not hear, Ren would not tell him that they would be able to hear every word, "Phineas is going to be mighty sorry he missed a pair of breasts." Leon, Ren, and even Jayda, though she gave the boys an exasperated look, chuckled. It was the first bit of humor in the last few days. Alastor understood the joke but did not laugh. He was still quite annoyed about having been shot. He stopped for a moment and finally managed to yank the arrow head from his thigh. He examined it with a sneer on his face and threw it in the wilds.

Jayda couldn't quite figure out why everyone had been so quiet and tense on their travels. If she thought about it hard enough she could swear it was just on the tip of her tongue but just out of reach; so it was nice to see them laughing and relaxing a bit. They were led through thick and dense forest off the main road onto a smaller less traveled one. The group could not believe their eyes when they came to a breathtaking town built over a sparkling lake of crystal clear waters. Leon's jaw hung open. He was the most well traveled of the group, so he assumed, for Oberic did not talk much about himself. He whispered to himself, "Amazing!"

"Absolutely beautiful," Rennyn exclaimed as she agreed with Leon, "Are there baths?" Her voice was filled with longing.

The head archer spoke with a bit of snark and far too much pride in his voice, "I think you'll find our home more than accommodating. Pleasures and relaxation await you and your friends. You may thank The Lady for her kindness when you are properly greeted."

"Pleasures and relaxations," Jayda said as she looked at Oberic, a sultry look in her eyes, "Doesn't that sound glorious?" She smiled as she watched him turn from his normal pale color to a deep pink.

"No pleasure I need from any Elf," Dwim said, "No offense meant!"

The archer called back. "All offense taken."

The town was very dream-like; even the homes which were merely trees grown in such a way that they formed buildings. They were carved and etched elaborately. True to their Elven nature, everything was very natural and in this world of nightmare creatures and holy orders; a world of cursed wolves and magicians, a world of Hunters and the hunted; this was pure. The Lady met them at the first bridge leading into the town. "I welcome you to our home. We will speak of your journey later when we feast in your honor. We do not gather many visitors so please, allow our people to show you our hospitality." She turned and led them across the natural bridge of intertwined trees that must have taken centuries to grow. Ren's excitement was bubbling inside her. She couldn't wait for a good meal and a hot bath. Jayda hugged Oberic's arm before letting her hand fall and grip his. They were both lost in the majesty of this place. Servants threw flower petals in front of them as they walked. Dwim thought to himself that a Dwarven parade was just as glamorous. Alastor had no thought on the matter. He was still fuming about having been shot.

They were led to a lane of small but lovely homes for each of them. Jayda squeezed Oberic's hand and leaned up to whisper in his ear. "Stay with me." She pulled back with a soft smile. Had anyone been caught between their gaze they surely would have burst into flame.

Oberic couldn't help but think of how he was unable to say no to her even when he was fully aware of how terrible an idea it was. "I can never say no to you. Do you know that?"

Jayda looked at him with emerald eyes, once filled with lust and desire, that filled with adoration and love, "I do now," she said with a whisper. With his hand in hers, she led him into one of the homes and shut the door behind them. The others looked at each other. Nearly all of them, except Alastor, were on the verge of letting their giggles spill from their mouths.

Alastor had of course not joined in on this but instead turned to the Lady and asked, "Are these tree houses good for keeping sounds inside? I do not want to be woken by those two mating." The others finally broke and laughter spilled out. Even the Lady could not help but smile. Alastor did not understand what was so funny about his genuine question.

The others went into their own little homes and they all marveled at the beauty and detail that was crafted into each. Ren was so delighted to have found the bath that she let out a squeal and set herself up for a hot bath. She slipped into the basin and let out a long sigh. She would soak away the terrors she had experienced so far. She had her eyes closed when she heard the voice of another woman in the room with her. "Would you like to be bathed?" Ren's eyes shot open and spotted an Elven woman who was barely dressed standing there..

Ren shook her head, "No?" She had no idea why she answered with a question. She decided to try a more firm approach. "No. I am capable of doing that myself. I will take some fresh clothes if that is possible."

The Elf nodded. "All shall be provided."

Other Elven women tried offering the same to the others. Leon politely declined. Dwim had made it clear no woman without a beard was going to wash anything of his. When the servant who was to take care of Alastor walked in and saw how ugly he was she immediately begged his pardon before she performed a series of apologetic bows. She would leave the Orc in a confused state but once she was gone, he shrugged his shoulders and laid himself on the floor. Jayda and Oberic were naturally offered the same thing. Oberic blushed, feeling awkward in the room. Jayda grinned playfully at him. She turned to the servant and nodded slowly, "I would love that. Do you happen to have any clean clothes for us?"

The servant bowed her head like the one had for Ren, "All will be provided." Jayda went to the tub and climbed in. The Elf had come in and washed her as she was instructed to do. Jayda had no issues allowing herself to be pampered and cleaned. Every inch of her body was scrubbed and polished. When that was done, the Elf worked on her hair; washing it and then brushing it out for her. Oberic was asked to wait in another room while they took care of her. Oberic felt he had been waiting quite a while and when the door finally opened, the servants gave Oberic a bow before leaving. Jayda took a shy step out of the room. Her cheeks were still flushed with the warmth of the hot water. She was dressed in a long white gown, thin flowing material; not as sheer as the clothing that was seen on others but a very stark contrast to what Jayda would usually wear. Her hair was pulled back into multiple braids and from each one was a small silver ring with a gem that dangled. Oberic stood there completely speechless. When he finally gained his composure, he spoke with such anxiety it was as though he were a young boy seeing a woman for the first time, "You're breathtaking."

Jayda glided to him and Oberic could not help but see the desire in her eyes and he knew she could see it in his own eyes. Her chest rose and fell as she wrapped her arms around his neck and leaned up to kiss him. The burning they felt for one another in this moment could only be described as an inferno. Her nails dug into his neck as his arms wrapped around her. He pulled her close against him. Even with his overcoat she could feel him beneath it. Their tongues intertwined and Jayda pulled away from him just after biting his lower lip.

"It's been twenty and some years since I've known a woman," Oberic said, "will you still have me?" The flush in his cheeks made her smile. She thought to herself that if their first time was nearly as fun as when they fooled around in the library then this was going to be amazing. The man was not known to be nervous about much, but he stood there trembling inside at the prospect of the two of them having one another.

Jayda nodded and moved back in to take him for herself. Just as her arms wrapped tighter around him her stomach growled. She pulled herself away with an embarrassed look, "I'm sorry!"

Oberic could not help but laugh. Maybe it was for the best that they had stopped. There was no telling what sort of fire they may have lit in that house. "Get dressed," he said smiling at her, "I am certain we can find something to eat. Our time will come when it's ready."

Jayda twirled around in the gown, something Oberic would have never expected from her, "I actually thought I would wear this for dinner and something," she thought for a moment and bit her bottom lip, "less modest for desert." Her eyes sparkled as she took his hand. "Let's go find everyone. I'm positive Rennyn will be very much at home here." He took her hand and the pair of them left the small house to find the others.

Dwim was in a fuss when he barged out of his home and nearly ran Oberic over. Servants chased after him from the house, insisting they braid his beard since he denied the bathing service. Leon was already outside and looking as handsome as ever. Alastor was also there waiting. His servant returned after calming herself down and insisted on him wearing Elven clothes, something he was not happy about, he stuck out like a sore thumb. She did not offer to bathe him. Rennyn was the last to come outside. She wore a dove gray gown similar to Jayda's, but hers was adorned with silver chains and delicate embroidery in a darker gray. Her red hair was loose and in waves down her back with a small fine chain of silver sitting above her ears like a crown. She wondered if her mother wore outfits like these.

They were all smiles when they met except for Alastor who promptly asked, "Where is the food?"

A servant appeared behind him just as he asked and bowed her head, "Please follow me. The feast is ready for you."

They followed the girl to a wooden pavilion covered in bright flowers. There was a single long wooden table on which bowls and plates of fruits as well as succulent meats awaited them. Leon pulled out a chair for Ren who blushed and thanked him. He sat next to her and Dwim sat next to him. Oberic and Jayda moved to the other side of the table and like Leon, he pulled a chair out for her. She thanked him and sat down and when she did, he joined her. The Lady sat at the head of the table and other Elves, who stood around the pavilion, watched them. Alastor was still standing as he reached out and took hold of a fruit unfamiliar to himself. He bit into it, sending juices flying and dripping from the crevice of his lips. One of the Elves cleared their throat, but The Lady laughed. "They are hungry. Let them eat. There is no need for formalities here." Alastor eyed the Elf who was offended and kept mashing the fruit between jagged teeth and glared at them with yellow eyes.

The Lady stood at the head of the table and raised her arms. "Blessed be the waters! Blessed be the earth!" All the Elves in attendance chanted some Elvish reply. "Eat and be merry. For this day we have visitors and this night we shall celebrate for we break bread with outsiders." The Lady was applauded as she sat down; her servants nearly tripped over themselves to serve her. She motioned for them to eat.

Dwim stabbed a piece of meat whose aroma had enticed him long enough. Ren and Jayda had reached for the same type of fruit and both let out a similar noise of appreciation with Jayda saying, "Oh, that is divine!" Leon had torn off a piece of bread and even Alastor was sticking his hands into different dishes, making sure to grab handfuls of it for himself. Oberic however did not seem interested in the feast and simply sat there.

It was several moments of feasting before servants brought out pitchers of dark Elven wine. Goblets were filled and they all seemed to relish the flavor except Dwim who would have argued that Dwarven wine was better if he wasn't so polite. Oberic still had not eaten or drank. The Lady looked at Oberic and found he was eyeing her. She cleared her throat and began, "You must be wondering-"

Oberic cut her off, "Wondering why you're being so generous to outsiders? Yes, that very thought had crossed my mind." The others immediately stopped what they were doing and stared at him. Jayda flashed a look at him and placed her hand on his arm. "Forgive me, but it is not like your people to so freely open your home. You've either broken tradition or you need something."

Dwim's eyes grew large, "Lad! Yer being insulting!"

"You seem to know quite a bit about my people, sorcerer." The Lady said. Oberic raised a brow in surprise. "Yes, I sense it in you as you no doubt sense it in me. You've called out my ruse so let us not play each other for fools any longer. You're right. We do not so commonly welcome outsiders."

Oberic surprised the group, except Rennyn who already knew, by speaking perfect Elvish to the Lady who let out a cackle and raised her goblet to him, "Your words, not mine." She took a long drink from her goblet and set it back down. Oberic would later tell the group he let her know that he knew that they were nothing more than lesser disposable beings to them. "Our generosity would not normally be wasted on your sort. We, however, do have a need for your services."

Oberic leaned back and let out a sigh. "What do you want-"

"Silence," The Lady snapped, "Your service is not needed." She eyed Jayda and pointed a finger at her to drive home her point. "You're a Hunter from Marrenval, aren't you?"

Jayda didn't like the tone she took with Oberic. She was feeling wonderful and sexy until this Elf spoiled it. Jayda cast emerald eyes to The Lady, "I am, yes. The best one there." Her declaration was full of pride and confidence.

The Lady sneered, "I do not believe you. I am sure there are better Hunters, but I am in no position to be picky. I have a quest for you." Jayda went to open her mouth to argue, but The Lady held up a finger. "I will reward you of course with whatever you wish, so long as it is in my power to give."

Jayda had risen to her feet and went to speak again, but Ren hissed out to her, "Don't. . ." Jayda took a deep breath and composed herself.

"What kind of quest?" Jayda asked through her clenched jaw.

"My daughter, Na'mia," all the Elves lowered their heads at the mention of the name, "has been kidnapped by a creature. Man maybe? I do not know. It is told that he was once one of our kin as well so at this point no one is sure. This does not matter for he has taken her."

"How is that no one knows what he is? How did he just kidnap her?" Jayda asked, looking rather annoyed.

"The thing must have fooled her into thinking she loves him. He keeps her hidden in a temple deep in the forest. It used to be a place of worship for the Wild

Gods many generations before me. We have sent many of our best, but they all return confused and disoriented. It is as if the creature hypnotizes." The Lady shook her head. "Surely you must have hunted such magicians before?"

Jayda retorted with a sneer of her own, "I have lost track of all I have hunted. Blood witches, wizards mad with power, conjurers trying to bully a town, this idiot," she jabbed a finger at Oberic who furrowed his brow and mumbled something about the remark being uncalled for, "even monsters when I have hunted all the others and there was nothing left. I am confident in my abilities." Her eyes lingered on the Lady and they flashed with anger. "I won't be fooled by parlor tricks. I wouldn't make such a mistake."

The Lady glared at Jayda, not appreciating for a moment her insulting the ability of her people, "Name your price."

Rennyn looked at the group and Dwim spoke up, "Maybe we should discuss this as a group. This seems pretty dangerous, lass."

Jayda raised her hand to Dwim and he silenced immediately, "I want you to find our friend, Phineas, and remove his curse."

"Curse?" The Lady barked a laugh. "Have your sorcerer do it. If that was a price I could pay I would gladly, but it is simply not in my power." She leaned back and placed her hands in front of her. She laced her fingers together and put on a face of confidence and assurance. "Now find him? That may be possible."

"If you can guarantee that you can find him then we have a deal." Jayda's eyes did not leave The Lady. She had laid the offer on the table and waited for the response.

The Lady drew in a deep breath and gave her answer, "You have my word that I will do my best to have your friend found. I have one condition to add to this quest."

"That is?" Jayda asked.

"You will go on this quest alone." The Lady said. The group erupted in protest. 'Your friends will remain here so that I can ensure you return with my daughter."

Jayda was pissed off now, "Fine." The group argued again, but the Lady raised her hand and archers stepped in again aiming their arrows at the group.

"Make no mistake, Hunter. Your friends are my prisoners until you return with my daughter" The Lady was leaving nothing to the imagination with her meaning.

Dwim stood up and shouted, "Now listen here, woman!"

"Silence!" The Lady called out, not raising her voice but somehow it was deafening. "Be thankful we have been this generous so far. You and your people will be treated as well as you are now while she is on the quest. I trust the Hunter and Hunter alone. Fail and we leave you to rot outside our sanctuary. Succeed and you shall have what you asked for and possibly more. Do we have a deal?"

"Oberic! You can't let her do this!" Ren pleaded, looking from him to Jayda. Oberic actually had no issues with Jayda going. It was not that he did not care about her safety, but that he knew what he himself was capable of. If she could take him down, and he had no doubt that even if he was trying she could still have done so, then she would have no problem handling some spell caster in the wilds.

"That's enough, Ren!" Jayda barked. Ren cowered down but glared angrily at her. Jayda lifted her goblet, finished the wine, and slammed it on the table. "You have a deal."

The Lady stood up, "I will have a map prepared, food rations, water, and a horse ready for you at the break of dawn." She smiled, one that each of them hated now, and stepped away from the table. "Enjoy our hospitality." The Lady left the pavilion. It no longer felt like a feast as the other Elves left as well. Alastor had not stopped eating and would not stop until he was ready to burst.

Rennyn pushed her plate back, suddenly feeling sick to her stomach. She stood up and yelled at Jayda now, "We are supposed to be in this as a team! You made a decision without thinking about the rest of us!"

"This quest is mine and mine alone. You want it then maybe you should have been the Hunter. This is the type of work I do!" Her eyes cut through Ren. "I will find her daughter and we will get Phineas back. Then we can leave this place." She looked around in disgust. The pavilion, once beautiful and full of life, felt ugly and gaudy. She was overwhelmed with the colors and smells. "I'm done here." She gathered her gown and stormed off back towards the house.

The others found that their appetites had gone. One by one they all left the table. Ren first, storming off to her own house. Leon left next followed by Dwim. Oberic and Alastor sat at the table alone together. The two looked at each other. Alastor continued to shovel food into his mouth. Oberic shook his head, half disgusted and half amazed, and stood up. "Good night, Alastor." Alastor nodded to Oberic and continued on with the feast.

Oberic walked back to the house where he and Jayda were staying. He placed his hand on the door knob and then paused. Would she still want him to stay with her? Even if he was unsure, he decided to go in anyway. He wanted to make sure she was alright and as he entered the small house he called out, "Jayda?" He removed his hat and placed it over a chair.

Jayda was pacing back and forth, running her whip through her fingers. "All of a sudden I am this weak woman to them?" She looked at Oberic. "I am stronger than Rennyn! Stronger than Dwim, Leon, Alastor! Even stronger than you!" Her eyes were filled with anger.

Oberic stood there and allowed her to release her emotions at him, "I do not believe they meant it that way. You are their friend, like it or not. They care about you. I care about you. No one wants to see you get hurt; myself included."

A frustrated sigh escaped her lips as she threw her whip to the bed. Her hands reached up into her hair, trying to pull out the intricate gems and braids. "I don't want to wear this anymore! I don't want any of their things!" She pulled harder and harder until her eyes filled with tears.

Oberic stepped closer and raised his hands, only halting for a moment, before he ran his fingers through her hair. "Be easy. I wish I could be angry, but I have to admit I suspected something when she first welcomed us. I am sorry I did not say anything. Not so much sorry that I didn't tell the others, but sorry I didn't say something to you." His fingers gently plucked the intricacies from her hair. "She is trusting you and it's for a reason. You have grown as a person, but that does not mean your skills have changed. You are a Hunter. This is exactly what you trained to do."

Her eyes raised to his and a few tears ran down her cheeks, "Oberic, I am scared. What happens if I fail? What happens to the rest of you?"This was something she never had to worry about. If she died while bringing someone in, that was it. She died and everyone would carry on. For the first time in her life, there was more at stake for her hunt. If she failed her friends could possibly be harmed because of her folly.

Oberic gave her a gentle smile. It was one that many people would never see for it was reserved for moments like this. It was sweet that even now she was thinking of her friend's safety. "You mouthed off to my ex wife. Some nut in the wilds won't be an issue. This is the time where you remember Angus and all that he taught you. He lives on in you. Always. No matter how much you change as a person."

Jayda laid her head against his chest and stood there quietly until her hair was free and flowing again. His fingers in her hair gave her chills and she looked up at him. Their eyes connected and she smiled. He made her feel safe, not that she needed anyone to do that, but it felt nice. Jayda stepped back and untied the gown just a little. It slid off her shoulders and fell to the floor, crumpled at her feet. Not a word was spoken as she stood there, exposed to him with her cheeks flushed and her lips parted slightly.

His eyes explored her body, wonderful creation it was, taking in the absolute perfection that was her firm and curvy form. He stepped to her and took her into his arms. He placed his lips against hers. The fire burned hot in both of them once more. They had each other for the first time. The love making was slow and passionate. Their bodies glistened with sweat while their eyes never left one another. Once they were done and he filled her, they rested. It wasn't long that they laid in each other's arms before they took each other again. This time it was wild and heated. Their cries of pleasure no doubt echoed in the night.

Jayda woke up early the next morning entwined in Oberic's arms. She very carefully slid out from the bed, got dressed quietly in her Hunter gear, and pulled her hair back tightly. She coiled her whip and placed it on her hip. She set her daggers along her belt where they belonged. Once her cloak was on, she slid her sword in its scabbard on her back. Her dark outfit was a vivid contrast to all of the bright colors that surrounded her. She looked down at Oberic's sleeping face with a sad smile. She had decided she wouldn't wake him. She thought that the goodbye would be too painful and so she walked out silently, shutting the door behind her with care.

The others should have been sleeping but every one of them, save Oberic who was worn out from her through the night, was there to see her off. Even

Alastor had decided to show up. He grabbed his ax and then took her hand with the other. He drew the blade across her palm, cutting her hand open. He then did the same to his own and once they were both bleeding he grasped her hand. "We are blood kin now. You and your man have earned my respect, my loyalty, for your bravery. The strong stick together." He then handed her the ax. "Cleave some flesh for your blood kin."

She tested the weight of the ax in her and then looked at Alastor, "I'll put it to good use."

"We have faith in you, Jayda." Leon said as he patted her on the shoulder.

"You'll be the light in the darkness, lass. Keep yer' chin up." Dwim said as he gave her a soft salute. She smiled at the both of them and returned Dwim's salute. She then stepped to Ren and tipped her head up with her fingers.

"Please don't be angry with me, Ren. I can't bear it." Her eyes provided proof of her sincerity and Ren smiled.

"Not angry; worried." She replied.

"I'm trusting you to take care of everyone while I am gone," Jayda said, "Oberic especially. Will you promise me that?"

Rennyn nodded slowly and whispered, "I will. Please be safe." Jayda leaned in and gave her a quick kiss on the cheek.

Jayda turned and headed over to The Lady who stood near a beautiful cream colored horse. She looked just as breathtaking as before but spoke coldly, "Come back with my child or be the reason your friends meet their end." Jayda climbed up the saddle and threw her leg over. When she was sitting comfortably, she commanded the horse forward.

The way was cleared for her and though they had mostly forced her to take the quest, the eyes of the Elves met hers with respect. Jayda was a true Hunter, and though they would never admit it, they were in awe that she was in their presence. She was on her quest to retrieve something precious for them. They all lowered their heads as she passed, a sign of their respect, and kept them lowered until she was across the bridge, out of their sight beyond the trees.

Oberic startled awake in bed and by the time he ran outside, fully nude, she was gone and his heart ached for her. He stood there, on the bridge leading out of the town, amongst what he knew as his friends now. He stared out into the wilds, unable to move himself as he remembered her taste. That was followed by the memory of her scent and her touch. He was lost and hopeless, not fully understanding how deep she had crawled into him.

Alastor placed a hand on Oberic's shoulder. "She is stronger than you. She will not die.

Rennyn turned around after losing sight of Jayda and blinked as she took in the sight of Oberic. "Oberic Wintersong!" She covered her eyes as her face turned red. "Where are your clothes?"

Oberic looked down at himself and blushed. "Ah, well, you see. . ."

Dwim shrugged, "I've seen bigger hammers on a Dwarven lass." He started to walk off. Leon looked puzzled and turned to follow him.

"What in the world is going on with your women, Dwim?" He called out with a half laugh.

Oberic turned and ran back to the house that he and Jayda shared. Ren peeked through her fingers and once she saw that he was gone, she caught up with Leon. She elbowed him and then smiled, "Took them long enough." The pair laughed.

CHAPTER 18

Na'mia, a tanned and tall Elf with brass colored hair, walked through the forest as she did every day of her life. Her teal eyes took in all the wonders of nature before her. She sat down on a moss covered hollow log with her harp in her lap. She took a deep breath and her fingers began to play the strings. The music she produced was slow and would have put even the wildest beast at ease. She opened her mouth and began to sing a woeful song about a man who loved a woman far above his station in society. The man gave the woman his heart and though she felt the same, denied him her love. The man, after giving her all that he could, died of a broken heart and the woman lingered on forever in sorrow.

Na'mia had no idea that she was being watched from a distance. A creature unknown to her had heard her harp and was called by it. It peeked out from behind a tree and stared at her with amber colored eyes that looked to have specks of gold in them. As it listened to the song, it felt its own heart breaking. It was unsure if it was the mournful song itself or her haunting voice. The creature came from behind the tree timidly. It crept towards her in awe and when it had come close enough it spoke, "What song do you sing?"

The girl stopped playing abruptly and looked to where the voice had come from. She cowered away as she saw the creature standing there. It was tall and half of it was man and the other half animal. It's legs seemed to be something similar to a goat or a deer. It's fur was coal colored and its skin, which started just below the abdomen, was a blue black tone. It's hands had long fingers that were tipped with black nails. It's lips were black and in it's mouth sat small pointed teeth. It's brow and forehead were elongated and protruded out. Dark brown hair that curled draped from it's head and hung over two black horns that rose and twisted back.

The thing flinched as she cowered away, "I am sorry," It said, "I have scared you. I only heard you playing and it called to me. What is your name?"

She sat there examining the creature for a moment, "Na'mia. Do you have a name?"

The creature thought for a moment as though it could not remember, "They called me Minnaar long ago I think."

"You think? You do not know your own name?" she asked, a bit baffled by the thing.

It shook its head. "It has been a long time. I was left to guard the temple."

"What temple?"

Minnaar pointed back in the direction he had come from. "That way. Deep in a hidden grove. A temple once used to make offerings to the Wild Gods."

"Why aren't you guarding it?" she asked, still feeling uneasy.

The beast flinched from her again and turned its head from her as if her words caused pain. "No one goes there. I only wanted to see more." It slowly moved to face her again."Will you play again?"

Na'mia thought for a moment and while she kept her eyes on the thing she started to pluck at the strings. She watched Minnaar sit and place it's hands on its knees. She had never seen such a creature before. "Are there others out there like you?"

Minnaar answered swiftly. "Not here, no. I am the last brother of the forest here. In other groves, yes. The world is big."

Na'mia played the harp for Minnaar who sat there listening, nearly on the verge of tears. It wasn't long after that she stopped and stood up."I must be going home, Minnaar."

Minnaar climbed up. "I do not wish you to leave."

"It does not matter what you wish of me, Minnaar. I simply must." She turned to walk away and hoped he would not follow.

"Will you come back? Will you come and play for me again?"

She turned and smiled at Minnaar, "Maybe."

Minnaar watched her leave the area until she was out of sight and then turned himself to face back towards the direction of the temple. He ran back into the wilds to his home. After a bit of running, he decided he would not return to the temple, but instead linger around the area in hopes that Na'mia would return. A day passed with no signs of her return. He assumed she had been scared by him and would never come back. He had pranced around the area for quite some time when the sound of the harp called to him again. He darted out in that direction and found Na'mia sitting on the log once more. Her eyes caught a glimpse of him and she offered him a smile. Minnaar sat down across from her and listened to her play.

This carried on for months. She would play and sing for him and he would sit and listen. There was one afternoon where she played a song for him and after she finished Minnaar called to her, "I love you, Na'mia. You love me too."

She looked at him curiously, "I do love you, Minnaar. We have grown very close and you are dear to me."

He crawled to her and placed his hands on her legs. "Let me keep you. Stay with me at the temple. Play for me forever. Please."

Na'mia winced as he squeezed her legs, "Minnaar, you're hurting me."

"I love you, Na'mia! I refuse to let you go!"

"You don't love me, Minnaar. Perhaps you think you do but it is not so."

"If you will not come with me then I will take you with me." Minnaar stood up and looked down on her.

Na'mia looked up at him with bright teal eyes,"If you do that Minnaar then we will not be as good friends as I thought we were. I do not wish to go anywhere. I have enjoyed our time here in the forest."

Minnaar had heard enough. He scooped her up in his arms and started off towards the temple. She beat at him with her fists though it did not seem to help the situation. She begged and pleaded with him to let her go but he would not. When she became too much trouble for him to carry he muttered words she did not understand and she slipped into dreamless sleep.

Some might think it is good to have dreamless sleep. Imagine if you can, rest without the burdens of life weighing you down or terrible nightmares plaguing your dreams. Surely then, dreamless sleep would be wonderful. Consider the possibilities of all the wonderful dreams you might miss. All the days spent with a lover, no longer there. They might be painful memories, but you would be glad to have them. Those days you celebrated with friends and family, all gone. Those would all be missed in a dreamless sleep. The ups and downs of life and the visions created within the heads of those dreamers would all be lost to nothingness. That is the slumber that beautiful Na'mia slept.

Na'mia would open her eyes and find herself laid out on a stone slab bathed in sunlight. She shielded her eyes and once they adjusted, looked around. She was inside ruins of some sort. From the shadows of the mossy ruins she saw the two amber eyes watching her. "Minnaar?" she called out, "Where have you taken me?"

"To the temple. You will stay here with me. You may not love me now but you will. I will be good to you." Minnaar crept into the light. "Play for me." He held out the harp to her.

"No. I do not wish to play for you anymore, Minnaar. You have taken me against my will." She crossed her arms and glared at him defiantly. He crept back into the shadows.

"Roam the temple as you like. Settle into your new home. Then you will play for me." Minnaar's eyes vanished into the darkness and Na'mia was left sitting there bathed in light. She threw her legs over the slab and climbed down. She spent the next few hours exploring the ruins. The place was littered with bones of animals and skeletal remains of beings more like herself. The place was overgrown and reclaimed by nature. As she explored she often wondered if it were her people who had built this temple long ago and then wondered why it was abandoned. They still worshiped the Wild Gods so why did she not know of it until now.

There were many rooms in the temple. Some were quarters for sleeping, another seemed to be a sort of banquet hall, and others she had no idea what they may have been used for. In the banquet hall she did come across the stone bust of a man who had the facial features of an Elf, ears as well, but large antlers protruding from his head. She knew this was the bust of Ezrel, Lord of the Hunt and Guardian of the Clearing beyond. She now at least knew one of the Wild Gods worshiped here.

Minnaar would try to get her to play for him again later as well as the days following and each time she would refuse him. She sat on the stone slab bathed in light when he approached her again. "Please play for me." he said, holding out the harp to her. She shook her head and Minnaar's anger grew. He thrust the harp into her hands and yelled at her. It was something he had not done before. "You will play for me!" Na'mia flinched from him as his face twisted. Her own anger grew now. Anger, as you might already know, is very contagious. She took the harp and threw it away from herself. The harp played its last notes as it struck a fallen column and several of its strings popped.

Minnaar backed away from her and released a heartbreaking and mournful cry; one that made Na'mia soften. It made her feel terrible for what she had done. Minnaar's cry was not for the harp though. He would have been happy to listen to her voice speak. Instead, he felt terrible for having yelled at her out of anger. There was no doubt in the beast's heart that what he experienced around her was love. It thumped so hard in his chest just at the mere sight of her. The fact that he not only yelled, but frightened her in the process, was something he never intended to do and would be eternally angry at himself for ever causing such a wonder of creation such pain. He cried out because he knew now that she found him vile and horrible.

Still, even in his understanding of what he was to her, he could not let her go. He was aware that it was selfish. He was aware it was unkind to both her and himself, but nothing he told himself would allow his heart to set her free. He stepped up to her and muttered the words he had done before. Her eyes grew heavy and she fell back on the slab. Minnaar took her hands and rested them on her stomach and then he brushed her cheek with his finger tips. Tears fell from his amber eyes. He knew, without a doubt, she would never love him.

Jayda's journey was nearly four days long and she had constantly checked the map she was provided as well as the sky to keep her bearings. There was an area marked on the map in Elvish that she could not read, but thought the image drawn looked like some ruins and so she decided that would be where she went first. When she did arrive she stared at the crumbling ruins of a once great temple, or so it looked like that to her. There was something special about this place and she could feel it. It was as if the area itself had a magical aura to it. Now and again she could have sworn she saw sparkling creatures flutter about in the treetops. She shook her head and released the thought. She had a job to do and if this was the place; she would do it.

She dismounted her horse and tied him up to a nearby tree. She gave him a pat as she examined the ruins with her emerald eyes. There were so many points of entry for her to make that it was hard to choose. She stood there for a long time before she decided to just go in the first entry she saw at the front of the ruins. She would no doubt be seen, but she wasn't made to sneak around; she was made to hunt.

"Where is that damn bird when you actually need him," she muttered to herself as she crept closer to the ruins, "Why we left him in Hadryn is beyond me." She could have used an extra pair of eyes for this particular quest. She listened as carefully as she could for any sounds that might be whomever she was hunting. She entered the ruins and found there was no need to search hard. Far in the back she saw a beam of light coming from a hole in the collapsing roof. It shined down on a beautiful tanned Elf with brass colored hair; almost as if it were a beacon making note of her objective. She knew not to go darting after the girl though. She uncoiled her whip and continued to scan the dark room.

Near a brazier of dying firelight sat a shadowy figure. It's amber and gold flecked eyes watched Jayda just as she watched it. "You've come to take her away from me, haven't you?" The sound of an out of tune harp being plucked came after the question.

Jayda nodded, "You took the girl and her family wants her back. This doesn't have to end ugly; it just has to end. Give me no trouble and I won't have to put you down."

"Have you ever seen such a creature?" The figure asked. It stood and moved from the dying fire and towards the beam of light. It entered and Jayda nearly gasped at the vision of the thing. It was something she had never seen before herself and she found it looked terrifying. The creature brushed the backside of his hand against Na'mia's face. The thing drew in a breath that was mixed with a sob. "The finest thing to ever walk this mortal world. Why won't she love me?" It looked at Jayda with such an expression of sorrow and despair that even Jayda, momentarily, felt pity. "I love her."

Jayda shook her head and moved closer, one slow step at a time, "You may love her. I can see why. She is very beautiful, but I have a feeling she doesn't love you. You need to let her go."

Minnaar looked back at Na'mia, "Why do you think she does not love me? What gives you that impression?"

Jayda stopped. "Sometimes love isn't returned. It's sad and it hurts, but life goes on. If you truly love her, then why is she asleep on some slab looking like some sort of sacrifice? You've put her under some kind of spell. That Elf is coming with me." She began to walk towards him again.

The beast knelt beside Na'mia now and gazed at her lovingly, "Have you been in love? Have you known a touch that both chilled and heated you?"

Jayda was starting to get annoyed, but if diplomacy was going to make this easier she would play along. "Yes." Her answer was short but honest. She did not feel the need to go into detail about what she had known of love.

The creature looked at her again. It had tears slipping from it's eyes and Jayda could almost swear that they were illuminated but only barely. "Would you give them everything? Sacrifice everything? Have you looked in their eyes and seen your unborn children?"

Jayda thought about Oberic for a moment and then pushed the thought away. He was trying to play on her emotions. She snapped her whip on the floor. It made a terrible crack that caused the beast to flinch. "I'm taking the Elf. You can either get out of the way or you can get hurt." She moved towards the slab no longer interested in trying to be cautious. She reached out to shake the Elf. "Wake up, Na'mia. We're leaving."

Na'mia mumbled something in her forced sleep and the creature hissed "Do not disturb her! She is mine and you are not worthy of her!" Jayda ignored the thing and this time grasped Na'mia's arm and jerked it. "Stay away from her! She is mine!" Minnaar shouted in a voice expressing pure agony. He threw out a clawed hand meaning to slash Jayda in the face.

Jayda leapt back and prepared her whip for an attack. The beast snarled as he watched her take her fighting stance. He pointed a clawed finger, the nail black and sharp, and began to mutter his spell that kept poor Na'mia asleep. This was Jayda's specialty. She moved so fast that a word barely left his sneering lips when the whip lashed out and stuck him in the mouth. He coiled back and felt his lips. The blood that poured from the wound was bright. Jayda wagged her index finger at him, "Tsk tsk. None of that shit." She wore a confident smirk on her face and a gleam in her that said she was ready to fight.

Minnar stepped back into the shadows and turned his gaze from her. Being so close to the beam of light she could not see very well and decided that she too should slip back into darkness. Jayda tried to keep low as she waited for her eyes to readjust to the darkness. As she prowled, she felt the wind of something pass just before her face and then hit the ground. She immediately thought the bastard had shot an arrow at her and if that were the case then she needed to see better. She took off at a sprint towards the entrance she had come through. She could easily pick up the clacking sound of hooves on stone as the thing chased her down. Jayda ran out into the sunlight and was temporarily blinded; what she could see however were trees all around her and so she darted to one and slid behind it.

The beast came out with a bow drawn and ready to fire. "You are in my grove, Human. The Wild Gods offer no protection for your kind! I will find you!" He marched forward sniffing at the air. "Your fear gives you away, girl!" He charged forward and swung around the tree she was hiding behind only to be met by the black haired Hunter ready for him. Her sword was drawn and pointed up so that as he rounded the tree it jabbed against his neck. He froze in place and sneered down at her while blood still poured from his lips, "You think you have won?"

"Won? Yes, but we're only just getting started. Just remember that you chose this when you tried to claw at me. Drop the bow." she commanded him. He did as she said and just as another smirk appeared on her face he thrust out his hand. His clawed fingers wrapped around her neck. He squeezed tight as he lifted her and began to slam her against the tree. Her hands went to his as she tried to pry herself loose. She started to change color in the face and her struggle became less. He was the one sneering now and he pulled her from the tree and threw her against another. She hit the tree and slid down. She was on her hands and knees gathering her breath when she saw her sword laying on the ground not far from her.

"I will rip you apart! I will sacrifice you to the Wild Gods for their favor!" He lifted a hooven leg and stomped down. Jayda rolled out the way just in time and grabbed her sword. She could feel the impact of the hoof slamming down into the earth. She scrambled to her feet and took off back towards the temple. Her blade in one hand and her whip, dragging along, in the other, she did best to keep her sprint up hoping to outrun the lovesick creature. She looked behind herself and was alarmed to see the beast was catching up to her. She knew he wasn't very close, but there were moments as she ran that she felt his breath against her neck. He was gaining on her as she approached the sleeping Elf. She was running as fast as she could and with every stride he was closing the gap.

Jayda dropped her whip and sword. The metal made an eerie chime against the stone in the silence of the temple. Just as she reached the stone slab, she climbed up with a leap and propelled herself up and back. Minnaar had caught up to her and swung his arms together to grab hold of her. He had missed and watched as she had launched above him. It was a risky move but Jayda landed it perfectly. Her legs, narrowly missed being gored by the horns, landed on his shoulders and she herself leaned forward to start clawing at his eyes. He stumbled back and forth trying to remove the little thing from himself. He let out yells of anger and woeful cries of pain as she dug her fingers into him. Jayda thought it was now or never; it was time to finish this. She pulled one arm back and grabbed the ax Alastor had given her. She brought it around Minnaar and chopped at his throat with it. It would not be enough to cause serious injury, that she knew, and so once it bit into the flesh she dragged it across his throat.

Jayda had pushed herself off the back of him and landed on the stone floor with a grunt. She looked at the ax's blade and noted how it shined bright red. Her emeralds moved up to look at the beast. It stumbled forward and placed a hand on the stone slab. He turned to face Jayda and stared at her a moment with amber, gold flecked, eyes that were slowly losing the light behind them. His lifeblood spilled down his chest and stomach in a constant flow. He let out a gurgled cry, it wasNa'mia's name, as he turned and reached out for the Elf.

Na'mia opened her teal eyes and looked at Minnaar who had now fallen to his knees. His hand was stretched out to her and the Elf looked at him with a heart of sadness. "Minnaar!" She looked behind him and saw Jayda sitting there with the ax. The girl knew then that whoever this person was, she had been sent to bring her back and she frowned as she petted the beast's hand. "None of this had to pass. I am sorry, Minnaar, my friend." She crawled forward, took his face in her hands, and placed a kiss upon his brow. Minnaar closed his eyes and fell to the stone floor.

Na'mia sighed and Jayda, from where she was sitting, thought the Elf did truly look sorry that it had to end that way. Jayda got to her feet and stared at the girl who was freshly woken from magic slumber. "I am Hunter Jayda. I was tasked with bringing you back home to your bitch of a mother." Na'mia looked at Minnaar's body once more and then nodded to Jayda. Jayda walked to Minnaar with her ax and grabbed a handful of his hair. She pulled up on the creature's hair to extend the neck and lifted her arm to strike at the neck again.

"What are you doing to him?" Na'mia asked frantically.

Jayda looked at her annoyed, "I'm taking his head back as proof that he won't be an issue any longer."

"Hasn't he suffered enough?" her tan face flushed with anger, "Isn't it enough he died for nothing?"

"He died because he stole you and would not return you." Jayda said in a growl.

"He died because he loved me. A misguided love, but it was true and I will not be angry at him for having that. Only angry that he would not see reason. Please, I beg of you mighty Hunter, do not make mockery of his heart anymore than needed."

Jayda looked at the corpse and swung her ax downward. One of the horns from the beast's head fell to the floor with a clatter that echoed in the empty temple. She picked it up and stashed the ax behind her once more. Jayda walked over to the girl, bent to grab her whip, and then coiled it at her hip. She bent once more to get her sword and slid it into the scabbard on her back. Jayda waited for the Elf to understand they were leaving and when the girl nodded, they walked out of the temple together. Not a word was spoken between them as they approached the horse. Jayda helped Na'mia on the horse and took one last look around the grove where the temple sat in ruin. It was a strange feeling that came over her; she felt as though the aura that she felt coming in had now gone. She shook her head, looked down at the horn of the beast, and stashed it away in the saddle bag. She climbed on the horse and gave it a tiny kick to start a trot. Na'mia looked back at the temple and stared. She felt terrible about how Minnaar, a beast she cared for, met his end. There was a brief moment as she stared at the ruins that she would have sworn she saw a ghostly apparition of Minnaar walking side by side with a tall, antlered, Elf and just as fast as the moment was, it was gone. She said a prayer for Minnaar hoping the Wild Gods would hear it and look after him in the clearing.

Jayda looked at the map as they rode off and mumbled, "Amun would have been useful right now. I could have had him bring Oberic a note for me saying I was headed back."

Na'mia decided to try and make small talk as she knew it was going to be a long ride home, "Who is this Oberic?"

"Oberic is my," she paused for a moment unsure of what they were. No declaration had been made, "well, we are. It really is quite a story and we have a long ride so I suppose I can tell it if you're interested." Jayda told the story of how she and Oberic met. She made sure not to leave out the fact that she roughed him good. Na'mia exchanged her own tale of how she came to know Minnaar. The pair of them were eager to get back and both agreed to take control of the horse while the other caught some sleep. Jayda's original four day trip was far shorter this time as there was no need to stop for sleep.

It was their luck that it was just before dusk two days later when they approached the bridge of trees leading into the lake town. Elven archers called out their approach when they were spotted and a large number of the Elves had rushed out to greet the pair, if only to see the return of their beloved Na'mia. Among those narrow and pointed faces Jayda spotted her friends; and among those friends a bearded man in a pointed hat.

Elves rushed to them and helped Na'mia off the horse. Jayda climbed down herself, not that she was offered, and her feet started running to him without her even realizing it. She pushed past Elves and when she reached him, threw her arms around Oberic, collapsing into his arms. He lifted her in a tight embrace and spun her around. He placed kisses on her face.

"So, the Hunter was successful." The Lady stood there with her daughter. They both walked towards Jayda, the other Elves cleared the way. "I was wrong to doubt you, Hunter. You have kept your word and I must keep mine." She clapped her hands signaling several Elves dragging a monstrously large wolf bound in the tightest of knots. "Your friends described the beast and our hunters, accompanied by this one," she nodded to Leon, "tracked him over the week. I can not cure this curse of his, but I have him here just as our agreement dictated."

"Yes, you were wrong to doubt me." She glared at The Lady with angry eyes. She turned from Oberic and headed back to the horse. Jayda opened the saddle bag and pulled from it the horn she collected from the beast. She walked back to Oberic and tossed the trophy at The Lady's feet. "But I thank you for letting my friends stay and for finding Phineas for us. There's your proof that it has been taken care of for good." She held tightly to Oberic; the exhaustion was starting to hit her.

Na'mia looked at the horn, frowned, and excused herself from the group. The Lady watched her leave and then spoke to the crowd of Elves in their tongue. When she was done, they cheered and The Lady held her hands up again to silence everyone. "It is time you rested. Please, you have earned it." The Lady dipped her head and turned to go and join her daughter. The Elves surrounding them all dipped their heads as well and headed to do whatever it was they did.

Oberic swept Jayda up in his arms and carried her off to their little home for their stay. She smiled up at him and they laughed as they headed away from the rest of the group. Dwim, Leon, Ren, and Alastor were staring down at Phineas. The wolf struggled against its binding and then barked at the group. Alastor leaned down and then roared back at him.

"Go," Alastor grunted, "let him loose. I would like to fight the beast."

"Quite possibly the dumbest idea you've had." Ren said, staring at him. Alastor only looked at her and sighed.

Ren pulled out the silver amulet and studied it, "What do we do with it?"

Leon shrugged, "Just hold it against him. See what that does." Ren crept over to the wolf's head. "Not there," Leon warned, "there's a chance he could bite you. Get him on the hind or something."

Ren nodded at Leon. He was right, she could have been bitten if he snapped at her. She looked at the others with big purple eyes and drew in a long breath. She leaned down and placed the silver charm against the wolf's hind. It flinched from her and whimpered. Ren took this as a good sign that it was working and pressed the amulet further and harder against him. The wolf struggled as it tried to get away from them but the binding was too tight. The four of them watched in amazement as the wolf let out a single howl before it shifted before their eyes to the man they knew as Phineas and as per usual, he was naked.

Ren hurriedly tied the amulet around Phineas neck and then dusted her hands. She placed them on her hips and smiled at the others, "I really thought that would have been harder. Welcome back Phineas."

The naked man groaned as he laid there on the ground in front of them. Leon grimaced, "I've seen that man's bits more than I'd like."

Dwim agreed, "Aye, me too, lad."

"Well," Ren said, "we should get him into a bed so he can sleep it off. Hopefully with Jayda back, we can be on our way in the morning."

Dwim pointed at Phin's legs. "You take the legs, I'll get his arms."

"I'll do it." Alastor said and grabbed Phineas by the ankle and simply dragged him to the cluster of homes they were staying.

Leon watched the Orc drag the naked Phineas and looked to the other two. "What kind of people do we travel with?"

Ren shrugged, "The best kind of misfits." She smiled and took his arm softly. "Come on, admit it! You wouldn't pick anyone different. Would you?"

"I could be alright without most of them," Leon gave her his most handsome wink, "but you? I'm too fond of you."

A soft blush creeped across her cheeks as she looked up at him and met his big brown eyes."I'm pretty fond of you too."

Leon did not blush because Leon as a man was far too smooth to blush when flirting with a woman. "Rennyn, honestly, I'm crazy about you. You're beautiful and fun to be around. There hasn't been a moment I've never been happy to see you." Ren's eyebrows raised at the surprise admission, but she smiled and pulled a strand of her hair behind her ear. Leon continued, "I can't move at the speed that Oberic and Jayda have in that small time. Maybe you want more and I am sorry about that. I am crazy about you though. You make every day easier and honestly I can't fathom exploring this world without you. If," he cleared his throat, "if that is acceptable, I'd like to explore this with you."

She stepped up on the very tips of her toes, Leon still had to lean down a bit, and she placed her lips against his. The kiss was quick and that was fine. When she pulled back from him, she whispered softly, "We shall take out time."

He smiled playfully, "You sure? There's always Phineas and his business waving in front of everyone. Not even a little enticing?"

Ren shook her head with a giggle and smiled up at him again, "I've only had eyes for you, Leon. From the first day I met you."

He offered her a handsome smile and then his arm, "I think this is the start of something good."

She took his arm and they walked together, spending the rest of the evening talking and laughing; learning everything they could about each other. As they stayed up late into the night talking in one house, Jayda slept in another. Oberic had carried her in earlier and laid her in bed. The Hunter had earned her rest and she fell asleep immediately. In her dreams there was a strange itching. She dreamed of the crumbling ruins and then dreamed of other things that felt more like memories than dreams. It was so strange that they felt so real, but she knew, even while she slept, there was no way they could have been real.

Time passed deep into the night with only the stars and the moon illuminating the land. Everyone in the town was sleeping. Jayda woke herself up with a scream that died as she sat up. She was drenched in a cold sweat and looked around the room. She spotted Oberic, his eyes nearly glowing, sitting in a chair.

"Shh," he said softly and moved from the chair to the bed beside her, "You're safe. I'm here with you."

Jayda's hands frantically scratched at her arms trying to push away unseen hands grabbing at her. She screamed out, "Get them off me!" and kicked at the sheets tangled around her feet. Her body shook as she tried desperately to get away from the terrors that weren't there except for in her mind. Oberic knew what was going on and without a moment's hesitation he lifted his hands and weaved his magic near her head. He concentrated hard to pull the false memories from her. If she was to no longer care for him then it was something he would accept. Using magic to escape reality was never good for anyone and the thought he was doing more harm than good for her made his heart ache. Jayda sobbed as her hands went to her head and batted him away.

"Stop! Stop please!" She cried out. She covered her ears and shut her eyes tightly. When she opened her eyes, she was looking beyond him. She swore she could see a rotting man with a cleaver lodged in it's head and it's neck twisted at a terrible angle. Jayda dove from the bed and grabbed her dagger from her belt. It was barely loosened and in her hand before she swung wildly at the air. Oberic moved out of the way to avoid getting cut. If there was ever any indication of how strong minded Jayda was, she had in her dreams, started to break a spell that he cast on her. A spell, from a school of magic, that he specialized in.

Oberic took a deep breath, "I'm guessing marriage is out of the question after this." His hands danced and for Jayda the home vanished completely. She was left in darkness with only her vision of the dead man. Jayda spun in circles, her screams echoed loudly as she looked for Oberic. She backed away from the dead man with her arm holding up the dagger in front of her for protection.

Ren was stirred from her sleep from the commotion next door. She knew it was Jayda screaming and so she went to wake Leon. The pair of them rushed into the home Jayda and Oberic shared. Ren looked at Jayda with concern as she was on the floor with her dagger screaming at nothing. "Oberic, what's going on?"

"Stay back," he called out to the pair, "I think the memories started to resurface in her dreams. I told her this was dangerous." He ran his hands through his hair and took a deep breath. "She's just going to have to face it and overcome it." Oberic stepped closer to her and weaved his hands again. "Jayda, see me. I am here beside you." He hoped that his voice would allow her to see him through the illusion he was casting.

"Please make it stop!" Jayda sobbed as she backed away and then curled into a ball on the floor. She wailed out pitifully, "Oberic please! Help me!" Her eyes were unfocused as she called out for help only able to see the dead man.

Rennyn wanted so badly to go to her friend, "Oberic! She can't fight it! Look at her!" She made to run to Jayda, but Leon grabbed her and pulled her back.

Oberic dropped to his knees near her and his fingers danced their dance near her. He fought with himself over what the right decision was right now. Rennyn's hands went to her mouth as she watched Oberic work. Leon rested his hands behind his head. As Oberic worked, the dead man became nothing more than a ghostly image to Jayda before it slowly faded away. As Jayda watched on, the room began to return to her while she felt a prickling in her mind again. Without even thinking of it, the library scene flooded her mind. She laid there, panting in exhaustion, while sweat ran down her forehead and mixed with her tears.

"Oh, Oberic." Ren whispered as she looked at Jayda with sad eyes. Leon put an arm around her as he watched Oberic slide his arms under Jayda. He lifted her up and turned, placing her back on the bed. He grabbed the blanket and covered her up.

Oberic turned around and faced the pair after letting out a long sigh. As Oberic's gaze fell on them Leon had the feeling Oberic could be a terrible enemy if he wanted. There was danger in those angry eyes. "I should have never done this," Oberic said to them, "It's cruel." Ren and Leon both knew he was not angry with anyone other than himself. He grabbed his hat off the chair and slammed it down on his head. "I'll be back soon. I need to walk and get my head straight or something." Oberic stormed past the pair of them and left the house.

Ren watched him go and looked up at Leon. He returned her look and simply asked, "Non stop around here, huh?"

Ren sighed and nodded, "Yes, I doubt it will ever stop." She took his hand and squeezed it softly. "I am going to stay with her until he comes back. Just in case she wakes up."

Leon thought that was a good idea and gave her a nod. "I'll see if I can find him." He gave her a smile and headed out the home leaving Ren alone with Jayda. Ren dug around until she found a cloth and soaked it in cool water. She rang it out and climbed on the bed with Jayda. The Elf rested the cloth upon her friend's brow. She hummed to her softly as her fingers played with her hair lightly. She pondered on the ways she could help so that the responsibility of this didn't fall to Oberic only. She closed her own eyes and thought of her knowledge with herbs and potions.

Leon would spend several minutes looking before he found Oberic staring into the clear lake water, "You okay, pal?"

Oberic shook his head, "I should not have used such a spell," he sighed and looked at Leon, "but affection has a way of making us do stupid things. I think you'll learn that soon."

Leon crossed his arms, "Might already know." He shrugged and continued, "She needs you in there, Oberic. You know that, right? Everyone with a pair of eyes can see the way you two have been looking at each other. Even before we got to Hadryn."

Oberic nodded, "I know. I'll go back. I just needed a moment."

Leon continued to look at him, "Are you sure? I didn't peg you as the kind of guy to walk out of a situation like that."

Oberic looked at Leon for a long moment before speaking, "Do not mistake my needing a moment to clear my head as a sign of abandonment. I waited around for a woman for twenty years knowing she was never coming back; I think I'll be able to return after a small walk and fresh air." Oberic headed off, shouldering Leon as he went. Leon watched him head off and sighed.

Ren had been sitting with Jayda for a little over an hour. Jayda shifted and nuzzled into Ren's touch. The cool cloth brought down any temperature she may have had. She was resting peacefully and Ren was thankful for it. She hated seeing her friend go through such an ordeal. She had come up with a few ideas, but decided to save them for when her and Oberic could discuss them.

Oberic soon returned and stood there after shutting the door. He removed his hat and held the brim within his hands, "I'm sorry," he offered Ren an apologetic look, "I lost my head for a bit. I should not have put you in this position."

"We're all a team here," Ren replied in a soft tone, "We'll get through this together. Everyone has different ways of handling things. I suppose Jayda's strength and will to defend her friends as well as her drive to fight to protect us, it also means that her fears are just as strong." Ren slipped out of the bed carefully. Jayda let out a whimper, but seemed to rest peacefully again. Ren straightened herself out and then offered a smile to Oberic, "I will give some more thought to the situation to see what I can do to help if sleeping becomes an issue."

Oberic nodded, "I've known some talented alchemists in my younger days. If I ever get back to my home," he laughed, "not the hut on the beach, I've got a large collection of alchemical goods you're free to take."

Ren walked over to Oberic and smiled, "I would like that very much." She looked back at Jayda and sighed, "I know we started off not liking each other-"

"Not liking each other?" he asked, "I'd say you both hated each other."

Ren held back a laugh, "We did. I think though we have grown to love each other. She's like a sister. She's fierce and has so much fire in her heart." She placed a hand on Oberic's arm. "I know she will get through it. She'll just have to learn to accept our help which I think we both know will be tough for her."

Oberic looked at Jayda and mumbled, more to himself than to Ren, "Evelyn wasn't wrong. I do like the fiery ones." He looked back to Rennyn and offered her a smile. "I'll take good care of her. I promise."

Ren nodded and gave him a soft hug, "I know you will." She let go of him and exited the home. Oberic shut the door behind her and moved to the bed where Jayda lay. He climbed up next to her and ran his fingers through her dark hair. He admired her beauty for a moment before speaking quietly, "When I was a boy we were taught about all the stars that litter the sky above and the legends that go with them. The Aegis and the Lady Love were two that were quite popular. They were believed to have been mere mortals at some point." He shook his head. Oberic didn't really believe in most of the old stories. They were stories for children and young lovers. "Foolish stories, I'm sure. The Aegis was a master of all magic and The Lady Love, to The Aegis, was the center of all creation. It is said though that she was his companion through all his adventures. She was said to be strong and you bare her name. Perhaps you were named after the stories; maybe you are her reborn." He thought for a moment as he admired her more. "I don't know if any of that is true or even matters. I do know, for certain, that I am a foolish man who made a mistake, but I swear to you I will eventually make this right for you somehow."

She nuzzled, sleepily, into his hand with a smile on her lips as she slept. The night passed and the sunlight eventually came in the window. The light kissed her face and warmed her skin. She let out a yawn and opened her shining emerald eyes. She stretched long, much like a cat, and found a soreness in her body that confused her. She looked around and noticed her dagger sitting on the floor. "Odd. . ." she mumbled. She rolled over and found Oberic sitting up in the bed leaning against the wall. His head was dipped and he was fast asleep. She thought it was strange that he was still fully dressed. She did not know of course that he had stayed awake through the night to watch over her. She smiled and scooted closer to him. She pushed herself up and whispered in his ear, "Wake up, sleepy head." She climbed into his lap, not remembering a single thing about the events that took place in the early hours of the morning where only the moon shone. She nuzzled her nose into his neck where she placed long kisses against his skin and lastly a nip at his ear. "I'm ready to get out of this place."

Oberic's eyes opened slowly. The man was beyond tired, but he would never let her know that. He offered her a smile and reached up to touch her face. "I think we are all ready to get out of here." His hand brushed her cheek and left her face. Both hands found themselves on her hips and he gave her a tight squeeze. "Did you sleep well?"

She smiled at him and nodded, "I did, though I am aching this morning. You must have put in some work last night." She bit her lip and gave him a grin. "We must have knocked my dagger off the table. We'll have to be more careful. Someone could get hurt." She remained blissfully unaware.

"Yes, that's what happened. I guess I forgot to pick it up. Too sharp for me. Wouldn't want to cut my dainty fingers." He smirked at her as she rolled her eyes with a laugh. "I hope the others are ready to go. This place," he sighed, "well I'm done with it."

Jayda leaned back and rolled off, pulling him with her so that he laid over her. She offered him a sly grin, "Maybe the others can wait just a little longer?" She wrapped her arms around his neck and pulled him close to love her. What had started as a morning event turned into hours as the two of them enjoyed one another once more. Even when Ren banged on the door a few times they did not stop.

It was the third time Ren banged on the door. "Enough! We're tired of waiting on you two!" She laughed as she said the words. She looked to her side and saw Phineas, who was back to feeling like himself, trying to peek into the window. "What are you doing?" She asked, horrified.

"Lucky bastard! She's got a great body! I'm just trying to get a glimpse." He licked his lips as he squinted.

Alastor grabbed Phineas by his ponytail and yanked him back from the window. "We do not intrude on their privacy, worm!"

The pair inside had finished their love making and both were satisfied to the point neither wanted to get out of bed. Jayda, now sore for better reasons, slowly dressed herself. She pulled her hair over her shoulder and twisted it quickly with nimble hands into a long braid. She hooked her weapons onto her belt and her sword on her back in it's scabbard. She was a Hunter once more. Oberic's dressing took less time as the man traveled with less weaponry. They looked at each other, smiled, and left the home together with a bit of a pep in their step. They were shocked to see their friends there waiting for them.

"Uh, sorry," Oberic mumbled. A slight blush crossed his face. He cleared his throat, "Let's get out of here hm?"

Oberic walked off from the group no longer able to take their smirks and grins. Jayda however smiled at Phin and gave him a hug just before punching him in the ribs softly. "Don't run off again! We had no idea where you were!"

Phin smiled and gave her a shrug. Ren had thankfully clued him in on Jayda's memory situation. "You know me; I gotta keep myself entertained."

She shook her head and turned from him to follow Oberic. Leon had come up next to him. "Really? Keep yourself entertained?"

"What was I supposed to say? I love nature so much that I just need to be out there?" Phin threw his hands up. "Don't want me to say something stupid then you come up with the lie."

""Come on," Dwim said, "They're waiting for us to leave and I'm happy to oblige."

The others caught up with Jayda and Oberic. Each was glad to be gone, some for other reasons. Phineas was busy staring at most of the near nude Elves. The entire town had gathered near the bridge and in that crowd the Lady stood in the middle. "You have saved my only child, Hunter. I know our welcome was a ruse and full of guile, but I hope that our goodbye is more genuine and satisfying for you." She nodded and several of the Elves brought forward to the group beautiful white stallions with braided manes. Each wore a hand crafted saddle with large saddle bags. The saddle bags themselves were stuffed with oats and grains for the horses as well as fried meats, food, and water skins for them. Another bag filled with some gold, not much, but just a nice reward on top of it all. "Please take these horses and gifts as our thanks."

Jayda looked at the horses, as did the others, and gave a slight nod. The rest of the group seemed to appreciate them a bit more than she did. "I gave you my word that I would bring her back. We thank you for your gifts and your," she paused and tasted the word on her tongue before speaking it with a hint of bitterness, "hospitality." She climbed up on one of the horses and looked to the rest of the group. Jayda seemed to have, at least in this moment, taken command of their party. She gave them a nod and the rest climbed up on a horse as well.

Alastor grunted as he sat on the steed, "This horse is a waste of a good meal." It was of course well known that Orcs would eat horses, as well as nearly anything that had meat on it's bones.

"One last thing," The Lady said, "You do not know how much it means to me that you brought her back. We are eternally grateful." She, and the other Elves, moved out of the way of a large tree that made up part of the natural bridge. The base and trunk were carved throughout the night and had been turned now into a living statue of Jayda holding her whip in a stoic pose. The statue starred up into the sun's light while lush green leaves lived above. "We will forever remember. We have seen to that." Jayda's mouth hung open. Her face flushed a deep red as the embarrassment flooded in. She simply had no words.

Alastor stared up at the carved tree, "It looks like Jayda."

Everyone, including the Elves, looked at Alastor for a moment. Phineas was the first to break the silence with laughter and thus started the chain reaction of everyone laughing. Even Jayda had forgotten about her new idolization and laughed at the dim witted Orc. She started to move across the bridge on her horse. The Elves bowed their heads so deeply this time as she passed by them she thought they might topple over.

"Be well!" Yelled The Lady, "And know that my people shall always call you friend!" The Elves stayed on the bridge until the group disappeared into the trees and vanished from sight.

CHAPTER 19

The group traveled on the small, nearly hidden, path that they used to get to the town of Laru'el N'stir. Once they found the main road, if you could ever really call a path through the woods a road, Oberic asked them, "I guess we head back to Hadryn?"

Dwim nodded, "Aye, we've been out here too long, lad."

Ren agreed with the Dwarf, "We really should get back to the High Priestess and discuss our trip." She looked at Jayda hoping that nothing she was saying would bring any memories up again.

They traveled slowly at first; when the path began to clear and widen, they'd move at a faster pace. The trip would not take nearly as long now that they had horses. When they passed through the dead wood, as it had been called by the Elves, Oberic did his best to keep Jayda distracted. They even sent Phineas ahead to drag any corpses that remained on the road through Oakember out of the way so that their memory impaired friend would not see them and relapse into another fit.

It only took them another day and a half before they neared the gates to the White City. The guards standing on the walls shouted for the gates to be opened. When they were, they were met with armed guards who made sure that none of them seemed to be the living dead. They were then allowed to enter the city. The group followed Oberic as he made his way through the city. Jayda and Ren chatted amongst themselves. Jayda had a strange nagging feeling that something was off about the trip that she couldn't quite figure out. She wondered why the High Priestess had even sent them out in the first place. Everytime she would ask Ren, or the others, they would just change the subject or someone would distract her.

Amun was the first to greet his friend. He circled Oberic and cawed wildly before he settled on his shoulder. Evelyn had just stepped out of the palace as the group rode up. The guard had passed along the word across the city walls and it made it back to her. She placed a hand over her chest and as Oberic climbed off the horse, she ran down to him and threw her arms around him. "I'm happy you've returned! I was worried you fell to the darkness!" Jayda scowled and threw her leg over her saddle. When she touched down, Ren quickly got off hers as well and grabbed Jayda's arm.

"Jayda, let's go work on some spells. There is a new one that Oberic taught me that I would love to test." Ren pulled at Jayda to drag her back.

Jayda looked at Ren, confused as to why she was being pulled away, and then glanced back at Eve and Oberic, "But. . ." She looked back to Ren who had done her best to give Jayda big sad eyes. Jayda groaned, "Alright. Alright." She let herself be dragged out the way, but she continued to throw glances at Oberic and Evelyn, who still held him in an embrace. Evelyn, over Oberic's shoulder, had seen Jayda walk off and found herself pleased, though her embrace itself was no ruse. Evelyn was genuinely happy that they had returned safely.

She pulled away from Oberic and looked up at him, "What did you learn?"

Oberic, Dwim, and Leon explained to Evelyn everything that happened. Every bit of detail from Oakember, to Oberic giving Jayda false memories, to the Elves, to Jayda having to save The Lady's daughter, and their trip back. Alastor only listened to the conversation and Phineas, bored within the first minute of being there, wandered off. Evelyn scowled at Oberic when he told her what he had down to Jayda. She reminded him that it was foolish and stupid; he agreed with her as he tried to calm her down. Jayda had watched the interaction and wondered what Oberic said to make Evelyn so upset at him. She had hoped he told her about the nights they spent together. She couldn't help but smirk now.

"Are you paying attention?" Ren asked.

"Of course," Jayda said just as a gust of wind nearly pushed her down, "alright! I'm paying attention now!" She wanted so badly to know what was being said, but instead worked with Ren and was as gentle as she could be with her whip to help hone the girl's skills. Jayda looked over at the pair again. Evelyn looked discouraged and that made Jayda smile. She was then nearly knocked over again and shot Ren a dirty look.

"What now?" Evelyn asked.

Oberic shrugged, "Honestly, your guess is as good as mine. At the moment I think it has gone elsewhere, this Wintergrave," he hated saying that, "how it travels is beyond my understanding. I have no way of knowing anything about it. I think I need to get home to Maer'lyn."

Jayda paused in her training to cast another glance at Oberic and Evelyn, "Ren?" she looked at the little Elf, "Everyone is acting so strange and I feel as though I am missing something. Like there is a gap in my thoughts."

Ren met her eyes and put her hands down. She smiled and told her friend such wonderful lies, "I'm sure everyone is just tired and ready for some more rest. I can draft something for you to help you rest tonight if you need it." Jayda thought it over and nodded. Ren smiled, happy to be of use, "It won't take me long to make. A little secret between us girls, right?"

Jayda nodded, "Of course. Just between us." She looked back at Evelyn and sneered, "And just between us I really want to kick that bitch's teeth down her throat."

Ren grimaced, but let out a little chuckle, "Maybe not the wisest idea at the moment."

Phineas's voice came from behind Jayda and she jumped. "Ha, yeah I wouldn't mind getting a hold of her mouth after she's lost some teeth, know what I mean?"

Jayda threw a single arm around Phineas neck and jerked him close to herself, "Listen mutt, you can do much better than that prude."

"You offering?" he asked, giving her a grin.

"Aw, that's adorable. No." she released him.

"What secret were you talking about?" he looked between Jayda and Ren now.

"If it was any business of yours, mutt, we'd have told you. Now excuse me. I don't like that they've been talking this long." Jayda pushed past Phineas and made her way to the others who were talking with the High Priestess.

Ren dropped her voice though there was no one else around to hear it, "I can whip something up to help her not dream at night. It won't work long term, but it may help until Oberic figures something else out. Don't tell him, please?" She looked at Phin who waved her on,

"We've all got our little secrets." he lifted the amulet on the rope. "So, you interested in sneaking off for a little bit and finding out what kind of wild animal I really am?" He offered her a perfect smile.

Ren, had she not known Phineas for what he was at this point, might have fallen for that smile. The scoundrel, she admitted to herself begrudgingly, was extremely handsome. "Not ever." She shook her head and walked to the others as well.

"I'll ask again tomorrow!" he called out to her and turned to go find something in this terribly boring city to do.

Jayda walked up to Oberic and slipped her arm around his and clung to him tightly, "I hope I'm not interrupting anything." Her emerald eyes met Eve's crystal blues and the pair of them simply stared.

"Nothing you'd be able to assist with." Evelyn retorted. She looked from Jayda back to Oberic and put on a beautiful smile. Jayda could not hide her sneer now as she took in the beauty of that smile. She could absolutely see why Oberic would have fallen in love all those years ago. Her stomach twisted and she prayed he was not falling in love with her again. She looked up at the older man and sent all her thoughts of *please fall in love with me* in his direction. "So," Eve had started, "you're wanting to return to *our* home in Maer'lyn?"

Jayda inhaled sharply and glared at Evelyn who seemed to take pleasure in how Jayda reacted. She bit her tongue hard, tasting the metallic tang of blood in her mouth. She felt the anger hit her like a wall, but she stood beside Oberic quietly and kept it under control.

Oberic frowned. "*My* home, yes. Can you help or not?"

Evelyn's good cheer flushed from her face when Oberic had made the comment. "Yes dear, I can help you. I have the mirror locked away because I do not associate with those kinds any longer. I'll have to activate it but once it is, you..." she glowered at Jayda, "and your friends can use it if you'd like."

Jayda's arm dropped and she took his hand tightly in hers. She needed to feel grounded or she was going to go off on this terrible woman. She took a deep breath, her eyes never leaving Evelyn's face, and said, "You at least own him that much."

"Well," Evelyn stood up tall and lifted her head up so that her nose was quite literally in the air, "aren't we tough? Having seen horrors that shake great sorcerers and yet, you come out unscathed."

Oberic let out an exasperated sigh, "Evelyn, don't."

Eve did not listen. "Almost like magic." She wore a triumphant look on her face and then she turned. "Gather your followers, Wintersong. I'll get you to Maer'lyn."

Jayda stared at Evelyn's back and knew for certain the woman would drop dead if her glare could burn holes. She then looked up to Oberic, "What did she mean by that?"

Oberic drew in a deep breath and was nearly about to tell her the truth, but decided this was not the time or place for such a discussion. He was certain Evelyn wanted them to argue and he was not quite sure why she would act that way, but he refused to cave in. "She's being a bit of an asshole," he whispered to her, "jealous of you is my guess." Oberic had no idea if any of it was true, but he knew it would be enough for her to let it go at the moment.

Jayda smiled softly. That was a very fine answer for her. "Her loss. My gain" She faced him completely and placed her hands on his shoulders. "You make me happy, you know that? I have never needed anyone to make sure that I am safe, but you make me feel both safe and cared for." She laid her head against his chest. "It would be wise of her not to push me too far. I'll kick her down these fucking stairs."

Oberic let out a good laugh and put his arms around that fiery woman, "Play nice if you can. That mirror is our ticket out of here." He let her go and stuck his fingers in his mouth and blew a high pitched whistle. The others, who were never that far off to begin with, came to the call and joined the pair. Oberic explained to everyone that the plan was to go to Maer'lyn. He finished explaining with a command, "Go gather the horses, we can take them through the mirror as well."

Phineas scoffed, "How fucking big is this mirror?"

Dwim nearly turned purple in the face as he went off on Phineas, "I swear by me grandpappy's beard, if ye' mumble one more obscenity in this holy city I'll. . . I'll. . ."

Phineas looked down at the Dwarf, "You'll what?" The Dwarf only responded with a yell as he leapt at the golden haired fool. He nearly had his meaty hands around Phin's neck when the others pulled him back.

Ren took charge by grabbing Leon and Phin. She dragged them along to help her round up the horses and make sure they were all ready to go. Jayda couldn't seem to get Evelyn's words out of her head. *Almost like magic.* What was she talking about? She watched quietly as Oberic worked on calming Dwim down while the others did their part in the preparations. She had everything she needed on her person. Evelyn returned with several guards and together she escorted the entire party, horses included, into the palace basement. They were careful taking the horses down the steps which were, by the grace of Olm, wide enough. Once they reached the bottom they were led down long hallways that led to other halls as well as rooms.

They finally reached a door that had several locked upon it. After a few minutes of unlocking the security devices, then having the large timber that kept it bolted shut removed, Evelyn spoke words of power. As she did so, special runic markings appeared on the door and glowed a brilliant white. Unlike the others, Oberic was able to see the runes all along. When the door was finally unlocked completely, Evelyn opened it up and entered the cold damp room that smelled like mold. Inside was a wonderfully tall object draped in a large sheet. Eve nodded to the guards who then pulled the cloth down revealing a massive mirror showing their reflection. It was encased in a wonderfully ornate frame carved with Angels holding the mirror up in place. Evelyn walked up the impressive thing and placed a hand on one of the Angel's swords. The eyes of every angel glowed a brilliant golden color. The mirror's surface, once still, began to ripple as if it were water. "There. It's activated. Once you go through I will shut it down again."

Rennyn, ever polite, looked at Evelyn and dipped her head, "We all thank you for your hospitality while we were here."

Jayda muttered, "Speak for yourself." She gripped her whip in her hand. It was always a comfort.

Evelyn smiled brightly at Rennyn and dipped her own head, "You have all done this city a great service and I thank you for that."

Oberic stood in front of the mirror. The others looked at him, awaiting some sort of explanation. Dwim stood next to Oberic and looked up at him, "Well, lad?"

"Sorry," Oberic said, "I forget I'm the only one who has ever done this. It's pretty simple-"

Evelyn moved swiftly to Jayda and grasped her arm tightly. Jayda shot her an ugly look, but Evelyn leaned in to whisper to her anyway, "Oberic Wintersong is a good man. I have been petty with you. It is not out of some endearing and longing love that remains. I just do not like you. For that, I will be sure to punish myself later. It is beneath me and my order to hold grudges-"

"I've got it!" Phin shouted. He walked forward at a confident pace and ran face first into the mirror. His nose mashed against the glass and then he fell back on to his back.

"That's not how that works." Oberic said.

"I wish you would have opened with that." Phin rubbed his face. Jayda had turned her head just in time to see it all happen and grinned. Still, Evelyn was talking to her and she didn't care for a damn thing for what she had to say.

"-he was a man I loved dearly, but not the man I think he could have been," Evelyn continued, "If you find happiness with him," she sighed, "and I hope you do. Please, push him. He can be so much more than that of what he lets on. Oberic is no fool and he can beguile the quickest of wit. Pleasant journey." She released Jayda's arm, stepped back. Jayda gave the High Priestess a curt nod. Evelyn lowered her head and said a prayer for the group.

Phineas stood up and dusted himself off. Oberic stared at the mirror again. First, they would all see many faces flashing in the reflection. They morphed into others just as quickly as they appeared. The faces seemed to melt away and were replaced with a beautiful sky with black storm clouds in the distance. The area in the foreground was paved with carefully carved brick. Beautiful pink and yellow leafed trees casted shade on the ground while falling leaves danced in the breeze. A man and a woman wearing white robes and white pointed hats stood in front of them now. Each carried staves painted white and adorned with crystals.

"You've activated Maer'lyn's portal, friend!" The woman said with a friendly face. "We are ready to receive you!" They both stood aside and held their arms out in a welcoming gesture.

Oberic turned to his friends and nodded, "It's time." Oberic held his hand out to Jayda who took it and offered him a smile. Ren reached out and took Leon's hand in hers. Phineas, seeing everyone else do this, reached out to take hold of Alastor's hand. Alastor jerked his hand away and growled at Phineas.

"Yer' an idiot, lad." Dwim groaned.

Oberic and Jayda were the first to walk into the mirror. As their bodies met the reflection, the surface ripped around their forms. Jayda, a Hunter who never in her life would have thought she'd be involved in such a thing, expected to feel something wet or possibly some sort of force pushing against her. There was no such feeling as her body passed through, however, as her head went through, there was a very brief moment where she felt she was being watched. On the other side of the reflection the feeling went away and the two of them stepped out in the wondrous city of Maer'lyn. Amun, who had been on Oberic's shoulder, must not have liked the transition. He shook his body and then took off from his friend's company. He went off on his own adventure in the city.

The next two to come through would be Leon and Ren. Each tugged their horses along with them. Both had the same sensation Jayda did. Dwim and Phineas went next with their horses. Alastor would bring in the rear walking three horses, his own as well as Jayda and Oberics.

Portals and mirrors are a mystery to even those who can use and create them. One would assume you simply appeared in one spot from another. They might be alarmed to know just how delicate the fabrics of reality were and that they were passing through tears in dimensions that connected two points. The sensation of being watched accompanied with the feeling of absolute dread and doom was no mere act of travel sickness. There was no way to escape that feeling when traveling through the space that lies between existence. Once you entered that space between realities, the mind simply desired to unravel and throw itself to the void. The need to give in to the madness of uncreation and the terrible things that lived in the nothingness could be overwhelming. Once you were on the other side however, you forgot there was ever a thought at all about it.

"Welcome to Maer'lyn." The portal guards waved their hands to the expansive view. Ahead of them were long fields of grains and other crops. The edge, which seemed to stretch for miles, looked as if it curved to their eyes. On the edge sat a long drop that was walled. Over that walled edge rested a sandy beach where waves washed upon it, reaching far up the shore before retreating back to the ocean. Beyond the blue ocean, surrounding the entire city from what they could see, a terrible storm raged. That wall of black clouds, wind, and rain would never move. Upon turning around and facing the grand mirror they exited from, they could see buildings. Most likely homes. Above that, an upper tier of more buildings.This pattern carried on until the very top tier where a tower reached far into the clouds.

Rennyn looked around, bright eyed, trying to take everything in, "Do you need a guide, friend?" the lady guard asked.

"No," Oberic said, "I live here." The guard lowered her head and stepped out of the way. Oberic led the group to the stables where they had their horses taken care of and put up for the duration of their stay. Oberic then led them up several tiers. He explained that the city itself was one giant tower. The group found the streets to be rather narrow, but everything was so finely detailed that it didn't seem to bother them that much. The buildings reached high into the sky. Shops and homes were all crammed together with small alleys that looked as though they could facilitate two people in them at most.

On the fourth tier up from where they had come, Oberic led them to a rather small looking home. As he approached the door, it unlocked itself and swung open. He stopped and faced the others. "I have not been here in twenty years. Forgive the mess," he looked at Jayda, "and other things. Keep in mind I was married at the time."

Jayda gave him an understanding nod. She had been fairly quiet ever since she was pulled aside by Evelyn. The bitches words lingered in her head and she was far too distracted to really take in her surroundings, which given her background might have been a good thing. Ren smiled brightly, "I am more than happy to help clean up. I'm sure after all that time, it's going to be a bit dusty in here." Ren was nearly shaking with excitement. She was in the city where magic was abundant and thrived.

As he led them inside, candles that lined the walls lit themselves, and the room filled with light. Jayda looked around the room and examined it to get a glimpse of what Oberic might have been like before she had met him. Any table surface that was there was covered in books and documents. Ren had no problems rushing in and picking up some of the books to thumb through them. Most were written in languages that she did not understand. They might not even have been words at all but symbols or runes. Dwim and Leon admired the banners, most with unknown sigils, that hung from the rafters. Alastor found nothing of interest, but at least Phineas was curious enough to snoop around. Jayda spotted a painting on the wall and stepped closer to get a better look. A teenage Oberic and Evelyn sat together. She was nearly curled up in his lap and they both wore smiles while they looked adoringly at one another. Jayda had to remind herself this was forever ago. It was strange seeing Oberic without a beard and even though she thought he wasn't overly handsome in the painting; she also found he was the most handsome man she had ever seen.

"What can I do to help clean up, Oberic?" Ren asked.

Oberic waved his hand which caused a closet door to open allowing a broom to come out. It stood on its bristles as if waiting for a command. Just behind the broom, a duster appeared. Once they were both there, Oberic weaved his hands again and both began to do their jobs. "It'll clean itself. Rennyn, follow me please." Ren followed him down a simple hall where there were a few doors. Opening one gave way to a large storeroom. At this point, some of the party had figured that the dimensions inside the house could no way fit inside the tiny home they entered, but Rennyn was absolutely sure of it when she saw the storeroom. "This is my alchemical and enchanting storage. Feel free to take what you desire." He pointed to a bookshelf. "I didn't care much for alchemy, but I enjoyed collecting knowledge. You can have those books if you like as well."

Ren let out an excited squeal of happiness that had Jayda covering her ears tightly. Ren hugged Oberic which nearly knocked him over. When she released him, she ran inside the storeroom. Her fingers danced over book spines while her eyes scanned and took it all in. Jayda sighed and looked to those she was still in the room with. "Guess we lost Ren now. We'll never get her out of there."

Leon and Dwim chuckled. "I'm never leaving this room," Ren screamed out.

"See?" Jayda smirked.

"You called it," Leon said.

The sound of some sort of pottery breaking caused them all to turn and look at Phineas who looked as guilty as could be, "I didn't do it. Alastor did."

Alastor uncrossed his arms and looked very insulted, "You lying swine! I'll remove your heart for such an offense!"

Dwim held his hands up to Alastor, "Calm down, lad. We all know it was him. Relax."

Jayda snickered, "Feel free to break anything that belonged to Evelyn." There was another breaking sound and Jayda turned and hissed at Phineas, "I was joking! Stop!"

Oberic opened another door that led into another large storage room. Bookcases lined the walls; each filled completely with books. They were organized by school of magic and topic. Shelves in the middle of the room were lined like a library. Each carrying an assortment of bottles whose contents were colored liquids, vapors, and powders. Crystals were scattered on shelves and even the floor. In the center of the room stood the very staff he pulled from his hat in Hadryn. Oberic looked around and spoke to himself mostly. "Might as well pack some of this up. I don't plan on coming back after we leave."

Jayda had made her way down the hall and stood near Oberic, peering into the room. "You won't be coming back?" She looked into the room at all the bottles and books. These were all the things she was taught to fear as a Hunter. She knew the magic in here was strong and for a moment, she felt a sinking feeling that she had lost her roots; that perhaps she had forgotten something, or someone, very important.

"No," he sighed, "It's not a home I wish to keep. Maybe I'll build something elsewhere." He shrugged, "Maybe with you?"

All her concerns and fears faded with his words. She looked up at him and met his eyes. Her face blushed deeply as she smiled, "Really?"

"If you decide to keep me that long," he nodded, "sure. The thought had crossed my mind. I know it's only been about two weeks but what can I say? I'm hopelessly head over heels for you."

Jayda had thought about the conversation her and Na'mia had when she saved her from the beast. She had asked who Oberic was to her and Jayda decided now was the time to find out. "Oberic, what are we?"

He raised his brow, "What do you mean?"

She drew in a deep breath, "You and me? This thing between us? Is this just a fling?" She prayed he would not say yes.

"I assumed we had decided that we were together. You know, long term," he cleared his throat, "meaning more than just a fling. Was I wrong to assume that?"

Her feet pushed her off the ground as she threw her arms around his neck and leaned in to steal a kiss from him. Sadly, Ren appeared on the other side of her and ruined the moment. "How will I ever have time to read them all?" Ren asked. Jayda sighed and rested her forehead against Oberic's chin.

He was fighting back a laugh, "Nearly twenty years gone and I haven't reached in that hat enough to drain this room."

Jayda looked up a bit confused. Ren seemed to have gotten it though. She inquired, "Is this where your hat connects?"

"It is," Oberic said, "take a look." He removed his hat and slipped his arm inside it. The two women watched as a ghostly non-corporeal hand appeared in the room. It moved to Ren and plucked a book from her arms. The hand drew back towards the ceiling and simply vanished. Oberic pulled his arm from the hat and drew from it the book. "See?" He held the book out to Ren who took it with a look of awe.

"Amazing!" Rennyn ran off again, excited noises came from the other room.

Jayda looked at him, "There is a lot of power here, isn't there?"

"In the city, sure. In this room? No. Not really. Just an advanced enchantment." He pulled her close to him again now that Ren had left. "You know, in Normoon there's a city called Basile. The city is covered by eternal night. Clearly some sort of enchantment, likely an illusion because crops somehow still manage to grow. It's so ancient though, whoever cast it must have been powerful beyond belief. Of course the legend is that The Aegis did it when he was mortal," Oberic scoffed at the idea, "they love telling those around here."

She smiled half heartedly, "You'll have to forgive my hesitation. I am trying to be open to all of this, but in truth, I can see how my mother became obsessed. The bottles and jars are beautiful and it's building a curiosity in me that I didn't know was there. Then I think of," she paused, unable to put a name on her tongue, "well I think of all that I was taught about how magic was horrible and how I grew up with such a hatred of it." She pulled away from Oberic and wrapped her arms around herself. "I don't want to become her. I don't want to forget about the people I lo-" she stopped herself and glanced at him briefly then down to the floor "the people I care about."

Oberic gave her an earnest look, "Maybe it was a bad idea to bring you here. I'm sorry. Will you tell me how I can ease your mind?"

"Please don't let me become her," she whispered softly and looked up at him.

"I'll do my best." Already another lie. Twice now he had helped pull bad memories from her. He hated the taste of those words in his mouth. "Maybe some fresh air?"

"I would like that. Will you show me around?" She did her best to put on a smile for him.

"It'd be my pleasure. Maybe leave the whip behind though. Just so we aren't asking for any unwanted attention." He offered her a smile.

She pulled the whip off her hip and handed it over to him. He removed his hat again, slipped it inside and shoved it back on his head. Jayda looked in the store room and watched as the whip positioned itself neatly on a shelf. "Hm. I really didn't like that."

"It's safe there. I promise." They left the doorway and headed back down the hall where the others were. "You all feel free to make yourselves at home. I'll get us an audience for Phineas and bring back some hot food. I think we could all use a bit of relaxation."

Phineas peeked up from digging in a drawer. "Did your wife happen to leave behind any sexy clothing?"

Oberic drew in a deep breath and simply shook his head. He gave no response and exited out the front door. Jayda was following until Oberic was out the door. She turned and like a flash of lightning, grabbed a book and hurled it at Phineas. "Knock it off!" She then adjusted herself, put on a smile, and followed Oberic out the door. She felt her heart lighten nearly immediately as she inhaled deeply. The warm sun felt good on her skin. She did feel guilty about being the reason he was leaving his own home just to try and make her comfortable, but she was going to spend the rest of the day with Oberic; no life threatening errands like saving damsels in distress in the way. She decided she was going to push past it and enjoy their time.

As they walked he pointed out interesting little shops that belonged to adventuring magicians who would travel the world and collect oddities. They passed by a grand tower shaped building with a sign that simply read *Library of Maer'lyn*. Oberic pointed at the library, "I used to work there when I lived here." Though they did not venture up to higher tiers, he would point out the main schools and then the smaller schools dedicated to certain magics. There was no forbidden magic here. Even magic like necromancy had its place in Maer'lyn. One of the city's council members who led the city was a practitioner of such magic. As Jayda learned more, her comfort level began to improve. She visibly relaxed and the smile, her real smile, reappeared on her face along with a laugh that escaped her lips every so often.

She peeked into the window of one of the shops and spotted a necklace with a vibrant green pendant attached to a silver chain. Her eyes lit up and she looked at him, "Can we go in?"

"Of course!" He moved to the door and held it open for her, "After you."

She stepped inside, Oberic after her, and took in the smell of the shop. It smelled like old well loved books and sweet flowers. Her eyes danced as they examined the trinkets and gems. She ran her fingers over soft furs and old books. Jayda looked at the old woman behind the counter. She offered her a smile, it was returned, and then she knelt down to look at a display of rings and jewelry. "I think Renyn would love this place!" Her eyes traveled back over to the necklace she saw in the window, "I love this place."

The old woman came from around the counter, slowly, and asked, "Can I help you dear?" She had large brown eyes that were nearly covered by the brim of her pointed hat. She turned her gaze up at Oberic and her smile turned to something of bewilderment, "You look terribly familiar." Oberic shrugged. "You're not that boy that made it rain in my shop for several days, are you?"

Oberic blushed, "No ma'am. Never been here before. What's that?" He pointed to a random gemstone and the old woman forgot her question. She immediately went into the sales pitch. Jayda looked at him with a bit of accusation and then burst into laughter. This was the first time in a long while that she laughed as hard as she did.

"I was just looking at the jewelry!" She smiled and tried catching her breath. She pointed to a thin chain of silver with two gems, one a light purple and the other a vibrant green, entwined between golden leaves."May I see that one?"

"Good choice! Nice selection!" The old woman pulled the item from the window and placed it under a magnifying glass. "Crafted from Moon Tears collected from the dunes of Mahir! That's Desruc craftsmanship there."

Jayda had no idea what any of that was. She had never left Marrenval and didn't even know what a Desruc looked like. "And the price?" She knew that the price would not matter. It was the perfect gift for Ren.

"Two hundred gold coins, young lady. That's a bargain!"

Her heart sank and she thought of everything that money could go towards with the group. It seemed unfair of her to spend such a sum without discussion first. Just as she was about to decline the so-called bargain, Oberic looked over her shoulder and commented on the necklace. "That's not Desruc crafted."

The old woman's eyes narrowed and she snapped at Oberic, "And how would you know?"

"Because there is no silver near Mahir. Desruc crafted jewelry is often done with glass or lesser metals."

The old lady grumbled, "twenty five! That's the lowest I'll go." Oberic pulled out his coin purse and dumped the coins out. They made an unpleasant noise on the glass top. The old woman thought it would have sounded better if it were two hundred of them. Oberic started counting them while the old woman stared at him. "Are you sure you didn't flood my shop when you were a boy? Your eyes look familiar."

"Wasn't me. Jayda, would you kindly finish counting this for me? I need to do something other than this right now," he left the coin purse, turned without making eye contact and stepped outside.

Jayda went to protest, but nearly started laughing again when he acted that way. She scooped his gold back into his coin purse and took out her own from her own bag. She paid the twenty five gold and gathered up the chain. She looked it over again and nodded her thanks before leaving the shop. She found Oberic across the narrow street and looked at him with half a grin on her face. "Oberic? Everything alright?"

"I can't believe that hag still remembers that," he gave her a mischievous smile, "It's not like that sort of thing was uncommon with students."

The half grin became full, "Of course you were the one who did it!" They started to walk again and she handed him his coin purse. "I didn't feel right using your coin so I put it back and used my own."

He shrugged, "Coin doesn't mean much to me. I don't have much need for it"

"I can't wait to give this to Ren. She's going to love it!" She held up the necklace and examined it in the sunlight.

The night was coming and as it did, lanterns around the city lit themselves in bright vibrant colors. Pinks, greens, blues and purples; all casting a wonderful glow on the streets and buildings. They spent the evening talking while they walked and learned about each other even more. She felt closer to him somehow as he pointed out places he would go as a kid. She eventually stretched and let out a yawn, "Maybe it's a good idea to head back? Have some warmed ale before bed? It's been a long day."

He nodded, "Yes, I'll escort you home first, then I'll head to the tower and try to get an audience for Phin." They walked back towards the small home on the busy street. "Would you prefer a room at the inn?" He stopped and gave her an apologetic look. "I do not want you to feel uncomfortable in the house. If I am being honest, I don't care much to be there myself."

Jayda bit her lip, "Will you be upset with me?" She knew she would feel more comfortable, but she didn't want to hurt his feelings. She couldn't bear to stay in the house, knowing that Evelyn had sat in the chairs and slept in the bed.

"Not even close." he walked with her to an inn that he knew of that was rather nice and cozy. "I could stay with you. If you wanted me to."

"Do what you need to do this evening and come back as soon as you can." She squeezed his hand. "If you are going back to the house, could you give this to Rennyn for me? It reminds me of her and I. The purple and the green of course. Makes me think how our destinies are now intertwined."

"I think it'll mean more if you gave it to her yourself." He paid for the room, gave her the key, and leaned forward to place a kiss on her cheek. "I'll return as soon as I can."

Jayda smiled and watched her man head off down the street from the inn's window. Once he was out of view, she sat at the bar and ordered a warm ale. She drank slowly and thought on the lovely day they had together.

Leon, Ren, Dwim, Phin, and Alastor were still in the house. Phin had exhausted himself digging through Oberic's things. He didn't find anything worthy of blackmail and seemed to be pouting about it. Leon looked at the others and then looked through the window at a sky that only seemed to be getting darker. "Do you think they're coming back?" Leon turned and looked at the others. "Seems late."

Phineas opened a drawer, "Probably doing something kinky," he moved things around and then slammed the drawer shut, "for a wizard this guy has nothing fun in this house!"

The other four responded in unison, "He's not a wizard."

"No one gives a shit!" Phin fussed. He gave up his search and sat on the old couch. As he flopped down a cloud of dust rose up. The magic duster immediately attacked Phineas.

"You should not be snooping anyway," Rennyn declared, "it's rude. Oberic has opened his home to us." She was on the verge of laughing as the duster continued to swat at Phin who kept batting it away from himself. "It is quite late though. I wonder what's keeping them."

Dwim chucked, "Honestly, the lad might be right on this one. Those two can't keep their hands off each other. Happened real fast too." They all agreed, even Alastor who had never really given input on any such talk. "Is she attractive for a Human?"

Leon, Phin, and even Ren, all agreed that Jayda was indeed attractive. Phineas of course took it a step too far, "Thick ass. The things I would do to her." Ren groaned and rolled purple eyes.

"Personally," Dwim went on, "a woman needs a thick beard to get me forge heated."

"They are in love," Ren smiled. "Leave them be."

"I'm sure they're fine. I'm going to turn in." Leon stood and stretched. Dwim stood and headed into the kitchen. He didn't suspect he would find food, but perhaps he would get lucky and find an old bottle of wine. Leon only made it to the hall entrance before he turned, "Ren, as the lady, I think it's right that you take the bed."

Phin immediately protested, "Just because she's a woman? I've got a bad back!"

"You're a dire wolf! You've slept in worse places than a couch," she said as she folded her arms, "I think you'll be fine!"

Phineas smirked, "Yeah, but my dick hangs so low that I hunch over a lot." Rennyn closed her eyes and gave him a look that expressed how done she was with his nonsense.

"By my beard!" Dwim shouted from the kitchen. "No one is going to sleep!" They all looked in that direction as Dwim came around the corner rolling a large cask in front of him. "Look at what I found! Twenty year old wine!"

"We can't just drink his wine!" Ren said.

"Lass," Dwim had pulled a tap from his own bag that he carried with him. It was a tool every Dwarf carried; his was even personalized. "Oberic said to make ourselves at home. There's nay a better way to relax than with a few glasses of wine!"

Alastor stood up, "I will drink with you, Dwarf."

"Aye! Ye' sure will, lad!" Dwim ran back into the kitchen and returned with five large mugs a few minutes later. "We're all set!"

"Sure," Leon said. "Few glasses wouldn't hurt."

Dwim filled each mug to the top and passed them around. He smiled and lifted his mug up and out to them. "To Olm's guiding light!"

Leon lifted his mug and tapped it against Dwim's, holding it there. "To adventure!"

Ren followed along, "To bettering ourselves!"

Phin thrusted his against theirs, "To luck being on our side!"

Alastor was the last to join in, "To you, my friends."

They all cheered and shouted, "To friends!" They all tipped their mugs back and drank. They drank their mugs and agreed to another mug full. Once that one was gone, they agreed another wouldn't hurt. What started out as a toast and a drink to relax ended up being a wild night of fun for the group.

We could venture together into the minute details of that night. We could look at all the deep and meaningful conversations shared between the five of them. We could also view moments that are tender and helped strengthen the bond between them. However, those moments are not as interesting as the moments where things had become out of control. We will not spend much time on these moments and there are many moments yet to come, but perhaps it would do well to shed some light on the shenanigans that were had, and needed greatly, by the group.

Five mugs in the group had started stacking books to see how high they could leap over them. Dwim was the first to lose. Leon was next though he swore Phineas tripped him. Ren came next. Phineas's jump was impressive, but the small framed Alastor astonished everyone by leaping over a tower of books that got higher every round several times before he crashed over them. They all cheered and drank.

Nine mugs in and Phineas, along with his accomplice Ren, had found some quills and ink. They drew all over Oberic and Evelyn's painting while giggling like children. Ren colored in a mustache on Eve while Phin drew a penis coming from Oberic's lap that was ejaculating all over the place. They all had a good long laugh. Alastor had fallen over from laughing so hard which in turn caused everyone else to laugh.

Thirteen mugs deep and they were standing around the cask, not even remotely close to being empty, and swayed side to side with their arms thrown around one another. They proudly, and loudly, sang all the drinking songs they had ever known. Alastor found he enjoyed this activity and swore to his friends he would never forget these songs. He forgot them the next day.

Fifteen mugs deep and Ren was starting to crash hard. She continued to hang in there as long as she could though and the men congratulated her on her attempt. Alastor helped Rennyn brush up on her hand to hand fighting by teaching her just where to hit for the best result. She swore she would never forget the lesson. She forgot the next day.

Seventeen mugs in and Ren had convinced Dwim to let her braid his hair as well as his beard. He looked lovely.

Eighteen mugs in and Ren had passed out. Phin had suggested they lift her shirt to get a glimpse and Leon punched him. Phineas fell over, not that it was hard to make happen at that moment. Leon picked Ren up and carried her down the hall. He accidently knocked her head against the wall on the way towards Oberic's old bedroom. He kicked the door open and carried her over the threshold. He laid her in the bed and covered her up. He returned to the others and they continued to drink.

Twenty mugs in and Phineas had cut a hole in the painting where Oberic's mouth was and stuck his own up to the hole. With his lips moving where Oberic's used to be, he made gross comments while pretending to be Oberic which made Dwim nearly choke with laughter. Alastor and Leon had found some knives in the kitchen and were having a competition to see who could hit the bullseye that they had drawn on the wall. Leon won every single round.

Twenty two mugs and Leon had passed out on the couch. Phineas took great pleasure in drawing a massive penis on his forehead.

Twenty three mugs in and both Alastor and Phineas had passed out on the floor. Dwim drew a penis on Phin's face and chuckled to himself. He looked at the other men laying there, each passed out and snoring. He put his hands on his wide hips and held his head up proudly, "Amateurs."

Oberic had returned much later than he had hoped. He did not stop by the house to check on the others. He was unaware of the party that was going on and had he stopped would have likely been dragged into it somehow. He went to the inn after coming back from the tower on the top tier of Maer'lyn and headed up to their room. When he entered, a single candle lit itself. Jayda was in bed sleeping hard. He smiled as he crept to the bed and undressed himself. He slipped in beside her, watched her beautiful form for a while, leaned in to kiss her cheek, and pulled the blanket up over them. The candle unlit itself. They would all sleep hard that night, some more than others.

The morning came and with it the beautiful rays of sunshine that filled the room. A soft groan crossed her lips as she pulled the blanket up over her head. "Not yet," she mumbled, "I've only just fallen asleep."

Oberic lifted his head and looked at her curiously. His long hair was disheveled as well as his beard. "You've been asleep all night. Very soundly."

Jayda sat up with a gasp. "When did you get here? I didn't hear you come in!" She still looked tired.

"You were already in bed sleeping when I came in. Kissed you goodnight and crawled into bed. Are you alright?"

"Yes, I'm fine." She smiled slightly. "I just don't remember going to bed. I must have been more tired than I thought." She got up out of bed and began to dress herself.

He threw his legs out of bed and started slipping his pants on. "I managed to get us an appointment with an Archmage who specializes in curse removal. She has never done a curse like this but doesn't see why it would be a problem."

Jayda smiled, "That's great!" She stood and pulled her cloak around her neck. Oberic looked back at her and smiled. There wasn't a moment he didn't find her breathtaking. "Should we get the others?" She asked. "I'm excited to give Ren her gift. Maybe we should bring them something to eat."

He nodded, "They'll very likely be hungry. They probably didn't venture out." He felt bad about that but had really enjoyed the alone time with her. They left the room and on the way back to his house, they stopped at a bakery to grab several breakfast pastries as well as some hot sausages from a street vendor. When they reached the house, the door swung open for them. Both Oberic and Jayda found themselves frozen in the doorway looking at the wrecked front room. Their eyes took in the absolute mess that was made then looked at the men sleeping on the floor and couch. Dwim however was wide awake and gave them a hearty wave.

"Morning!" He was rather cheery and Jayda tilted her head unsure if she was seeing him correctly because to her it looked as though his hair and beard were braided. Oberic and Jayda stepped in and shut the door behind them. They walked in and dropped the food on the small table in front of the couch.

"What in the world happened in here?" Oberic asked, though he wasn't even remotely upset. Jayda had looked down, spotted the many dicks drawn, and bit back a laugh.

"Lad, would ye' believe these people can nay drink?" Dwim shook his head. "I hope ye' nay mind, but we dipped into yer' wine there." He thumbed to the cask.

Oberic shook his head, "Not at all." He looked at the crude drawings on the painting. "Phineas' work?" Dwim nodded. A door in the hall opened and Ren groaned the entire way down the hall.

"Can you all please quit yelling?" she asked in a hoarse whisper while she held her head. It felt like it was going to pound right off her shoulders.

Jayda raised her brow, "You too?" she walked over, grabbed her face and looked her over. "Sure hope you didn't make any poor choices."

"Nay, lass was put to bed by Leon who was a perfect gentleman." Dwim commented.

"Well, I'm almost sorry I have to wake you all up." Oberic said.

Ren growned, "I thought you were supposed to be the drunk in this group, Oberic." Her eyes went large when she realized just what she said and immediately she apologized. "I'm sorry! That was rude!"

Oberic held his hands up to show her that it was alright. "It's fine. You're not wrong there." The truth was, ever since he and Jayda shared that first kiss, he hadn't felt a desire to drink at all.

Dwim clapped his hands, "Come on, lads! Time to wake yer' asses! We've got business I suspect!"

Leon pushed himself up with a groan of his own, "I haven't drank like that in a long time."

Alastor sat up as well, "I have never drank like that before." He looked at Leon and pointed, "Your face has been drawn upon."

Leon glared at Phineas who was also just now getting up. As he exposed his face they all saw another crude drawing on his face as well. Dwim flashed a toothy smile and disappeared into the kitchen. "Well well well," Phineas said, "if it isn't Jayda and the guy who stole her from me." Phin teased, unaware of the drawing pointed in the direction of his mouth. "Little romps around the city huh?"

"Don't make me eat your food." Jayda said as she held up a box full of pastries, "because I'm hungry enough that I will." Phin reached out to grab one and she jerked the box back. "Go wash your face first."

"Aw dammit. Someone drew one on me too, huh?" He shook his head. "That's like my thing. Can't believe you guys stole that from me." He got up and headed off down the hall. Leon stood and joined him knowing he needed to scrub his face as well.

Rennyn walked further into the room and sat down on the couch. Jayda held out the box to her. Ren reached in and grabbed one. Jayda, nearly prancing, sat near Ren. "I got something for you!" she said. Ren had bitten into the pastry and looked at Jayda with a mouth full of delicious pastry. Jayda pulled out the necklace and held it out to Ren. Ren's big purple eyes got bigger and she made an undistinguishable mutter of words. She threw her arms around Jayda and let out a happy sob.

Alastor had grabbed a juicy sausage and bit into it. "Why is she crying?" he asked with a mouth full. The juices ran down his chin.

Phineas had just come back into the room no longer wearing the drawing but a red spot on his face where he scrubbed. "Don't know much about women, huh?"

Alastor looked at him quite seriously and said, "I know that you are the prettiest one I have seen." Dwim cackled madly at the insult.

Leon had come back out just in time to hear the exchange, "Nicely done, Alastor."

Alastor walked to Oberic, "Most of us are not welcomed here. Let us do the business we came to do and leave."

Oberic nodded "Everyone ready then?" They all devoured the food before they would give him a definite answer. Once they were stuffed, and Dwim was on his sixth mug of wine for the morning, they agreed they were finally ready to go.

CHAPTER 20

Rennyn talked Leon's ear off as they left for their appointment, but he did not seem to mind one bit. Oberic had pulled Jayda's whip from his hat and told her to keep it. She looked at him a bit puzzled and asked if he expected trouble. Oberic only told her to always expect trouble. She didn't care for that answer, but she did as he said and placed the whip at her hip where it belonged. There was a nice breeze this morning and the wind kicked up her cloak every so often making her weapons visible. They could all feel eyes upon them as they were a strange group of companions, even here in Maer'lyn.

What were once happy faces in the street turned to scowls and whispers. Fingers pointed in their direction. Every now and then the word *Hunter* floated on the air to their ears. None of them, except Oberic, really had an idea how big the city of Maer'lyn was. It took them quite a while before they made it to the top tier where the tower kissed the sky. As they neared the large wooden double doors that led into the tower, two guards stepped to the center of the doorway, grabbed the large iron knockers, and pulled the doors open for the visitors. They entered, following Oberic who seemed to know what he was doing which was good because the others had not a clue.

The room they entered on the first floor was absolutely silent. Their footsteps on marble flooring echoed in the chamber. A plump woman in a pointed hat sat at a lone table. She looked up from a large tome and smiled, "Can I help you?"

"We have an appointment with Archmage T'ar." Oberic said simply. The plump woman stood and escorted them to a rune on the ground. She politely instructed them to stand in it. As they did, she cast her magic and they appeared in another room within the blink of an eye. The room was decorated in a style that both Oberic and Rennyn would be familiar with. Elven crafted furniture and other decorative things filled the office like room. The group spread out a bit and looked around. Jayda, feeling her anxiety pick up from being so drawn into the world of magic, stood by the window and lost herself at the sight of clouds passing right by the window. She assumed they were very high up the tower. She called to Ren who then joined her and the two of them admired the majesty of being so high up.

Pineas had picked up something off the desk and considered pocketing it when the rune began to glow and a rather short Elven woman appeared. Her hair was yellow and braided down to her bare feet. "Archmage Oberic Erelas

Wintersong!" She held out her arms as she spoke with excitement. "One of Maer'lyn's finest!"

Oberic shook his head, "Just Oberic, please. My friend here," he motioned to Phineas who immediately put the object back down on the desk, "is cursed. He turns into a direwolf and can not control himself."

The Elven woman draped in a heavy white cloak moved to Phin and stared into his eyes. "Does anything set the wolf loose? Stars? Certain nights? Words?"

Oberic shook his head, "Seems to be of its own will."

Jayda watched Oberic and the Elven woman talk. She strolled over to Phineas and whispered softly to him. "Ready to be rid of the wolf? Maybe it will help you to not be such a pest." She took his arm and laid her head against it. She would never admit to him, but she adored him.

Leon was off looking at some paintings that were hanging on the wall. There was one in particular of an Elf with long pointed ears and yellow eyes. He wore a black leather overcoat and had a rapier drawn out in front of himself. Under the painting was a plaque that read *Sebastian*. "This guy looks like an ass," he mumbled to himself.

Ren had joined Leon at the painting. Dwim and Alastor simply paid attention to the conversation. Jayda stepped forward and looked at the Elven woman. "Do you think you can help him?"

The Elven woman, Archmage T'ar, was honest. "I can't say for sure. I have never actually seen a curse where someone turned to a wolf." Jayda nodded her understanding. She was getting hot in the room and decided to remove her cloak. She untied it and let it fall. She caught it on the way down and folded it over her arm. Her weapons, and her bracelet with its blue stone, were now completely visible. The Elven woman narrowed her eyes. "Is this the company you keep, Oberic? A hunter?" You dare bring her ilk to Maer'lyn?" She spit at Jayda's feet. "Have at me then! Hunt and meet your doom!"

Out of pure habit, Jayda's hand instinctively went to her whip and her eyes cast a dark stare at T'ar. Oberic interjected, "She has come here with no ill intent and I demand you apologize for she has not wronged you, yet you insult her!" Oberic's eyes fixated on T'ar.

·"I had hoped that the rumors I heard about you were not true. You were supposed to be some young prodigy that carried the blood of the High Men. I see now you are a weak fool." She spit in his face.

Oberic wiped the spit from his face and for a tiny fraction of a moment had the urge to bring ruin to the entire city for her offense. However, he regained himself and spoke to T'ar as calmly as he could though his eyes burned into her. "Remove the curse as you said you could."

T'ar scowled but turned to Phineas and without warning cast a ray of light towards him. He was lifted into the air and while it held him, visages of both Phineas and the wolf seemed to fade in and out with one another as if fighting for the right to exist. The Archmage seemed to struggle as Phineas started to yell out in agony. "What kind of curse is this?" she screamed at Oberic.

"I'm not the expert here!" he screamed back at her.

Dwim shouted out, "Yer hurting him!" Even Alastor had stepped up looking angry.

Jayda growled low, the whip uncoiled at her feet. "Stop it!"

After their exchange, T'ar had elected to not tell them that the process was going to be painful. However, she found that she was struggling badly. She focused as hard as she possibly could before her spell let Phineas go and she found herself being flung back against the wall. Her head made a horrible knocking sound. She sat there for a moment, very still. Phineas dropped to the floor and groaned. Alastor and Leon helped him to his feet.

Jayda had watched the two forms phase just like everyone else had, but when she saw it she remembered something else. She had visions of the wolf in some dark and dead looking forest chewing on a body. Was that right? How could she possibly forget something like that? Evelyn's words replayed in her head. Almost like magic. She turned, her eyes met Oberic's and she blinked for a moment, having a strange sense of distrust take over. She shook her head and looked back to Phineas; he was her concern at the moment.

Ren had started to head to T'ar to check on her when the woman groaned. She felt the back of her head and pulled her hand away and saw it shined scarlet. Still, she was well enough to stand. "That curse, it fights back."

Phineas could feel the wolf fighting to get out harder than it ever had before. The silver amulet still kept it at bay though and he was thankful for it. The thumping in his ears was almost deafening. T'ar stood up, nearly stumbling over as she walked. She held her head as she took another step. Ren also reached up and touched her own head. Leon had seen it first and asked if she was alright. Ren nodded but as she did so the room began to spin and both her and T'ar dropped to the marble flooring with their eyes wide open.

While the others rushed to both women to see what was wrong, they found themselves in a saturated forest grove. They looked at one another unsure of what was going on and unknowing that their bodies were convulsing on the floor. They both stepped further into the grove and could feel the magic of this place vibrating deep inside them. Little winged creatures that shined brilliant colors, each different, flew high above them in the tree tops and both women recognized them for what they were, faeries. A mist rolled out from behind the trees and with it emerged a wolf who looked to be made of clouds or perhaps a vapor. Tendrils drifted up from its body, but the creature never lost form. Behind him, a tall Elven woman whose hair looked much like the wolf's fur, stepped out and she stared at them. The woman's voice entered their heads and made them cringe. They dropped to their knees. The words spoken were in Elvish and yet Ren somehow understood what was said. "Not a curse," the voice said in a soft sultry tone though it still made them both feel as their skin was trying to remove itself, "a gift." The women found their vision becoming oversaturated with light once again and then found themselves in their own bodies. Everyone had them surrounded and was looking awfully concerned.

"Ren!" Leon called out to her. She was slowly coming to now. "Ren, can you hear me?"

She sat up and rubbed her head, "What in the world was that?"

T'ar stood up, nearly fell, and gained her composure again, "The curse can not be removed."

Dwim questioned her, "And why is that?"

"Because it was a gift from the Wild Gods." She slowly walked to her desk and sat down behind it. She lifted a hand and said something none of them, but Oberic would understand. A book flew from its shelf to her. She laid it down on the desk and opened it. A thin finger pointed to an illustration, "Here! Girl of my kin! You recognized her, didn't you?"

Ren got to her feet and felt ashamed to say it. "I don't know much about the Wild Gods. I was raised mostly around Humans." Ren moved to the desk though and looked at the book. T'ar had pointed to an Elven woman wearing furs and by her side a ghostly looking wolf. Rennyn's mouth hung open for just a moment before she yelled out, "That's what I saw!"

T'ar grimaced, "A warning! I will not work on this man, blessing or curse. To do so is to anger the Wild Gods."

Oberic raised his voice, "This is getting out of hand. Isn't there someone else we can talk to who is not superstitious?"

T'ar looked at him angrily but answered, "I will not take part in this, but we will go see Master Kaj'r." She stood and headed to the rune on the floor. It lit up for her and she stepped into it. She vanished before their eyes.

"Oberic," Ren said softly, "I wouldn't lie to you. I did see what she said it was. It was the strangest thing." Oberic thought it over and nodded at Leon and Alastor. They helped Phineas walk into the rune and they too vanished. Oberic and Ren followed them and vanished.

Dwim looked up at Jayda with a frown on his face, "Something is wrong here." She nodded in agreement and they followed their friends through the rune.

The room the group found themselves in felt like a throne room of sorts mixed with an office. On the elaborate chair that rested in the center, sat a figure in a purple robe with its hood drawn up. Its face could not be seen except for two glowing red eyes. A thin gold crown rested over the ears and kept it place. A voice whispered, but it was as if it was speaking directly into their ears, "Why have you brought these outsiders to me, girl?"

T'ar stepped forward. "Forgive me for intruding, Master Kaj'r." She bowed her head. Jayda's fingers held the handle of her whip so tightly that her knuckles were white. She felt energy coursing through her body as she kept her eyes on the glowing red eyes. Rennyn hid herself behind Oberic. "This one," T'ar pointed to Phineas, "has a blessing from the Wild Gods that I can not lift."

Kaj'r's laughter was deep and monotone. He drew in a deep breath as if smelling the magic in the room. "There are no such things as Wild Gods. This spell hails from another realm. That is why you can not lift it, stupid girl."

"Can you do it?" Jayda asked, anger clear in her tone.

"I can." Kaj'r said as he slowly stood up. He was nearly seven feet and seemed to glide towards T'ar.

"Will you?" Oberic asked.

Kaj'r reached out a ghoulish looking hand and grabbed Archmage T'ar. "No." Kaj'r responded. Immediately T'ar's skin wrinkled and her body shrank. When she fell to the ground she was little more than a mummified corpse. Dwim ran to T'ar, but already knew there was nothing that could be done for the girl.

"What did ye' do to her?" Dwim shouted in a thick accent.

Kaj'r reached out those ghoulish hands and spoke. "I have been here for many, many years," he glided closer to the group,"and I need to feed. You've come so willingly into my city only to find death." He drew in a deep breath and each member of the group felt as though their life was being sucked away. They all dropped to their knees and gasped for air. Ren held up a hand and tried to conjure the elements, but found that she could not focus her mind enough.

The room faded from everyone's sight. Kaj'r, who had been around for no less than a thousand years, was a master of illusions. Nightmares did not have to be scary, according to him, they just had to cause pain. Each and everyone one of them lived another nightmare like they had done in the dead wood.

Rennyn found herself in a cavern with a natural hot spring. Light shone down from a hole in the rocks and cast a beautiful light on a small patch of earth covered in grass where wild flowers bloomed. "Hello? Jayda? Leon?" She spun around once. "Where am I?" She spun around again and this time saw that Leon was laying naked in the bed of flowers.

"What are you doing here?" He asked, pulling a flower to his nose and smelling it.

Ren blushed and stammered, "I think I was looking for you." she bit her bottom lip. "I'm not quite sure though, I thought I was somewhere else for a minute."

Leon rested his head on a hand and posed for her, "Do you like what you see?"

With a shy nod of her head she whispered, "Yes."

"Good. Then they will too." he nodded behind her. Ren turned and saw five Elven women who were completely naked as well, coming towards her. "Now get out of the way so I can have some fun." The girls passed Ren and knelt down in the grass with Leon. They were all much taller and more beautiful than Rennyn was.

Her lips parted slightly and she did her best to hold tears back. "Leon, why are you doing this?" She watched the women cover his body and handle him right in front of her.

"Why? Because why in the world would I want to be with you? These ladies are far more attractive. If I was even remotely interested in you, wouldn't I have fucked you already?" Leon laughed. "You're nothing to me." The women became more bold with their sexual intentions. "You're nothing more than a glorified bar keep. Good job on mixing those potions I guess." Leon tilted his head back and enjoyed the women. "Mmm. That's good stuff." Ren's chin trembled. "What are you going to do? Make the wind blow? Get out of here and go cry. Better yet, make yourself useful and mix me and these ladies up some drinks."

Tears filled her eyes and she bit back a sob. She held her hands up, trying to cast anything at all, but nothing happened. She finally broke and let out a cry. She turned and took off running away from Leon. Her feet pounded on the ground as the tears ran down her cheeks, but no matter where or how fast she ran, the image of Leon loving other women and laughing at her followed. Ren stumbled and hit the ground. She sobbed into her arms as she lay on the cold cavern floor, feeling as though her life were being sapped from her.

Jayda found herself standing in a candle lit bedroom. In the center was a four post canopy bed where sheer curtains shaded two figures in the bed. She walked closer to it, glimpsing down to see flower petals had been thrown all over the floor. She swallowed nervously as she got closer. She could hear, very clearly, the sound of passionate love making. The curtains pulled themselves back and revealed Oberic laying in bed with Evelyn on top of him. Oberic's face was in pure ecstasy. Evelyn turned to Jayda and smiled. "We're in love and got remarried." She held out her hand and showed off a gorgeous ring as she continued to have him. "All it took was a silly little girl to make him realize that he needs a *real* woman and not some whore with a whip." Evelyn then pulled out a whip of her own. "We did keep that part though. He likes it." Oberic didn't respond at all. He was lost to the pleasure Evelyn was providing and hadn't noticed Jayda was there at all. "I guess you lose again, bitch." Jayda felt as though her heart shattered. She spun and looked for a way out. She ran to the wall and banged her fists against them trying to block out the loud noise of their pleasure.

"No!" Jayda screamed as she continued to beat on the wall but the noise just became louder. She fell to her knees.

"I doubt he ever had feelings for you. Oh! Here it comes!" Oberic and Evelyn climaxed together. He made noises that he had not made with her. Evelyn laughed merrily. "Oh! I think I'm going to have a baby!"

Alastor found himself standing on an Orc encampment. A woman was bent over a log, being raped repeatedly by the monsters. Alastor walked around the group of Orcs to see who the woman was and was not surprised, but terrified all the same, to see that it was his mother. She screamed and struggled against the Orcs who violated her. Alastor ran towards the group, meaning to avenge his mother, but every step he took forward the scene seemed to draw backwards. "It's okay, Alastor," she cried out, "this is a much better outcome than giving birth to an ugly thing like you." He stopped running and looked at her in confusion. The Orcs had pumped their seed into her and when they pulled away, she stood up. Her stomach swole right in front of him and she spread her legs. A little gray infant slipped from between and fell to the ground. "Oh by Olm's light! Look how deformed this thing is?" She picked the baby up by the ankle. "I should have thrown you in the river, Alastor. You're the reason I died. You're the reason my father hated me. You deserved everything that has ever happened to you and I was punished for you being alive." Alastor felt light headed and found that he felt overly weak as if being drained.

Leon found himself in a similar situation as Ren. He found her lying there exposed to him, but as he got closer saw that Phineas was laying behind her. Leon looked away as Phineas had her leg lifted and was deep inside her having his way. Her head was tipped back and her hand was raised caressing his perfect face. "Can you believe Leon thinks I want him when I have this piece of meat?" They both laughed at him. Phin moved her into a different position and took her more roughly. Ren just smiled at Leon "I'll always be a nasty little whore for Phineas. Never you. You aren't worth it. You'll never be able to handle me like this big man behind me. Leon dropped to his knees feeling weak. He felt tired as if his energy had been drained from him.

Dwim found himself stepping foot in a cathedral. As he did so, his feet lit aflame. He swore and tried to run forward but found that he could not. He looked behind himself and saw that the door had locked itself. A chorus of voices sang out to him, "Betrayer! Sinner! Zerrick had every right to strike you down! Betrayer!" Every step burned him more and more. There was a beam of light at the altar at the end of the room, but no matter how many steps he took he could never reach it. He fell to his knees and as his hands hit the floor, they too burst into flame. Dwim understood this was no regular flame though. It was a holy flame and he was the unholy being smote. He cried out to Olm to show mercy but no words left his lips. The beacon of light vanished from his sight and he knew that he had been forsaken.

Phineas, who may have had the strangest fear play out before him, was in a brothel with all the women he could ever desire and for some reason could not make the magic happen. The women promised him any desires he wanted and continually grabbed at his member which continued to remain as flaccid. It wasn't long until the mockery began. They pointed and laughed at his small, and now shrinking, penis. Phineas stood and tried to escape the women, but as he ran away he found a hall of mirrors. Each carried the face of a laughing woman letting him know they had faked everything. He ran faster and the faces he saw were no longer women but his own. Yet at the same time it was not him at all. He stopped and stared at the man in the mirror and the reflection was Phineas, but an ugly Phineas. The mirror Phineas spoke to him earnestly, "This is you. You know that don't you? You're as ugly as can be on the inside pal. All those women that ever loved you, you lied and used them. You ruined your family. Left your brother to die. You're just the worst." Phin placed his hands against the mirror and felt himself become weaker.

Oberic was on his knees in front of Jayda who told him she never really cared for him. "I'm just biding my time," she said, "Until someone younger comes along. You can't keep up with me. You don't really make me happy." She stepped behind him and wrapped her whip around his neck and started to choke him with it. His fingers tried to wedge themselves under the leather but he could not. "I'm going to leave you soon. Just like Evelyn did. You know why? Because you're nothing. You're a nobody! I might not be able to cast any magic but at least I was respected. Does anyone respect you?" The whip got tighter around his neck. "Let me clue you in, they don't. None of us do. You're great with books but you can't even tell that I'm playing you for a fool." Oberic gasped for air as he fought against her.

The illusions vanished and they found themselves on the ground weak and exhausted. Kaj'r loomed over the group like a lighthouse at sea and let out a low laugh. "How very pathetic. Please, relax and know that while you will certainly die on this day, your lives will fuel my own for quite a while longer."

Ren looked at Leon and felt heart broken though she knew now it was nothing more than an illusion. Leon returned the look, unable to get the idea of her and Phineas out of his head. "Why do this?" Ren asked.

"I have been here for so long. I have watched civilizations rise and fall. I was there as fabled heroes were born and died. It may be easy to assume then that my body reached it's expiration long ago. I have to feed to remain here in this realm. I'll not give up until I can find his spell books."

Oberic struggled to get up. "Whose spell books?"

"The Aegis, you fool!" Kaj'r shouted. His voice never raised though it seemed like it was deafening to them. "The master of all magic! Powerful enough to travel between worlds!! The fool could have conquered this world, possibly the stars, but he was too stupid to use it."

"That's just a story!" Ren screamed out. Most of them were still hung over and the day had already been too much for them.

"Story?" Kaj'r laughed. "I was there! There were several of us after those books. Alas," his cheerfulness had vanished, "we were not powerful enough to win. He petrified his own son and banished the others. I have survived by draining the life from others"

Jayda got to her feet, "Enough of this!" She struck out like lightning with her whip. The leather bit into the robe but seemed to hit nothing.

Kaj'r laughed again. The ghoulish hand appeared and ran a boney finger down the robe. The robe tore apart down the center and then he grabbed the crown upon his head and lifted. The hood fell away first revealing a black skull with decaying flesh still attached to it. It was runny and insects crawled upon his face eating the flesh. The eye sockets were filled by a red glow. He placed the crown back on his head and shifted his body. The rest of the robe fell and revealed that his upper body was much like his head. Decaying and wet; mostly made of bone. There were no organs beneath the rib cage but one. It was a tiny and petrified looking heart that did not pump. His lower half was nothing at all.

Rennyn let out a shriek and cowered. Jayda's stomach lurched but she swung out again, aiming now for his neck. She had the feeling she had done this before but when? The imagery of a wolf chewing on a dead body appeared in her head again. She shook it out. This was not the time for that. The whip wrapped around the dead flesh. Kaj'r gilded towards her. "You must have liked what you saw, girl. I can show you again; in much greater detail."

"I won't let you in my head again!" Jayda growled at him and prepared a dagger as he moved closer to her.

He laughed at her once more, "We'll see!" Kaj'r, and the world around her, vanished once more. Just as he said, a more and very detailed scene played out in front of her. Kaj'r's laughter echoed in her ears all the while. Jayda screamed as she found herself trapped in the room again. She slammed her fists on the walls of the room that had no door. Ren screamed her name trying to get her to snap free from the illusion hoping to bring her back to the here and now but it seemed to be useless. Jayda felt a cold and grimey touch wrapping around her neck. Her hands immediately dropped the weapons and went to her throat. The illusion vanished once more as she was lifted from the ground. Kaj'r hoisted her up so that they were face to face. He squeezed her neck tightly, which may have been hard to believe given the state of decay of the thing. "I will devour you first," his whispering voice said, "just so he has to watch."

Alastor stood and charged at Kaj'r. He dived at the undead creature, but the thing simply lifted into the air further. Alastor fell flat with a groan. Dwim was nowhere near as tall nor did he have the ability to really leap up and grab the thing. Leon and Phin stood and tried to grab the monster just as Alastor did; they both failed. Oberic screamed out for Jayda and weaved his hands. The same ball of blinding energy appeared and began to dart into Kaj'r. The undead thing let go of Jayda as it was blasted back a bit. Jayda fell and landed on top of Alastor. She gasped for air and immediately clawed at the floor to drag herself to her weapons.

Kaj'r pointed at Oberic, "Your holy magic will not save you! You're not nearly as powerful as you think you are!"

Jayda's fingers touched the handle of her whip and she crawled to her feet. The Hunter was ready to lash out again. Oberic's spell vanished and he offered the thing a smirk. "I might not be powerful enough on my own, but all of us together? Well that's just trouble for you." Oberic weaved his hands again and the whip in Jayda's hand ignited in white flame.

Jayda looked at the whip and then to the undead creature with anger. "No more of this! You picked the wrong girl to mess with!" She lashed out at the creature and the whip made a connection with his sternum, or what remained of it. Kaj'r let out a shriek and floated back from her swiftly.

"You think you're so clever!" His hands pushed forward and started his draining spell on the others. Each of them slumped back down to the floor as they were slowly being stripped of the time on this mortal coil.

Jayda lashed out again and this time the whip wrapped around his neck once more. His spell was interrupted and he cried out as he tried to pull away from her. Jayda dug her feet in and tried to pull him back down to her level. She struggled, but as the creature burned against her whip she was slowly winning. Kaj'r stopped trying to fight the pain and instead turned to sapping her life from her. Jayda slowly began to sway as she was being drained. "You can't stop me," he hissed, "even if you beat me, do you think you could escape here?" Her friends got up and ran to her side, all of them except Oberic, who ran past her, leapt up, and clung to the floating monster.

Oberic began to pummel the creature while holding onto cold and wet decaying flesh. Kaj'r thrashed about, not really in pain from the attack, but more from surprise. He swung and glided around the room trying to loosen Oberic's grip on him. The others stood with Jayda and aided her in pulling the creature down. Everyone there had it in their head they were going to fight to the last breath.

When it was low enough, Alastor held up his claw-like fingers. "That man has giant testicles and a warrior spirit!" He ran and leapt onto the creature. The added weight caused Kaj'r to lower even more. He clawed at the monster and held on as tight as he could.

"I've got big nuts!" Phin yelled and just as Alastor did, he jumped and grabbed on to the monster. Leon and Dwim continued to help pull on the whip.

Ren stepped forward and held her hands out before her. She mastered her emotion and focused on the things Oberic had tried to show her in their spare time. The small flames that burned the wicks of the candles in the room flickered and vanished. Between Ren's hands sparked a fire that continued to grow. "You mess with one of us and you mess with all of us!" Ren shouted.

The undead thing spit out a strange substance that was a mixture of liquid and vapor. It splattered the ground and from that toxin crawled strange hybrids of roaches and spiders. The little nasties scampered around the room taking snaps at anyone they could.

"I nay think so!" Dwim shouted as he stomped on several at a time. They made a hideous pop noise and left behind an outrageous amount of blood. It squirted out from beneath his feet like a projectile.

Jayda started stomping what she could but there seemed to be far too many. Ren shouted up at Oberic as she continued to build the fire in her hands "Oberic! Let me blast this piece of trash!" Oberic dropped from the lich and landed on his back. One of the little bugs ran up to him and snapped. Leon stomped on it right before it could get Oberic. Leon, however, did not get so lucky. One had crawled up his leg and bit into him. He let out a cry and swatted the insect away leaving only the gash in his leg. Alastor and Phineas also let go but they managed to land on their feet.

Alastor shouted, "Take your shot, Elf!"

Rennyn pulled her hands apart as the fire grew. She raised and held them above her head and thrusted them forward. They all watched as the flame flew forward at the lich. It shrieked and simply vanished. Jayda's whip fell limply to the floor and she rushed to Oberic, slipping on the blood that covered the floor from stomped bugs.

Alastor bent and picked up one of the remaining bugs and stuffed it into his mouth and chewed. He spat out the mush and wiped his mouth, "Does not taste well."

Jayda reached down and grabbed Oberic by his coat and pulled him to his feet. Ren stood there and grinned proudly. "I did it!"

Once Oberic was standing he took Jayda's face into his hands and kissed her hard and deep and whispered, "It's not over! We need to go!"

Leon looked around, "What now?" The others would have accused him of jinxing them had they had the time. The top of the tower began to collapse around them and as they all looked up they could only see two red eyes amongst the darkening skies. They could hear screams coming from the city below them.

"There is no escape!" Kaj'r's voice said ringing in the entire population's ears. Jayda cried out as she was knocked back down by the rubble and as she was holding on to Oberic he fell on top of her. Ren pushed Phin out of the way of a slab of stone falling and narrowly missed being crushed herself.

As Oberic covered her from falling debris he semi shouted at her, "If we die here today I need you to know I'm happy you kicked my ass when we first met! You have breathed more life into me these past weeks than I have lived in the last twenty years!"

Leon seemed to take note of Oberic's words and looked at Ren, "If we survive; go on a date with me?"

Ren nodded with a smile on her face and let out a mixture of a laugh and sob, "Now you ask? Of course I will!"

The others pushed themselves against the wall hoping to avoid being hit by debris there. Jayda held tightly to Oberic as he shielded her. She met his eyes and placed a hand on his face. "I love you, Oberic! I think I have since day one! You and that silly bird." Her hand dropped away leaving bloody fingerprints on his cheek as they were pummeled by another chunk of the tower.

There was a moment where the tower took a break from falling apart over them. "Now is our chance!" Oberic climbed off Jayda and grabbed her hand to pull her up. He then waved his other hand and the rune that brought them there lit up. "Go!" He made sure that each of them went before him. Once he appeared on the other side with them they all made their run for the doors.

They exited the tower and each member followed Oberic. Above them the skies had turned black and the red eyes loomed over menacingly. "I see you. . ." Kaj'r taunted the group. Insects, much like the ones they fought at the top of the tower, swarmed down from the clouds and began snapping at scared citizens.

A certain leadership quality had always laid dormant in Oberic for his entire life and it only seemed to arise when he felt he had to protect Jayda. As they ran down streets, passing by people who were being devoured by the insects, Oberic pulled her into a shop. The others followed in and shut the door. Oberic grabbed Jayda by the arms and forced her to look at him. "You must promise me you'll run. Do not look back; just run. Get to the stables, tie the horses together, and ride together through the mirror. I don't know where it will send you but you should be together at least."

She looked at him confused. The others looked out the window at the chaos in the city. "Oberic?" She asked, unsure of what he was wanting from her.

He placed his forehead against hers for a moment and then kissed her lips. "I swear on my life, I will find you again. Promise me you'll do as I have asked!"

Panic filled her eyes, "I can't do this without you! Oberic, I can't!"

"You can! You have to!" He shook her. "You are a Hunter! Now be the Hunter that hunted me down. I swear it on my love for you, I *will* find you, I promise." He did not give her a chance to respond and instead pulled his hat off and put it on her head. "I'll see you again soon. Keep them safe." he touched her face once more and gave her a wink with those dangerous green eyes. He pushed past the others and ran out the shop and back towards the crumbling tower. The others rushed outside to find that balls of fire had started to rain from the sky as the ghastly eyes hovered over them all. It was pure chaos now.

Jayda made to charge after Oberic, but Leon grabbed her arm and dragged her down the street away from him. They dodged what they could and jumped over those who already fell victim to the insects. They were making their way down to the stables as Oberic instructed; pushing through crowds of scared and screaming people. Jayda broke free of Leon's grasp and started to run back into the carnage after Oberic.

Ren yelled, "Phineas! You need to grab her! We need to get to the stables!" Phin nodded and did not hesitate to follow her command. He sprinted off after Jayda and ran past her. Jayda looked at him as he ran past, wondering what in the world he was doing. Phin swiftly turned and shouldered her in the stomach. She let out a grunt as the wind was knocked out of her and draped over his shoulder. He lifted her off her feet and ran with her back to the group.

"Gotta listen to the wizard, doll!" Phin apologized to Jayda who was beating at his back with her fists.

"He's not a wizard!" Dwim shouted back.

"Not the time!" Alastor yelled back.

They reached the stables finally where they found their horses rearing up and letting out terrified neighing. When Phineas put Jayda down she immediately launched herself at him and punched him with all her anger and sadness. "I could have saved him! I should have been with him!" Phineas took every blow and looked at her with sad eyes. He felt for his friend, the only one in the group who didn't treat him like a problem. Her punches grew weaker and weaker until she collapsed against him sobbing. "I should have gone and been with him! He can't be alone!"

Dwim spun Jayda around and grabbed her wrists, "Lass, I know ye' love him. Please, ye' have to understand something; they called him an Archmage. That isn't some title nobodies get, ye' understand? Oberic is far more powerful than he lets on and I think ye' already had an idea of that. I trust his decision and so should ye'. Now he gave ye' a chance to run," Dwim released her and grabbed Oberic's hat. He made sure to tug down on it so that it was nice and snug on her head, "time to make him proud, lass."

She looked at Dwim, and though he felt such sorrow for her knowing that Oberic was surely going to die, he remained as neutral as he could. Jayda nodded, "Tie the horses together. Leave one behind for him!"

Dwim nodded and barked the order at the others. They worked together and got the horses ready. Each mounted one and Leon called out from behind her, as she was the first in the procession. She was at this moment at least, the new leader, "What now?"

Jayda looked back at the one horse left and felt the burden of responsibility on her shoulders. "We go back to the mirror and go through it just as Oberic said. We should all end up together so long as we're tied. Do not get off your horse, understand?" The others cried their understanding and Jayda accepted it. She kicked the horse and their gallops led them to the mirror. As they rode she, along with the others, looked back up the tiered city and watched as a tornado of fire appeared. Oberic's magic? The lich Kaj'r? None of them had any idea of knowing.

Alastor called out from the last spot in the procession, "Where will this mirror lead us now?"

"Hopefully somewhere safe," was all she replied. Once they reached the mirror they saw hundreds of others pushing and shoving their way through the rippling glass. So many different images were flashing that there was no way to determine what was being seen. "Together! As close as possible!"

The horses were forced to walk very slowly with the crowd of people surrounding them all trying to get through. They neared the mirror and Jayda took one last look up at the red eyes. Amun had flown right above her and she reached out and grabbed the crow. He pecked at her hand and cawed wildly but she refused to let him go. The group walked through the mirror on their horses. That strange feeling returned to them. The sensation of being watched accompanied with the feeling of impending doom and dread. Ren would have a strange vision in that short space and time between worlds. She saw a dove in a tree and it looked at her with shining blue eyes. "Find the baby," it said to her, "heir to the crown of your home."

The dove flew off and was replaced by a ghostly image of Oberic, "Tell her I will find her and that nothing can ever keep me from her. Tell her nothing else if not this; I love her. Tell her that for me." His words echoed in her mind and Oberic vanished only to be replaced by the Dove who appeared right in front of her face.

Ren nearly fell off her saddle from the sudden appearance of the dove. "The baby will always be in danger. The snake can not protect the baby alone. The accursed of your kin can not protect the baby alone. All must come together under the stars!" The dove flew off; reality returned to her as a large field of green and charming blue sky appeared to her eyes.

The party had appeared in a field, none of them knew where. As Alastor came through, being the last of the group, the horses bucked and threw them all off. The six of them fell as the horses galloped away from them though never really leaving their sight. Jayda hit the ground and Amun flew from her hands and ventured off on his own making a big fuss as he went.

CHAPTER 21

Rennyn got up slowly and with a groan. She tried to make sense of what she had seen. It felt like it was nothing more than a fraction of a second and yet she felt it was something important. The others stood up as well and dusted themselves off. Leon had moved to Ren to check on her, but Ren pushed him aside as it started to come back to her. Ren grabbed Jayda by the shoulders and forced her to look at her.

"I saw Oberic," she started, "while we were passing through the mirror. He said he loves you and that he is going to find you." Even just being the messenger, Ren's eyes started to water. Jayda finally broke and fell into Ren's embrace. She hugged Jayda tightly and allowed her to get everything out.

Leon and Alastor went and rounded up the horses again while Dwim and Phineas went off to find wood for a fire. Camp needed to be made and a plan needed to be plotted. The horses walked through the field and Leon knew they would not go far from them. Once they were calmed down they were very well behaved. The fire had been made and they sat around it quietly. Jayda was staring into the fire looking dead to them.

"When we passed through I was also told something about a baby." Ren finally said, breaking the silence.

Jayda looked up, "From Oberic?"

Ren shook her head and felt a bit silly for what she was about to say, "A blue eyed dove told me." She did not feel silly afterall. Of all the strange things to have happened to them, her being granted a vision from a blue eyed dove seemed like a pretty normal thing. She went into greater detail about what was told to her and together, excluding Jayda who held no interest in it, they pondered the meaning.

Alastor, in a matter of fact tone, stated, "You were granted a vision from the goddess Alitria."

Ren looked at Alastor, "Alitria? Are you sure?"

Alastor nodded. "My mother told me she is often seen by those worthy as a dove or a half dove half woman. She is the goddess of fertility, love, sadness, and fates." Alastor's mother, Ren knew, had taught him all about the gods that Humans worshiped. She was familiar with them herself.

Phin looked at Leon and asked him a question as the fire crackled, "Any idea where we are?"

Leon shook his head, "Not until I see more landscape."

Jayda looked up at them coldly. She had grown tired of their discussions about babies and locations or anything else they could think to discuss. Oberic was gone and had a sinking feeling he lied to her when he said he would find her. He had a record of throwing himself to the flame if it meant saving others. She wrapped her cloak around her and spoke in an angry tone, "We will need to get an early start in the morning. I'm going to sleep." She got up and moved a bit away from the others and laid down. When she was on the earth and facing away from them, she cried herself to sleep.

Rennyn moved closer to the others so that they could continue talking without disturbing Jayda. "Do you suppose you will know once we cover more land?"

"I can only hope," Leon said, "land mostly looks the same until I can see some landmarks. Even then we may be in a land that is unknown to me."

Dwim stroked his beard. He still had the girly braids that Ren had done for him the night before. "Ye' think we should take shifts tonight?"

Alastor answered his question, "I do not think we are in any danger at the moment. I believe that magic mirror put us in a random location. We should all be able to rest tonight and be fresh for the morning light."

They all sat there for a while longer before they all turned in, one by one, for sleep. Jayda was the only one to have bad dreams. If not for the strange feeling that certain things weren't real to her, she would dream of Oberic. Even though her eyes were closed and she was sleeping heavily; she cried.

The morning came and brought with it a light rain. They had lost their weapons, except for Jayda who carried hers with her everywhere. Leon asked if he could borrow one of her daggers and she handed it over without saying anything. She did not want to talk nor did she care what happened at the moment. Leon went off and returned a little later with a few rabbits. He had hunted them down and with his incredible aim managed to kill them by throwing the dagger at them. He skinned and cleaned them with Ren's help. They then roasted them over the fire. The meat was handed out to everyone and they ate very fast except Jayda who took a bite or two before throwing hers into the fire.

The sun stayed behind the clouds that day and it matched the mood of the group. Jayda silently packed her stuff and prepared her horse. She just wanted to get the day started regardless if she had any real idea of what she was doing. She reached down and pulled her whip from her hip and looked at it for a long moment before setting it back where it belonged. She held up Oberic's hat and looked at the ragged thing. She smiled, but her eyes filled with tears again. She had slept with it pulled against her chest all night. She stuffed it in the saddle bag and with a jump, she mounted her horse. She sat there waiting on the others.

The others noticed this and as soon as they had finished their meal they too packed up what they had, which wasn't much, and mounted their horses. They traveled for two days through fields of green and wild flowers before they found a road. They traveled that road for another two days with no one saying much of anything at all until Leon finally shouted out, "We're back in Normoon!" he pointed off to a mountain range, "Near Basile I bet."

Phin rubbed his hands together excitedly, "Finally! A brothel! I need to get myself wet if you know what I mean!" He elbowed Alastor who did not know what he meant and so did not reply, but only glared for having been elbowed in the first place.

Rennyn, who next to Phineas, had the best attitude and disposition in the group had her mood soured by Jayda's attitude over the last few days. "Phineas, that's enough."

Jayda turned and snapped at them both, "Both of you, knock it off! We will find somewhere to stay while we are here. I don't know how long we will stay though." She looked back ahead and returned to her silence. Another day of travel passed before they reached what was once the capital of the kingdom back in the old days when North Normoon was nothing more than a stronghold for the royal family. Basile was large and crowded and just as Oberic had told them, covered in eternal night.

As they approached the city, the sky above them turned from blue and beautiful to black and filled with stars. They all looked up rather amazed except Leon who had seen quite a bit on his travels. The city was decorated in red, pink, and purple lanterns to emphasize it's ideal destination for couples or those looking for a bit of romance.

Ren smiled as she rode next to Leon, "Isn't it just beautiful here? A perfect place for a date?" Jayda turned back to look at her and shot her a death glare. Ren cowered under Jayda's eyes.

Leon said nothing, but reached over and gave her a reassuring squeeze on her hand. "I miss the mountains." Dwim said, sounding rather homesick.

Phineas patted the Dwarf on the back, "My friend, I'm going to get you laid."

Dwim pushed Phineas arm away with his elbow, "I nay need yer' help, scoundrel."

"No one is going anywhere!" Jayda yelled suddenly and turned her horse around to face them. "We're all sticking together!"

Rennyn snapped back and narrowed her eyes at Jayda, "You know what, Jayda? We all miss Oberic! We all wish he was here with us, but you're being mean and rude! I don't know who you are right now!"

Jayda returned the gaze, "I can't lose anyone else. My heart can't handle anymore than it already has." Her voice had dropped as she began to choke on her words. Sadness overtook her face.

Leon rode up next to her and placed a hand on her shoulder, "I know you're hurting. He saved us all." He reached back and motioned to the others who all nodded. "You need to try and do some sort of living though. I don't know if he will return, but I do not wish to see you live in the past."

Coldness replaced her sadness as she spoke to him, "He *will* come back to me. He promised."

Leon removed his hand and surrendered. He rode back to the others and joined them again. Alastor was not so easily shaken, "And if he does not? Will you waste your youth waiting on a ghost? He may very well be dead already." Jayda glared at him, shocked at his boldness and choice of words. She found that she had no reply so she turned her horse around and rode ahead of them.

Ren looked at Alastor and whispered, "Do you think he made it?"

Alastor looked at Ren and frowned, "I saw fire raining down upon a city of magic from an undead creature that a handful of us did not defeat. I am just being realistic."

Ren nodded and sighed softly. They came across a nice inn and Jayda took charge of going inside to get rooms. She was only able to get three rooms and when she walked back outside she let them all know they were going to have to double up. She tossed a key to Leon who caught it. "You and Ren." She tossed another key to Dwim. "You and Alastor." She held up the last key. "Phin, you're with me." She wore no friendly look on her face and the entire group hoped Phin was smart enough to not say something stupid.

They could hope and pray all they wanted, but Phineas Lightfoot was a simple selfish creature. "I'll help you forget about Oberic." He let out an exaggerated pur. Jayda's face fell and she walked away. She took her horse to the stable and headed back inside the inn determined to get herself a drink. The others waited until she was inside before they brought their own horses to the stables.

When they were all off their horses Leon slapped Phineas across the back of his head, "You're a fucking idiot!"

Alastor and Dwim grunted their agreement. Ren jabbed a finger at him, "You better behave yourself with her in that room, Phineas!"

Phineas looked at all of them and shrugged, "Everyones getting upset with me? For what? Because she's hung up on a dead guy? Some new dick in her life might make her feel a little better."

This time Rennyn slapped him across the face. Phin flinched back and rubbed his cheek. She looked at the others, "Maybe someone else should room with her?"

"Relax!" He cried out looking rather annoyed that he was slapped. "I won't make a move. I sleep naked though and once you get a glimpse of the real beast, well, there's no denying the need after that."

They all walked into the inn and found Jayda sitting at the bar. She called out for another one and the barkeep obliged so long as she kept supplying the coin. This was Basile afterall and many lonely hearts drank away their sorrows here. The others grabbed a table instead of sitting with her. Her terrible mood and attitude made them not really want to be around her very much. Leon went and got them drinks and they sat together making noise and getting a bit rowdy. Phineas had gotten up and put the moves on some thin woman who nearly immediately took him away upstairs to her room.

Jayda called for another and drank alone. She could very clearly hear the others having a decent time behind her but she did not care. She was hurting and none of them would ever understand how badly her heart was broken. She felt that she could give in at any moment as it seemed to beat less and without conviction. She had another. Dwim had come to the bar to get another tray of drinks for them and said nothing to her. She didn't even glance in his direction and she called for another.

Alastor came and sat next to her at the bar. Jayda was slouched at the bar staring into her mug. He looked at her for a bit before he spoke to her. "I do not know romantic love. I do not know that I ever will. I am not sure it is in me."

Ren and Leon said goodnight to Dwim and headed up the stairs. Dwim finished his drink and headed up shortly after. Jayda's words were jumbled as she looked at him "Love is fucking painful. Look where," she hiccuped, "it got me." She took a swig of her drink.

He had no experiences in love of his own and so he asked, "Where did it get you?"

She looked at him and raised her mug, "Sad. Sad and fucking drunk."

He asked her a simple question but in the Orc's mind it was very deep. "Did you feel loved when he held you? Did you feel desired?"

"Like I never have before." She looked down at her drink and watched her reflection in the mug.

Alastor nodded at her words. "It may be sad that it is gone, but perhaps you should be thankful that you felt that. I have never felt that. I doubt Phineas has ever felt love though I do not doubt he has made procreation attempts with many women." Alastor shrugged as he tried to work out the situation in his head. "Is it better to have loved and lost than to never have loved at all?"

Jayda snapped at him, "Everyone talks as if he is already dead! As if we have buried his cold body!" She stood abruptly, "Have you all given up so soon?"

Alastor did not retreat from her anger, "Maybe he survived. Maybe he did not. We can not know. What I do know is that he was a trickster. He spun pretty words. Maybe he told you what you needed to hear to get you to safety." He shrugged. "I could be wrong. I just do not want you to long for ghosts that can never appear."

Jayda looked at Alastor, his words had hit home for her. Maybe he was right. Were they the words she needed to hear? She finally agreed. "You are right." Her acceptance was but a whisper. Jayda picked up her mug and finished it. She gave him a nod and patted him on the shoulder. "Goodnight, Alastor."

He mumbled his goodbye and watched her leave. He did feel some sort of sorrow for her though it was not much. He liked the man she had fallen for, but he himself did not believe Oberic survived.

When Ren and Leon entered their room she immediately sat down her satchel, one of the few things to have survived everything so far, and removed her wooden chest. She opened it and dug through the many tiny vials of liquids that she had labeled. She lifted one, read it, and shook her head. She placed it back down and repeated the process several times while mumbling to herself. She was looking for something tasteless and when she lifted another bottle and examined it she smiled. "Time to put Jayda to bed, Leon."

Leon cleared his throat, "Is that a good idea?"

Ren turned around and looked at him, "What do you mean?"

"Oberic struggled with what he did. Is it wise to keep doing that?" Leon looked genuinely concerned as he sat down on the bed.

Ren pondered the question. "Oberic made her forget and that was wrong. I'm just helping her to rest without dreams" She saw that Leon looked unconvinced and she stepped forward to defend her idea. "You have heard her during the nights over the last week. The crying that she thinks no one can hear. His name on her lips as she cries out from her nightmares." She looked at the vial in her hand."I just want her to feel better."

He nodded. "I understand that, Ren. I really do. I still think she needs to deal with it. She will have to at some point because hellfire was raining down upon him. Chances are he never made it out."

Ren studied Leon's face and sighed. She turned and put the bottle back in the chest and shut it. "At least we will have a reprieve from her cries tonight."

Jayda stood outside the door of her room and leaned her head against it. She closed her eyes and prayed. "Please let him be in there waiting for me. I would give anything. Please. . ." She turned the knob and pushed the door open. She intruded on Phineas crying like a baby.

As soon as he realized she entered he dried his eyes and cleared his throat. "Accidentally punched myself in the balls."

She stared at him and blinked. "Oh Phineas. . ." She broke into tears again and ran into his arms. She sobbed, finally letting go of everything she had been feeling since they left him behind. Her body was racked with sobs. She cried and cried until her sobs turned into tired whimpers and then into silence as her body gave up from exhaustion. Phineas, very unlike himself, did not even attempt to put a move on her. He knew who her heart belonged to, at least for now, and there was no sense in trying to sway her. He cried with her that night, not because he himself missed Oberic, but because his friend had been hurting for days. He would deny it in the future if it were ever brought up. She fell asleep wrapped in his arms, needing to feel some sort of emotional protection. It was purely platonic and everytime she woke from a nightmare, he was there to ease her back to sleep.

Everyone slept late into the afternoon the next day and for days after as they stayed in Basile. Alastor, Leon, and Dwim had signed up for guard work to help take care of and finance the group since Jayda hadn't laid out any plans for them. Phineas, cunning thief he was, made a very successful living off of picking the pockets of tourists and stealing from nobles who were involved in businesses that they could not alert the guard about. Rennyn had picked up work in a small apothecary shop, helping out the old woman who owned it. Jayda spent her days wandering around town. She was often found in the forest training with her whip or at the inn where she drank and played cards with Phin, who she had become very close with. They shared a different kind of bond these days. This was their lives now and they slowly accepted it.

CHAPTER 22

A storm rolled over the cold dunes of Mahir, a desert located in the center of the same continent that Hadrym was located. The rolling thunder caused the woman laying in bed to open bright orange eyes. She blinked a few times and then sat up. She climbed out of her bed and walked to the window and opened it. She stuck her head out the window and breathed in deeply. The Mahir rarely got storms so it was a great pleasure to experience one. She slipped on some clothes made from a strange silk collected from the worms that burrow in the dunes. She exited her room and stepped into a cold stone hall. Torches lit her skin. She was colored a mixture of dark blue and purple. Her lips, plump and beautiful, had a natural rosy hue to them. Her hair was brown and it was long and braided behind her. Her ears were quite long.

The woman walked down the hall and took a turn up a set of stairs that led to a high wall. She walked along and gazed at the raging sea that lay a bit aways. Her people, the Desruc, had once been nomadic, but as their population grew, a need to find a more stable home had arisen. This city, like other Desruc cities, was built on the coast. They were able to gather the water easily. Using the sun and the temperature of the Mahir, they were able to purify it. Her orange eyes spotted an older man looking through a telescope. She smiled having recognized the old man and she approached.

"Late night for you, V'ma?" The old man asked in their native tongue, not looking away from the telescope.

She nodded, "And for you, Fesk?"

"Oh yes," he pulled away from the telescope and looked at her. He smiled at her. His skin was wrinkled terribly, but its dark gray coloring hid it well, "I had come out to track the stars. Trying to see if I could find anything interesting other than that black star that appeared a while back."

"It bothers you?" V'ma asked as she leaned on the half wall that kept people from falling.

Fesk nodded. "It does and it does not. You know the plight of our people. It gives us strength but rarely is a black star appearing a good thing." He could see V'ma was not paying much attention and he smiled. "You still having those dreams?"

"I am. Some stupid white bird with blue eyes keeps trying to speak to me, but I can never hear what it says." She breathed in deeply. "Nonsense is what it is."

"Ah I wouldn't say that. Dreams are both nothing and everything. It could be some sort of warning. Perhaps destiny?"

"If it were something important then Kalina, mistress of dreams and the night, would grant me proper vision."

Fesk continued to look through the telescope, "Our mistress is great and powerful. You are probably right. It might be nothing at all." He stood up straight and stretched while looking at V'ma, "Come here, young one. Gaze across the water."

V'ma moved to the telescope and bent to look through it. Her eyesight was amazing and even with the telescope she could barely see the tower jutting out from the sea. The clouds surrounding the tower were red and she thought she might even see fire raining from the clouds. "What's going on there?"

Fesk shrugged, "No idea. I hope it does not come this way. We have enough problems of our own."

V'ma stood and the wind caressed her body. "What is that place called again?"

Fesk appreciated her curiosity. "They call that Maer'lyn. Home of magic supposedly. Not that any of our kind ever go. There were a few though who were skilled enough to make something of themselves."

"Such as?"

Fesk placed his hand on his chin and thought hard. He dropped his hand to his hip when he thought of a few examples, "There was Maru the Bold. She was a skilled illusionist. Before her there was L'adik who claimed he could raise the dead. Pa'ru the Equalizer who would drain the life from prisoners and transfer it to the sick. Kaj'r the Devil of the Sands who was by all accounts cruel and terrible, but that was about a thousand years back. I'm sure there are more, but I can not think of them. I am an old man, V'ma."

"Such impressive titles they hold and yet our people remain exiled to the harsh sands of the Mahir"

"That's what we know now. It is who we are."

V'ma hated that answer. Her people could be so much better off if they were just allowed to make a home outside of the desert, but with each attempt they made their colony was burned and her people killed. Their rivalry with the Elves ran long and deep. V'ma had heard once that the Desruc were once Elves themselves, but cursed by one of the so-called Wild Gods for some crime that no one quite remembered. She knew that it was such a terrible thing that several families were stricken by the Wild Gods and they lost their communion with nature. Their skins would eventually darken as well as their hair and their eyes.

The thunder rolled again and Fesk looked up just in time to feel a drop of rain dab his forehead. "Ha! I am blessed on this day for I have been kissed by rain. Let me sleep eternally, having been so lucky."

V'ma looked up as well and a drop fell against her lips. She tasted the water and smiled, "We are both blessed. I will return to my chamber now, Fesk. Sleep well."

Fesk kissed his fingertips and held them to his chest. "You sa well, V'ma."

She turned and traveled back along the wall and down the stairs where she would venture to her room. She shut her door, undressed, and climbed into bed. She closed her eyes and fell asleep to the sound of the storm. Her dreams were once again plagued with the white bird with blue eyes, but still she could not understand what it was saying.

Her eyes opened in the morning as the sun began to heat her room. She slipped from her bed and stretched. She was tall and curvy. Her body was built firm and muscular; considered to be an extremely attractive woman among her people. She had not known a man's touch and refused several suitors who had tried to take her as a wife. She dressed herself in sheer cloth that helped protect against the stinging sands of the Mahir and when she was done, she slipped two Desruc crafted daggers into her belt.

She left the room and walked out into the small city. Their streets were made of sandstone and even though they were constantly swept, they seemed to always be buried under more sand. She passed through the outdoor market and though she was greeted several times she acknowledged no one. Today was a very important day and she could not be late. Their leader, Rodea, was picking a new leader to keep the Desruc people safe. V'ma had worked hard doing whatever she could to secure this position and the only other person who could possibly take over was G'zeera, who she knew to be a venomous fork tongued snake.

She entered the council room where the Balva, the leader, sat on a jeweled chair being fanned by two servants. The Balva welcomed V'ma in and offered her a chair. G'zeera had already arrived. V'ma took the chair near G'zeera and looked over to the snake with unfriendly eyes. His skin was a dark olive tone. Both his eyes and hair were a burnt orange color.

"May the wind bless you, V'ma," he kissed his fingers and touched his chest, "I had perhaps thought you decided it was best that I run our little city. Afterall, it would be for the best. It would be unwise to let a woman like you lead us."

V'ma did not smile, "May the sands bury your bones, G'zeera. I would never allow a little sneak like you to rule over these people unless I was interested in seeing the slave trade start again."

G'zeera smiled at V'ma. His teeth were yellow and wet. "Well, fortunate for us all we have such a protector in you."

The Balva clapped his hands, "May the winds bless you both," he kissed his fingers and touched his chest. Both G'zeera and V'ma returned the gesture. "You both know I have watched your careers here with great interest. I believe you both have great plans for our people though you both take different paths. I am afraid I had a hard time deciding. On one hand," he nodded to V'ma, "we could use your cool and level headed thinking to try and build diplomacy with the Elves again. It would be such a wonder to know that we could walk the forests once more without worrying about our people being harmed. On the other hand," he now raised a hand to G'zeera, "we have been exiled far too long and your ideas of taking land by force seem to make sense to me. I agree we have been pushed around far too long. Generations of our people have known nothing but the sands."

V'ma and G'zeera glared at each other. The Balva continued on, "This is why I have decided to let the Balvas of the past decide."

G'zeera dipped his head, "Such a wise decision my Balva. Let the ancestors choose."

V'ma very much wanted to roll her eyes but smiled, "Yes. A most wise decision."

The three of them were escorted to the deep tomb of which the entrance was merely a stairway leading under the burning sands of Mahir. They walked down the long staircase for several minutes. The tomb itself was cold and was a nice change from the burning heat above. Guards lit the torches in the tomb and once they were lit both candidates looked at the urns holding the ashes of the Balvas before them. In the center of the tomb was a little square pool with a pedestal. The current Balva headed to the pedestal and uncorked a vial. He showed it to both of them. "Kalina's Mist!" he said triumphantly. "Offer your blood to the Balvas and then drink from the vial. You will be granted a vision. When you are done, tell me your vision and I shall know who to choose."

V'ma stepped up to the pedestal and pulled a dagger from her belt. She cut the palm of her hand while making eye contact with G'zeera. She held her hand above the pedestal and turned her hand into a fist. She squeezed tightly and let the blood stream down into the small basin. She then took the vial and took a drink from it. G'zeera had opened his hand and V'ma was quick to slice his hand open for him before he could even reach for his own knife. G'zeera eyed her and gave her a fake but polite dip of the head. He squeezed his blood into the basin and it mixed with hers. He then drank from the bottle as she had.

They stared at each other, both knowing they hated one another. V'ma blinked a few times and felt herself sway where she stood. G'zeera prayed that she would fall and hit her head against the basin but was disappointed when she lowered herself to the tomb's floor to lay down. He started to feel light headed himself and did the same as her. The Balva watched them both seeming quite pleased with the events so far.

Kalina's Mist could be used in several ways. Ingested, such as they had done, but in a greater dose it would induce long and deep sleep. This would allow someone to relive dreams on command. Then there was the way it was used when Dwim and Ren were able to live the dreams of another. Now though, they ingested and did not sleep and so dreams, random at best, became life-like and danced in front of them so real they might have been able to reach out and touch them.

G'zeera called out loudly, "Yes! Oh thank you for such a vision, ancestors!" V'ma had no idea what he might be seeing, but what she was seeing annoyed her. It was the white bird with blue eyes. It fluttered around her head and she reached out to grab it. The Balva watched this behavior and wondered what she was reaching for. V'ma sneered as it continued to circle her.

V'ma figured if anything this was a great time to find out what the bird might have said in her dream. She asked the bird, "What did you say? What were you trying to tell me?"

The bird flapped its wings right above V'ma and stared down at her. The voice that spoke was so amazingly clear now that it startled her, "You must protect the baby. The snake can not protect the baby on it's own. Protect the baby and you may yet lead your people out of the burning sands and into the green wilds. South of the northern moon is where you will find the baby lingering in a grove on the verge of day and night. The constellations draw close." The bird vanished and V'ma sat up right away. G'zeera was still making a lot of noise about whatever it was he was seeing.

V'ma got to her feet and waited as patiently as she could for G'zeera to end his entertaining little show. He seemed to have decided it was going on too long and got to his feet as well. The Balva approached them with anticipation clear on his face, "Speak to me your visions! Let us see who the ancestors have chosen!" The Balva looked to V'ma and smiled, waiting for her reply.

V'ma had no idea if she should tell the truth. It had nothing to do with her current situation and if the Balva thought it wasn't good enough, he would choose G'zeera thus everything would fall to ruin. Then she thought about her conversation with Fesk and what she told him. Kalina would guide her and did she not hear the bird's words after drinking Kalina's Mist? V'ma swallowed hard, "I must find a baby and protect it. Only then will I have the chance to lead our people out of the desert." She felt absolutely stupid for saying it out loud but it was too late to recant now.

The Balva raised his eyebrow and nodded slowly. He did not know the meaning of that, but it was not up to him to decipher. He turned to G'zeera who was standing there with a terrible grin. "Great Balva," the snake started, "I have seen the future! I have seen you giving me the crown of our people! I will rule long and proud! My riches shall be uncounted! Great fortune and prosperity will befall our people! The ancestors have shown me this!"

The Balva nodded and then rubbed his chin, "I have made my decision." He looked at both of them for a long moment. The tension seemed to heat the cold tomb. V'ma wished he would spit it out already. "G'zeera," a triumphant smile appeared on the snake's face, "I know you will support your new Balva, V'ma, and give her all the respect she deserves."

V'ma looked up and smiled. She wanted badly to rub it in her competitor's face. She bowed her head low to Rodea, "Thank you, Balva. You honor me."

"What?" G'zeera shouted, "I have seen our people thrive and she talks about a baby and you pick her?"

The Balva frowned, "I believe you saw what you did, G'zeera, but I believe your heart is not ready to lead a people. You seem to be far too obsessed with the glitter of treasure. V'ma's vision, though I do not understand it, gave her no gain other than our people leaving the desert. Even if it does not come to pass, I believe I have made the right choice. Come."

The Balva led the two of them out of the tomb. They traveled up the staircase in silence and once they were back out in the sun he spoke to them again. "Tomorrow, V'ma, when the sun casts no shadow; we shall crown you Balva and I will be glad to follow your rule." He turned to her then kissed his fingers and placed them on his chest. "May the winds bless you."

V'ma returned the gesture, "And you, my Balva."

When the Balva left, G'zeera faced V'ma and growled, "Well, it would seem you have fooled him into dooming our people."

"Let us be thankful he was able to see through your guile," she retorted.

G'zeera nodded and smiled, "Rest well tonight, V'ma. Tomorrow is going to be a very long day."

V'ma eyed him as he walked away from her. She did not care for the way he had said that. She walked around the city for a while and decided that the nagging feeling that he was going to try and have her assassinated that night was far too strong. V'ma and G'zeera were both assassins by trade. They were known as Black Blades in the Mahir and an assassin knew to trust their gut when it came to other assassins. When she got to her room, she immediately dressed herself in her assassin's clothes. They were dyed black and covered her body completely. She slid small daggers into her boots and then set herself to work on rigging a trap on her door. When the door would open a bell would trigger and wake her so that she could fight back. Happy with the set up she laid down in the bed and waited for the sky to grow dark blue and the cool air to flow in. She slipped her daggers under her pillow, covered herself, and drifted off to sleep.

V'ma had fallen asleep with ease. No one ever attempted to enter the room, but if they had they would find themselves bleeding out rather fast. V'ma was exceptionally skilled. What she did not anticipate was someone already being in the room when she came home. When she had been asleep for some time a figure clothed in black slowly slid from under her bed. They could have ended her then and there, but the orders were to bring her in alive. The only thing V'ma saw when she startled awake by the sound of a man grunting was a fist wearing metallic knuckles.

When she opened her eyes later it was the morning and she found herself naked and in a cage. She quickly studied her surroundings and found she was in some sort of arena. She looked up and saw G'zeera and a few of his assassins standing there looking down. "Oh good! You're awake! May the wind bless you!" They all laughed. "You must forgive my rudeness for taking your clothes, V'ma. I know you too well to know you would have weapons. I was originally just going to have you killed, but that would be too obvious! Instead I have another surprise for you!" He pointed across the arena where a gate was slowly opening. V'ma got chills, even in this heat, as she watched a full blooded Orc step out into the arena. She knew exactly what was about to happen to her.

"You coward," she yelled out, "G'zeera, I swear I will end you for this treachery!"

"No," G'zeera laughed, "You won't. Goodbye, Balva. Your reign was short and sweet."

The gray skinned Orc with stringy greasy black hair came charging at V'ma. It grabbed her cage and easily lifted it. She was as prepared as she could be and immediately sprinted away from him. It threw her cage at her and when it hit the ground it shattered. None of the pieces of wood were good enough to use in the fight and as she thought hard about what to do she could see the beast growing erect. It charged at her again, it's member swung between its legs as it did so, and she ran once more to avoid the beast knowing she would be violently raped before she was killed. Unfortunately, she had no idea what to do. She had no weapon and wasn't sure if the thing would tire out from chasing her. She knew that without a weapon she could not match the thing physically.

As she ran, her foot connected with something in the sand and she tumbled forward. Her nipples hardened as they touched the burning sand and she looked back and saw the Orc already climbing over. It's erection rode up her thigh and she struggled to get up. The Orc grabbed her head and slammed her back down in the sand, pinning her where she was. She threw an elbow and it did nothing. The Orc laughed at her attempts and V'ma did the only thing she thought she had left and grabbed a handful of sand and thrust it back at the Orc's face.

The Orc released her and cried out as it covered it's eyes and rubbed at them. She scrambled to her feet and turned around to make her stand. She knew now she was going to die here but if she could get the thing to kill her before it took her then that would be the best way to go. Her eyes fell to the ground where she tripped and saw a skull sticking up out of the sand. How many people had G'zeera done this to? Women? Children? Certainly runaway slaves.

The Orc continued to whine as it dug at its face. This would not last for long and she looked for solutions. She looked up at G'zeera who at this point wasn't even paying attention and saw that one of the guards had a spear. She licked her lips and ran forward. She grabbed the skull and kept running to the Orc who could see but just barely. She dropped down on her thigh and slid right under the Orc's legs. The stench that she passed was awful, but she had no time to think about it. She jumped up and let out a hiss as air hit the new scraped area on her thigh. There was no time to be concerned about it. She ran forward enough that she could be sure she'd hit her mark. She veered to the right a bit and as she approached the wall of the arena, she jumped, propelled herself off the wall with her feet and after spinning in the air released the skull with a hard throw.

The woman was fast as the throw even faster. The skull met the side of the guard's head. He stumbled forward and teetered on the edge of the wall. V'ma's heart dropped. If he didn't fall she was done for. The guard's arms waved around frantically before he fell victim to gravity. He fell off the ledge and landed on his neck. V'ma ran to guard and grabbed his spear from the sand. The Orc chased her down again and she ran once more. When the Orc reached the fallen guard, who was still alive, he picked him up and tore his head from his shoulders and threw the body at V'ma.

She dodged it easily enough and used the momentum of the dodge to turn around. Her speed dropped only for a moment before she charged at the Orc who was still carrying an erection. As she neared him, she jumped and slashed from side to side with the spear, meaning to cut the Orc's face as fast, and as many times, as she could. The spear sliced into the beast's face and sprayed hot blood on her body. When she landed, she was hit in the head by the Orc who used the guard's head as a weapon. The sound of skulls connecting echoed in the arena. She flew to the side and tried to shake the stunned feeling off.

The Orc charged once more. V'ma got up, let out a yell, and charged at him as well. Just before the two would collide V'ma spun and threw herself on her back. She slid towards him and cried out at that familiar sting of sand grinding against her skin. As she slid, she angled the spear and at just the right moment, she thrusted up. The spear head split and dug into the flesh just under its hardness. She twisted the spear and shoved it in deeper. The Orc let out a terrible roar of pain or perhaps it was anger. The monster grabbed her by the waist and yanked her up. She tightened the grip on the spear so as to not let it go. When she was lifted into the air, she yanked the spear free and jabbed it into one of its eyes.

The Orc dropped her immediately and like a true assassin she rolled from the fall; not injuring herself even a little. The Orc fell to its knees and covered its face. V'ma ran, leapt onto its back, and shoved the spear into the back of it's head. Her strike was hard and the Orc whined no longer as the tip of the spear pushed through it's brain all the way through until it protruded through it's thick forehead a tiny bit. She twisted the spear for good measure and then pulled it out. The Orc was dead, she was safe from it, and now she was going to kill G'zeera.

There had been shouting from the wall of the arena and V'ma turned to see the gate being raised to allow more guards to flood in. This was her escape. She charged at them with the spear in hand and as she met one she ended them swiftly. V'ma may have very well been blessed by the wind on this day for her movement was so graceful that it may have resembled a leaf dancing on a breeze. There was an elegant flow to the carnage she wrought upon those who tried to stop her and one by one each guard fell.

G'zeera had already ordered the other assassins to kill her. The gate started to lower. V'ma made a sprint for it as the other assassins leapt down into the arena. She dove under the gate just in time as it bit into the sand and shut. The assassins banged on the gate as she stood and ran. G'zeera turned and walked to the other side of the wall watching V'ma run into the desert. "Raise the damn gate you fools!" There was no answer though. V'ma had slain every guard. G'zeera climbed down the wall and opened the gate himself. He looked at the three assassins and made sure that his orders were clear. "Kill the bitch! If you don't, it's your head!"

The assassins began to track Balva V'ma, but the winds of the Mahir were cruel and her tracks were covered in minutes. They of course would not return to G'zeera empty handed and so they would continue to search, never knowing if they would find her and she continued to run never knowing if she would see her home again. The only thing on her mind as she ran, eventually slowing to pace herself, was that she had to find a baby south of the northern moon.

CHAPTER 23

Days turned into weeks for the group of friends in Basile. Weeks turned to months. Unsure of what to do next they remained in the city. It had become a life for them. They had changed and became hardened; nearly forgetting, at least a few of them, their past life and what had happened. Ren closed up shop for the night, it was always night and time simply did not make sense here. She had a long day (night) and stepped outside, ready to go home. It was raining and business was slow. She drew her hood over her head and made the walk to where she knew Alastor, Dwim, and Leon were stationed. She had brought them some warm stew and drinks earlier to fill their stomachs.

Jayda had just returned to the city dragging a tattered looking man through the gates by his bound feet. The man's face was swollen and bloodied, a sure sign of her handy work. She dragged him to the shop that requested he be brought in and opened the shop door. "Here's your thief." She held her hand out for her payment. The shop owner gladly paid her and praised her for her fine work. Once she was paid she'd stash the coin away and grab the thief again. She walked to the guard outpost to turn the criminal in and to see if they had any new bounties.

When she arrived she half smiled at Dwim. "Here you go. Got anything else?"

Dwim removed his helmet. "Already done?" Jayda nodded. Dwim chuckled, "Aye. Should have known. Ye' always get them." Leon counted out the reward and handed it over to Jayda who promptly stashed it away. She had no need to double check it with Leon. "Yer' the top bounty reclaimer this month. Has to be some kind of record."

Jayda didn't have the sparkle in her eyes that she once did, but she smiled a little more, "Just keeping busy. You know how it is." She wound her whip back up and put it on her hip. Leon squeezed past her to grab the beaten thief and put him in a cell for transfer later. She spotted Ren sitting inside the outpost with the boys and gave her a little wave before leaving again without a word. She still struggled seeing her and Leon together and often got angry that Oberic had been taken from her.

Jayda had mostly given up on the idea that Oberic would return, but anytime that she had a bounty where it was mentioned that magic was involved, she got her hopes up and each time she was let down. Alastor ran up beside her,

"We have another bounty if you are up for it. Found it stuck under your completed bounty."

"Of course," she said, pushing wet hair from her face.

"Something called a Desruc," he handed her the wanted poster, "no crime committed but overly suspicious. Some sort of dark Elf is the way they explained it to me. They were last seen in the woods outside of the city. It will be a few days of riding . Do you think you can find them?"

She let out a cold laugh, "Have I ever failed?"

Alastor returned her coldness with his own, "You are a beast inside your heart. I respect your prowess. They are offering five hundred gold for this one. It seems like Desruc are not commonly seen here if they are that concerned."

A handsome reward she thought. That would feed them for quite a while. She gave Alastor a pat on the arm, "See you in a few days then, my friend."

"Travel well," he said, slamming his fist against his chest.

The ride out to the wilds was long but nothing she hadn't experienced before. Leon had taught her much about tracking and she had become quite good at it. There were tracks she found unusual that she followed, eventually leading her to a forest clearing where a tiny makeshift hut of mud and leaves sat. She crouched low as she took careful steps to minimize the noise she was making. She drew her daggers and held them in her hands crossed behind her back. She crept closer to the hut and stopped, frozen in place, when she heard the soft crying of a baby. Confusion rested on her face. She saw no signs of anyone around. Surely no one would leave a baby on its own like that. She stood up and walked slowly to the hut.

Once she reached the hut she slid against the wall to keep herself in the shadows as much as possible. She saw, swaddled in cloth, not a newborn but a baby at least six or eight months old. It whined in a woven basket on the ground. She crouched low again and glanced round the room. It was small and though she saw no one there, something felt off. She reached out slowly and touched the child's hand. Tiny fingers clasped her finger and the baby made happy cooing sounds. Just as she let her guard down for a moment she heard a hiss. A snake's head lifted from the basket with it's mouth opened and poised to attack.

It had large fangs that looked to be dripping; Jayda assumed it was venom. It raised to Jayda's face and the two stared at one another.

Jayda pulled the dagger from behind her and made sure not to break eye contact with the snake. Slow movement was key; she thought she remembered hearing Leon say that once. The snake wouldn't make a great meal but a snack for the road would be nice. The snake lunged forward, but not at Jayda. It launched itself past her and Jayda turned in time to spot a man of dark navy blue skin, dirt colored hair, pointed ears, and red eyes. He had daggers drawn and was ready to pounce. The snake lashed out, but the man was far too fast and within the blink of an eye had moved out of sight. Jayda slipped her daggers away and gathered up the baby. She backed slowly out of the hut. The snake hissed at her once more as she tried to leave with the child. This wasn't her mission, but she couldn't very well leave the baby out here and alone to die.

A dove perched itself on the makeshift hut and stared at Jayda holding the baby. The snake lunged forward into the clearing towards her and within a moment was no longer a snake but a raging bear who roared loudly. Just as the bear started to move towards Jayda, a dart flew past it's face. The dark skinned man appeared again and took several slashes at her with his daggers. She ducked and dodged every swing. Her feet moved like a dancer taking peculiar and unfamiliar steps to avoid injury. The baby squirmed in her arms and she held on to it as tightly as she could without hurting the thing.

The bear swung wildly at the man and seemed to actually be assisting her. The man was fast, and while Jayda could certainly have kept up, it was proving difficult with the baby. The man was trapped between them now and while he did his best to attack Jayda, he also had to defend himself against the bear that was once a snake. "Save yourself the trouble and accept death," said the man in a strange accent she had never heard. "You won't be able to keep up with a young one in your arms." The voice had come from behind her and for a moment she could have sworn the man flickered in and out of existence. The bear took several more swipes and when each of them missed it changed its form once more, within the blink of an eye, into a vulture. It flew at the man trying to gouge his eyes.

The man may have been fast but now that he had a vulture on him he was starting to slip a bit. He swung at the bird now too. Neither Jayda nor this shape shifting thing knew that the blades of this man were coated with a poison that would kill them with a single scratch and it was lucky of them to not have been slashed.

A dark violet skinned woman dropped from the trees silently and glared at Jayda with bright orange eyes. Her brown hair was in a knot at the back of her head to keep it from her face. "First I am going to kill this fool," she pointed her own dagger at the man, "then you are going to hand over that child!" The woman moved much faster than Jayda. She and the other man danced around each other as if they knew the next move that was going to be made by the other. The fight between the two Desruc was, at least Jayda thought, almost entertaining. Their speed and agility was uncanny. Even the vulture had quit its attempts at attacking and shifted back into the bear and planted itself in front of Jayda and the baby. The male Desruc did his absolute best, but the woman was a far superior fighter. She dodged one of his swings and stuck her daggers into his gut; not once, not twice, but at least twenty times at such a rapid speed it seemed brutal. The man hadn't even had time to fall when the woman placed both blades against his neck and slit his throat. His life blood sprayed all over the woman and he gurgled out something in another language before he dropped to his knees. He knelt there in the dirt for a long moment before he leaned forward and his face planted itself into the ground. V'ma twirled her daggers in her hand and turned to face Jayda but only locked eyes with the bear.

Jayda held the baby close to her as she looked at the woman and the dead man while hiding behind the form changing beast. She was unsure of which of them was the bounty. The bear let out a huff of air from it's snout as it stood. Jayda backed away from both and asked, "Why was he after the baby?"

V'ma looked to the dead unnamed Desruc, "He was not after the child; I am. Now hand it over. It is my child to protect. It has been asked of me and so it shall be."

"I don't think so," Jayda said, "I'm taking the baby with me."

The bear shifted forms again, but this time to that of a man. Once changed he looked like a beggar with long and wild brown hair and a beard to match, but he had kind blue eyes. "Actually," he said in quite a friendly tone given the situation, "I've been looking after that baby since his mother died. He is mine to look after." Both women jumped back from the sudden change and odd demeanor of the man. "I'm not afraid to kill either of you."

Jayda made slow steps backwards still. She had planned to jump on her horse and make a dash for it. V'ma was having none of that nonsense. She unhooked a bola and slung it at Jayda's feet. It wrapped around her ankles and did it's job, causing her to fall back as she tried to move. The baby was held in the air, though she had not let go of the child and clung to it with determination and care. The man dashed forward and plucked the child from her hold, "And I thank you!" he said in a remarkably snide tone before he shifted back into a bear that cradled the baby. He let out a roar that slung spit across the area.

Jayda cursed loudly and yelled, "oh come on!" She sat up and fought with the chain and weights wrapped around her legs. The bear had moved further through the clearing. When she finished unwrapping herself she tried to stand, but found that the Desruc woman had a dagger held to her throat.

"You have cost me the child. Now I have to kill that beast as well. I have killed bigger and stronger. I can not allow a pretty thing like you to get in my way. I have been granted a vision and I must fulfill it." Her orange eyes met with Jayda's emeralds and Jayda could immediately see that the woman meant business.

Jayda closed her eyes and for a moment accepted that she was going to die. While it scared her there was also great comfort in the thought. She would at least have a chance to see Oberic on the other side of life and that helped ease her woes. Just as she was about to tell the Desruc to do it, something else slipped from her lips. "A white dove with blue eyes told you to find the baby, didn't it?"

V'ma narrowed her eyes and lowered her dagger, "Yes. It said the snake could not protect the baby alone."

Jayda pointed at the bear, "He was a snake when I found the baby!"

The Desruc woman turned and eyed the bear who then shifted to his Human form, "I am perfectly capable of protecting this child. I have done so and provided for it since the winter. What madness are you two going on about?"

Jayda stood and dusted herself off, "If we are all wanting to protect the baby then there is no sense in us fighting each other."

V'ma held her daggers up, aiming one at each of them, "Unless it is you who the baby needs to be protected from."

Jayda rolled her eyes, "If that were the case then why would I have that information?" V'ma considered it and then lowered her daggers once more. The dove that had been watching from the roof of the hut fluttered over to them and landed in a spot where it could face all three of them. They each studied the dove curiously and just as they all noticed it had blue eyes; they found themselves blinded by a brilliant light.

Each of them were knocked to their backs and the baby, swaddled still, was held in suspension. They all sat up and looked at the blinding light. A creature whose lower half was that of a woman and it's top half that of the dove. She spoke to their minds and while each of them were fearful, they felt at peace, "Poisoned was the crown! A mother exiled and slain! A son left to die! The gryphon will protect and in turn reunite kingdoms under one! An alliance between many will be forged under this golden age if the boy survives and claims his birthright!"

Just as suddenly the bird woman was gone and with it the blinding light. When their vision cleared they were able to catch one last glimpse of the dove flying away from them. Jayda groaned and rubbed her head.

V'ma got to her feet quickly and looked at both of them, "What does that mean?"

The man sat up, "I guess you both heard that as well?"

V'ma walked to the baby who was still suspended and reached out gingerly. Her hands deftly plucked the baby from the air and she took it into her arms. The man walked forward and looked at the baby. "He is a sweet kid." He held his hand out. "I'm. . ." he had forgotten his own name. The man did not use it and so had no reason to recall it. "Augustus!" he blurted out.

Jayda joined the two and looked at the baby. Neither of the women took his hand. Jayda simply looked at the man and responded, "Jayda," she followed up without really understanding why she did it, "Wintersong."

V'ma did not look up, "My name does not matter. Just because we have seen the same vision does not mean I will not end up with this child."

Augustus narrowed his eyes, "Then we have a problem. I'm not going to leave the child with anyone else."

Jayda sighed and rubbed her forehead in frustration, "Listen," she looked at both of them again, "I don't know much about what's going on, but we need to come to some kind of agreement here."

V'ma looked at Jayda finally, but her words were no kinder than before. "It's simple. Let me take the child."

Jayda shook her head, "Not going to happen. None of us seem willing to part with the baby. Why don't the three of us take the baby back to Basile? I have a group of friends who may know more about this than we do."

V'ma gave a mocking laugh, "Yes! Let us follow you to your friends who will then ambush us and take the baby. How exactly are we supposed to trust you?"

Jayda shrugged, "I guess that's up to you. We're at a stalemate here otherwise."

The three of them stood there silently as the baby cooed and kicked his little legs inside the wrap. Augustus sighed, "The baby doesn't leave any of our sights. Agreed?"

Jayda agreed to that condition and V'ma, reluctantly, did as well. "Fine," the Desruc said, "but at the first sign of either of you trying to run off with the child, I cut your throats." They stared at one another again and then she finally gave her name, "You may call me V'ma."

Jayda offered a fake smile and then motioned for them to follow, "My horse is this way. We can all walk back. It'll be a few days."

They traveled back to Basile. The baby was watched between the three of them and they remained uneasy with each other on the journey. They did adhere, however, to a strict schedule about taking the baby. Jayda felt a sense of purpose again and it felt good to have some bit of life breathed into her. She still thought about Oberic and knew that perhaps she always would, but at least she had something bigger going on that could keep her mind busy through most of the day.

When they arrived in Basile Jayda called a meeting for the group. They sat at a large table in the inn with the baby placed in the center of it. They had shared all their stories that led them all to this point. Both V'ma and Augustus slowly understood that something larger was at play. Dwim, who none had known was a father as well, took to the baby quickly. He held the little bundle of joy up and declared that the boy would have a mighty beard someday. They had finally come to an agreement that they, all of them together, would watch over the baby.

Ren asked happily, "What's his name?" There was silence around the table.

Augustus shrugged, "I never thought to give him one. I've lived amongst the animal world for so long that I never had a need to use one."

Phineas, who had his pinky jammed so far up his nose that he might have been scratching his brain, made a suggestion, "How about Graham?"

The group looked around at each other and then at the baby. Alastor nodded and claimed, "Graham, yes. That is the name a king would have."

Baby Graham would be loved and protected by every one of the members, perhaps not so much by Phin who made it clear he didn't like kids. V'ma and Augustus made the decision to stay in Basile if only to keep an eye on the baby. They had taken the vision very seriously and they, like Jayda, would refuse to abandon that duty. Once again, the days turned to weeks; weeks turned to months. Spring, summer, and the fall had all come and gone and the cold harsh winter had returned. Nearly a year now since the incident in Maer'lyn happened.

The group had long since moved from rooms at the inn to renting small homes in one of the more modest districts of the city. Amun had returned to them and would occasionally be with Jayda but seemed more often than not to fly off and do whatever it was that crows did. Ren and Jayda shared a home, but Jayda found herself alone most of the time as Ren had taken to sleeping at Leon's place. She was sitting at the small table in the kitchen tickling Graham's feet and listening to him giggle. He was the one small joy in her life and all the time she would have spent thinking of Oberic, she gave to the boy. His laughter made her heart happy again. V'ma sat across from Jayda at the table and watched the exchange. At least Augustus was friendly enough to talk when spoken to, V'ma was not. She often stayed quiet unless she had a need to voice herself for one thing or another.

The women were not friends by any means, but they were civil with one another. Augustus was often around in his snake form and seemed to prefer to be an animal more than himself. Jayda often wondered what his story was but never asked. When Augustus had the child for his time, Jayda and V'ma found relaxation in combat training with each other. V'ma taught her more about being an assassin and Jayda taught her how to handle a whip. They could at least admit, if nothing else, that they admired the other's skills.

Between the three of them, Graham was over protected. No one spoke of Oberic anymore either. That did not mean Jayda had forgotten. Though most of her day was hunting down bounties and taking care of Graham; at night she held Oberic's hat close to her as she slept. The others had of course continued with the things that kept them busy before Graham was found. The boys were enjoying their guard work and Ren was happy to be mixing once more. Phineas was doing better than all of them and lived quite lavishly. He would drink constantly and spend most of his time at the brothel.

It was snowing heavily on a winter's eternal night in Basile. A knock at the door interrupted Jayda who was preoccupied with holding Graham's tiny fingers as he worked out standing and possibly walking. V'ma grabbed her dagger and held it ready as she opened the door. Her hand moved fast and held the blade to Augustus's throat. He smiled at her, this was common with everyone V'ma greeted, "Hello, V'ma! I've come to see Graham." V'ma did not greet him and instead only stepped out of the way to allow him to come out from the cold. The man shook the snow from himself and walked to the table.

"He's doing so well!" Augustus said proudly. "I saw the guard had another bounty posted up for you."

Jayda did not look at Augustus as she gave Graham encouraging words as he tried to make progress. His balance was unsteady, but Jayda made sure to keep him up. "V'ma, can you take this one? I'm making great progress with my little ray of sunshine here." She talked sweetly to Graham, "Say mama! Mama!"

V'ma glared at her, "Why would you get that honor? Why should he not call me mother?" The two women began to bicker and Graham started to cry.

Augustus rolled his eyes and looked over the bounty he had brought for her. "Seems like some street magician in a pointed hat is out there harassing people." He rerolled the bounty and tossed it between the two arguing women.

He did not hurt people. He was one with nature and his only concern was the baby.

Jayda sat Graham down softly and grabbed the bounty, "I'm sorry, did you say magician?"

V'ma had reached for Graham, but Augustus snatched him up first, "Out there performing tricks and begging for coins. I don't see why it's a big deal, but they constantly go after these street performers." V'ma sneered at Augustus who was now holding Graham up above his head and making baby talk at him. Jayda grabbed the bounty poster and gave Graham a quick kiss on top of his head where golden threads of hair had started to grow. She said nothing else to the others and left the home as soon as she slung her cloak on and had her whip at her side.

"Why is she obsessed with the street performers?" V'ma asked as she stood up. She plucked Graham from Augustus and nuzzled her nose to his. Augustus shrugged and continued to smile. V'ma now worked on getting Graham to call her mama instead.

Jayda found herself running as she always did when it came to any bounty that mentioned a magician. She opened it up to read the last known whereabouts of the magician and when she noted it in her head, she took off at a sprint. It had been almost a year since Oberic had been gone from her life. She did not forget him ever and had always dreamed he would show up, but Alastor helped her understand that he was likely dead now and she had made some peace with that. Still, with every magician she found that her hopes still rose and would ultimately be let down when she would find that it was never him. Over and over his words replayed in her head *I will find you*. He promised he would. He swore it. She knew Oberic was able to talk around the truth, but she did not believe Oberic would say that to her if he did not mean it. Still, as she ran at full sprint in the snow covered streets, Alastor's words made sense. She was chasing nothing more than ghosts now.

The year's end celebrations had kicked off and many people were out, even in this blizzard, making merriment and having a good time. The romantic colored lanterns were replaced by more festive colors. Her run had come to a stop and she now walked among the people, scanning the crowd with sharp emerald eyes. Her hand rested on her whip as it always did. *I will find you* repeated in her head again. How often had she dreamed those words? How many nights did she wake with wet eyes and tear stained cheeks? How many times had Ren heard her call for Oberic when she was sleeping? The lingering hope that lived inside Jayda hurt her. With every bounty that failed to be the man she loved, her heart broke all over again. She knew this was going to be no different and yet the love she had for him said she must never give up hope; Oberic would never give up. He loved a woman who did not love him for twenty and some years. Imagine what he would do for a woman who did love him.

The wild snow blowing in all directions made it hard to see much of anything. Young couples built snowmen on the side of shops and others threw balls of snow playfully at one another. There were drunks wandering in and out of the street making it difficult for horses and carriages to get through, but no one seemed to be in a terrible mood. How could you be at this time of the year? Jayda knew exactly how you could be in a terrible mood. Her nerves were being racked by emotion as she looked high and low to get any sign of the magician. One man with a mug full of something frothy bumped into her and spilled a bit of his drink on her cloak. He made to apologize, but Jayda simply put her hand in his face and pushed him out of the way. He greeted her after she passed with a rude gesture and a condescending wish of a happy holiday season. She had come to an area where there were several street food vendors and even performers. These were all locals who were well known to them and there was no need to go after them.

Her hope had started to falter as she looked around. Not only did the snow seem to become heavier along with the wind that bit the bone but thunder had rolled in the sky. It caused the mass of people out and celebrating to let out a cry of surprise. Jayda looked up and saw, even against the night sky, rolling black clouds and the occasional flash of lightning in them. This blizzard was about to get worse. She passed a vendor, one of her favorites, who was selling fresh roasted spiced chicken on a skewer. The aroma filled her nose and she felt a pain in her chest. She wished many times that Oberic was there with her to experience the city. She passed another vendor who sold small winter shrubberies that resembled pine trees and were decorated for the season. She thought to buy one for Graham, but that would come another time. She had to find the magician. There was a group of people singing a haunting hymn out in the snow storm. She recognized the song immediately. It was the very same song her and Oberic heard when they had first visited the cathedral together. The hymn was about the passing of seasons, time, even life and how each gave way to new beginnings. She felt she could drop and cry right now. Even if she did, her tears would freeze upon her face. She was ready to give up. Thunder rolled again and the crowd cheered. She thought that was odd to cheer a storm, but then the crowd cheered again and she narrowed her eyes. Just above the crowd she spotted the tip of a pointed hat in the center. The crowd were cheering for them, not the thunder.

Her heart thumped hard in her chest and she strode in that direction. She was not kind as she pushed and pulled members of the crowd out of the way. *I will find you* Oberic said in her head once more, *I promise*. People complained about her rudeness, but this was the season of giving and what they would give her was forgiveness. She fought through the crowd and once she reached the center she called out, "Oberic!"

An old man with a missing leg and no teeth stood in the center of the crowd. The hat he was wearing was tattered and torn. The thunder rolled over head again and he held out a hand, "Coin, lady? For a flower perhaps?" The old man waved a hand and from his long sleeve, a sleight of hand trick that Phineas did quite often, pulled a flower for her. Her heart dropped and she felt it rest in her stomach. She was on the verge of tears. She had no idea why she continued to do this to herself other than the words that repeated themselves in her head. *I will find you, I promise*. She swallowed hard and composed herself. She pulled the bounty and let the poster unroll itself as she held it up at him.

The old man cowered away from her knowing now that he was in trouble. She sighed as she watched the old man. "What am I supposed to do with you?" She just wanted to go home and see Graham and hope that with his cute little face that she would not find herself crying into a mug for the rest of the night. *I will find you, I promise* repeated the voice. She shook her head and whispered to herself, "Shut up. He's not coming back."

The old man, not even dressed for such a blizzard, raised his bushy brow and asked, "Sorry? What was that?"

She had gotten her hopes up again and found herself more angry than she had been in a while. She removed her coin purse and threw it forcefully at the old man. It banged against his chest and fell at his feet near a wooden bucket where others had been depositing coins. "Take the coin and get out of here, old timer. Don't let me catch you around here again. If I do I'll bring you in and you'll be rotting in a dank dungeon with shit covered walls." The old man stared at her wide eyed. This seemed to anger her more and as thunder rolled once again she kicked snow towards the bucket and the coin purse. "Take your coin and get out of my sight. Don't return here! I'm sick and tired of you assholes ruining my day!" The old man scooped up his bucket and threw the coin purse in it. He hobbled off with his crutch as fast as he could.

She stood there for a long moment taking in deep breaths. She knew she was going to cry, but she refused to do it here. Snow had blanketed her cloak and black hair and the wind had made her nose and cheeks cherry. The crowd had watched her send the old man off. The thunder rolled once more and she crumpled up the bounty and threw it. Oberic's voice spoke to her once more and she weeped silently, "I don't know how he was so easily able to run from someone as beautiful as you. I had a hard time doing it myself."

This was unfair, she thought. Now she was making up things he had never said in her head. Her tears ran down her cheeks and frosted against her skin. The sky, filled with dark clouds and the occasional flash of light, echoed thunder that grumbled low and long. "I can't do this anymore," she said to herself as the crowd decided to move away from the crazy woman.

"I told you I'd find you." his voice said again. Jayda's chin rested on her chest and she thought about the words being spoken to her.

"You promised," she weeped, "you promised you'd come back."

"And here I am." Jayda raised her head. There was a sinking feeling that the voice was not in her head at all and as she slowly turned around she wondered if she had gone insane. It felt to her that the voice was coming from behind her. She prayed to the gods that she was not going crazy. This might just be the night that her mind blew out the last candle. She drew in cold air that pained her lungs, but that pain was nothing compared to her heart ache. She was giving in; giving up the hunt for the ghost, at least for tonight. She turned around to head home. The thunder rolled again, shaking everyone in the area to core. Lightning lit the sky as it broke free from the storm clouds above and her eyes fell upon a thin man with long unbrushed hair and a terribly shaggy, wild beard. Most importantly, he had the most dangerous green eyes she had ever seen.

"I'm dreaming," she whispered, "or I really have gone mad." Her voice was low. The snow swirled around them both as they looked at one another. She saw him standing in front of her in torn rags and boots that were barely sewn together.

Tears welled in his eyes as he spoke in a low apologetic tone, "I'm sorry it took so long." His voice choked midway through the small statement. "I never gave up though."

She walked to him slowly. She still did not believe her eyes. They had fooled her so many times before when she thought she saw his face in a crowd of people or when she went to her bedroom and saw him, if only for a moment, waiting in bed for her. She reached up and placed a shaking hand to his cheek. She expected her hand to pass through his face, but her hand rested firmly against it. Her tears became a deluge once she understood the man was there in the flesh and she threw herself against him. She cried hard against his chest. Her hands gripped the rags, then his face, and then draped themselves around his neck, trying to find the right position to hold him as close as she could to herself. "You came back! You came back to me!"

He wanted to lift her. He wanted to spin her around, but the man was far too weak at the moment. Time and the journey back to her had not been kind. There had been so many days where the man had found himself in peril and on the verge of death; where only his sheer determination to keep his word to his love allowed him to be able to be there with her now. He held her as tightly as he could, "I said I would. I gave you my word."

She looked up into his eyes and her hands explored his face again. She pulled at his beard and touched his hair as she drank him in. "You're real. You're real and you're here. You came back."

"I'm real and here," he said somewhat jovially. His eyes found her so terribly beautiful in the snow. He cleared his throat, finding he was on the verge of choking on his words as he asked a question that plagued him day and night for nearly a year, "Have you found someone else?" He swallowed hard, doing his best to prepare and harden his heart for the pain she was going to deliver him.

She placed her hands on the sides of his face and forced him to stare into her eyes which still streamed tears; tears for once that were born of happiness and not grief. She leaned up so that their lips were nearly touching and she whispered, "Only you. It has only ever been you." She kissed him gently, and when the taste of her tears fell upon both of their lips, she kissed him harder. Lightning lit the sky once more as they kissed one another deeply. Each moment turned the embrace and kiss into something far more passionate. They had together accepted that the long journey and wait was over and finally each heart was where they belonged once more.

She pulled away from him and touched his face again. She looked him up and down, studying his thin frame. She remembered him being a bit thicker, but it did nothing to change her love for him. "I'm not ready to share you yet. Come home and I'll get you fed. We can get you new clothes and a rest. We can tell everyone else in the morning perhaps," she looked up into his eyes once more and kissed him again, "but tonight you belong to me only."

His chest swelled with a deep inhale and the lifting feeling of being in her embrace. He let out a happy sigh of relief and simply responded, "Anything you wish of me. So long as I am yours once more."

CHAPTER 24

Jayda tried to remove her cloak to put it around him, but the sorcerer in nothing more than rags, denied her and she remembered just how wonderfully stubborn they both were. It made her smile and she rushed him to the home she shared with Rennyn, making sure to not put a strain on him if she could help it. Jayda opened the door and found the entrance room, a small little kitchen, was empty and that a small note had been left on the table. She ushered Oberic inside and closed the door behind him. She grabbed the note, read that V'ma and Augustus had taken Graham, then threw the note away. Graham was safe and that was well; she now had all her attention to give to Oberic.

She wanted desperately to bombard him with questions, but knew there would be much time for such things. She found some clothes that the other men in their little group had stored there and laid them out for Oberic. She lit the small fireplace and placed a pot of soup over it to warm up. She grabbed a smaller pot of water and placed it over the fire as well so that he could wash up when he was ready. She kept throwing glances at the man, even now still unsure if he was really there with her. Would he disappear again before her eyes and leave her with the realization that she had indeed snapped?

Oberic warmed himself near the fire. Jayda found that he looked even more wild than the first time she met him on the rocky shores of Marrenval. She wondered what happened to him. She thought about asking again, but she knew in her heart he would tell her exactly what happened to him. His tale was an interesting one though filled with danger and peril. His messy and nearly botched escape from Maer'lyn led him to being lost at sea. That in turn led him to being rescued off the coast of some desert where he was then imprisoned and forced to do things against his will. He would escape imprisonment and trek through the sands of the desert then travel through the wilds before he found himself in Hadryn once more. He would barter passage with a merchant ship that brought him to Karren's Call and from there he simply went in the direction that something in his heart told him to. He had no idea if he'd ever see her again, but knew he would continue on until he did.

She left him alone near the fire for a moment and returned with a bowl, spoon, and a ladle. She dipped the ladle into the pot and poured its contents into the bowl. She handed him the bowl and went off to grab a chair for him. She returned once more and sat it in front of the fire after forcing him to sit. He did not argue. She knelt there near him and watched him sip the soup. "Oberic there were days that I had given in and accepted you died. That sounds terrible, but you were gone for so long. Hope burned inside though and every time that something vaguely reminded me of you I felt you would return. I had those hopes swept from under me so many times, but I knew deep down that you would return. I'm thankful that Phineas was around. He has surprisingly kept me grounded."

A tinge of jealousy arose in Oberic and he wanted to ask if that was all he did, but he fought it, mostly just being too tired to even bother with such emotions. "I told myself that death would have to wait until I saw you again." He lifted the bowl and drank from it greedily.

Jayda smirked, "Phin was a perfect gentleman," Oberic wondered if she could see the concern on his face, "Don't tell him I told you but we often cried together." Her smile, one that he missed, was playful.

He laughed. The idea of Phineas crying like that was both believable and unbelievable. "I'll try not to bring it up." Soup had lingered in his wild mustache and dripped into his beard. "The others? Everyone survived?"

Jayda nodded quickly, "Ren and Leon are moving slowly, but still very much together. We have all picked up jobs here in the city. Added a couple of newcomers to the group as well. You will likely meet them soon when we find the others," her emerald eyes shined bright and the sparkle had now returned to them, "and Graham! You will get to meet him too!" Her body language and tone changed. She seemed uplifted by the idea of them meeting, "He is the image of perfection. His laughter can instantly brighten your day."

Oberic felt the soup suddenly not sit well. In the time he had been gone not once did he feel hopeless until now. She had told him there was no other and yet here she was speaking of someone new. "Oh," he feigned calmness, "is that so? Who is he then?"

She took the bowl from him and placed it on the floor. She then took his hands and urged him to his feet. "Come, I'll show you." She picked up a lit lamp and pulled him further into the house. She opened a door across the hall from her own bedroom and pulled him inside. She placed the lamp on a small table by the door and it illuminated a room filled with wooden toys that sat soft furs on the floor. There was a handmade wooden crib that rested against the wall. Inside it, a small stuffed animal rested tucked under a quilt. Jayda picked up a small frame and handed it to him. Oberic examined the image inside the frame and saw a very well colored sketching that a traveling artist had made. The wonderful work of art was of Jayda and a bald baby swaddled in cloth.

He studied the picture and looked up at her nervously, "Yours?", he mumbled even more quietly, "Ours?"

She shook her head, "Not by blood. He was found in the woods outside of the city here. We can let Augustus explain that story though." She smiled softly and took the frame from him and placed it back on the table, "but children? I suppose that hasn't been something we ever discussed."

"No, it wasn't, but we were also only together a short time before circumstances forced us apart."

She took his hand and nodded, "I can't wait for you to meet him," Oberic could very clearly see how much she was in love with the child and found that somehow it made him love her even more, "you must be exhausted," she gestured across the hall, "this is my-," she corrected herself, "our bedroom. Ren sleeps upstairs when she is here."

Oberic admitted that he was indeed exhausted, but the ragged look on his face was more than enough to show that he was. The man was malnourished and lacked a good sleep for nearly a year. He told her that he would like to clean up a bit and so she gathered the hot water and a cloth and he stood in a basin and washed himself. He hadn't cleaned himself like that in all the time he was away and when he was done he felt like a real person again. Jayda helped dry and dress him, then brought him to their bed. She laid him down and then climbed in next to him. She covered them both with a few heavy blankets of fur and rested her hand on his chest. Her head was propped up on her other hand and they stared at each other. His voice shook as he asked, "Am I the one dreaming?"

She looked at him and let out a soft laugh, "If you are, I promise I'll not wake you from it." She leaned down and kissed him tenderly. She wanted to climb upon him and have him inside her, but she placed her own greedy desires aside and let him rest. He fought to keep his eyes open, never wanting to lose sight of her again, but his body gave way to the comfort of the bed. The fact that he was now back to her as he had promised put his mind at ease. When his eyes finally shut, he slept deeply for the first time since Maer'lyn.

Oberic slept for the next three days, at least Jayda assumed since there was no day or night cycle; just the ticking of a clock that hung on the wall that she never checked. She laid there in the bed with him every moment she could watching him sleep and still believing this was all in her head. She noticed that strands of his dulling blonde hair had actually gone gray and that wrinkles had formed around his eyes. She wondered just what put the strain of time on him like that. Every now and again he would call out in his sleep the same words she would hear in her head, "I will find you, I promise" and then he would return to deep slumber. If he dreamed at all, there was no sign of it. Ren had stopped by the house on several occasions, but Jayda quietly urged her to come back another time, giving her excuses that she was unwell. She exclaimed she could come and see everyone once she felt better. She missed Graham terribly, but Oberic was her concern right now and she knew the baby was being watched over. She had meant what she said when she told him that she was not ready to share him with the others just yet.

Jayda had changed in the time that he was gone. She was still the powerful and feisty Hunter he had known; V'ma only added to her skill with their training sessions. Still, there was a new trait that had emerged that she had never thought would and that was that she had a strong, fierce motherly quality now that Graham had come into her life.

It was at some point during the fourth day (night) that Oberic grasped her hand that rested on his chest and his eyes shot wide open. "By the gods!" he turned his head and looked at her with a stupid smile on his face. "I didn't dream it!" She could not help but smile at him as he sat up. His face seemed to look less worn with time now that he had rested though around the eyes she could see the crow's feet had remained. His eyes were just as vibrant as ever and she could see in them that he had seen much on the journey back to her. "I feel better already. Just a few hours of sleep was all I needed."

She squeezed his hand and chuckled as she looked into his eyes, "You have been sleeping for days now, love."

He raised his brow and said rather gravely, though she knew he was joking, "Well, maybe I needed a bit more than I suspected."

"Do you think it is time to tell the others you are back? I think Ren is getting concerned about my health. I haven't left your side since you've returned." She leaned in and kissed him before she excused herself. She left the room and returned a bit later with a mug of warm ale. She handed it to him and climbed back in the bed with him. Oberic lifted it to his face, smelled that it was ale, and lowered it away from his face. He would not drink it, but held it in his hands to not be rude and he thanked her for it. The man hadn't drank a drop since they shared their first kiss and there was no longer any hurt left inside for him to bury down.

"If you think it's time," Oberic nodded, "or if you would just like to get out of the house for fresh air, I understand that too." His eyes fell on the table that sat next to her side of the bed and he saw his hat that he placed on her head before leaving her in Maer'lyn.

She turned her head to see what he was looking at and then she looked back at him with a loving look in her eyes, "I kept it with me every night." Oberic could not express into words how much that simple gesture meant to him. He lifted a hand and stroked her cheek with his thumb while his hand rested against her face.

His words were filled with honesty when he spoke to her, "Thank you for keeping that candle lit. I feared for many nights that it would burn out and you would never want me again."

She reached up and grabbed his hand and slid his fingers to her lips where she kissed them. She was doing her best to not cry. She was tired of crying and there was no longer a need to do it. He was home, with her, where he belonged. "Are you ready to see them?"

Oberic shrugged, "I imagine I'm as ready as I'll ever be."

"You realize if I tell them to come here and surprise them that way, this house will be filled with our friends," she smiled and her eyes sparkled brightly, "I don't think I can even imagine the mess they would all make."

"Then I suppose we best go out and see them instead. I just need a few things first."

She tipped her head, "Name it."

"First, I need your kiss," he placed the ale on the table near him. She smiled as she leaned in and kissed him deeply. Her kiss gave him energy. It gave him life. "Wonderful. Next, my hat if you don't mind?"

Jayda turned and grabbed the hat. She examined it and turned back to Oberic. She almost handed it over to him, but decided she should be the one to plop the hat on his head like he had given it to her. She pulled the brim so that the hat sat on his head tightly. "Oberic Wintersong, you're starting to look like your old self again."

He laughed and removed the hat and jammed his arm deep inside it. Jayda's mouth opened and she wondered why in all the time she had why she never thought to do the same thing. Maybe she would have found nothing, which was very likely, but the thought simply hadn't crossed her mind. He had caught her expression and assumed she was just wondering what he was doing, "I returned to my home before I made my escape from Maer'lyn and stashed most of what I thought I needed or could into my storage room." He pulled his arm back out and with it a fresh set of clothes. "I'd like to see a barber before I see the others. So that I can feel normal before I see them."

"Of course. Get dressed and we will head there right away." She gave him another kiss and headed out of the bedroom to prepare her own things. She went to a basket of folded laundry that Ren must have dropped off. She dug through it and only found the clothing she wore as a Hunter; something she did not stop doing so that she could keep herself busy. None of it would do. She wanted to look more like a lady for Oberic. She of course knew Oberic wanted her no matter how she dressed, but it was something she wanted to be when she was with him and on this occasion, she felt it was required. She did not find anything she was wanting and headed back to the bedroom where she found Oberic already dressed. He had slipped on some light brown linen pants that were tucked into chestnut colored cuffed boots. He had on a long sleeved linen shirt that resembled something Phineas would wear as it was slightly opened at the chest. Over his arm rested a heavy overcoat dyed green. The hat on his head was colored the same as the coat and as always, pointed and bent so that the tip faced behind him.

She smiled. He was almost looking like himself. She grabbed him and shoved him out of the bedroom and slammed the door. He stood in the hall with a surprised grin, "I'll just wait out here I guess!" She smirked at his comment then turned and dug through her dresser. She ended up finding the perfect dress. She had bought it, never wore it, and decided now was the right time. She slipped the soft brown dress on and pulled her hair from the ponytail she always wore it in. She brushed it and her raven locks rested over her shoulders. There was a thin belt she fixed around her waist and she then reached, out of habit, for her daggers and whip. She stopped and reminded herself there would be no need for them. Not right now.

She stepped out of the room and into the hall where Oberic was still waiting. He watched her come out of the room and time stopped for him. She was just as breathtaking as she ever was.

She stepped to him and took his hands in hers, "I still can't believe you're home." They squeezed one another's hands and walked out of the house together.

Once outside, Oberic slipped his coat on. The blizzard had passed and buried everything in nearly two feet of snow. He remarked on what she had said inside, "There were nights when I thought all was lost so I understand what you mean."

She guided him down the street to the barber that Dwim frequented, "Did anything help? To keep you going, I mean."

He looked at her. The answer was obvious to himself, "I had only one quest, Jayda; to find the woman who lit a fire inside me again." She smiled and blushed. She held onto his arm and they made small talk until they arrived at the little barber shop. Oberic went inside after Jayda said she would wait for him. She had strolled around the small little shopping district in such a better mood than she had been in a long time. She returned some time later and saw through the window that Oberic had just gotten out of the chair. He paid the barber and exchanged a hearty handshake. She stepped in front of the shop to greet him as he exited.

Oberic came out with his hair cut short and the front long enough to be somewhat fluffed and swept back. His beard was also finely trimmed and Jayda realized this was the first time she had ever seen him look so clean. She found herself throwing out a line that she had often heard Phineas say, "Hey good looking! Going my way?" Oberic laughed and slipped his green hat upon his head. She would lead them back to the district where they were currently living to another house further down the street. Jayda knocked on the door and called out, "Ren? Leon? Are you home?"

Even with them standing outside in the lightly falling snow, Jayda could hear Ren raising her voice from inside, "Jayda, we have been worried sick about you!" Ren swung the door open as she continued to fuss, "Where in the world have you. . ." Ren's voice trailed off as she looked Oberic dead in the eyes.

He removed his hat and smiled at her, "I am afraid that is my fault. She has been playing nurse to me again."

Ren was shocked, as was evident by her silence as well as that if her jaw had hung any lower it would be resting on the floor. She closed her mouth, opened it, closed it, and opened it again. She fought to find words and finally came up with, "We thought you were. . ." she licked her lips, "No one thought. . ." She turned and yelled back into the house, "Leon! You're going to want to see this!"

Leon's voice called back from inside the house though he did not appear, "If it's Phin being thrown out of the brothel by an angry mob of patrons for trying to take all the girls to bed at once again it's not a big a deal! It's happened several times now and honestly, him naked in the streets has happened so much that he and the guards all know each other by name!" He finally appeared around the corner and stood next to Ren. For a moment he stared at the pair in the doorway. He recognized Jayda of course, but the man she stood with seemed unfamiliar to him and then it dawned on him. "You dog! You're alive!"

Jayda smiled happily and Ren could see the sparkle had returned to her eyes. It made her so happy she almost wept for her friend. "I'll let you catch up," Jayda said, "I'll try to track down the others and bring them." She leaned up and kissed Oberic on the cheek and whispered softly to him, "Welcome home. I love you."

She had walked off before he could reply and so he turned and shouted to her as she walked away, "I love you!" He turned back to Leon and Ren and then looked up to the enchanted sky that caused the city to be forever in darkness. "How curious we would find ourselves reunited here." They both agreed with him of course and decided they simply could not wait for Jayda to return. They both grabbed coats and cloaks to keep themselves warm and walked with Oberic to the guard outpost where Leon knew Dwim and Alastor would be.

Jayda had got to them first of course and as she entered the small outpost she saw Alastor sharpening an ax. Dwim leaned back in a chair with his feet kicked up on a desk. He had a big mug tipped back to his thick lips. She was far too excited to be calm and she shouted very suddenly, "He's back! Oberic's back!" She gave an excited spin which was very out of character for her. Upon hearing the news Dwim let out a surprised yelp and tipped back in the chair. He fell back and onto the floor spilling his mug all over his face. Alastor, who remained neutral, looked back at Dwim and grunted out a laugh. The Orc'oth, thanks to his friends, had started to develop a sense of humor.

Dwim sat up with soaked hair, a wet beard, and a face drenched in beer. His fat hand reached up and wiped away the drink, "Is he really, lass?"

She nodded, nearly jumping in place, "He is! He is with Leon and Ren right now! I'm going to go find Phineas and share the good news! Meet you guys there?"

Even Alastor smiled now, though it was an ugly one, "If you can contain your excitement, I have an idea that may be fun. Fun for us," he motioned to the three of them and then amended, "the others as well. Not so much for Phineas."

Jayda grinned at him. She was curious as to what he had in mind, "I can certainly try."

"Phineas is at a tavern that he goes to often. He always takes a chair near the window to watch for victims passing by. Allow Oberic to tap on the glass. I believe he will scream like a woman." Alastor nodded, "This will make a good laugh for us. Not for him."

Jayda clapped her hands in front of her mouth and pressed them to her lips. "That," she paused for a dramatic effect, "sounds like a wonderful idea. Let's head over and collect them!"

Alastor nodded and stood. He followed Jayda out into the snow and Dwim shouted out to them, "Who is going to watch the outpost?"" He waited for an answer. but got none and then shrugged. He shut the door and left with the pair. They were headed back towards Leon's when they met the three of them who had come to meet them. Jayda had Alastor explain the plan and they all thought it was a wonderful idea. Oberic of course was quite happy to oblige and they decided to head to the tavern together.

As they approached, the tavern's window was frosted from the heat inside, but a very clear circle had been wiped in the window so that Phineas could look through it. The golden haired man could very clearly be seen there having a drink. Like Dwim, his feet were kicked up on the table, and he had a drink tipped up to his mouth. He waved at some woman who passed by the tavern and she returned the wave with a flirty smile. He put his drink down and held up a coin purse. He started dropping coins inside it looking quite pleased with himself.

Oberic adjusted his coat and stepped forward. He turned back only for a moment and said, "Let's hope this gets the reaction you wanted." He continued on his way to the window. The others followed closer to get a better view. Oberic reached up and knocked on the window. Phineas looked up and gave a nod to Oberic, then looked back down to his coin purse. Not a moment had passed before he looked back up in shock and just as Alastor had said he would, he screamed like a girl. His hands flew into the air and he flipped backward from the table, landing with a very audible bang.

The group bursted into laughter having seen and heard it all. Phin's head popped back up in the window and his jaw hung open. He stood up and ran to the tavern door. He swung it open and came outside. He stood there, not clothed for such cold weather and he yelled out, "You dirty bastard!" He put his hands on his hips and let out a good hard laugh. He motioned down to his crotch, "You made me piss myself!" His pants were indeed freshly wet.

The group laughed some more. Phineas happened to spot V'ma walking up the street and called out to her, "V'ma! Go get Augustus! We're celebrating tonight!" She did not answer him and continued to walk away. Phin grumbled, "Stuck up, bitch." He shook his head and then waved to everyone, "Come in here! We're drinking!" They all followed Phineas inside and gathered at the largest table in the center of the room.

Phin went to the bar and ordered an outrageous amount of drinks. When the tavern keeper asked how he planned to pay for it all Phin simply said, "You know I'm good for it, but if that isn't enough then maybe we can go talk to Marge about you and her sister. How does that sound? I got a feeling it sounds like you want to get those drinks going, am I right?" The tavern keeper sneered but nodded. "Good boy. Put it on my tab. I'll take care of it."

It took the tavern keeper several minutes to complete Phin's order. Once it was done, he advised he'd be back again as there was much to celebrate. As he headed to the table with the large tray, V'ma and Augustus came in. Augustus was holding Graham in his arms. The group was whole once more. After introductions were made between Oberic, V'ma, Augustus, and of course Graham, they drank together, they laughed, and they shared fun stories. They had made a bet to see who would end up smiling first, V'ma or Alastor, since neither did much of it; V'ma did so less than Alastor. Graham had been passed from Augustus to Jayda who then showed Oberic the bundle of joy that had kept her sane. Oberic was pleased to meet Graham and saw in Jayda the happiness the baby had brought her. He hoped to someday share that experience with her. Dwim would take the baby from her later and V'ma would take it from him.

Ren had noticed the way Oberic was looking at Jayda when she held the baby and she elbowed him, "I bet you never thought you would see or hear that sort of thing coming from her, hm?"

He smiled at her and mumbled a reply, "Something that may have only crossed my mind in dreams."

Jayda had reached out and plucked Graham from V'ma. The Desruc gave her a glare. The Hunter cuddled him to her and inhaled the sweet baby smell. Oberic leaned closer and stuck a finger out for Graham who promptly grasped it. "I hear that you've stolen my darling's heart." Graham giggled and smiled at Oberic.

Jayda's smile could not have been any bigger at that moment, "Can you say hi, Graham?" Graham let go of Oberic's finger and reached his chubby hands out for Oberic's hat. He tugged on the brim for a moment and then reached out to Jayda.

"Ma," Graham babbled as his fingers wrapped around her inky hair and tugged. She bounced him happily and spoke to him in soft baby voices.

Ren eyed Oberic and smiled, "One day soon, I'm sure of it."

Oberic had never thought of being a father. He was a destroyed and crippled man when Evelyn left. When he met Jayda, he was still a mess, but from the moment she kissed him he had started to feel whole again. She kept him going. Now that he saw her with the baby, there was no doubt in his mind that he wanted that kind of life with her and if they could find each other after so long of them both being in the dark, then surely anything was possible. He smiled at all of them and loved that they were all so jovial. He did not have the heart to tell them all just how much things had gone from bad to worse. He would tell them his story soon enough though and they would understand what was to come very soon. Right now they, himself included, needed this moment.

The night carried on and they drank more. They all had a great time. Ren filled Oberic's ear with everything she had learned while he was away. She told him, proudly, that she had been working on her spell casting and that it was improving. She asked if he'd still be willing to assist with her training and he naturally agreed. V'ma eyed Graham like a vulture circling the dying. She was not interested in making a new friend on this day.

The tavern door opened and, along with the fat man who entered to have a drink, a crow came flying in. He fluttered over to the table and landed on Jayda's shoulder. Graham let out a happy shriek as he saw the bird. Amun cawed angrily at Oberic who in turn offered him an apologetic smile, "I'm sorry, old friend." Amun didn't accept the apology and comically turned away from him.

Graham reached for Amun's tail feathers. Jayda slowed his hand down, "Gently love. Remember Amun doesn't like to be pulled at." She gave Amun a quick kiss on the head, "Forgive him, Amun. Neither of you will be happy until you do."

Amun cawed and flew to Oberic's shoulder. He ripped a hair from Oberic's beard and flew off. "Ouch!" Oberic rubbed at his face and watched Amun perch himself on Augustus's head. "That bird really holds a grudge."

Jayda gave a half smile, "We didn't even see Amun until a few months after we came through the mirror. Soon as we were in the field he flew off. I had thought that he wouldn't return without you."

Graham reached out towards the air, pulling away from Jayda's hands. "Little guy seems antsy," Phin said as he tried to get close to the baby. Graham let out a cry and Phin leaned back in his chair, "Every time."

V'ma moved fast and was already at Jayda's side pulling Graham from her hands, "Leave the boy alone, filth!" She pulled Graham close to herself and eyed Phineas with a look that dared him to talk back to her.

Jayda frowned and looked up at the Desruc, "I had it under control, V'ma."

Phin lifted his drink and mumbled into it, "If I'm such filth why don't you come over here and lick me clean." V'ma almost launched herself at Phineas, but remembered she had Graham in her arms.

"You're from the Mahir?" Oberic asked.

V'ma nodded, "Yes."

Oberic raised his brow as if the next part of the question should be obvious, "Why are you here? Out of the Mahir, I mean. That's not common for your people."

"I was given a vision to find and protect Graham. I will do it and then return to the Mahir as Balva and lead my people out of the desert." V'ma's answer was short and to the point. She did not have time for stories.

Jayda pointed to Augustus, "She, him, and myself saw a vision out in the clearing where we met Augustus and Graham. Ren had the vision on the way from Maer'lyn." Augustus had come around the table and hovered near V'ma. Graham's three protectors would not let anyone else in on the special group.

Rennyn rolled her eyes, "It's too bad none of you included me in the raising of the child even though I had the vision too."

Oberic nodded apologetically, "Things continue to get stranger and stranger. What are they planning to do with the baby?"

"That's where nay a soul can seem to agree," Dwim said as he wiped a bit of froth from his beard.

Ren piped up, "Everyone thinks that they can just go on day to day as if this mysterious child didn't just appear in our lives. They seem to think he has always been here."

V'ma scowled at Ren, "Watch your tone, Elf!"

"I think you've got that right, Rennyn." Oberic commented. Ren smiled up at V'ma who looked ready to slap it off her face.

Oberic turned and looked at the baby in V'ma's arms, "Why are you so important?" Graham looked at Oberic from her arms. His bright baby blue eyes met Oberic's and the two stared at each other for a moment before he let out a wail.

"Here we go," Ren smirked, knowing a fight was about to start. Jayda and Augustus immediately started to harass V'ma about giving Graham to one of them.

"I can take him," Jayda said, "I am better of the three of us at soothing him." Jayda moved forward and V'ma stepped back.

Augustus argued back, "The boy likes my fur. Give him to me!"

Oberic looked at Leon, "What does that even mean? Is he cursed like Phineas?"

Phin shook his head, "He might be able to change his form at will but his dick isn't nearly as big as mine."

"Always a one track mind with you, isn't it?" Leon groaned out.

"That's not fair!" Jayda protested, "What child wouldn't love to cuddle in the warmth of a giant bear?"

Ren crossed her arms with a sigh, "Maybe now that you're back we can finally figure out what to do with this mess."

He watched the three of them argue and looked at Ren, "You've got the right idea. Tell me the exact details of this dream you had if you can remember it."

V'ma yelled, "I don't trust you, snake!" The three protective parents continued to bicker as Graham wailed in the middle of it all. Ren explained the vision she had when coming through the mirror to him in surprising detail. She wasn't able to recall it when it first happened, but as time went on it became more clear and it wasn't something she thought she would ever forget.

When she was done, Oberic folded his arms and leaned back in his chair, "You've all been touched by the gods. The baby needs to be protected and the crown is in danger somehow. Graham was found here? In Normoon?"

Ren nodded. Jayda finally managed to pull Graham back into her arms. She cooed softly to him as she held out her finger to him. Graham reached out and grabbed it. "I found him," the Hunter said. She was smiling at the baby, "all alone in that cold, dirty hut! Yes I did!"

V'ma glared at Jayda, "I was right behind you, girl!"

Augusutus threw his arms up, "I was already there in the hut with him and had been looking after him for a long time already!" They continued to bicker.

Leon shook his head, "These three. . ."

Ren nodded in agreement with Leon, "Oberic, it never stops."

Jayda bounced Graham softly, "You were a snake, Augustus! I should have sliced you up into pieces!" She meant the words, but said them in a loving and sweet tone to keep Graham from crying out again.

"A snake that saved you from getting stabbed by that other fellow!" Augustus reminded her.

V'ma snapped back at them both, "An assassin who was only using Graham to draw me out of hiding! An assassin who I promptly put an end to!"

Oberic stroked his beard and spoke to the ones who were still being level headed, "I think we need to have a very long and hard talk. All of us. Even the newcomers."

Ren nodded in agreement, "I'm very glad you are back, Oberic. We missed you." She placed her hand on his shoulder and offered him a gentle smile, "If you'll excuse me,"she glared behind her at the three arguing, "I have some work sitting on a table I need to get back to." Ren got up and as she was leaving, kissed Leon on the forehead.

Leon smiled as she left and once she was gone, he took her place next to Oberic, "You don't have good news, do you?"

Oberic shook his head, "No, I do not. And this baby? Well I think that will complicate things."

The arguing stopped as Jayda held up a hand to the other two, "Not good news?" Worry filled her eyes, "What do you mean?"

Alastor snorted, "It is like a woman to only hear the bad things. This is correct?" V'ma and Jayda shot him an ugly look. He pointed to Phineas, "He has told me this."

"You're a dick," Phin complained.

Leon clapped Oberic on the back. He was not going to get involved in that and he moved out of the chair taking his spot next to Dwim again. When he sat, he and the Dwarf shared a look that expressed happiness that they weren't Oberic right now. "Jayda," Oberic started, "it has been good to be with you once more. There are things we need to discuss though. Soon," he looked at all of them, "all of us. I want to meet outside of the city in the wilds. Where you found the baby. We will make camp there and we shall have our long talk."

Jayda looked at Oberic and sat down in the chair next to him again. She felt her heart sinking fast, "Tell me you aren't leaving me again. . ."

He looked saddened by the thought, "I left you in Maer'lyn like I did for a few reasons. I would not have done so if I didn't think they were good reasons. You escaped as I hoped you would, my love. Know that my heart could not bear not having you. I could only let you go under the most dire of circumstances."

Her hand reached up and touched his cheek softly, "Your voice in my dreams is what kept me going; that and this little sweetheart." She placed a kiss on the top of Graham's head and then on Oberic's cheek. "The little one is exhausted. I will return home and settle him down. Once he has had a sleep we can all pack and leave for the wilds."

"Prepare the baby as well. I think he needs to be there too." Oberic was interrupted by Amun's loud cawing. He flew back to Oberic and landed on his shoulder. Oberic smiled, "Forgive me?" Amun nipped at Oberic's ear. "Ouch!"Oberic rubbed at his ear lobe, "Guess not."

CHAPTER 25

They all returned home and packed some heavy winter clothing. There seemed to be an understanding of how important this must be and with Oberic back there was at least some kind of plan forming. Ren was happy to have such a thing happen. She did enjoy living this simple life with Leon, but she knew they had more important things to worry about at the moment. Perhaps someday they would be able to relax with their work done and consider children of their own. She prepared her satchel and loaded it with vials wrapped in cloth to prevent them from smashing together and breaking. They were elixirs and potions to keep any sickness at bay as well as to help keep them warm if they needed it. She had also prepared a bottle of Kalina's Mist that she took from the shop.

Leon had gone out and purchased thick furs that he would weave into canopies so they would have some sort of shelter out in the snow and cold winter nights as well as some extra furs for them to use as blankets. While out, he was also smart enough to grab some thick and hard wooden poles to prop the furs so that these canopies and tents would have a chance to remain standing in the wintery conditions. Phineas had gone along with him and acted as the financier since he was the only one who could actually afford all the equipment.

Alastor and Dwim gathered the horses and prepared them by packing everything as they were brought to them. At some point as they packed, Alastor suggested they buy a wagon. When Leon and Phin returned with their equipment the suggestion was floated to Phineas who rolled his eyes and complained he wasn't spending all his hard earned gold just to hear some wizard, they reminded him he wasn't a wizard, tell some stories and talk about what they needed to be doing. After he was done fussing, he turned and made Leon go out with him and buy a wagon. They returned later and attached two horses to it.

Jayda had collected some of her warmer Hunter gear and packed it in a bag. Oberic did not own much of anything at the moment and protested anytime she suggested they go out to buy some. He assured her he would be fine. He carried her bag out to the wagon. Jayda wrapped Graham in thick furs to ensure he was warm on the journey.

V'ma had nothing really to her name other than some extra clothes she bought so that she had fresh clothes to change into. When it grew colder, she buckled and got a thick fur cloak. She was the first of the group to be fully ready and waited outside near the wagon for the others. She was a strange beauty looking much like a dream standing there as the snow blew around her. Her brown hair had been let down and danced in the wind.

Phineas came out next and threw a bag into the wagon. He admired V'ma standing there alone and gave a sharp whistle. The Desruc turned and looked at him. He offered her a smile and asked, "How much do I have to pay you to have you sit on my face with that jiggly ass?"

V'ma sneered while she walked over to him. She reached out and grabbed him by the shirt, "Speak to me like that again and I will bury you out in the wilds. No one will ever miss you." She released his shirt and walked away from him.

"I'm willing to go as high as two-hundred!" he called out. She turned and glared at him again. He raised his hands to say he was only kidding. He mounted his horse and stroked the stallion's neck. Dwim and Alastor came out next and did the same as Phin. They threw their bags in the wagon and mounted their horses. Leon and Ren came afterwards and repeated the process. Last was Oberic, Jayda, and Graham. Jayda wore a sling around her that Graham rested in nicely bundled up. Oberic helped Jayda on her horse and then slung himself up behind her.

V'ma looked at all of them, "Who am I riding with?" Phineas wiggled his brow at her and she groaned, "Anyone other than him?" Alastor offered out his hand and even though she had no issue with Alastor really, her fight with the Orc that G'zeera released in the arena put her off from really being around him. She ignored the offer and pointed at Leon, "I ride with you." She walked to him and climbed the saddle with grace. She settled behind him and placed her arms around his waist. Ren was not happy about it.

They started for their destination. When they reached the gates they met Augustus. Oberic told him that someone would certainly give him a ride, but Augustus declined the offer and before Oberic's eyes changed into a vulture. He flew off into the air and would arrive at the spot days before they would. Oberic watched the change happen, finding that he was only able to mumble something about that being rather impressive. Amun did not join Augustus in flight and would instead ride with Oberic perched on his shoulder.

The snow made the trip rough. There was low visibility. Even Jayda and V'ma, who had been there, were having trouble heading in the right direction. When they finally made it out of Basile's range, the enchantment no longer darkened the sky and they were happy to see a blue sky again. It took them six days to find the clearing. When they arrived, they found that Augustus had already made the spot for a campfire and had been sleeping in the little hut. They made camp while the sun was up and the light was good.

No one got to slack. Everyone gave time and energy into setting up the tents and gathering wood. Leon had brought his bow and arrows and was off gathering kills for dinner. He returned later dragging a large buck behind his horse and the camp applauded the meaty kill. Alastor assisted in skinning and making cuts of meat. The fire was built, but was not putting out much heat. They sat there shivering and grumpy. Rennyn dug in her satchel and pulled out one of the vials. She advised them all to stand back and when they did, she tossed it into the fire. The Vial shattered and sprayed the wood with a liquid that seemed to hold a fire and not burn away. The fire blazed hard and hot. They all thanked her and she smirked; she felt quite happy with herself.

They cooked the meat and as they ate Oberic drew in a deep breath before he spoke to them, "Augustus, you said you were the first with Graham. How did that happen?"

Augustus told the story of how he had been flying through the woods near North Normoon scouring for forage. He had just about given up when he saw a girl running through the snow with a thin cloak on. He could see that she was holding on to something and it looked as though she were trying to protect it with the way she held it close to her. He circled away to see if there had been something chasing her and when he saw the guard had his bow drawn he swooped in to help. He explained that he had flown around a tree to land and when he did, he changed to the bear and came out to attack the guard. The woman had already been shot and there was nothing he could do to save her. The guard ran away and the woman said her final goodbye to the bundle after slipping a scroll into the wrap. Augustus said he grabbed the baby and took it off into the wilds to watch over it. They traveled further south until they reached this clearing. It was a good enough spot since there was fresh water nearby and he himself was able to communicate with animals and so there was no shortage of milk for the little one. He then explained he was with Graham by himself up until Jayda had come poking around.

Oberic sat there and listened to the story with interest. When Augustus was done, Oberic asked where this scroll was. At first Augusutus did not understand why that was important and his face changed as though it was something he had not thought of before. The truth was Augustus hadn't thought of it because Augustus could not read and did not think that the scroll had carried any important information. He got up and left the fire and entered the small hut. He dug around and shouted out that he found it and returned to the group and handed it to Oberic.

Oberic examined the scroll carefully. The seal had not been broken at all and he immediately recognized it as the royal crest of Normoon. He broke it and unraveled the parchment. He read it out loud.

Dearest Clarissa,

I am filled with sorrow to say that my wife knows about our love affair. She is understandably angry and I regret having hurt her so. Our love blossomed like a flower in spring and your beauty would not allow me to tell my heart no. We have loved one another in secret for two years now. I wish it were as simple to leave her and take you as my queen instead but politics are a dirty and treacherous game and the peace between Normoon and Marrenval are too important. It is more than just you and I.

Please do not for a moment ever think that my love for you is not real. My body aches for you and you alone. You know my heart and my dreams like none other. Please follow my instruction carefully and do not tarry in doing so for time has been cut short and I know not her plans.

She knows you carry my seed and I fear what may come of your safety. With this letter you are being delivered a chest of gold. Take it, my love, and head to South Normoon. Purchase a home and raise our child. Teach them to be as wonderful and kind as you are. Included in this letter are coordinates to a very special treasure. When it is time and they are ready, they can find this treasure and prove they are my heir and they may then take their rightful place by my side as Prince or Princess and eventually take my throne with my blessing. Please do as I have asked of you and do not hesitate to leave as soon as possible.

My heart, you will haunt my dreams for the rest of my life. The sun will never be as bright without you. I am willing to suffer that loss though if it means you and the baby are safe. May all the gods in the world watch over you both. May the stars shive favorably upon you.

My heart and love forever yours
Dorian

Oberic had skipped over the information regarding the location of said treasure and rolled the parchment back up. They all looked at Graham in awe. In their presence, raised by three over protective parents, was the rightful heir to the throne of Normoon. Oberic stuffed the parchment into his coat. There was a long silence before Oberic decided to push ahead. "Thank you, Augustus. Now to tell you and V'ma our stories so that we may understand how things happened." Oberic let Phineas start the story. Phineas, who lowered his head in shame, explained the events in Karren's Call. Once his story was done, Oberic nodded to Ren and Alastor. They told of the murder that led to the fire and their escape to Whiterock. Alastor said he left Ren with the Dwarves and Dwim vouched for the statement. Dwim and Rennyn then went on about the prophecy the Oracle had but were sad to say at this point they did not remember much of it. Leon joined the conversation now. The Dwarf and renowned adventurer explained how they all met Phineas and the sequential confrontation they had with Phineas and his brother.

Next, Oberic and Jayda told their own story that had started about the same time as the others had left for Marrenval. They spoke of the burning of Lilly Tree and their own adventure that led them to Sirentide. This of course was where the party met together. Oberic talked about how Phin had managed to get them on board a ship and how Alastor had been snuck on, unknown to the crew. Jayda took over and spoke about how the ship was sunk and they nearly lost Oberic. She told of them being dropped off at Hadryn. Phineas picked up from here and described Oberic's ex wife in very intimate detail before Alastor took over and discussed their quest into the wilds. He, like Oberic, skipped over the parts about the undead. Even after so long Oberic remembered what he had done and Alastor was wise to follow his ruse. Jayda took over once more and discussed her travel from the Elven city and the thing she fought against. Phineas discussed how loud Oberic and Jayda had been in those nights and everyone yelled at Phineas to shut up. Ren talked about their trip back to Hadryn and eventually to Maer'lyn. Leon finished explaining their escape and led up to where Jayda met V'ma and Augustus.

It was a very long story and they were all getting tired. Night had come a long time ago and they all thought they were honestly quite tired of the dark. Still there was much to be discussed and Alastor was the one to say it. "It is time to hear your story, Oberic Wintersong. Will you tell us of your escape and what happened between then and now?"

They all looked to Oberic now. They were all quite eager to hear what he knew or been through. What had he seen that he felt was so important that they all come out to the wilds and discuss it in the freezing cold? Oberic understood they wanted to hear the story and he was going to tell it to them. "Where should I start?"

Jayda answered him, "Start when you told me to leave you in Maer'lyn. Where did you go? Why did you run back to the tower?" Oberic nodded and agreed that it was as fine a place to start as any and so he told his story.

Oberic's eyes watered as he ran back up towards the tower. He had only known her for a while and already she was inside his heart. He knew she'd be there just as long as Evelyn had been if not longer. Everything in his body told him to go back to her. He knew very well he could escape with them, but there was that risk of them all being captured together and it was something he could not allow. He had always heard dark rumors about prisoners of Maer'lyn and it was not a fate he would allow them to share.

He had tired already of running and his breathing had become labored. He was fighting against a current of people trying to escape as his friends were. Now and again as he ran, he would cast a glance up at the eyes in the sky. He wondered if he could actually be seen or not. He had a feeling that it was nothing but an illusion and if the dead bastard wanted to find out just how powerful Oberic was, then Oberic was willing to show him.

He neared the tower and no longer found himself fighting against a crowd. All that wanted to escape from the upper tiers did. He slowed his run to a walk and tried to collect himself. He stood there staring up at the looming tower and considered his options. As he pondered his predicament one of the insect hybrids had crawled up his leg and bit into him. He let out a swear and brushed the thing off of him. As soon as it hit the ground he stomped on it. This victory was short lived however as he watched hundreds more swarm towards him. Oberic weaved not only his hands but his arms danced as well. Flame appeared at his feet and began to swirl around him. It was a simple and thin circle at the beginning but as he continued to dance inside the flame, it pulsed and slowly spread out further; swallowing up any and everything.

The fire lifted up into the sky and began to twist its body and move wildly, though the base did not move an inch other than spreading and covering more ground. The insects caught by this whirlwind of fire were cooked immediately. The ones who did not find themselves burnt fled away from the spire of fire and Oberic was glad to see that because he himself was growing weak from channeling the spell.

He let the spell fall and the fire pulsed one last time like a blast wave and the tornado of fire vanished. He fell to his knees in the one little area that had not been scorched. He did not like to use his power and always feared becoming one of those who constantly sought after more. He did his best to never really use it and so when he did, he often found himself drained from it.

"Get up," he told himself. He got one foot to the ground and continued to kneel for a moment longer before getting to both feet. He walked forward and back into the tower. Just as he entered he was already over the situation. Sitting at the desk where the plump woman had been sitting was Evelyn.

"She's going to die out there, Oberic. You know that, don't you?" She asked with a sweet smile.

Oberic shook his head, "Enough with the games, Kaj'r. You've already played your hand and I'm here to, as my good friend Phineas would say, party." Oberic reached out and grasped at the air and pulled as if removing a sheet from some old furniture. Evelyn vanished with it. "Now come out here and show yourself or don't you have the spine? Pun intended." The rune lit up and Kaj'r appeared once more wearing his torn robe with the hood pulled up. "Why even hide it? You don't think these people will figure it out?"

Kaj'r laughed, "You really are a fool, Oberic. A city full of skilled casters and you think you're the only one to know? They all know. They all feed into it so long as I help them flourish! The unwanted? The undesired? All of them brought to me." They glared at one another and without warning Kaj'r thrusted his ghoulish hands forward. A bolt of black fire propelled from his hands towards Oberic. Had Kaj'r been battling anyone else this surprise attack may have done more, but the one mistake Kaj'r would make was that he underestimated the sorcerer. Oberic caught the flame and spun around, compelled to do so by the force of the blast, but as his eyes looked and saw Kaj'r once more he backhanded the spell right back to him.

Kaj'r captured the spell and it vanished, "Cute," he said, not sounding the least bit amused, "you're one of the High Men, aren't you?"

"It's been discussed once or twice. Does that scare you?" Oberic asked, calm as ever.

Kaj'r laughed, "I fear nothing! That's just one more of you to die before myself!" He glided like a ghost at Oberic.

Oberic nodded, "That's good because I want your full attention." Oberic's hand frosted over and from his hand grew a long icicle that he would swing just as Kaj'r reached him. Oberic swung it like a mace and clubbed Kaj'r on the side of the head. The icicle shattered and Oberic wasted no time in pummeling the lich once more. Both of his hands were now covered in ice and with each hit they shattered. Chunks of ice spilled to the floor as Oberic took the offensive. With every punch, ice shattered and it left his hand bare. So he would strike with the other hand while the bare fist regenerated its frozen weapon.

Kaj'r had no time to fight back. One punch after another kept him from being able to get anything out. This was not how casters fought, or at least not how he had always known. Kaj'r fought through the beating and began to float from the ground. Oberic had lost the upper hand and he smashed his ice hands together. The shards of ice dropped and though his hands remained frosted over he was free to grab onto Kaj'r. His hands tightened around the robe and he was lifted off the floor. They were both in flight.

Together they twisted in the air and Kaj'r swore at his new foe. Oberic's hands shifted from ice to flame and the robe he held onto started to smoke. After a moment of the burning grip, it caught fire. He let go and fell to the floor, landing on his back. He let out a groan as he watched the lich fight his own burning robe. The fire burned the undead thing and when he freed himself of the burning cloth he flew around the room as fast as he could to extinguish the fire on his decaying flesh. The red eyes locked onto Oberic once he was free of flame and he flew down meaning to attack again.

Just as the lich came close Oberic threw his foot out and bashed Kaj'r in the skull. The kick was powerful enough that it would have surely knocked the crown from Kaj'r's head if he hadn't thrown it off already with the robe. Kaj'r was only temporarily stunned. When he gathered himself again he grabbed Oberic's leg and started swinging him in circles. Oberic felt his stomach turn as he was spun and closed his eyes, simply telling himself that he was not allowed to vomit in the middle of a fight. Kaj'r released him, slamming Oberic against the wall and the sorcerer dropped to the floor.

Kaj'r laughed, "What did you think you would accomplish here, boy? I have lived lifetimes. I have watched mere mortals turn to legend! I survived the Aegis! What chance do you think you have?"

Oberic pushed himself up to his knees, "Yes, yes I hear you. You survived a bedtime story. We all did. Congratulations."

Kaj'r flung another bolt of black flame. Oberic pulled it from the air and shook his hand. The fire flickered out. Oberic then climbed to his feet. Kaj'r was getting frustrated. In all these years he had not met anyone who so easily usurped his power and let it go as if it were nothing. Oberic swung his arms about once again; pillars of fire began to shoot upwards from the floor in random places. Kaj'r dodged them as best as he could but soon found himself burned not only once, but several times. Kaj'r yelled out and cast another illusion. Oberic was surrounded by darkness. Kaj'r should have learned his lesson the first time. He closed in on Oberic who stood there trapped in the illusion. His hands reached out and he fully intended on draining Oberic of every bit of life he had. There was only one problem, Oberic was no longer there. In fact, nothing was there. Kaj'r looked around and saw that he himself had been surrounded by darkness.

"You think you can use my own spell against me?" Kaj'r screamed out. He spun around and looked for a sign of the sorcerer.

Oberic's voice called out in an echo, "Wouldn't dream of it. It'd be rude. This is actually my spell."

"Come out," Kaj'r called, "and face me like a man!"

"Half a man," Oberic laughed, "though I'm not sure you're even that."

Kaj'r had done just as Oberic did and pulled at the darkness like a sheet. The darkness vanished, but Kaj'r's excitement was short-lived. Oberic sat there in front of him at the desk. He also sat on the desk; as well as standing near the desk. Kaj'r looked around the room and found that there were many Oberics standing around. Some of them were talking to each other casually. Others played a game of catch with Kaj'r's crown. Kaj'r growled out, "What is this?" He clawed at the air and tried to pull the illusion away but had no success this time.

The Oberic sitting at the desk was wearing spectacles and pulled them down his nose to look at the lich over them, "Excuse me sir, I'll need you to keep your voice down. We have a meeting of great minds in session at the moment." He leaned forward and whispered, "Between you and me, they're all a bit pissed off right now." He leaned back and removed the glasses from his face, "If you'd like to leave your name and have a seat, I'm sure that I'll be right with you and will then be able to discuss how you'd like your ass kicked today."

Kaj'r had enough of the mockery. He grabbed the desk and flung it from between them. The Oberic sitting behind it vanished with a plume of purple smoke. Kaj'r floated to another pair of Oberics and slashed at them. Each vanished with a plume of smoke of their own, yellow and blue. Kaj'r turned to another Oberic who smiled, "You look upset." Kaj'r swiped at him and he too vanished in a plume of red smoke. Kaj'r felt something itching at the back of his rotted mind and he clawed at his skull. He tried to shake the feeling and when he looked back up he no longer saw any of the Oberics.

Kaj'r was surprised to see one of his own memories being played out before his own eyes. He watched himself enter a vast library filled with ancient books, but there is only one in particular that he is interested in. He observed himself, not a lich then, approach the center of the room where a single book sat on a podium. He heard someone talking, but the sound was muffled. It was a conversation he could no longer remember. He watched himself reach for the book and his voice called out, "I have it! The book of mastery!" Just as he rushed to the door to make his escape, he was confronted by someone. The memory faded as Kaj'r slowly regained control of himself. When it vanished he found that he was again surrounded by the Oberics. One walked up to him with a smile. Kaj'r yelled out in frustration, "Another of your stupid little images!"

Oberic shook his head, "No, it's me this time." He thrusted his back and low. When it came forward, another spear of ice formed and it was pushed under the lich's jaw, then upwards through the skull until it broke through the top. Kaj'r thrashed about and let out a terrible scream that could never be human. The other visions of Oberic simply faded and Oberic made a run for the exit.

"Come back here you coward!" Kaj'r called out as he tried to pull the icicle from his head.

"Would love to, but you're looking for that book and now that I know it's actually real, I'm going to find it first!" He ran out and down the steps leading to the lower tier. He sprinted as fast as he possibly could. He had it in his head to go to the mirror, but as he ran for his life he saw a child laying in the street crying. The insects had eaten away the flesh at her leg and left only bone. Oberic ran to the girl and slid to a stop. He dropped down to a knee and scooped the poor thing into his arms. He apologized for the pain as he ran with her in his arms. He looked back at the tower and saw a river of what looked to be blood come cascading down the streets. He was not sure if it was an illusion, but he could not take the chance with the girl. He dipped into a shop doorway and slammed his back against the door until it opened. Once inside, he kicked the door shut behind him and rushed to the counter where he laid the girl on it

"You have to quit crying! I know it hurts, but you have to be quiet or we're both going to end up dead!" Oberic tried to hush the girl. He was no medicine man and his ability in the magic of life or even nature was mostly very limited. As he tried to calm the girl down a few people came from out of the back room. They each held a weapon and made sure to point it at Oberic. He put his hands up, "Hold on, now. I didn't do this. I saved her. How about we-" he blinked as he began to sway, "-all just calm down." Oberic tilted forward and as he dropped, his head banged against the counter.

Oberic would wake up several hours later to find that he was laid out on a cot next to some crates in a small storage room. He sat up and rubbed his head. It ached terribly and he stood only with the help of the crates on which he leaned. He made his way through a door to find himself in the shop. The others were sitting behind the counter and the girl laid upon the counter still. "Did you give her something for the pain? Put her to sleep?" An old woman stood up and looked at the girl and then to Oberic with sad eyes. She shook her head at him. Oberic moved to the counter with long strides and hovered over the girl. Her face was drained of color and the light in her eyes was gone. Oberic unceremoniously slapped the girl's face, "Get up! Come on, kiddo! Wake up!" His voice raised with every plea and after a few minutes of trying to rouse her gave in and accepted she had gone.

Oberic brushed her cheek and moved strands of red hair out her face. Her eyes, though lacking the vibrancy they once did, were a beautiful emerald color and he immediately felt pain in his chest. He thought of Jayda and wished now, more than ever, he had just gone with her. He put his finger upon her eyelids and shut them. Oberic stepped away from the counter and looked around frantically. Everything that happened here today was his fault. Phineas was doing just fine with the amulet and yet Oberic brought them to Maer'lyn. He set up the meeting which eventually led to their fight with Kaj'r. He helped his friends escape and stayed behind to try and save the others, but here he realized he failed miserably. How many others died outside? No one had been saved by his hand this day other than his friends. He looked at the girl who now slept eternally and he fought to hold in tears that threatened to spill over his lids.

Oberic yelled out. He turned to the wall where a shelf of trinkets and other consumables sat. He ripped the shelf off the wall and threw objects across the room all the while he screamed out in anger. The others lifted their heads from behind the counter and watched the man tear the shop apart. He swore loudly, breaking everything he possibly could, but nothing eased his rage or the pain. He failed and what did he have to show for his ego? A little girl who suffered the feeling of insects eating her flesh before dying of pain or whatever it was that actually killed her. He reached into his dulling blonde hair and ripped out threads of it while he screamed again. This time the tears flowed freely as he loosened the grip on the removed hair and began to pummel the stone wall with his fists. He acknowledged the pain he felt as each punch left a bigger splatter of blood on the stone, but he deserved it. When Oberic was done he slammed his back against the shop door and breathed heavily. He slid down until he was sitting and hung his head.

"We'll bury her," said the old woman after a moment of silence, "when we get the chance to." Oberic did not look up. His hair hung in front of his face and hid the tears. "You saved her the best you could. If she had been left out there those things would have made slow painful work of her."

Oberic reached up and wiped at his face with both hands. His knuckles were busted open and he somehow managed to smear his blood across his face. He brushed his hair back and looked up at them. His voice was cracked and he was doing his best to remain as collected as he could, "What's the situation like out there?"

One of the men, the old woman's son, spoke up, "Mostly quiet for some time now. The city guard has been patrolling the street looking for someone. Looking for you." Oberic nodded. He was not the least bit surprised. "They came into the shop and asked if we'd seen ya. We told them we hadn't. They threatened to kill us if we didn't tell the truth and mom here told them we had nothing else to lose." The man looked at the dead girl on the counter and swallowed. "The guard must have assumed she belonged to us because they didn't give us any more grief. They left and went back to searching."

Oberic took a moment and got to his feet. He peered out the window and saw that there were indeed armed guards patrolling outside. He muttered a swear. The old woman was the next to ask a question, "What do you plan on doing?" Oberic shrugged. He had no plan. He thought himself cunning and crafty, but found out the hard way he was nothing but foolish. He could never leave anything alone. He couldn't just let well enough be enough and constantly had to dig down into something deeper. Maybe it was just his curious nature or maybe he just enjoyed the stress of it all.

"I'll leave you at nightfall. I'll head down to the mirror and try to get out of here" Oberic said finally.

"They broke the mirror, sir," replied the old woman's son, "Little while after you came in. We could hear the uproar from up here. People were sent back to their homes and no one else was allowed to leave."

"Well that certainly puts a damper on my escape." Oberic laid his head against the window.

"In a few days," the old woman started, "in the night we can take you with us down to the pier. We have a small fishing boat. You can take it and take your chances with the storm."

"Why would you help me like that?" Oberic asked. He did not pull away from the window.

The old woman pointed to the dead girl, "Because you helped her. You at least gave her a chance, mister. Let us give you a chance." Oberic did not respond, but turned and looked at the old woman for a long moment. He looked at the young girl and still could not help but feel responsible.

"Best to get out of here and keep you all from being tortured, I suppose." He slid against the door again and sat there quietly. The old woman and her son, possibly sons as the other did not speak at all, all sat back down behind their counter. Night had come now and the sky had darkened, but Kaj'r's eyes still remained in the sky and fire still rained down around the city though it did not seem to be doing any structural damage. Oberic stood and looked out the window again. The guards were still patrolling. He looked back at the counter and unsure if they had fallen asleep or not called out, "I'm going to try and sneak back to my house. I'll return soon."

Oberic opened the door and slipped out behind two guards that patrolled by. He walked as silently as he could behind them before he dipped into an alley and took off at a sprint. He stuck to the shadows as well as he could and by some wonderful miracle had managed to not be spotted. He had come to his home and as he emerged from an alley he was dismayed to see his door had been kicked in. He entered slowly and examined the destruction. Things had been pulled from the walls and shelves and he honestly had no idea if the guards had done it or if it was the party his friends had without him there.

He crept through the room and turned down the hall. There was no one there. He ran to his bedroom and grabbed all the clothes he could grab and carried them to his storage room and threw them in there without care. He then went to the other storage room and began to move all manner of things into the other one. All his alchemical and enchanting supplies as well as the books he kept on the subject. They were all thrown onto the floor. He had spent a few hours doing this and when he was done he decided to take a little rest. Just as he turned to leave the room he got an idea. He bent and picked up one of the books and threw it at the ceiling. It slammed against the roof and crashed back down to the floor. He had no idea what he was hoping for and decided to let it go. He went to the first room, remembered the door was busted open, and returned to his old bedroom. He pulled the old dusted blankets from the bed and laid on the floor.

He woke up some time later and decided it was time to head back to the shop. As he was leaving he saw the leftover pastries and sausages on the table. He grabbed them and snuck back to the shop. When he slid inside the shop, the others peeked over the counter. The dead girl had been wrapped in a blanket and placed in the storage room for now. Oberic threw boxes of stale pastries and cold sausages in their direction. It landed on the counter and nearly slid off. They accepted it graciously and shared the rations.

Oberic spent the next two days with them. No one really talked and the poor girl in the storage room had begun to decay. When it was time to leave in the night, he helped the men bring the poor girl outside. The old woman dressed Oberic in a long coat and a straw hat. She thrusted a flimsy fishing rod in his hands. She looked him over, "This disguise might be enough. They might not be able to see too well in the dark. Not down by the pier anyway." The old woman, Oberic, and one of her sons walked down the tiers of Maer'lyn until they reached the beach. A handful of guards were standing at their post and they stopped them.

"Where do you think you're going?" one of the guards asked.

"My son here," she gestured to Oberic, "is going to try and catch some fish. Since that nonsense happened a lot of us are starving in case you didn't know!" The old woman fussed. The guard tried to raise a hand to calm her down, but she batted it away. "Don't you dare touch me!"

"Calm down you old hag! Only one of you is permitted at the moment." the guard said as he yanked his arm away from her.

The old woman looked at Oberic, "Go on, son. Row out near the storm. The biggest fish are there." Oberic nodded his thanks and she smiled. She then turned and gave the guards another piece of her mind. Oberic walked down the pier to the little fishing boat with its oars neatly laid inside. There was a small mast with a thin sail attached to it and Oberic thought that would be useful in a bit when he neared the storm.

Oberic rowed out to the ocean. It was simple at first and the waters did not seem to be too choppy. As he got closer to the storm that never stopped though, the boat constantly threatened to turn over and Oberic cursed himself more than ever now for not leaving with Jayda when he could have. Oberic called out the words he needed to to make the storm calm. Nothing happened. He was sitting in the rocking boat wondering if he said the words wrong or if they weren't the right words at all. Hope faded from him fast. He just wanted to get out of there and back to Jayda. He jolted his middle finger at the storm and let out a string of obscenities. It was as if the storm heard his impatient swearing because the wind and rain seemed to lessen greatly before him. He dropped the sail and waved his hands to call upon the wind from the storm. It obeyed and thrusted the boat forward. He narrowed his eyes and muttered his thanks.

As he sailed through the storm he was hammered with fat drops of rain that stung his skin. The little boat took on water with every dip from riding down the crest of a wave. He waved his hands and cast the water out but no matter how much he did it the boat continued to take on more. Oberic looked around in the wind and the rain trying to think of any solution at all. He stood in the rocking craft and weaved his hands. The water beneath the boat lifted and seemed to carry it through the storm a bit better. He was going to make it through just fine.

Oberic narrowed his eyes as a strange howling sound filled his ears amongst the roaring thunder and crashing waves. He looked around ahead of him to see what it might be and only when he turned his head to the left did he see the tornado headed for him. His little boat was caught in the violent winds and lifted from the water. The boat tore itself apart and Oberic was caught in a whirlwind of debris. The tornado went out of the storm's ring and flung the sorcerer out into the ocean. The last thing Oberic remembered was crashing into the waters and sinking so far below that he did not believe he would see the surface again.

The fire continued to blaze brightly in front of the group and everyone seemed shocked by the ordeal. Phineas however did not and made it clear, "Then what? You obviously didn't die!"

"You seem disappointed about that," Oberic smirked.

"No, I'm just saying there has to be more to the story."

Oberic nodded, "There is." Oberic lingered a bit longer and just as he went to carry on something rustled in the woods behind him. Leon stood, notched an arrow, and pulled the bowstring back. From the bush peeked the head of a rather large but adolescent eagle. It's feathers were as white as the snow itself and it had piercing golden eyes. Leon lowered his bow and Augustus stood instead. He walked over to the little thing and knelt down. It cried out at him and he smiled.

"Little lady has no idea how she got here," Augustus called back to the others.

"Oh come on! This asshole can talk to animals?" Phineas was half amused by the idea.

Augustus looked at Phineas, "I talk to you, don't I?" He looked back at the bird and held his hand out. "Come on, friend. You're safe with me." The thing came tumbling out of the bush and Augustus stepped back, "Not a bird!"

The others stood up. "Then what?" Ren asked.

It ran past Augustus and revealed it's front half to be that of an eagle and it's back the body of a lion cub with fur as white as it's feathers. Leon declared with a lot of excitement, "A gryphon!" It charged past Oberic and ran straight to Jayda. She almost tipped over as it threw its body against her legs and seemed to nuzzle her for a moment before trying to claw up her leg.

"I think it likes me!" Jayda said finding the whole thing to be exciting. The gryphon, little more than a hatchling, squawked at her.

"Not you," Augustus pointed to the baby swaddled in furs, "Him. She says they are siblings."

Phineas dropped his piece of meat into the snow, "You mean that baby has been a gryphon this whole time?" The hatchling ran to the meat and snapped it up. Phin reached down to pull it away from the beast and was bitten by the little thing. "Ouch! Little bastard!"

Jayda knelt down in the snow and held Graham out towards the gryphon. It clumsily ran over and V'ma was nearly having a fit as she tried to get up and stop Jayda from performing such an insane thing. Dwim grabbed her and made her sit down. The gryphon rubbed her head against the furs and let out its own cooing sound. "The gryphon will protect and in turn kingdoms will be reunited. Or something like that," Augustus said. "In the clearing, remember? I think that gryphon is as part of this as any of us are."

The creature seemed to have no desire to hurt Graham and as Jayda pulled the baby back to herself, the gryphon followed. Ren smirked and grabbed one of the smaller furs and laid it out near Jayda. The gryphon screeched and then nestled into it and looked at them.

CHAPTER 26

"Please," Alastor said while everyone seemed preoccupied with their new guest, "continue your story. What happened next?"

"If I'm being honest," Oberic rubbed the back of his neck, "I don't know. At least I don't know what happened between that and arriving on the beach."

Oberic opened his eyes and saw nothing but a long stretch of beach as far as his eyes could see. He let out a questioning groan and rolled over on his back. His face was covered in sand and he wiped, but only brushed most of it into his mouth. He sat up and coughed up sand for a bit before he vomited a mess of water. He crawled up the beach under a palm tree and leaned against it. Oberic drifted in and out of consciousness for a while. The heat here seemed unbearable, at least when he was awake. He rested until nightfall had come again. The temperature dropped fast and deep. Still, he had to make his way somewhere. He walked along the coast hoping to come across a dock or harbor or some sort of town. The first two did not work out but he did come across a walled city. As he approached he was struck in the back of the head and he collapsed into the sand. He did not see who had done it, but felt two people grab him by the arms and drag him into the city. He was brought into a building of sandstone and dropped on the floor. Sitting in front of him was a man who had dark olive skin. His hair and eyes shared the same burnt orange color. The man sitting in the throne-like chair spoke to Oberic in a tongue he did not understand. Oberic got to his knees, looking quite ragged, and tried to explain that he did not understand what the man said. Oberic was struck in the face by a fast fist and collapsed to the side.

"I am getting real sick of this shit!" Oberic yelled out as he held his face. He flexed his jaw and tried to shake the disoriented feeling from his head.

"It does not matter what you are sick of, outsider. What matters is you have come stalking the night around my city and now find yourself at my mercy." The olive skinned man looked to have been woken up and alerted about Oberic's appearance. "Who sent you? Why have you come?"

"No one sent me, alright? I'm lost." Oberic tried to stand, but was forced back to his knees by those who had brought him in.

"So no one will miss you then? This is good." He turned his back to Oberic and looked out the glassless window.

"That's a strange thing to say, friend. And just who are you?"

The man turned and faced Oberic again, "I am Balva G'zeera, but you will address me as master."

"I don't believe I will." Oberic was struck again.

"What is your trade-" G'zeera clapped his hands together, "Ah! Forgive me. A thousand apologies friend. I did not catch your name."

Oberic faked his smile, "My name is Oberic, but my friends call me Oberic so you can go ahead and call me Oberic."

G'zeera sneered, "You have a sense of humor, Oberic-"

"Please, Oberic was my father's name. You can call me Oberic."

G'zeera cut eyes to his associates and Oberic was struck several more times in the face. "Your pride and humor will burn out here in-"

"You know this is kind of starting off like my first date with my lady. Busted face and everything." Oberic looked up at one of the guards, "She hits harder though." Oberic was struck again and this time collapsed to the ground.

"Take him to the pit. Chain him to the wall." G'zeera offered a little wave before Oberic was picked up and taken away. He was dragged down into a strange pit where the walls were slanted. He was laid down and chained so that his arms and legs were stretched out. Above him was a clear black sky with all the wonders of the universe dancing before him. The two men, wrapped in black, laughed as they went back to serve G'zeer.

Oberic laid there, not that there was much he could do about it, and watched as the sun rose the next morning. It started off with a nice warmth and then shortly after it had heated up the stone on which he laid. His back cooked against the wall and the iron cuffs around his wrists and ankles burned him. Oberic screamed himself hoarse and by the time the sun sat at its highest point he had no voice left. His skin had baked in the sun and he had already started to blister. It wasn't until much later in the day that he was visited by G'zeera.

He squatted near Oberic and smiled, "You do not look well, my friend Oberic. Perhaps you have reconsidered your attempts at humoring me. Yes?" Oberic was in such incredible pain that he could not even turn his head to look at the man. "Yes, I think you have indeed learned a lesson. Let us make sure that lessons sticks." G'zeera stood up and called out to whomever had accompanied him, "Leave him until the sun dies. Collect him then and we shall see if my friend Oberic, who was named after his father, is still as funny. And if he is, we will bring him back to witness the rebirth of the sun."

Oberic continued to be roasted by the unforgiving sun and heat of the Mahir. When the sun finally did set, he was covered in orange blisters that oozed yellow pus. He was retrieved just as G'zeera had commanded. Oberic let out a silent cry of pain as they handled him roughly. When he was dropped in front of G'zeera he looked awful and nearly unrecognizable. "My friend, Oberic! You have returned to me a new man! Ah yes, your mouth was so full of life just a night ago and the Mahir has changed your ways in the matter of a day. May the wind bless you!"

G'zeera sat in his chair and leaned forward, resting his forearms on his knees, "Friend Oberic, something in the wind tells me that you are something more than some Human who was unfortunate enough to wander into the Mahir and further into my city. We Desruc do not take kindly to outsiders. You have learned this." His smile was terrible. "We are of course two grown men and I am sure you are filled with ambition as am I! So let us begin anew, hm?" He leaned back and clapped his hands. "Friend Oberic, I will of course ask you in a few days once more who you are and you, I pray for your own wellness, will answer friend G'zeera with both honesty and love in your heart. Until then, friend Oberic, I will show you such wonderful hospitality." Two Desruc women entered the room wearing an outfit that resembled a bikini with a sheer dress that split down the hips. Their skin was dark and smooth; without a doubt enticing to anyone who laid eyes on them. "Ladies! My guards will bring him to special quarters. You will attend to his every need, yes?"

The girls bowed their heads and responded, "Yes, Balva."

Oberic was picked up again and he let out another silent scream. He was carried off to a room with a lavish bed and large sandstone tub. The guards dropped him to the floor and left. The women hovered over him and examined his cooked back, much darker and uglier than his front.

"You will go through much pain as you heal, but we shall aid you in the process." the one with dark green skin said.

"And when you are healed we shall give you pleasures if you wish of it," said the dark blue skinned woman. "We will return to you soon. Rest well. Maybe this will give you something to work towards as you heal." She slipped the coth holding her breasts up and let the large dark breasts with tiny nipples drop. She ran her hands over them and then covered them once more, "Soon." The women made their exit and left Oberic to lay on the floor crippled.

They returned the next day and found Oberic laying in the same spot. He had not moved, rather, could not move. The pain did not stop. Even when he passed out, he dreamed of the pain. Even his sweetest dreams were painful. Between remembering being stuck out on that hot stone slab being baked alive, he dreamed of her. He woke up from one of his dreams of her and willed himself to roll on to his back. As his roasted skin touched the cool stone he let out another cry, this one was not so silent. He breathed in deeply and tried to settle. The less he moved the less he would feel it. The two women came into the room and looked down at him.

Blue, who had a body Phineas would have messed the front of his pants over, licked her lips and spoke softly to Oberic, "You have moved. That must have been great pain. We have known the horrors of the scorching sun of the Mahir. We can help ease your wounds." She looked at Green and gave her a nod. Green left and returned a bit later with a large bucket filled with strong smelling powder. The stone basin tub had room underneath where a fire was lit to heat the stone and then the bath. They drew water for Oberic and poured the powders in. The water foamed and sizzled. When it was hot and ready to be used, they removed Oberic's pants before they begged his forgiveness as they lifted him. They were strong, as all Desruc women were, and moved Oberic with ease. He let out a long agonizing howl of pain and then screamed when they lowered him into the water. Blue and Green would stand outside the basin and undress themselves before getting in with him. They held him up and dabbed at his skin with cloths

Green looked into his eyes with her own yellow. Her dark red hair was pulled up above her head. "The mixture we have put in this water will seep into your flesh and you will go through much pain through the night, but I swear to you now that you will feel much better by this time tomorrow." She continued to wash him. She took care of his chest while Blue took care of his shoulders and neck. They both took care of his arms. Blue dabbed gently at his back and Green

391

gave him a seductive look as she cleaned his stomach and eventually grasped his manhood and washed him there. They bathed him over and over for nearly an hour. They made sure to work over every spot several times so that the medicine sunk into his skin.

When it was time to get out they stood up. Green made sure to stand in front of Oberic a while longer than she needed so that he could see the water running between her thighs and drip from her sex. They lifted him together and dried him. They carried him to his bed and laid him down. They were at least conscientious of his comfort as they fluffed a pillow as much as they could and they covered him in fine woven blankets. Blue leaned down and whispered breathily into his ear, "We will return to check on you. I am sorry for the pain that is to come, but when you are better we will make it worth your while." They dressed and left him.

The women did not lie about the pain that was to come that night. It felt like he was tied to the stone again, but the pain was so much worse. It was as if his own body was eating him alive. Every inch of his skin screamed in pain and he was only able to scream for a little while before his voice gave out again. He was forced to lay there with his mouth wide open in a silent scream.

Blue and Green returned sometime in the morning and uncovered Oberic. Green stroked his face as softly as she could to avoid causing the facial burns to hurt more than they were, "Your pain was great, but we know you will be better soon." They covered him again and returned hour after hour to check on his condition. When the evening came again they returned with a knife that had a thick blunt edge. "We are sorry," Blue said as they pressed the dull blunt side into his skin and then scraped down slowly. Oberic yelled out silently, but had he seen the results he might have tried to fight the pain. Where there was once roasted and burned skin that carried blisters was now bright red skin. Still burnt but a lot better than what it was before. They performed this process over every inch of burnt skin until his body was free of it and laid there bright red.

They finished up by mixing a cold cream and gently rubbed it into his skin. Oberic relaxed a little. The feeling was the first soothing thing he had felt in a few days. Green spoke to him, "You will rest easier tonight. Tomorrow night, we shall make your rest even easier." They were correct that he would rest easier that night. The pain was there and still excruciating, but he was able to move a bit. He watched as the skin darkened and blotched throughout the night. He drifted to sleep and dreamed of Jayda. This was the first night that he truly feared he would not get back to her.

Green and Blue returned the next day and repeated the process. The skin underneath the new peel was less red and once he was lotioned and taken care of he found he was able to move relatively well. When their care was done, Blue stood at the side of the bed and undid her clothing. They dropped around her feet and she took his hand in hers. She ran it over her flat and toned stomach. She crawled over his naked body with her own and straddled him. She bit her lip and stared down at him with her red eyes when she felt him grow under her. She slid his hands slowly up her body and helped him squeeze her breasts. Oberic's mouth moved and only the rasp of a man who had lost his voice came out. She leaned forward and put her ear to his lips. "You desire something. Tell me and I shall make this fantasy a reality."

Oberic's lips brushed against her ear and it gave her chills, not for the reason she would have thought though, "Please, I am begging you, no. I do not have the strength in me to stop you, but I pray that you understand my desire lies with one woman and one woman alone. With her in my heart; I could never. So please, don't."

Blue sat up and pressed herself against his hardness. She touched his face and leaned down again kissing his lips before whispering against them, "You are a good man. Your love will have your loyalty." She climbed off Oberic and bent to grab her clothes. She dressed herself in a hurry, not ashamed, but as a favor to honor the man's request. Before she and Green left, she looked back at him, "If you change your mind, you may take me." They left and shut the door. Oberic let out a long sigh and closed his eyes. He drifted off to sleep and dreamed of Jayda.

The girls returned for the days after again and each day they worked with Oberic to get him moving and functioning normally once more. Oberic was grateful for their care and assistance even if it was too hands on at first. After he told them he couldn't however, they were respectful of his love for another woman. G'zeera however had come to call and Oberic now knew this was not a man you played games with. Oberic was escorted to the Balva's building and offered a chair. He took it and sat looking at G'zeera. "Friend Oberic," the cruel bastard started, "you look well. The girls took care of all your needs, yes?"

Oberic nodded. His throat still hurt, but he was able to use his voice again, "Yes. All of them."

G'zeera raised his brow, "And?"

"And thank you," the next words were nearly unable to come out of his mouth, "Master."

G'zeera leaned back in the chair and clapped his hands. "Marvelous! Marvelous! Friend Oberic, you have come around to the thinking of G'zeera! Now maybe we can help each other!"

"How can I help you?" Oberic asked. G'zeera raised his brow waiting for that magic word, Oberic wanted to kill him, "Master."

"Tell me, friend Oberic, how does a Human come walking into the Mahir? There were no ships along the coast. There was no army you arrived with. You are not being honest with G'zeera. I can assure you, friend Oberic, that there are much worse punishments than the pit. So please," he smiled, "tell G'zeera the truth this time."

Oberic knew he could not be honest about what he was. He would never have a chance of getting away if they knew what his magic could provide, "I'm a scholar. From Maer'lyn."

G'zeera studied him for a moment, "And what are you a scholar of, friend Oberic?"

"Elven cultures. Forest Elves to be more precise." It was the first thing he could think of.

G'zeera sneered, "You find them interesting? Beautiful perhaps?"

"Quite wrong, Master. Stuck up and snooty. I am not sure how aware you are of the world outside of the Mahir, but Human and Elf relations have been poor for decades." G'zeera searched his face for lies. G'zeera was a man who could read deceit on a face, but Oberic was a man whose specialty was lying to the mind. G'zeera seemed satisfied.

"Friend Oberic, are your people as fond of riches as I myself am?"

"We've waged wars over gold. And women."

"My new good friend, may it be possible we set up a trade with your Human Balvas? I know that you enjoyed my slaves," G'zeera said. Oberic's gut turned. Those poor girls were being forced on him. It did not change anything nor would it have made him be any different with them, but he felt awful that he was their chore, "Let us be great friends now. As a gift and sign of my trust, I give you Misha and Wy'ya. They are yours to do with as you please! Beat them! Rape them in front of their families! It is no concern of mine!"

"I like to keep my perversions in the bedroom," Oberic said. "Thank you though. I will take this gift from you and I will put them to work at night." G'zeera's lips pulled back revealing big teeth. "Now, Master, what did you have in mind for a deal?"

G'zeera spent the next few hours speaking with Oberic about the booming slave trade that had, within the last week, picked up now that he was Balva. They worked out a plan together that Oberic, accompanied with several of G'zeera's assassins, would lead a slave caravan to the border of the wilds. He would threaten war with the Elves by telling them that they had contacts waiting for them just beyond and if they weren't met in time they would come to the wilds to burn them down. Once through the wilds, Oberic would take the slaves and present them as a gift to the leader of Hadryn. G'zeera wanted to know what kind of man this Locke fellow was. Oberic explained just how cruel Locke was and that he had a very deep mine they needed more muscle for. He even went as far to say that Locke would strongly consider an alliance if you present this gift and may continue to purchase slaves if he could produce high quality Desruc. He then noted that women like Misha and Wy'ya would be excellent sexual slaves for the Human nobles. G'zeera was hearing all the right things. Oberic knew however, a man like this needed to be persuaded further.

"One more thing," Oberic said, "I want a bigger cut."

"You are becoming a greedy man, friend Oberic."

"I think we can both quit playing coy with one another. I am indeed a greedy man, but so are you. You want into the wilds and you want more for yourself. I can help you with that. I want more too. More slaves. For myself. Both men and women."

"And what would you do with both men and women, friend Oberic?"

"I could use the men for labor and make a little extra for myself. The women, well, thanks to you I've taken quite a liking to your women. Do you understand?"

G'zeera clapped his hands and laughed, "Friend Oberic, you have yourself a deal." He clapped and had several dancers come into the room. "Friend Oberic, you will have all that you desire. Together we shall become powerful beyond our wildest dreams!" The women danced for them. Oberic did his best to pretend he was interested when in truth all he could think about was Jayda in one of those outfits.

Oberic was sent to his room with Misha and Wy'ya, who were both collared and chained. He led them to his room. When he shut the door, they dropped their clothes for him once more and he whispered to them, "No. Never. Understand? You were kind and took care of me and I will return the favor. Put your clothes back on. Do you trust me?" Both women, who had seen him naked and touched him more intimately than he desired, nodded their heads though it seemed they were uncertain to him. "Good. If G'zeera asks, you were both taken all night. Understand?" They nodded again. "Get some rest. The next few days will be trying."

"You will sleep with us, Master?" Misha, the dark blue skinned Desruc, asked.

Oberic shook his head, "No. I'll be fine on the floor."

The girls laid in the bed as told and spent most of the night wondering if this was a cruel trick or if he would get up to take them by force. They would fall asleep not knowing Oberic's touch and he would fall asleep scheming against G'zeera. He dreamed, as he would for every night here on after, of Jayda. *I will find you, I promise.*

Two weeks passed and the slave caravan was ready to leave. Oberic had been gifted another twenty personal slaves. He chose not to explain the plan to them so that he would not risk being found out. Misha and Wy'ya tended to Oberic's requests throughout the days and learned to love him, not a romantic love, but a love of his kind heart. On the day they were to leave Misha came to Oberic and dropped to her knees in front of him.

"Master!" Her palms placed together as she prayed up to him, "If your plan is true and you mean to be kind, I beg of you to get G'zeera to send my grandfather with us. Please! G'zeera will be cruel to him and he is an old but good man."

Oberic grabbed her hands and pulled her up, "I'll do what I can, Misha, but G'zeera is a mad man. Who is your grandfather?"

"Master, please, his name is Fesk. Bring him with us and let him see the wilds for once in his life."

"I'll do my best, okay? Whatever the outcome though, do not break. Do you understand?

Misha nodded, "Yes, Master. I will remain loyal to your planning. I am grateful that you will try."

 Oberic sighed, "Put your collars on. It's time to go."

They left the room together. Oberic held on to their chains and guided them around a corner. Misha quietly pointed him out standing on the wall with his telescope. He had seen Fesk about, but never spoke with him. Oberic nodded and when he met with G'zeera several minutes later he pointed up at the old man on the wall.

"Master, I wonder if you may bestow on me another gift as we part." Oberic bowed low as he knew to do now with G'zeera.

"Friend Oberic, you ask much, but G'zeera is in good spirits this day for you are about to help me gain fortune and by extension, my people! Tell me what it is you desire and I will consider it."

Oberic pointed up at Fesk, "I want him as a slave."

G'zeera looked up at the wall where he was pointing and let out a laugh, "The old man?" G'zeera did not wait for an answer and snapped his fingers. Assassins went up the wall and grabbed Fesk who just barely managed to pack up his telescope. When he was dragged down he was thrown to his knees beside G'zeera and in front of Oberic. Fesk looked up at Oberic and then down to the stone. "Friend Oberic, what could you possibly do with this old man?"

Oberic could not think of a reason to use Fesk and he smiled at G'zeera, "If I'm being honest I like to hear the old timers tell stories and I rather like his telescope there."

G'zeera nodded and looked down at Fesk. The Balva's hand was disgustingly fast as it drew a dagger of glass and slipped it across Fesk's throat. Before blood even slipped from the wound he grabbed the telescope from his hands and let Fesk fall where he died in the sun. G'zeera held out the telescope to Oberic, "The old man has no good tales, friend Oberic. He would be a burden on our very important mission. Please, accept his telescope as a gift."

Misha watched as her grandfather was murdered in front of her and as she promised she did not break from the plan. She lowered her head and said a Desruc prayer for his spirit. G'zeera walked away and yelled at everyone to get ready to leave. Oberic turned to Misha, handed her the telescope, and whispered his apologies. She took the telescope and said nothing

Oberic met G'zeera one last time before leaving. The Balva leaned in and spoke to Oberic quietly, "May the wind bless you, friend Oberic. I have placed a trust in you, do not betray me for I swear that we shall meet again and I will be no friend of yours. We understand each other?"

Oberic patted him on the arm, "Nothing to worry about, Master. Everything will fall into place."

Oberic and G'zeera exchanged their goodbyes. Oberic took his twenty-two personal slaves, some of which held large umbrellas to keep them from cooking under the sun, as well as a handful of G'zeera's assassins at the front of the caravan. A line of slaves walked behind as gifts to the cruel leader of Hadryn. They walked for days and slept in the cold dunes at night. There was no great detail to be told about this part of the journey other than the sun was cruel and that three of the gifted slaves in the back of the caravan had died on the journey.

They approached the border where the sand met dirt which would transition into grass; further along there would be trees. Just as Oberic suspected, Elven archers dropped from the trees with bows drawn and ready to fire. Oberic put his hands up and spoke to them in their tongue, a language he hoped none of the Desruc could speak. His words were spoken to them in a most angry and threatening tone, "Don't shoot! I am a prisoner! I am on good terms with the High Priestess of Hadryn! These Desruc with me mean no harm!" The assassins nodded approvingly of Oberic's angry tones. Oberic jabbed a finger out accusingly at the Elves, "I'm speaking to you angrily because they think I am making threats. The men clothed in black are assassins. The rest of these people are slaves. I am begging you, in your tongue, help free us by ending the assassins and granting the rest of us passage through your lands. We will not attempt to make home here, only camp as we pass through on our way to the White City. Do we have a deal?"

"Only camp," The head archer replied in Elvish.

Oberic jumped up and down throwing his hands all over the place in rage, "Absolutely! As you wish!"

"Deal. Kill the assassins." The head archer, and the others, made swift work of all the assassins they could see. All the enslaved Desruc crouched and hid themselves under their hands the best they could as they feared for their lives. One assassin however was at the back of the caravan and turned and sprinted back into the desert. "Let the desert claim him," he looked at Oberic and bowed his head, "I appreciate the respect you have shown by speaking our language," Oberic would of course not tell them he only did it to fool their wardens, "Keep to your word and move these people along and out of our wilds and I will respect you by not killing them."

The caravan looked to Oberic who turned around and spoke in the common language again, "It's alright. You're all safe. They are allowing us passage. We will go to Hadryn, but you will not be slaves. We will find you a place to make your own. I promise." The Desruc stood, most of them unsure if they believed him, but Misha and Wy'ya placed their hands on his shoulders and thanked him with their eyes. Oberic began to walk into the wilds. The Elves stepped aside and dipped their heads to him. Oberic, and his new friends, were getting out of the desert.

CHAPTER 27

If Jayda's eyes were knives she would have sliced Oberic and V'ma up several times throughout his story. She of course understood V'ma had nothing to do with Oberic's stay in the Mahir, but when Oberic had spoken of the two Desruc slaves and how they tried to entice him, all she could do was associate her Desruc co-parent with them. V'ma was of course exceptionally beautiful. If Phin ever got the chance to see V'ma naked he would lose his mind. Jayda did feel a little ease when Oberic made it clear that he did nothing with those women, but it did not clear the feeling. She wanted more than anything to cling to Oberic and make sure V'ma went nowhere near him.

V'ma had other things on her mind. Her face twisted into hatred as Oberic had talked about G'zeera. The worm had claimed himself Balva somehow and was already running their people deeper into ruin. She was even angrier when Oberic explained how those people were nothing more than an investment to him and how he was so easily able to trade them. It was quite the emotional ride for her. She felt her heart tighten as Oberic told them what happened to the old man, Fesk. V'ma commented, "Fesk was a good mind. Very kind and curious. I am sorry you did not have a chance to know him as I did." There was silence around the fire and then she decided she needed to add to her statement, "Oberic, I thank you for getting the slaves through the Wilds. Did you arrive safely at this Hadryn?"

Oberic nodded, "We did. Not a single Desruc soul was lost beyond what I have mentioned."

"At least you got some sort of break out in the Wilds, Oberic," Ren said with a smile.

Oberic shook his head, "No, not exactly. There isn't much of a story to tell at this point other than we encountered more of what we did in Oakember. Just the puppets though, no master. Do you understand?"

The original members of the group nodded except Jayda who promptly asked, "What does that even mean?"

Oberic danced around the answer, "Just that we ran into a spot of trouble along the way on a few occasions. There's more of them out there now." Jayda was unhappy with the answer, but she knew she would get it out of Oberic later.

Leon shook his head. He hated to hear that the terrible thing was gaining power again. He looked up at the sky to say a prayer for him and his friends. His chestnut colored eyes studied the stars and pointed up. He let out an excited yell,, "Look at that!"

Everyone looked up to the star littered void above them. They watched as stars slowly moved in the sky towards each other. It was something that none of them, even Oberic, had ever seen. The stars, set in constellations, were familiar to all and Rennyn whispered in a voice that sounded as if it was a little horrified, "The Aegis and The Lady meet again. . ." They were all mesmerized by the cosmic phenomena that was taking place before their very eyes.

Dwim watched with wide eyes while the stars in those constellations mingled and twinkled in the pitch sky painted with galaxies and nebulas. Something told him their business needed to urgently carry on. "Oberic," he interrupted their star gazing, "I think it's important that ye' finish yer' story, lad. And soon." There was no disagreement from the others. They all had that sense of urgency.

Oberic pressed on, "So we found ourselves coming to Hadryn. The barrier had been dropped and I took that as a sign of things being just fine there. I was absolutely wrong."

As the caravan of Desruc slaves approached the gates of Hadryn on the main road a voice called out from on the wall protecting the White City. Most of the Desruc paid no attention to his words as they stared up in awe at the buildings towering up towards the sky beyond the walls. The guard shouted out, "This some kind of raiding party? If it is, it's the worst I've seen! Just a bunch of half naked, well I don't know, but I do know you're not coming in!"

Oberic shouted back, "And how would the High Priestess feel about you turning away a bunch of runaway slaves?"

"Slaves? Where did you find them?" was the guard's reply.

Oberic sighed, "From the Mahir! Will you please just open up the gates and let us in! These people are hungry and tired. If I can be honest for just a moment, I've got shit I really need to do!"

The guard looked annoyed but called out, "Hold on. . ." and he vanished from the wall. After a twenty minute wait the gates slowly started to open and they were met by a platoon of well armed paladins. They came out and searched everyone for weapons. The Desruc all did as Oberic did and put their hands in the air. One of the paladins, whose face was covered by a helmet, addressed Oberic.

"I'm Cyrus, Captain of this lot. You'll forgive our rudeness, but we need to get you to the High Priestess. Any other time than now and this would not be an issue, but we are having hard days." He turned without another word and led the group, including the refugees and the armed paladins, down the streets to the palace. The Desruc slaves looked around themselves in wonder at how good life could be outside of the Mahir and only hoped that they would be able to obtain some sort of life resembling such. As they neared the palace Oberic could see Evelyn standing at the top of the palace steps and her eyes immediately widened upon seeing Oberic.

Eve ran down the steps and hugged Oberic, "You look dreadful! What has happened?"

Oberic gave her a friendly pat on the back and then broke free of her embrace, "I've gone and had myself an adventure. I need your help."

Eve looked beyond him at all the Desruc, mostly half dressed, and then noticed two of the females standing outrageously close to Oberic's sides. She looked at her ex husband, "Where is Jayda?"

Oberic frowned, "We've been separated-"

Eve cut him off and put on a false frown for him, "That's a pity, Oberic. I'm sorry things didn't work out-"

"No," Oberic stopped her, "We physically got separated. As soon as I help these souls I'm off to find her."

Evelyn cleared her throat and adjusted her shaw. Summer was nearly at its end and she did not care for the heaviness of her cloaks, but was far too modest to reveal any skin. She examined the Desruc girls again and gave them a curt nod, "And who are they?"

Misha and Wy'ya dropped to their knees beside Oberic and declared in unison, "We belong to the Master. We do as he wishes."

Oberic rolled his eyes and bent to grab their arms. He yanked them both up to their feet and let out a long sigh, "You are not my property. How many times do I have to continue saying this? You are free people. I do not have any desire to own any of you." He glared at Evelyn, "Please, can you help me?"

Evelyn Locke wore a face of horror at watching these two, very attractive women, throwing themselves down at Oberic's feet. She looked between them and Oberic, then hissed out at him, "Oberic I will not help you start some strange cult of perversion!"

Oberic had enough of it. He reached up and rubbed his tired eyes. When he dropped his hands, he stared hard at Evelyn. "For the last time, I am not doing anything but trying to fu-" he calmed himself, "I'm trying to help these people, Eve. Now your whole holy order is supposed to be about humility and helping those in need," Oberic pointed behind himself, "These people need help, Evelyn. I've done all that I can for them."

Eve glared at Oberic. She did not appreciate the tone that he used with her, but she acknowledged that he was correct and she was not being very helpful. "Oberic, I can try to find them a place here in the city, but how well will they adapt here?"

Oberic's face eased a bit as Eve had finally agreed to help, "I have another idea, actually." Oberic explained just what happened in the Mahir to him and went into greater detail about why Misha and Wy'ya were acting like that. He made sure to drive the point that he did nothing with either of them. Both Desruc women agreed that he was well behaved despite the many temptations they offered him. Then he explained about the deal he made with G'zeera and how he betrayed him to save these people as well as himself. Evelyn found a swelling in her chest and wondered to herself where this Oberic was when they were happily married and found herself angry that he would go looking for Jayda afterwards. "Anyway, I was thinking about Oakember. After that nasty business it's deserted. Let these people live there. Let them build a life of their own. Can you help with that?"

Evelyn looked over the group and then to Oberic, "As you wish, Oberic. Let it be declared now that Oakember will be the new home of these souls and Hadryn will provide them protection for a short while until they find themselves situated and in better spirits." She nodded to the Paladin Captain, "Captain Cyrus, get these people food and drink. Provide them a means to bathe themselves and then give them appropriate clothing. Let them rest at the inns and tell the innkeepers they will be compensated for the rooms. You will escort them tomorrow to Oakember and will help them start a life there." Cyrus nodded and waved at everyone and asked that they follow him.

Misha and Wy'ya looked at Oberic for confirmation it was safe to go with the armored man. Oberic gave them both a nod, "Go on. You're safe now." They both hesitated and then turned to leave with the others. He looked back up to Eve, "Thank you, Evelyn. I appreciate it."

Evelyn dipped her head, "You did a wonderful thing, Oberic. I am proud of you."

Oberic would have at one time done anything for her praise, but now found that it didn't mean much to him at all, "That's nice. I need another favor."

Evelyn had gone to ask what he could possibly ask for when they both heard shouting coming from the city square. "Not again," she muttered. She stepped down the stairs past Oberic and started walking towards the noise. Oberic, curious as to what might have her concerned, followed behind her.

The pair of them arrived at a crowded square where both citizens and paladins stood listening to a man shout. The man standing on a crate had dirty blonde hair and sky blue eyes. Bits of his face were horribly disfigured. Oberic and Evelyn watched on as he riled up the people around him.

"This is supposed to be the city of holiness! The capital of Olm's worshippers! Yet we stand here doing nothing? We wait around for nothing? What is the point of having a holy order if they do nothing?" the man shouted out. People in the crowd began to cheer him on. The man continued, "Look at my face! Do you know what happened to me? Betrayal. . ." He let the silence linger for a bit, "As I meant to put an end to a foul creature, an abomination to all that Olm stands for, one of my own brothers in arms watched me be attacked by an Elf! He watched me be attacked and he did nothing!" The crowd booed. "Ask yourselves this, brothers and sisters of Olm's love, do the Elves worship Olm as they should? Do the Dwarves for that matter?" He cuffed his hand to his ear and listened as they all yelled out their answers, all being no. "You're right! They do not! They worship some silly forest animals and call them Wild Gods! The mountain dwellers have faith in nothing but booze! It is time we rise up and show our High Priestess that we are ready to take our holy word of Olm to the Elves or anyone else who stands in the way of what the White themselves teach! We will show them the light of Olm or we shall introduce them to the darkness and let

Olm judge them himself!" Evelyn hid behind Oberic to hide herself in case things got out of hand. The man threw his arm into the air, "If you are ready for a crusade and are willing to really stand up for what is right, come with me! Together we shall bring the dawn!" He jumped from the crate and held his hand high. Dozens of men and women from the crowd followed behind him cheering. Evelyn was surprised to see that even several of her Paladins had thrown down their shields and followed the man as well.

Evelyn kept behind Oberic as she watched him go off with the followers, "He has been at it every day for a few weeks now. More and more of them leave and head out into the woods. They have an abandoned fort they've been repairing. Oberic they are going to do terrible things."

Oberic frowned, "Then why not stop them?"

"Because he isn't wrong. He believes, as I do, that all should follow Olm but I do not believe they should die for not doing so. That would be against our teachings. I can only protect my people, Oberic. I can only keep them safe and so far, no one in the city has been harmed. Not even the Elves."

Oberic sighed, "Eve, I would help you, you know that, but I need to find Jayda and the others."

She stepped out in front of Oberic and nodded, "My problems are not yours, I know this. How can I help you find them?"

He asked, "Any chance you can get me passage to Normoon?"

"Is that where they are?"

"I don't know," and he really didn't. He only knew that right now something inside him said to go there, "Just following a hunch."

Evelyn nodded, "I can get you passage. Go rest at the inn, Oberic." She placed a hand on his arm and left him at the square.

Oberic traveled to the inn and let the innkeeper know he was staying with all the Desruc that had come. The innkeeper was polite and provided him with a key. Once in his room, he laid down and dreamed of Jayda. It was such a sweet dream that he was having when he was disturbed by a pounding on the door. He jolted awake and for a moment forgot where he was. Once he regained himself, he got up and answered the door.

A short woman wearing Paladin's armor greeted him, "The High Priestess has made arrangements for you to sail with a merchant ship heading to Karren's Call in Normoon. You will be expected to work I am afraid, but they will provide you passage as a favor for the High Priestess." Oberic nodded his understanding. "Grab your things. They are ready to go."

Oberic turned for a moment, briefly forgetting he had no bags to bring, and simply followed the woman out. They left the inn and made it to the docks. As he walked down the pier to cross the gangplank, Misha and Wy'ya called out for him. He turned at the mention of his name and watched them run as fast as they could towards him. They were now dressed in more humbling clothing that didn't show off any part of their body. He was happy about that.

They both stopped in front of him. Misha asked, "Are you leaving us?"

Oberic nodded, "I am. I have to find Jayda. I've been too long without her as it is."

Wy'ya questioned him, "Why do you not take us?"

Oberic looked at the both of them concerned, "You do not belong with me. You belong with your people. You have a chance out here to not be chained to anyone, do you understand that?"

Wy'ya nodded, "We understand. We are not simple minded. We are just fond of a man who has saved us from cruelty."

Misha came closer and placed a hand on Oberic's face, "Be safe, Oberic. Be a good man to this woman you seek." Misha and Wy'ya took one of his hands into their own and placed a kiss upon it, "And if she leaves your heart shattered, you may find us again." They smiled and turned from Oberic.

He watched them leave. He knew he would miss them both and hoped their lives out in the wilds would be infinitely better than what they had lived so far. He boarded the ship and stood on deck. When the Paladin said that the ship was ready to leave, she wasn't kidding. The ship made birth shortly after he boarded and drifted out to the ocean. The sails were dropped later and Oberic would spend the autumn stuck on the water caught in storms that delayed the trip more than he would have liked. The captain of the ship worked Oberic hard, but the sorcerer didn't mind it. It kept him from thinking too much and so long as he had Jayda in his heart, he knew his adventure would soon come to an end.

When he arrived in Karren's Call he was greeted with the bite of winter. He did not stay long, or at all. As soon as he stepped off the boat he began walking. He had no idea where he was going but knew that he would find Jayda. He walked deep into the wilds for weeks and on occasion hopped a ride on the back of a wagon passing by. The snow had started and there were nights he was certain he was going to die and be left a frozen corpse. He kept himself warm by using his magic to create flame, but could never keep it up for too long. He would risk the dangers of being burned by sleeping far too close to fires he would make so that he could rest.

The blizzard had come and brought with it thunder clouds and Oberic found himself standing at the gates of a city cast in eternal night. He explained how something inside him made him absolutely sure he would find her there and while he did search for a few hours, he would eventually find his love threatening a one legged beggar. He smiled as he watched her from the back. His heart soared and everything he had gone through was worth it just to see her now covered in snow. He called out to her.

Jayda, once rigid with jealousy, found herself softening at how Oberic explained that he just followed his heart to find her. There was nothing in the world she wanted to do right now more than hide him away for the rest of their lives. She however was aware it would never be that simple. The group found themselves in the middle of something bigger than all of them.

Dwim mumbled, "And now we're all here."

Alastor nodded in agreement, "I think this youngling is to face great perils in his life. How will it survive if everything seems to be surrounding it?"

V'ma growled out, "We protect him!"

Ren saw the fire light change colors first and cocked her head to the side, "What's going-"

The fire burned brighter and hotter as the flames turned pink and red. Standing in the fire were the legs of a woman and the upper body of a dove. The legs were long and thin. They were bare and connected to wide hips. The torso had thick feathers that led up the rest of the body. Even heavy, but perky, breasts were covered in feathers. The arms seemed normal with hands at the end of them, but they were connected to the body by large wings. The head of thing was that of a dove and those who had seen the vision before, including Ren, knew exactly what it was.

"Hear my words, mortals!" The voice was booming but that of a woman. Everyone coiled back. Phineas fell over completely. The bird woman stared at them all with piercing blue eyes, "You stand at a point in time where much of history can be changed for better or worse!" V'ma had slipped into a fighting stance and Jayda had clutched Graham closer to her. "The crown of this kingdom is in peril! You hold the key to prosperity for generations to come! I can not tell you what to do beyond what I have! Before you is a choice that you must make! Regardless of your choice, despair, heartache, and tragedy lies in both directions! I have gifted you a gryphon! They are noble and kingly beasts! Let it be the child's sigil! Go forward! The choice is yours and I have done all that I may for you! From here, fate is yours and yours alone!" The dove woman vanished and the flames died down, returning to the colors they were before. Even though the vision said there was nothing she could offer them, a ghostly image appeared in the fire. Graham slowly grew before their eyes. First he was a young boy with rosy cheeks, golden locks of hair, and kind eyes. Then he turned to a handsome young man looking adventurous and brave. His next transformation showed him a full grown man who wore a crown on his head and a green banner with a white gryphon as its sigil. Behind the crowned Graham, stood images of older versions of themselves; all of them but Phineas. They all carried gray in their hair except V'ma and Ren who would live much longer than their friends and even at this time retained much of the beauty of their youth. Leon was a dark gray, but it looked rather handsome on him. Oberic, already starting to gray now, looked to be going white. Dwim however was completely white and looked like a wise old sage. He wore a crown of his own. Augustus was gray and maintained the wild man look. Alastor looked much the same but crankier. Jayda had a mixture of light gray and black in her hair still, but just as radiant and tough looking as she ever was. There were other shadowy figures standing with them that seemed to shift heights and sizes. These visions faded as well and all returned to normal.

They all sat there staring at the fire. Oberic, who did not believe a lot of the tales he had heard about gods granting visions, found himself at a loss for words. Ren darted her eyes to Oberic, "That scroll said he was the King's son!"

Alastor made his argument, "The gods are said to be tricksters. How can we take that vision's word?"

Ren glared at Alastor in disbelief, "She clearly said there would be risks if we did or did not protect the child."

Dwim nodded and agreed with Ren, "Aye! Regardless, lad, that baby is pure. We will protect it until we figure it out. If we all become damned by that decision, well," he sighed, "That'll just be our burden to bear."

Jayda, who had said nothing for a bit, looked at the others, "I did not see Phineas in the vision." The others had noticed, but did not think much of it until Jayda brought it up.

Phineas snorted, "You think I'm going to be hanging around the lot of you when I'm old? You're out of your minds. Probably ditched you people because you got too boring to be around. You all looked pretty stiff up there."

Leon narrowed his eyes at the man, "Or you end up betraying us."

"Eat a dick," Phineas scoffed.

Jayda glanced at Phin and felt most of what he said was bravado. Oberic took his turn, "Are we agreed that we can not just sit around and wait for something to happen?"

Phineas was mumbling to no one, "I'll be seventy and ruining some twenty year old. That's what I'll be doing-"

Ren nodded, "We need to continue on and protect Graham," she looked at the others with a worried grin, "I have a feeling we have only just begun to hear the arguing over his safety now."

"-You'll all be off playing with your crowns and whatever and I'll be balls deep in some action." Phineas finished and folded his arms.

Amun cawed and Augustus laughed, "You're right! They do sound like a bunch of old maids!"

V'ma glared at him, "Says the man talking to a bird!" She moved back to where she was sitting and tried to relax a bit.

Augustus frowned, "Well he said something first. It'd be rude to not respond." He looked over at Jayda and smiled, "Would you like me to take him? I'm sure you and Oberic would like some time alone to get reacquainted and I hardly get time to see him between you and her." Augustus pointed to V'ma. Phineas crudely made a hand gesture universally understood to mean having relations.

Dwim groaned and threw a handful of snow at Phineas, "What's the plan here?" His voice hinted at annoyance with the casualness of the group, "We were just spoken to by a goddess and yer' all talking about sleepovers and fornication!"

Jayda stood and walked to Augustus. She placed a kiss on Graham's head and handed him over, "Sorry, Dwim. You're right. We should discuss a plan." Augustus wrapped Graham up and sat down, rocking the baby in his arms. The gryphon, who had slipped into a sleep, woke and trotted over to Augustus and forced itself into his lap where it curled and laid down again.

Leon interrupted, "We don't have any reason to assume he is to be king of another kingdom, do we? I only ask because Normoon's banner isn't green. It's blue."

Rennyn gave a shrug, "I don't believe so? The scroll did say he was Dorian's son. Dorian was the king of Normoon."

"That's right," Leon mumbled, "Sorry. I'm not sure why I forgot that."

She offered him a smile, "It would be nice to be able to stay here. We have all built nice lives for ourselves this year." She looked at Oberic now and let out a soft giggle, "Although it appears I may have to find a new place to officially call home now that Oberic has returned." She looked up and spotted something peculiar growing on the underside of a tree limb hanging over them. Her eyes studied it for a moment and when she realized what it was she let out a soft but excited gasp. It was a rare flower used in alchemy. It was in full bloom and its petals were colored in such a blue that it looked like ice. In the center of the bloom, another flower that was deep red. She knew them to be called Winter Roses. She told herself she would get help collecting it before they'd leave.

Oberic nodded, "I think we can remain here a while longer. We need to focus on making some gold. If we are to protect this child and raise him then we need a more suitable home where we can *all* protect him." Oberic stood up and

410

looked at the others gravely, "I propose that on this night we come together, all sharing the one goal of raising Graham, and form a union under that cause." He looked at the gryphon that had moved to Augustus just to be near Graham, "For the protection of Graham, the founding of the Order of the Gryphon." He put his hand out, "Who's with me?"

There was no answer for a bit and Oberic felt discouraged. They had to agree to something or nothing would ever work out. Alastor stood up and growled out, "Who leads this order? You?"

Oberic hadn't thought about it, "If you have someone in mind, speak their name."

Alastor stomped over to Oberic and met him face to face. He stared for a moment, long enough that the rest of the group grew concerned that there was to be a fight, and then he slid his clawed hand into Oberic's, "I follow your lead, Oberic Wintersong. You have time and time again proven your heart is true. You saved your woman, those children," he motioned to the group, "all of us, and then those enslaved people of V'ma's kin. You are an honorable man and I will follow your lead and call you my blood kin."

Leon raised his hand and called out, "As do I! Things fall into place when you're in charge."

Ren called out her answer, "I agree. So I'm in as well!"

V'ma stood once more and casually agreed, "You have watched over my people and so yes, I will follow you."

Dwim cheered, "Aye!"

Augustus nodded, "I will follow as well."

Phin groaned, "I'll follow for now."

Jayda stepped to Oberic and placed her hands on his face, "I'll follow you to the ends of the earth with the very last of my breath."

Alastor drew a knife and grabbed Oberic's hand. He slid the knife across the palm and looked at Oberic, "We make the blood oath for it is the only oath that matters. Each of them took turns cutting their palm and took one another's hands to seal their pact. There was a sense of purpose and duty. One group bound together by the sole objective of looking after one orphaned child. They were aware, but had no idea of how dangerous the obstacles that laid before them truly were. In the course of the year they had made powerful enemies and more would come in time. The goddess had not lied when she told them there would be loss and heartache. There was never going to be a way to avoid any of it. Graham, rightful heir to the throne of Normoon, had an order formed for his protection and a blood oath sworn for his survival.

EPILOGUE

The night passed and the oath sworn under the rose as The Aegis and The Lady met fulfilled all that was seen by the Oracle, mostly, and it set the newly founded Order of the Gryphon on a road they could now not turn away from. The morning came to them after they all had some rest. The night was freezing, but the morning sun was warm and the wind didn't blow, which made them a bit happier. Ren and Leon cooked up more deer meat for the group.

Jayda and Augustus fussed over Graham while V'ma watched them silently from afar. The joyous sound of the child's laughter did force a smirk, a small one, on her face. The child's laughter lifted everyone. Phineas was asking Oberic to go into greater detail about the bodies of the two women he had spent time with; Oberic did not oblige. Dwim and Alastor were busy packing up camp and made it clear they wanted to go home as soon as possible.

Ren turned over a skewer of meat that dripped with grease and looked up shyly at Leon, "So last night when I mentioned that I may need to find someplace to go now that Oberic is back," she bit her lip and gazed at him with lovely plum eyes, "I know I stay with you often, but was wondering. . ." She paused, a soft hue of pink crossed her face, "Would you be interested in," she licked her lips, "Would it be. . ." She trailed off nervously, unsure of how to ask.

Leon smiled knowing where it was going. Their relationship, so far, was mostly good natured teasing, "Not going to leave clothes everywhere, are you? You know I like to keep my place very clean." This of course was a joke because it was exactly what he himself did. Ren would often find one boot near the door and the other under a table. The man lived as though he were a bachelor though he hadn't been one in a while. They were together. They went on dates. They kissed. They had nights of passionate love making. He winked, "I don't see why not. I'd really like having you around more."

Her blush darkened and she let out a giggle, "So long as I don't stop cleaning up for you, right?"

He let out his own laugh, "They are placed there on the floor for a reason."

"Oh? And what was that reason again?"

"That's where I took them off."

The two of them laughed and leaned in placing a kiss upon one another's lips. Ren pulled away, "How do you explain the time I found your boot on the table?"

Leon smirked, "I told you there was a spider."

"Which I had to kill for you!" She teased him playfully, "Big tough man!"

"And what's your excuse for being afraid of the bat that was in the attic?" Leon asked, but Ren would give no reply. She leaned in and tackled him to the wet ground where the fire had melted the snow. She tickled him and forced a laugh out of him, "That's cheating!"

Alastor approached the two of them with a frown on his ugly face, "You two continue to play games while the rest of us are hungry."

Ren blushed and allowed Leon to sit up. They both mumbled their apologies. Alastor turned his back and started to work on packing the camp again. Ren yanked a piece of meat from the skewer and threw it. It hit Alastor in the back of the head and he turned around with a growl. His yellow eyes watched Leon and Ren as they cooked the meat looking rather bored with the job. He sneered and turned away.

Ren shook from having to hold in her laughter. Her eyes studied Leon's handsome face and he offered her a smile, "Move in. I'd like that."

Ren reached forward and tangled her hands into his hair. She pulled him in for another kiss and nipped at his lip, "I thought you'd never ask."

The others had packed the camp up and once the breakfast was ready, they sat together and feasted on the meat. Jayda was eager to get back home and really have Oberic settle in. She felt there was going to be lots of time now that there was no need to travel any more than they already had. It was time to rest and to look after Graham. When everything was packed she took Graham and slipped him into the sling she made for herself. Oberic helped her on her horse and then he climbed up behind her. Oberic called out to the others, "Let's go home, gryphons!" The snow white gryphon had been packed up in the wagon and let out a squawk. They were all headed back to Basile, city of eternal night.

Jayda looked back and smiled at Oberic. This was their true start. She looked ahead and kicked the horse into a trot. Jayda was happy. She was a Hunter and she loved a sorcerer.